THE COMING OF WINTER
by David Adams Richards

An Oberon Book

1

Blood had dried to his hands by mid-morning, thin streaks of blood on his fingers and knuckles. He cradled his rifle, walking slowly over wet gully leaves, his jacket opened, his blond hair in sweaty knots. The stench of a headless yearling partridge, foot-strung and dangling, a splatter of its dried blood on his pants. He walked cautiously, almost awkwardly, hearing thin sounds in the quiet, sounds that became audible because he was alone and silent.

He hoped nothing would catch his scent or the scent of the bird. Another partridge perhaps fanning in the side gravel, digesting as he supposed this one had, uncertain whether to fly or straighten, and so sitting startled waiting. He hoped for a spikehorn late to the spring, insensible to the conditions of survival. He hoped for a fawn, easy and tender, easy to ground.

A warm sun over the slanted coloured birches and a fresh autumn sky. A perfect Saturday. Not a stir. The wind only slight on his face bringing all the day to him, the cleanliness and purification of the season, rotting spruce cuts along the side of the road, the road twisting and overgrown. He concentrated, peering into the shaded growth with a pang of excitement, wishing, wanting something, knowing that something might be there watching him.

He moved from the path now moving toward the spring, hearing it before he reached it, and then crouching when he did, crouching and resting his rifle on the stones. The spring water numbed his hands, the cold clear spring, its pebbles and mud that he sank his fingers into. When he raised himself the tightened thigh muscles ached. He stroked the back of his neck, feeling the wetness of his fingers.

He stood there with his rifle once more cradled, with the dead bird once more bleeding in small drips. And he stood there watching. Maples on the top slope swayed. He looked past them because the day was so unclouded, the sky clean. Moments elapsed, erased themselves before he began to move again.

When he did, he noticed how stiffened his small kill had

become. No longer a bird. Only some stiff cold thing. Earlier its warm breast to the sun, neck turned, feathers ruffled. And only the one. By now, late morning, he was unlikely to spot another. There would be little until dusk, and then he'd hunt the path again, slowly over the leaves and dead roots, watching the limbs of trees.

He moved uphill very quickly, his boots and pantlegs soaking from the water. But once the water warmed in his boots he would feel comfortable again. It was easier to wade the brook than walk the dam, he feeling unsure and clumsy on his feet. He hunched as he moved, grabbing limbs for support, decayed spruce gum sticking to his palms, frightened for his eyes, yet forever watchful. And once or twice he thought he heard a fanning, felt a pressure in his ears. He would stop to rest looking back over his shoulder, looking to right or left. Stop to rest hearing only his heart, his breathing.

Once uphill he moved more slowly so that his breathing slowed, and at the edge of the density peered into the field. If only it was dusk and a buck standing close to the shadows in the other corner, or a doe feeding. He slipped between the wires, tilting the ancient fence logs, and stood in the open. It was a useless empty field even on this day. Enclosed by a dark quarry, the long greyish brown weed and hay unkempt. It had nothing of the colour or smell of the gully.

He moved to its middle and sat down. The dry October weeds. He sat down to the musty smell of weed and brownish turned-down grass. Deer had lain here the night before, moved with the dawn downhill to the brook, fed and watered and now were somewhere in the back woods lazy and fed and hidden. He noticed the half-fresh droppings. He unlaced his boots, taking them off to pour out the water. He wrung out his socks, leaving them off to dry. It felt good to have his feet naked to the slight breeze. And it was Saturday; he did not wish to think of lifting crates, nor did he wish to think of Sunday when there was never anything to do but wait for Monday's shift. So for a while he thought only of the breeze, the white wrinkled skin of his feet.

He could feel sharp blades of undergrowth so he resituated himself once or twice, lying down finally and taking out his knife. The blade glinted in the sun, the sun with its faint autumn strength, and he severed in two some of the tall stems that rose around him, whistling to himself as he did. It was a

6

poor kill for a morning's hunt.

By noon he was up once more, retracing his steps over the pathways connecting the small irregular-shaped fields toward his truck, thinking that perhaps he might move from his position to hunt somewhere else, farther in perhaps. The day was turning cloudy, the breeze stronger, sharper on his wet pantlegs than before. But the tree colours seemed no less distinct, the day still carried in its breath all cleanliness and purification.

He passed familiar morning markings, empty cartridges on the wet pathway, bootsteps at the edge of listless puddles. The squirrel he had shot lay belly down on a spruce stump, cold now, tail cut off. He inspected it again, its bloody head, gatherings in its pouch, and threw it aside into the alders and undergrowth.

Then he stopped, silent, stiffened. No movement, not even shouldering his rifle, not even that. And his pulse, he could hear his pulse as it rushed everything through him. The deadened pale excitement of his face. Everything at that moment was weightless, his whole body, the one step lightly on the tinted leaves, now the one step closer to the alders, as if he must see, as if it had to be there. That instant he craved for it to be there, noticing nothing of the day, the field in view, but only the brown hide of the animal, the black heaviness of it through the thin twigs.

He heard the sharp sound of his rifle before he realized he had fired and then he heard its sharp painful sound again, twice to the head. The smell of powder mingling with other smells that he did not notice. And he knew that it was a cow, not a doe. The thickness of a cow's frame in the field bellowing and whining, not dead. He had realized it all before he had shouldered his rifle and now the rifle sounds were fading in his ears, replaced by that of the cow. At once he cursed himself for firing but he knew that it did little good to curse. And now it was bellowing, trying to stand again as if standing would heal the shot wounds, make the day as it had been before.

It was unexplainable but he knew he couldn't help firing. He also wished the day to be as it had been. He must kill the thing, must kill it! And he was very afraid now, felt the heaviness of his body, and could not shoulder his rifle again, wished to run but knew he couldn't. Couldn't stand the sick whine of the animal.

He cracked the limbs, the twigs with his heavy body, stumbling with his heavy boots uncareful of where he trod, his eyes fixed on his destination, a flicker of angry desperation on his face.

He stood in the open field, the wind at his back, the brightness of the coloured day surrounding him, the strong flavour of autumn once again. The cow lay on its side, trying to jerk upright every so often, falling to its side again, kicking its thick hind legs. It was bleeding very little. Perhaps it didn't notice he was there. Another cow stood a short distance away watching, not venturing any closer, its enormous eyes watching. He felt sick as he fired, shaking, uncertain of his aim. And he fired four times rapidly and then only live nerves twitching in a dead hide and everything was quiet. He cursed and he could not stop shaking, could not stop feeling sick. But he felt he must leave it there, forget it. And then he laughed nervously as he turned away.

He turned to walk along the field-path to his truck, but as he did he noticed that someone was watching him from the shadows near the opposite edge of the field. The man came no closer yet but only watched him as the other cow did with its lazy morbid eyes. He stood still and his sickness was replaced by a throb of terror. If he turned to run he would have nowhere to go. He thought of running, thought of hiding in the gully. But of course the man must have seen his truck. Yes, how could he ever reach his truck if he ran? And the man seemed to be staring past him, staring at the carcass, or staring at everything at once. The man seemed very calm; everything in fact seemed very calm now.

It was the man that finally moved but when he did he did not move along the path as would be expected but rather he moved in shadows at the edge of the field, disappearing among the trees so that it was uncertain where he was. Only one thing was certain: he was moving closer. Time passed, his body reappearing every little while, his gaze still fixed, and then disappearing into the shadows again. He seemed to be circling the entire area. Then he was in the open not a hundred feet away, standing heavy, tall and strong in the sunlight.

"Good afternoon," he said in a very calm voice and with a heavy river accent, a very calm, almost kind voice. "What's your name, boy?"

"Kevin Dulse." The boy spoke softly, also trying to be sure of himself, trying not to fall under the man's gaze—or he intimidated by it, frightened by it. He still cradled his rifle, his jacket open smelling of the woods and animals he had hunted. Waiting.

"That your truck?"

"Yes."

"Nice old truck—what year?"

"48 International. Belonged to my grandfather."

"I see," the man said moving closer, moving past the boy at a distance of a few yards and standing next to the carcass. Kevin turned to face him as he did. The man crouched near the head of the cow. There was a strong smell of dung in the air now. The other cow's tail slapped against its rump and it moved no closer. The man wore breeches, his brown coat also opened, pipe in his shirt pocket.

"Hunt much?"

"Saturdays," Kevin answered feebly, hating the expectation of it all and yet standing there, not running, not running to his truck. The man was at least 50, a close crop of greyish hair, stubble of greyish beard on his coarse face, heavy wrinkles on his brow and near his eyes. His large right hand smoothed the cowhide.

"Not much in the woods these days but hunters," the man said. "But I see you've got a bird."

Kevin had forgotten the weight of it dangling on its string and he looked down at its headless greyish form cold and stiff along his leg. He didn't answer. The man stood again, taking his pipe from his pocket. He filled the bowl and lit it, the fine aroma of pipe tobacco on the air. He kept the pipe in his mouth as he talked.

"I'm not so rich a man that I can afford to lose cows to hunters."

"I didn't say you were," Kevin said, his voice sharpening a little, not understanding why all of a sudden it had sharpened the way it did but knowing that he must not be fearful of the man, that he must not ask forgiveness even in the sound of his voice. "I thought it was a doe," he said.

The man smiled angrily, showing yellowed broken teeth. He seemed to be searching out the lies on Kevin's face. And Kevin knew they were there in plain view but he never turned

9

away. There was something about the man, about the way he approached the subject of the cow, his dead cow, that made him more than interesting. There was this about him Kevin thought and he couldn't turn away. Such a calmness to him, little driblets of cow's blood on the cold ground, and the smell of soft smoke on the soft October air. Kevin felt a haziness come over him and in this haziness he tried to picture what he had done. He couldn't feel it now; he couldn't feel the way he did when his body, weightless with its own energy, stood near the alders listening to its pulse. The man stepped closer to him shaking his head at the lie.

"I ain't seen no deer in this field in five year. I keep my cows here though. Everyone knows I keep my cows here, but I don't keep animals for people to come and butcher."

"I told you—," Kevin began again, his voice sounding like someone else's, not like his own.

"Son of a whore," the man said. "Ya just kilt my cow; how can ya stand there and lie?"

"Not lying," Kevin said.

"Then what was ya doin huntin' doe with a fuckin' .22?" His voice was calm once more, the hard scrutinizing look in his eyes. The man would not strike him, Kevin thought, would not lift his hand, but would try to humiliate him without doing that, with his words, with his voice that seemed to tolerate every injustice. The man was preaching, preaching with his dry, calm voice, and Kevin not hearing exactly what the man said but looking away into the shadows of the nearby spruce. After a time the man stopped staring and turned to look at his cow, the small bloody wounds on its face, its fat domesticated hide.

"Well, what do ya want me to do?" Kevin asked finally, not sure whether he should ask anything. But he did ask and now the man must answer him. Kevin was no longer frightened; he felt there was nothing to be frightened of any more.

"That's what court's gonna decide," the man answered.

"Court?" Kevin stuttered. The man continued to look at his dead animal, his pipe still loosening its soft white smoke. And then he turned and walked away, walked to the field-path and moved along it.

The boy watched after him until he had reached the far side and had disappeared. Then, after a time, he too began to move along the same pathway and in the same direction. He

10

cursed, wishing to say things to the man he had not thought to say when the man was present. If the dialogue had been more abusive Kevin might have found words to say, things to utter, but as it was he felt gutless; his action little justified.

He remained in the shadows at the other edge of the wood for some time thinking that it might be best to go to the man's house. Yes, to talk it off his chest would be the best remedy and though he did not know the man by name he knew where the house was situated. But then he would be giving in to something he could not give in to, as if in his worst moment he was admitting defeat. It was better to go before the man came back for the carcass, go into town as if nothing had happened, and wait—wait until something did.

He returned to the truck, the sun still warm and bright on the gravel, the smell of stale heat inside the cab. He sat there with the door open, his mud-laced boots on the runner, drinking coffee from a thermos which was too hot for his thirst and surveying the quiet peacefulness of the day, feeling the breeze on his woodshirt. Sounds of shots in the distance echoed something of the remarkable solitude of the land.

"I've killed a cow," he said to himself. "I've killed a cow," and his body shook with uncontrollable nervous laughter, spilling coffee on the stiffened headless bird.

It was not glee, or was it? He couldn't actually tell just how he thought with everything wandering inside him, how he felt. At moments he was sober, painfully sober, fearful, frightened of the consequence, of court. And even though he was driving on the loose gravel road he would shut his eyes tightly as if clutched by an inner torment seeing the old farmer stepping calmly and stiffly toward him, the carcass of a cow. He would almost cry out with its anguish, and then in an instant he would be relaxed, become happy, intoxicated, would laugh until he coughed, until his eyes blurred. The cow, the stupid old cow.

There was still good light to hunt left, the best hunting time left. The birds would be in the trees in an hour and it was always peaceful hunting at dusk, the brooks were always so dark, the land quiet and stiffened, the shadows so inviting, familiar. Being in the woods alone at dusk was fulfilling, walking the pathways watching the birches, hunger.

If he had missed with the first shot perhaps he would not

11

have fired again. The cow had stumbled and groaned under its own fat weight. And it was such a fine day to hunt. It was not his fault; it was not anybody's fault. He would not blame himself. The man, why hadn't the man yelled?

But he returned to town now driving along the main highway slowly, watching the river—spotting geese. Saturday night was a good night, the best night of the week, and he would drive out slowly checking fields, looking down side roads. His legs shaking. The smell of dust in the cab.

When he reached the railway tracks the day seemed much colder to him than it had been, the few afternoon clouds spreading themselves over the sky, the wind increasing, the flattened dull green of the churchyard. He had to wait here for a freight to pass, its rusting cars spread for a thousand yards. He could smell it from where he sat, smell the old grease-ridden men that worked it, smell the jerking couplings. He tore the partridge from its string and threw it on the floor. To wait—he hated to wait. Small children were walking the lane, looking cold.

He walked through the town for some time before setting out toward the tavern, leaving his truck parked and locked. And as he walked he was once again very happy, excited, nervous. He laughed at people he met though they did not know him and turned to watch girls stride briskly away from him. He smelt of blood and huntsclothes and he felt it was proper that he did for it gave him a wildness and a roughness, an uncontrollable energy. He wished to tell everyone what he had done. He wished to confront a stranger, a middle-aged man or woman and say:

"I was out hunting today, you know, and in this field I met a cow—." Yes, he wished to say it but couldn't so he decided instead to go to the tavern where friends of his would be.

This exuberance he felt made him walk strangely and he was under its influence when he reached the grey-barred tavern doors. He hammered on them thinking that there must be someone inside, cursing under his breath in disappointment. Spitting. And it was only after a moment's thought that he realized it was supper hour. The place closed for supper hour. Grey dusk over the streets, the lamps over the stores were burning, people moving in the half darkness toward their homes. He should be in the woods, the best time for moving along the gully. Saturdays were so infrequent that

12

he should not waste one, he thought. He remained on the tavern steps.

Sitting as he was, looking at the step dirt, all excitement and promise of the celebration left him, and he felt limp and miserable once more, pressing his hands over his face smelling squirrel. He had not really thought of the man phoning the police. Now that he did the act didn't seem significant to him. They couldn't do that much to him because it was rather like a joke. And yet he was frightened again, almost numb with fright, numb throughout his tired body because of what the man had said, what he intended to do. And, damn, the man had moved through the shadows toward him, through the undergrowth and pine, and then had said nothing to him—nothing! He wished to sleep on those steps, the dirt and the gobs of spit from the diseased throats of old men. He was tired and it didn't matter. The other cow watching him, its morbid brown eyes, its tail swishing the ticks and flies from its heavy rump, watching him as if it were inevitable what must be done.

For half an hour nothing moved, the square and the streets were silent, parked cars in front of the town hall, flags almost limp on their tarnished poles, an ore-boat docked on the listless water, the huge black ore hills covered by tarps. He drowsed, half asleep, his side leaning against the chipped cement wall. He did not notice when Charlie came, walked up the steps past him and unbarred the door. He was startled when Charlie spoke:

"You must be thirsty."

He shivered, sat up quickly. "Oh ya," he said in answer, not knowing for a moment where he was, "ya." Charlie laughed, leaned against the inside wall and scratched at his bald head as if digging fingernails into his skin. A man of 60 with a cigarette in his mouth.

"Thirsty?" Charlie said. Well he was not so thirsty as he was hungry. Charlie stood holding the door for him smiling at him and so he rose slowly to his feet and entered, moving past the man. He took a corner table near the wall. The lights went on, dim tavern lights with everything shaded, clean table-tops in a gigantic room. Charlie moved to his tap and pouring a draft, brought it to the table and sat down. Kevin shoved 40c his way, slouching in his chair, grateful for the comfort. Still the smell of blood and huntsclothes and the smell of the

13

tavern, the taste of draft. Charlie blinked through his cigarette smoke at the boy.

"Hunting?"

"Yes."

"Where'bouts?"

"Upriver a ways."

The tavern was quiet, only their voices. He did not like such a quietness in the place, the bareness, clean unspoiled ashtrays under the lights.

"Get much?"

"Bird."

"Not much going," Charlie said.

"All hunted out," Kevin responded, swallowing and then sitting upright moving his outstretched legs inward. They seemed to be shaking slightly. The old man was trying to talk but trying not to look at him, didn't know him.

"Father hunt, does he?"

"Not much anymore—fishes a bit."

"Still have his nets."

"No more," Kevin shook his head and finished the glass, resumed his slouching position. Charlie went to his tap and brought another glass over. Then he went about dusting the clean table-tops, whistling. Kevin sipped at his beer. His hair was matted and coarse and dry now and his face was smeared with the dirt of hunting.

Another customer came to the entrance and peered in. Small and thin with black curly hair, sunken sore-blotched face, he stood inspecting before he too moved to a corner table across the room and ordered a draft. He had ugly vacant eyes. Kevin stared at him and he stared at Kevin but as their eyes met their staring shifted to the floor. They knew each other only well enough to make sitting near each other uncomfortable and so there was no conversation. It was like Charlie and him. In fact the three were strangers in that sense. Charlie went behind the bar and picked up the morning paper to read once again. Randy came through the back entranceway and put on his coin pouch and stood silently.

"Randy," the customer called sharply as soon as he had noticed him. "Hear about the accident?"

"When?"

"Some crazy young bastard wrapped his head around a pole."

"When?" Randy asked again, "Who was he?"

"That young Turcotte that drives the Dodge."

"Dead?" Kevin asked.

"About an hour ago," the customer said without flinching at Kevin's question.

"Hour ago," Randy repeated coming over to sit with the man. Charlie also moved from the bar and walked over. "Anyone else in the car?" Kevin sat sipping his beer looking vacantly at the three of them.

"Just let the slut out and started home I guess. It's pretty bad—still tryin' to get him out."

"Where was it?"

"Up at the underpass."

"He must have been doin' some awful jesless speed," Charlie murmured.

"Oh Christ," the man said loudly. "Walkin' it right to her, the boy had no sense at all." The man looked across to Kevin who stared blankly and mutely at the man. "Know him there, Dulse?"

Kevin rose and walked to the other table carrying his beer.

"Andrew—ya I know him, is he dead?"

"Now what would you be," the man answered, "if you was wrapped around a pole?"

Rain drizzle on the dark streets, the cold rain drizzle on his face. He moved slowly and sorely, his body aching from so much movement. He walked close to the buildings sheltering himself from the cold and drizzle but actually he felt neither. He felt nothing save the tired soreness, the bad taste of his mouth, the shallow feeling. Others on the street also, winos sitting on building steps shouting at the young girls as they moved through the square. The girls returning laughter.

There would be a dance later. Saturday night there was always a dance. He would have to be drunk before he went and then he would sit in a stupor on a bench watching the moving contortions of those young girls, the stink of flesh in a heated room, the smell of stale wine puke on the floor. And he was not drunk now; rather he was sober. The news had turned him cold inside, the beer having no effect on his empty stomach.

He was circling back over the streets walking to his truck, but he did not wish to be alone, did not wish to savour the

15

impact of such knowledge alone. Excited faces standing near the death car in a pit.

And he didn't want to see it, told himself inside that he would rather stay in town and wait, and yet he was walking to his truck, walking to his truck to go there. He could not stop from going. Friends of his would be there and he became agitated, walking faster and more clumsily, hunching over, staring at the ground.

The soft rain drizzle gave the town a gloom—a death-like appearance in itself and even the shouts seemed muffled. He passed the streaked restaurant windows, the smell of food, onions and gravy and the sound of agitated voices in the parking lot, as he walked toward them without seeing who they were.

"Dulse, hear 'bout Andy?" John yelled. He walked to them without speaking, not looking at them until he was in the circle. They stood hunched and shivering and spitting in a circle near his truck.

"Ya—dead?"

The rest nodded without looking at each other.

"Pretty bad," Bruce said.

"You been up?" Kevin asked.

"Oh ya—just got back, where were you today, huntin'?"

"Ya."

"We were with him all day, then he left to pick up Julie."

"Where are you going now?"

"Back to the tav I guess—comin'?"

Kevin looked at them; he had wanted to go up but not alone, not now. He looked at them; there was nothing else to do and so he nodded.

"I feel like getting pissed anyway," he said.

It was eight o'clock. The sound of the mill whistle as the three walked closely together, Kevin cramped by the others' shoulders walking in the middle. The streets were dark and windy, the rain lashing against their faces. He could see the others shutting their eyes because of it, looking as if they were in some terrible pain. He too squinted his eyes.

The tavern was filled now so that when they entered, they moved to the farthest corner of the room and squeezed among the other labourers. They listened to the loud sounds of cursing and laughter but said little to each other. The round was brought to the table and they drank. Kevin undid his damp jacket and sat in the same position he had sat in when Charlie had talked to him; one moment he would sprawl, the next, he would be upright in his chair staring directly in front with little idea of what was being said. It was good to be out of the rain; he could still hear it lashing out, could hear it in the alley-way on the tin barrels. It was good to be in a dry room.

The man directly across from them was asleep, his head slumped, his hands folded together on his belly, cigarette in his hand. Others at his table were trying to wake him but with little success because they also were quite drunk and did more giggling and cursing than anything, which of course did not wake him. The man asleep smelled of heavy liquor and being dressed in his finer clothes seemed to have come from a celebration, a wedding perhaps. All of them were dressed this way, their black suits and tight narrow ties. They spoke French and Kevin could not understand what they said nor was he listening. He looked at them only now and then but whenever he did he noticed the man's cigarette burning closer and closer to the skin. They did not seem to notice.

Bruce and John were talking about the accident. Kevin sipped his beer, his face contorted a little. He listened for a while and then looked at the man's cigarette again. He couldn't just let the fingers burn. Nothing worse than a cigarette burn, he thought.

"I thought Boyd and Terry were coming," Bruce asked after looking toward the door.

"They were with us in the parking lot," Kevin answered turning around, "they could be anywhere."

"I hope they didn't go up there again," John said.

"Nothing to see anyway, probably all cleared away."

Kevin turned back in his chair to peer at the man with the cigarette. Still asleep. Still talking French, the thing still burning unnoticed. The man's mouth open as if he were about to snore. Burning him would wake him Kevin thought but then there was nothing worse than a cigarette burn and if the man was very drunk he mightn't feel it right away. Why didn't he notice it?

"Hey," he shouted at the man, not at the man's friends but at the man himself, bending across to shake him as he did. "Wake up—your smoke!" The others from both tables stared, and the man grunted, rolled his head and partially opened

17

his eyes. "Hey," Kevin yelled again but with little success, "your smoke." One of the man's friends seeing what Kevin was yelling about opened the fingers and took the butt away, burning himself and cursing, and making a gesture as if to strike the sleeping drunk for the trouble he had caused. The man slept on and the others at his table ordered more beer, grinning their thanks to Kevin who turned back to his own.

"Well how was your hunting?" Bruce asked. "Anything back there?"

"Oh I shot a bird," Kevin said looking at his draft glass. He had waited too long. If he had wished to tell, he should have done it long before, but it wasn't the time to tell them about it now. It was better to say nothing.

"One bird all day?" John asked.

"Yes," he answered. "Why?"

"Nothing—just it was a beautiful day for hunting—I'd have figured you would have gotten more."

"It turned windy in the afternoon," Kevin said. They were silent for a time, John tapping the salt-shaker on the rim of his glass.

"What time did he leave?" Kevin asked.

"About four—went to get Julie—drove her home, and that's that."

They were silent again. Kevin looked at them silently. He looked at John, the hand tapping the salt-shaker on the glass. The noise of the men leaving their table and stumbling to the urinal. The sound of the doors swinging.

"Some day we should all go out together—some weekend, stay at the camp," John said. "We haven't gone out hunting together in two years."

"No game," Bruce answered.

"So what the hell—it doesn't matter. Even if we just go out and get drunk—it doesn't matter. In a few years we won't even know each other. Last time we went out we never got a thing, slept in most of the mornings. But it was one hell of a drunk."

"Andrew was there then, wasn't he?" Kevin said.

"That's what I mean," John said, "that's what I mean—two year ago, last hunting trip we went on. Went out along the Renous looking for arses."

"So he's dead," Bruce mumbled, "it'll take a while to get used to it."

18

"Don't talk about it anymore," Kevin said nervously, staring at their grey faces in the dim light, "it doesn't do one bit of good to talk about it."

"Sure it does, Christ," John answered. "Anyway let's get pissed and go to the dance. I don't want to sit here all night." He called the waiter to bring more draft and he paid for it and drank his down right away, some spilling out of the corners of his mouth, and then he ordered more for all of them and paid for it all again. "Good stuff," he said.

The men across from them were arguing now in French, but it was clear that they disagreed on what to do with their drunken sleeping friend. It was as if they were afraid to touch him, to waken him or carry him from the place and also it was as if they were afraid to leave him. It was wrong to leave him. The heavy bulk slept, anointed with the liquor he had drunk and Kevin looked at him from time to time, looked at his friends also as they argued with one another in loud drunken voices.

Randy had been watching also and each time he brought a round to their table or to one of the tables beside them, he would curse under his breath. He was a very nervous fellow and it took very little excitement to put him on the phone. There were those in the town who hated him for this reason. His friends seemed to be the ones who sat alone drinking slowly without companions. The loneliest thing is to drink alone. Randy hated the rowdy confusion of large swilling crowds. When he brought the second round in a row to Kevin's table, he spoke in a nervous way, low and smiling.

"Little party boys?"

"Sort of," Kevin answered.

He leaned over to wipe the table taking his tip as he did so, speaking next to Kevin's ear.

"Too bad about young Turcotte—served him just before supper."

No-one spoke. He looked at them and then leaned over farther so that his chest was above the centre of the table, so that he was talking to all of them, as it were, face to face, hoping that one of them would reply, his eyes narrow as he spoke:

"I'd like to cut those bastards off."

"Who?" John said looking at him and burping.

"The frogs," he answered. "They're cut off, I ain't serving

19

them again—bothering you?"

"Who?" John said again taking his fresh draft, putting it to his mouth.

"Those French fuckers."

John looked over at them unconsciously. "No," he said. Randy lifted himself and moved away. Kevin smiled.

"Who's he talkin' about?" John asked and then in answer, "Those guys. Thought he was talking about us at first. I was all ready to call him a baldheaded prick."

"Good thing you never," Bruce said who was rising to go to the urinal. Kevin followed.

The washroom was small, smelled of urine and cheap soap, looked yellow and white. An old man was leaning against the urinals as they entered. He was dressed in a tattered brown all-weather coat and did not look at them as they entered but was aware of them and as he spit into one he spoke.

"Swill it inta ya and piss 'er out," he said. The boys moved around him to find their places.

"Swill it inta ya and piss 'er out," he said again.

"Yes," Kevin answered. "We all do that."

"Surely—surely," the man said, stepping backward almost tripping. His pant-legs soaking near his wet leather shoes. He stood against the sinks, spittle on his mouth. He had come in from the rain with the smell of wine on him, a green wine bottle tucked beneath his coat. He was still standing motionless, staring when they turned around again.

"I think John's going to get rowdy tonight," Bruce said.

"Ya, so do I." Then he added solemnly, "I don't think he should go to the dance; he'll get beaten half to fuck."

When they reached their table another round was ordered, John wishing to pay for all they drank. Of course neither of them would let him, feeling that they should stop him from being foolish—take care of him.

"You don't earn any more than us, bud," they said laughingly. John looked at them without saying a word and then he laughed also, and almost choked on laughing, his face turning very red and sick looking.

"Baldheaded fuckers," he said, "look at them—both of them."

Nobody at the other table was moving. They ordered another round but Randy shook his head and pointed to the door. They looked at their friend and shrugged and Randy pointed to the phone. Then they started cursing again but it wasn't loud this time, and nudging the drunk. Randy's face was like a little stone god, conviction and purpose on it, and John stared menacingly at him.

"Jesus, I hate that bastard," he said.

Kevin said nothing. He drank his draft as fast as his stomach would allow. And he wished to go, go out into the damp and sober up. See Pamela, he thought. He had not seen Pamela all day. Go out into the rain so that his mind would stop spinning, so that it would become quiet. Go to sleep. He realized that one of the men from the other table was coming over to him and he waited. He felt a hand on his shoulder.

"Hello bud," he said. The man extended his large hand and Kevin took it and smiled. The man stood there smiling, breathing heavily, his liquored breath.

"Speak French?" he asked.

"Sorry."

The man eyed them smiling. "I don't think that waiter likes us much," he said laughingly.

"Don't mind him," John said. He too looked very bad now and he eyed the man with vague drunken eyes.

The man said nothing more for a moment, a long moment in which he was content to regard the faces of the three boys. They said nothing to him either. The man stood stupidly for a moment and even in his drunkenness seemed to be embarrassed with coming over. Kevin swilled at his beer, trying to think of something to say. Randy watched from the counter, his stone face. But the man kept smiling as if he could not dare undo his smile.

"Our friend is asleep," he said. Kevin looked at the man asleep and nodded.

"Yes, you'd better get him home," Kevin said.

"Oh no—him." The man laughed waving his arms, "he would not go home." The man sat down in the empty chair and extended his hand again. The boys were uncertain and looked at each other a little cautiously, but John, having finished his draft, ordered another round.

"We're going to the dance, aren't we?" Bruce asked, trying to grab John's lifted hand but failing to do so. John shook his head. "After," he said. The man now seated at their table laughed and looked over at his friends. "Yes, they are all drunk and they do not wish to go." He said it loudly pointing

21

at them, waving his fingers at them. They made gestures at him and continued conversing.

"That is my brother asleep," he said. "He is a good person, you know that, a good person. He is crazy too."

"How is he crazy?" Bruce asked, winking at Kevin.

The man put his finger to his temple, tapping it, showing crooked white teeth that seemed pointed because of their crookedness. And he laughed. Randy came with three draft and set them down. Kevin took a dollar and gave it to him and Randy looked at the Frenchman in a severe manner.

"I ordered four," John said. No-one spoke. Randy looked at them, looked at John more than anyone else.

"He's cut off, remember that," Randy said moving away. John cursed under his breath. The other two Frenchmen were coming over to their table now and bringing their chairs with them. "Lucien," they were saying addressing the seated man, "Lucien," and they spoke in French and laughed and Kevin felt very uncomfortable. He felt uncomfortable not only because of the language but because they were drunken and menacing, and the man asleep was big and burly and perhaps retarded. Kevin, of course, did not know this but he did know he wished to go now that he felt uncomfortable. And John was drunk and liable to do anything at any moment.

"Let's go," he said finally eyeing Bruce. Bruce nodded and looked toward John.

"Well, you coming?"

John saw none of their frustration with him or with the group that had gathered, and was quite prepared to stay for hours talking to Lucien. Randy looked at them all from the counter and when he had to bring rounds to other tables he still concentrated on their group. John was describing the accident and Lucien, in sympathy, was shaking his head and muttering. He was drinking from John's beer, looking over his shoulder before he did to see where Randy was.

"Yes," he said finally pointing toward his sleeping brother, "Alcide crushed his arm in an accident and his daughter was killed you know. I hate to think of them," he said. "But you have to keep on living, eh Donald?" He smiled at his friend who took John's glass also and drank from it. Kevin and Bruce sipped from their own and made no effort to get their friend away but rather watched and waited in nervous anxiety. The men talked in French to one another again and John drowsily leaned back in his chair.

"Let's go," Bruce said to Kevin. "If he won't come, we'll leave him—goddamnit I'm not missing the dance." Bruce was half on his feet. Kevin reached over one of the men and pulled him down again. "Wait a minute," he said.

"One more minute," Bruce answered, "one more."

But already they had caused enough of a ruckus for the waiter to come back over and, seeing a draft glass in Donald's hand, he fumed.

"All right, you're all cut off. No more means no more. Now if you don't screw off out of here, I'll use the phone. Five minutes."

The men cursed at him in French but it was obvious that they would go. Lucien reached across and shook Alcide swearing, with the other men already on their feet ready to lift him if need be. They did not wish the police and felt they had pressed as far as they ought to under the circumstances. John was unmoved.

"Where's everybody going?" he said looking around.

Kevin was also on his feet peering down feeling quite drunk thinking of his morning experience. He looked at John.

"Come on, we got to go."

"Where?"

"I don't care, let's go."

"I want another draft," John said. The Frenchmen were already going, one stumbling toward the urinal and the others waiting for Alcide who was awake now and seemed harmless enough. The tavern was not filled with people now. Little groups sat together or old men sitting alone in darkened corners watched the proceedings with colourless eyes, colourless faces.

"I want a draft," John said loudly. "Randy, one draft."

Randy shook his head and then pointed to the door in the same fashion as he had to the Frenchmen. Stone face, unmoveable. John looked at him angrily and clutched the salt-shaker in his hand, half rising, half stumbling to his feet. Kevin and Bruce jumped for him and held him back but he managed to throw the shaker on the floor, spilling salt when it hit, its top coming off, a bit of splintered glass.

"You're coming if we have to drag you," Bruce said. They

23

both held him and he struggling and screaming. The Frenchmen standing watching and then moving to the door before any real trouble started. And the rest in the tavern looking on as if they were seeing a crazy man performing.

"Goddamn baldheaded quiff," he yelled. "Give me some goddamn beer."

And they were taking him to the door as he said this. He tried to swing at Randy. The Frenchmen were gone. Randy stood like a statue near the phone.

"Are you crazy?" Bruce was saying. "Are you crazy?" Kevin hanging on to an arm.

The rain had given up, the streets leaf-strewn, rotting leaves. And it was so black now that as they took him down the steps they tripped and all went falling onto the cement. Kevin put his hand out, his one free hand and cut it when he fell. He laughed and cursed weakly, lifting himself as the rest did, and looked across the street to the small damp shops each with their one light glowing yellow in the dark. He could not control his shivering.

"You wait," John was saying, "you wait," as he bent over to brush himself off.

"It'll be a while before you're inside again," Bruce said still holding onto him. John turned, twisted out of his grip and flared.

"It's none of your goddamn business, is it?"

"Now don't start on Kevin and me," Bruce said alarmed.

"I'm not starting on Kevin, bud; you've been at me all night, so just screw off."

Kevin said nothing and Bruce turned and walked ahead, slowly unstably with his hands in his pockets. John spit and walked to the side of the building where he urinated and coughed. Kevin stared first at one and then at the other, remained silent, remained unmoved. He shivered there with his hands in his pockets until John came back calmer and smiling.

"So what are you going to do?" John asked.

"Hell I don't know—you're not going to the dance, are you?"

"With him?" John said spitting again. "Screw him."

"It's better if you don't go," Kevin said.

And then they crossed the street and began moving slowly,

24

not speaking, Kevin closing and opening his cut hand feeling the pain in it, knowing that it wasn't bleeding but that it was scraped. And his eyes kept searching the road and the square, the few cars parked on the road, for the Frenchmen they had talked to. He was hoping he wouldn't see them but was wondering if he would.

"Well you're not going home, are you?" John asked.

"Pamela's," Kevin said. He wondered if his parents knew about the cow, if the police or the farmer had phoned. He became frightened once more and it seemed urgent that he get home. "Pamela's," he said again softly.

"Walking?" John asked.

"No, I'll take my truck—coming?"

"Sure—if she won't mind."

"Oh for Christ's sake," Kevin said.

They walked to the truck without speaking and no-one was in sight. John splashed his way through puddles wetting his pantlegs and cursing and laughing as he did. But they never looked at one another directly. The smell of the restaurant in the wet air.

"I don't know—maybe I shouldn't go," John said once more staring through the cab windows, Kevin's rifle between his legs.

"Oh for Jesus' sake come on, Pamela's doing nothing anyway and anyway I was supposed to be there at five. She won't bitch if you come with me."

"Women screw you up," John said.

Pamela had probably been waiting the whole evening in the apartment alone and now that it was growing late, she might have gone to bed. Kevin didn't answer John's remark until he had parked his truck on the lane outside.

"Ya well, we're going to have to be quiet," he said, opening the cab door as gently as he could. "I mean just until we get upstairs."

John nodded. He opened his door and walked around the truck stumbling and laughing quietly, stepping in the lane puddles unconsciously or deliberately but in any case not caring where he stepped. His pantlegs were soaked but he didn't seem to mind it or even know. And Kevin was frightened that he might start acting up before the apartment was reached. Pamela had complaints before, and the landlord who lived in the building across could easily come over himself at any time of the night whenever noise woke him.

So Kevin motioned for silence and they ascended the stairs. He felt the warmth on his face and heard John stumbling behind him and the warmth and the noise, the smell of heat made him sick. When he reached her door, he knocked but not so loudly that someone in the other apartment might hear. And they waited. No answer.

"I need a snappin' good piss," John said.

Kevin rapped again, loudly this time and called her name softly. "Pamela," he said, "Pamela, for Christ's sake." No answer for a moment and then her voice from behind the door.

"Kevin—that you?"

"Ya."

Then she opened the door standing in her nightdress, half asleep. And she stared at them for a moment before turning abruptly and walking from the door leaving it ajar so that they might enter. She went into her bedroom and slammed the door.

"Nice place," John said when he was inside looking around. Kevin bent over to take off his work boots, hoping that John would follow his example without being told, for he didn't like giving orders to anyone about anything. And so he glanced at John, hoping he too would take his wet boots off. John didn't but proceeded to walk to the other end of the small room with them on and then sat down with his knees crossed on the couch.

"You get a good view of the river here," Kevin said coming over himself to sit in a chair. Only the small table lamp burned. The place was old but very clean; Pamela kept it very clean and she had small prints on the walls of famous paintings but nothing good or original hanging. And she had her encyclopedias and nursing books, some high-school books also very properly placed in a small book-stand. Kevin didn't know anything about paintings and cared nothing for books except, of course, war magazines. He loved the famous battles.

"She coming out?"

Kevin shrugged.

"Where's the can?"

"That's a good idea—right through that door by the kitchen and you better take off your boots or she'll have a fit."

"Oh for God's sake."

26

"No come on, I don't blame her."

John looked at him and started laughing slyly but he did as asked even though he made it clear that it was a stupid request. He threw his boots to one side and stood, his socks and pantlegs soaking and walked unstably to the washroom. When he came out, Kevin went in. His head was a little dizzy, nothing to eat all night. He had hoped Pamela would make him something. She wouldn't now. She was lying on her bed wide awake, listening, angry, unwilling to come out until John left. So maybe they would only stay a moment.

John sat with his hands over his face on the corner of the couch, and Kevin came back to sit in the chair again wide-eyed and listening for sounds. From this floor he could hear the wind begin again driving the dead leaves to the ground. It was a good view of the river—see all the way to the bridge. In the winter they skated just below the wharf on the rough uncertain ice and in spring though warned by their parents they went out on the floes spearing the first dull Tommie-cod for sport. He had not done either in some time.

"Want a coffee or anything?" he asked.

"Anything to drink?" John said looking up from his hands. "Wine or anything."

"Maybe," he reflected glancing toward the bedroom door. And then he lifted himself once more and went into the kitchen. After a moment he came out shaking his head. "Sorry—nothing, coffee?"

"Shit no, come on, let's go get some wine."

"Now? It's damn near eleven."

But John simply groped for his boots, grunting. Maybe it was best to let him go or go with him, leave him somewhere, anywhere and come back later. Pamela might be in a better mood later. He would come back to cook the partridge for her later; toast and partridge and coffee to stay awake. He felt his hunger. Any wine and it would be difficult to see. So he didn't want wine but he would go along. He wished that Bruce was still with them. Two could handle it better than one because with two there seemed a bond. More of intense excitement on how the whole thing would end.

"Naw," John resumed, grinning and standing, unbalanced and tilted to one side as he spoke. "Naw, we'll get a couple of quarts, bud and just dancer in the park." Grinning. Kevin stood, looked at the wet marks John's feet had made, looked

27

to the bedroom door. He grinned a little also, a tight little grin.

"Okay," he said. He turned out the lamp and put his wet boots on in the dark, smelling the dark apartment, hearing the wind from so high up, John beside him leaning on the wall.

Once outside again the wind was not so bad but it was cold, colder than before and the streets were soundless, wet and autumn dead. They walked. John insisted that they walk, and Kevin obliged, listening to the drunken shouts of his friend. Only the heaviness of his friend beside him stepping through puddles in some needless exercise, splashing Kevin as he went along.

"I think I'll climb a pole," he said at one point, running ahead. "I'll climb a pole," and he latched onto it and tried to shinny up but failed and fell backward uncontrollably and laughed, lying on his back until Kevin reached him and helped him to his feet. "Goddamn pole," he giggled.

"There, there my good man, take 'er easy," Kevin said cautiously. He felt the damp mud on John's jacket as he lifted him. "You're a little wet."

"My hair's a little wet."

"So is your ass."

"My ass and my hair's a little wet."

"So be it."

"It be so."

With that they kept walking, John laughing and cursing through all the side lanes that they took, grabbing onto branches and trying to swing. Singing. But when they passed the police station he was at once sober and contained and normal conversation resumed.

"I don't think you need the wine."

"Oh yes I do and so do you—she won't talk to you the rest of the night so you may as well stick with me."

Kevin was silent.

"It's my fault, isn't it?"

"What?"

"That she won't talk to you."

"Christ no."

"That's what you think, that's why she slammed the door."

"That's stupid. She's mad because I didn't take her out."

"I still know she doesn't like me."

28

Kevin was silent again but his silence provoked John into speaking.

"I never liked her too much either, if you want to know the truth. She's too bitchy. You should kick her ass."

"Okay," Kevin said.

"Well, it's just my opinion."

They were both silent for a moment.

"Sure but I go with her, you know that."

"So?"

"So just watch what you say," Kevin said finally, unsure of his voice.

"Oh don't be so fucking serious about it."

And again they were silent until they came to the square. There was nobody in it. A few girls loitered on the far side of the street that they were approaching. Waterfront, the black rotting timbers of the wharf. And there in the shacks the old men hard on rubby, telling stories of the war. Kevin loved the stories of the war.

"So you really want your wine."

"Yep."

"I'd rather get something to eat."

"Later."

"Can't afford to do both."

"Wine will fill you up."

They proceeded across the street and down an alleyway by two stores, each walking on one side because of the puddles and then moving along close beside each other across the dirt parking lot. In front were the black depths of the channel water and at the upper left the small shacks with their lights on. They turned and walked along the waterfront as long as they could, hearing the waves lap against the ageless timbers, and then began moving up another pathway through wet frost-killed burdocks and weeds.

"Hope they have some wine—two quarts of Napoleon."

"One quart, one quart is all we need, all we can afford, at least all I can afford."

"See those girls back there did you?"

"Yes—so what."

"Wait until I get a bit of Napoleon."

Sometimes they crawled, aided by grabbing onto branches with their hands because the path was steep and shale-ridden and they moved carefully for fear of sliding. Then once on

29

top of the bank they had a view of where they had come from and of the buoys out in the dark water and the far side of the river glowing also. But they turned and went toward the shacks outlined in the darkness. Tall, oak-lined, the far side of the field. Kevin had hunted squirrels here when he was younger, armed with a pellet gun that the police one day took from him. That was before his family had moved downriver. Now the place had changed, old things had died and new things been born, and it wasn't the same coming here for wine. No matter how many times he came here for wine he couldn't help feeling that it was not his place any more.

In front of them was the rotting skeleton of a car defaced in the muddy dooryard, its hood toppled back in undergrowth a few yards away, large cement blocks here and there on the short brown grass. The door to the shack being slightly ajar, they ventured up to it, John knocking.

"Nice smell," he said under his breath.

Kevin was back from him a little and he could see through the window a man coming to answer. And soon the man was there in his undershirt opening the door cautiously as they all do, his burly half-bearded face staring out at them through the light. On recognition he smiled, but not broadly, just a careful understanding grin and without so much as a word motioned them through. They stepped inside. The smell of stale awfulness. Not that all bootleggers' homes smelt of this, but his did. It smelt of the yellow light, the yellow sweat, the dark grease from cars, the blanket partitions separating the kitchen from the living-room, the living-room from the closet and the toilet, and the small paper-streaked walls, water-damaged as if at some point there had been a fire.

The wood stove was burning. They came in and sat by the stove because they had always done this and it was an accepted thing to do, tracking mud and wetness over the browned floor, sitting on paint-chipped stools and seeming as much at home as they could possibly be although they weren't.

"Wet one tonight," said the woman sitting there with them. Her husband stood beside the table with an orange faded table-cloth, oil-cloth—cups and saucers not cleared away and a loaf of bread not cleared away. She sat, housedress below her knees, torn near her bulging thighs, nylons down around her ankles and her thick black veins protruding like meat gristle along her legs.

"It is, Mammie," John answered. She laughed and coughed, swollen double chin. But her husband looked at them now without so much as looking as her, or listening to her. He was a small man, but with a rough broad face and thick dark arms and his hair, which was turning grey, was short and uncombed. He was standing in a dirt-streaked undershirt before them, his right hand stroking his chin, his brown pants too long and too baggy, and the belt he had on was drawn to the last hole.

"I don't have no beer," he mentioned. "I don't have no hard stuff either."

"You know we always get wine, Walkie," John said looking toward him and then to Kevin, who nodded in agreement. Kevin looked at him also, looking past him. The large Virgin on the windowsill in that blue gown of hers and that white angelic face. A large Virgin and a pin box with beads, the plastic window curtains pinched back by the table ends.

"Not always," he said looking finally toward Mammie. "Eh Mamm," he smiled. "Not always—but anyway I don't know if I want to sell my wine tonight."

"Why?" John questioned.

"Well supposin' I want a drink, you fuckers never think that someone else might want a drink, no sir, you never think of that, eh Mammie?"

"Well if you can't sell none, you can't," Kevin said getting to his feet to leave, happy enough to leave.

"I ain't said nothing about not selling any; it depends—it depends."

"All's we want is a quart of Nap," Kevin answered before the question was asked.

"Hardly seems worth it then," Walkie said.

"Worth what?" John questioned.

"Worth me going into the closet to get the son of a whore, eh Mamm."

"Well, Kevin wants a quart and I want a quart."

"Two quarts," Mammie said. "Walkie, they want two quarts."

"One," Kevin said again.

"Jesus you can't even make up your mind."

All were silent for a time. Walkie went into the other room and came back a moment later with a quart half emptied, one

31

he'd been drinking from, and began to sip nonchalantly. He passed it around and they all had a mouthful. It tasted sickly sweet and warm. Kevin wished to go.

"You buy one and I'll buy one," he said to John. "Okay, we'll have two."

Walkie looked at them and grinned a little and then motioned to his wife who disappeared behind the partition and came out a moment later with them in her hand, placing them on the table and sitting back down.

"Seven dollars," he said.

"Three-fifty each," John said. "Seven dollars?"

"It's the cheapest you're going to get it here," the man said.

They were outside again and walking along the path again. The sky was rolling with black wintery clouds and they were moving back toward the square through burdocks and dead weeds.

"Be careful—if you fall, you'll break your neck."

"Or the wine," John said looking back over his shoulder. "He was in a good mood wasn't he?"

"Never like that before, never was and I've seen him drunk out of his mind before, but tonight he was retarded."

"Ya and seven bucks is a bit of a burn," John said running the last few paces downhill and coming to a stop on the muddy roadway, looking back again. Kevin came up behind him holding his green full bottle under his hunting jacket. Wasted money. Now he was broke and already intoxicated, he needed no more. He needed no more on his empty stomach. "Where are we going?" he asked. John already had his top off, and drank and shuddered and spit and passed it over. The sick sweetness of alcohol and fruit. He did not smell it as he drank, rolling his head back to the sky and closing his eyes, its warm too-sweet taste in his mouth.

"We'll walk to the wharf," John said already heading in that direction. "Save yours till after," he shouted back. And Kevin felt the cold again. It was as if Walkie had made him buy the extra quart; it was as if he had been forced to buy it. What would they need with a Virgin statue? What would they need with beads? The smell! As if her veins themselves were roasting in the fire. He had never been that way before, never, but she was always the same, always sitting, always ugly, but kind and passive.

Kevin sat with his feet dangling over the timbers, looking

down into the water black and uncertain seven feet below him, being cold and frightened by it. Depth. A hideous liquid encasement. He had seen them take a youngster from the water the summer before. Three days in water tangled in construction wire under the bridge; ripped and swollen body, its bloated purple face. And he had run to see it; he, frightened by the depth and blackness of the bay, frightened on the floes, frightened on his father's drifter as a child, had run to see.

John sat beside him, his legs also dangling, staring not down at all but across to the lights on the other shoreline and drinking from the green bottle at intervals and passing it over to Kevin. They spoke very little the first few minutes. It was getting later and later and he was thinking that Pamela would be waiting. The more they drank the drunker they got, and being drunk they began to talk. Kevin was no longer cold. His stomach was burning but he felt tired and comfortable and fixed in the certain place that he was he didn't wish to move. He felt very heavy.

"Last time I'll go to Walkie—son of a whore," Kevin said.

John lay back on the wharf and began looking at the sky.

"Well where else is there?"

"Taxi's."

"They don't sell to everybody."

"Jes' he's a prick lately."

"He was tonight," John said.

"I heard he hires Mammie out—can you imagine, who in Jesus would want to screw that?"

"I would if I was drunk enough."

"Holy sweet fuck bud, ya'd have to be awful drunk."

"Just drunk enough."

They both laughed slightly.

"Things screw you up," John said after a short while.

"What do you mean?"

"Well they do; when you stop to think of them, they start screwing you up is all I mean. My old lady's always bitching about my drinking but what in hell's name is there to do?"

"Worst thing is to start thinking about them when you're drunk, bad enough to think of them sober."

Silence again for a long period. Kevin took the last swallow from the first bottle and threw it into the water. It buoyed there ten feet from the wharf. He stood to find a rock but when he had he could not see the bottle any longer so he threw the rock into the water also. He felt dizzy and sat down again. He took the top off his bottle and passed it to John.

"Last time I'll go to that bastard," John said, and then added sitting up, "what do you think of Bruce anyway?"

"He's all right, I don't think he meant anything tonight."

"Oh hell, he's always shouting his mouth off, you just don't see. His old man does everything for him—everything for him and he's gutless and I can't stand gutless people. Why did he graduate? It was his old man. Why did he get on at the mill? It was his old man. And that Jesus car of his, who pays the gas? His old man." John said all this rapidly and then drank again as if he needed a drink and then passed the bottle over.

"Maybe," Kevin said and drank also.

When they had finished half the bottle they were on their feet once more, walking back over the parking lot, John carrying it and stumbling along through the puddles again, still talking loudly and cursing, Kevin slightly behind him, answering the curses with curses of his own. When they reached the alley between the stores John turned around. He was standing in the middle of the large puddle and turned around as if he didn't even know where he was, didn't care where he was and said, "she's pregnant."

"Who?" Kevin asked starting.

"She is—Julie is," he said, and when he said it, he sat down the bottle clutched in both his hands; he sat down in the water so that it flowed in its murky coldness all across his legs. Kevin stood stunned not by what John had said but by what he had just done. John sat there tipping the bottle to his mouth. "She's pregnant," he said again drinking from the bottle once more, "and I'm the only one who knows, the only one alive who knows."

"Andrew told you?" Kevin asked.

"Two days ago and then zap he's gone, so what in hell am I going to do?"

Kevin reached down and helped him to his feet. He was soaking and looked frightened and Kevin couldn't say anything, couldn't answer. John passed the bottle to him and he drank. They were both standing in the middle of the puddle.

"Do you know Julie?" Kevin asked.

"Oh hell I know her, ya but I wouldn't know what to say to

her. I mean I wouldn't know how to act or anything, especially when Andy's just dead."

"Well what was he going to do?"

"That's what was screwing him up—that's what screws everyone up—I don't know what he was going to do!"

The town clock showed just before two. They had come up out of the alleyway, out of the puddles. The wine was gone and John was coughing continuous short coughs and was drenched and cold. Kevin also was cold but in his drunkeness he felt more sick than cold. His stomach was turning and he could taste the wine that he had consumed.

They walked unsteadily along the street and then crossed it to sit on a park bench. They did not talk now. They sat. The two girls they had seen earlier were still loitering, this time on the other side of the park by the statue, laughing and singing as if they were drunk themselves.

It was true that Kevin had often hunted girls but now he felt little like doing so, and since John for the time being didn't mention it he said nothing. He felt that they must continue their walk and go back to the apartment—that he must take John back with him and dry him out and then drive him home.

"What time is it?" John asked.

"Time to go—it's after two and you'll freeze to death in those clothes."

John willingly assented and they rose again, both stiff-legged, and began to walk not in quite the same way as they had earlier in the evening, nor for that matter, as they had before they came to the bench. No, this walk was different and the more disagreeable since both were wet and cold and so dull-brained with liquor that they felt like sleeping on the spot. And John was more than wet, he was drenched and his hair mud-ridden, and so he stepped almost mechanically in front of Kevin, water still dripping from his clothes.

The girls, half way up the statue, clinging to its arms, stopped their yelling as soon as they noticed the two and then began a bird-like tittering and laughing between each other. Kevin wished to pay them no mind. They were drunk, and far too young, and he would not go out on a limb for girls so skinny and stupid. Pamela was at the apartment and he would go there. Even if she was angry he would go back to her.

Reassuring apartment with warmth and clean walls and sleep.

John was the first to come below them. He stopped when he had and looked up at them, snorting in a horse-like fashion which made them titter even more. They were fourteen or so Kevin thought; yes, no more than fifteen. No he mustn't do anything, say anything. He felt very dizzy and could not look up at them because he was so dizzy.

"John," he said.

"Look at the ass," John said turning back to him. The girls jumped from the statue, very young and small with saucy faces. They no longer tittered. Kevin moved closer and tried to pull him away but he didn't budge.

"Where did ya get wet—swim the river?"

"Yes," John said.

"Sure ya did," they both laughed.

"Fall in a puddle?"

"Up yours," he laughed, grabbing the girl nearest to him and hugging her cruelly with his right arm. She had long dirty hair and her face was puffed, her pug nose red from the cold. His clothes wet hers and she screeched for him to let go and kicked at him so that he did, he cursed at her once again, telling her that she was a bitch, that they were both bitches.

"Christ John, come on," Kevin said, grabbing him by the arm and finally leading him away to the other side of the fountain. The girls were laughing, laughing saucily, and John wanted to go back to the one and hit her.

"What are they here for if they won't screw!" he yelled, his face at once maddened and contorted.

"Now come on John," Kevin said dizzily, his words coming from far inside him, holding onto John's wet clothing. And the girls no more frightened than they were on the statue, laughing, hideously laughing so that John became all the angrier.

"I want to know," he said, twisting out of Kevin's grip finally and standing where he was, standing, shouting at the girls because of the liquor in him. "Saucy little sluts," he roared. Kevin wished to turn and walk away but couldn't. John did not know how to handle himself now, did not know how to act. It was obvious by the way he approached the whole subject, by the way that he had talked to the girls that he was in a drunken fit. He was roaring at them and they were roaring back.

36

"Sluts," he was saying.

"Prove it you bastard," one of them yelled back.

And when he could stand it no longer and apparently losing all self-discipline he jumped into the fountain and began to cross it screaming at the top of his lungs so that the whole town must have been awakened by it. It was all so ridiculous. What was it for? Kevin stood petrified at the noise and the girls ran off screaming into the darkness. John wished to kill them it seemed but could do nothing more than slip and slide into the knee-high water until his shouts gave up and he sat to his neck, exhausted.

John didn't speak but rather shivered like a sick old man as if his whole life had been spent by the one exhausting tumult that he had showed in the fountain. All anger, frustration seemed absent now, only the shivering, the coughing, the squeaking boots. Kevin also was muted and though he was searching for something to say was searching vainly. Pamela must wake to feed them he thought and John must take a bath to get the dirt and the wet from him or he would wake with pneumonia in the morning.

They walked the same quiet streets back to the apartment. Half-naked trees tossed above them in a sky still rolling with winter clouds. Kevin smelled the winter in the night, the coming of winter. And they walked around the puddles now, puddles so still that one would think they were already covered with ice, the half wisps of smoke from brick chimneys, and the lonely shadows of dogs running. Here and there a sound in the alleyways.

But it was only October—his birthday not too far off—so it meant a long freezing season, an empty sterile season ahead, hauling crates through the snowdrifts to the factory door as he had done the winter before, his hands so blistered red that even through his mitts he could feel the burning itch of pain. He hated where he worked, the smell of tarps, the boxcars, the taste of lime and salt. Often he would neglect his work to watch the yellow filth from the pipes flow and seep through the discoloured ice of the river and stream hovering like mist for a quarter of a mile. And in the morning especially with the bright sun over the sharp motionless treeline it seemed like the greatest crime if he didn't stand motionless also, for a moment at least, and watch.

They had no more passion for the night, no more for

37

drinking or talking out loud, no more for cursing their way along. It was very uneasy walking in such quiet after such a scene. They ascended the stairs solemnly, Kevin going back for a moment to get the bird from his truck and then returning to find John leaning against the door shivering like a sparrow half dead from fright.

"No answer?" Kevin asked.

"Don't know—didn't knock," John answered, abruptly stepping backwards a little to let Kevin in and coughing deeply. A hoarse cough in his lungs. "Your job to knock," he added silently.

"Hope we don't have to wake her," Kevin sighed, knocking rapidly and loudly as if it was his intention to wake people, knowing that at this time of night she mightn't even answer the door. Frightened if she didn't John would freeze before he got home. His responsibility. And his stomach turning now like crazy because he was in the warmth of a building and there was no air to stop him from becoming dizzy or sick.

Reluctantly he knocked a second time and a third and finally called her name as loud as he dared before he heard her footsteps. And when she opened the door she stood there silently in her nightdress again, her eyes half closed again and he and John walked past her into the room.

They stood by the door when she closed it, motionless. John dripping on the small mat that she had. No-one spoke for a moment. John seemed too tired to speak and Kevin undid his boots with one hand while holding the bird in his other. He took his socks off also because they were wet and placed them on the floor beside his boots.

"What time is it?" she asked.

"After two I think," he said. "Ya it's well after two—John needs a hot bath."

"Hot bath?"

"Ya."

"No I don't."

"Sure you do—you'll freeze," Kevin said turning toward him and then turning quickly away, eyeing Pamela with desperation as if to say, Please don't say anything to him. She glared at Kevin and went to the couch to sit and John with his boots on walked over also and sat down, his head lowered and his face so deathly white. Kevin stood for a moment more and then went over also to sit between them and he put his arm

38

around Pamela, the feel of her soft bed warmth still on her. The partridge lay between John and him, hidden from her eye. She couldn't have noticed it—she noticed only their drunkenness, the smell of wine and wetness and John marking her couch with the outline of his clothes. She sat silently flinching because of her sleepiness but sitting straight and unmoveable, staring at those nice prints on the wall, at her nurse books in the corner.

"What time do you go in?" he asked.

"Four," she replied coldly, searching with her hand in her purse for a cigarette to smoke. "Four o'clock tomorrow afternoon," she said again. "Why?"

"Nothing," he said.

And if there was anything he detested, it was a moment in which he had to suffer the agony of her silence. He was never very good at playing the same type of game. Now with John there in his wet and filthy clothes it seemed improbable that she would speak at all. He had no idea of what to do. What must he do? He listened to the wheezing in his friend's nose and time passed and he became dizzier, seeing the light on the ceiling revolve before him ever faster and faster until he knew he must move, stand and move before he was sick on the spot. But when he stood, he did not know where he was going, could not see clearly—only the hot light blurring in his eyes, and he wished to clutch onto anything to remain upright.

But he fell onto his hands and knees and began crawling to the bathroom. She was screaming at him—he could hear her screaming. He remembered the soreness of his scraped hand and could feel her hands trying to pull him to his feet—hands under his armpits trying to pull him to his feet. And when she tried to lift him he was sick.

"Jesus Kevin," she said.

And already he felt better, felt himself emptying, the sick and clouded sweetness of his brain so that when he rolled away from it he lay utterly exhausted and relaxed wishing to sleep on the floor beside his vomit. She was crying—he could hear her cry and above her cry John snoring on the couch. He must waken him to take a bath and even though he wished to sleep he stood, his weak eyes glaring at the floor.

"It's not too much."

"It's all over the place."

39

"So I couldn't help it."

"Why do you always have to make a pig of yourself?"

"I don't."

"You do—you always do."

"Ya well, if you had just acted half decent I wouldn't have gone out—ya won't even cook the partridge."

"What partridge?"

"That fuckin' partridge," he yelled pointing to the couch.

John was now full across it and the partridge was covered. John's soaking body lying like a lead weight on the couch. Pamela went to the kitchen and came back with the bucket and mop and Kevin felt himself getting dizzy again but remained standing knowing what might happen if he fell.

So he stood bending over her as she mopped the mess with a mop and warm water making a wet giant circle on the floor back and forth, back and forth, never ending. And his dizzy wet eyes watched her as she mopped, unconsciously watching. He said nothing. Her frail little shoulders he thought. They were shaking; she was frightened and her body was shaking violently and she was angry with him and her body was shaking. Oh what a sickening sweet taste in his mouth.

"Your mother phoned wondering where you were," she said.

He was startled out of looking, straightened but said nothing.

"She phoned twice in an hour."

He went over to the couch and woke John, tugged at him until his eyes opened and he grunted nastily. He would die there if he did not get of his wet clothes. Kevin told him to get up and helped him to his feet and then moved along with him into the bathroom. It didn't matter about his boots any more—it didn't matter because that was only a little wetness and everything was wet and smelling. So they moved into the bathroom and Kevin ran the water.

"Where's the wine?" John asked sitting on the flush; asked it so it took a moment for what he said to be understood, to come through the air and be finally understood. And the wind was up again. It rattled the window so high above the lane and whistled through the slanting arches of the house so that it made the thought of sitting in puddles and swimming the fountain all the more horrible and cold.

"The wine—oh it's finished John, we've had enough wine."

40

"You puke?"

"Yes a little."

John laughed drunkenly, such a mean drunken laugh, and the clear water pouring in the tub and the wind so fierce on the outside against the house. Kevin laughed also and John coughed like his soul was coming up, forcing itself through his windpipe into the small yellow room.

Kevin reeled around and went away, with John still laughing faintly from behind his shoulder, from behind his soiled hair and the wind stench on his huntsclothes. He stepped over the wet mop marks on the floor and into the living-room into where Pamela was. His whole body ached now and he felt very sick, did not want to argue any more, wished to find some place soft and warm to lie down. But she turned to him now reddened at the cheeks as if about to curse.

"What the hell is this?" she asked.

"The partridge," he said alarmed. "The one you were going to cook."

"Cook?" she mocked. "At three in the morning."

"So."

"So there's feathers all over the place," she cried.

"Oh like hell."

"Well look at the couch—it's ruined, soaking wet feathers all ground into it. I'm throwing this out," she said and walked into the kitchen. Kevin ran after her and grabbed her by the arm; angry now for the whole evening, he grabbed her by the arm and squeezed at it so that it hurt her and she squealed. She glared up defiantly at him but he still squeezed.

"You're not throwing it out," he stammered. "It's my partridge."

"Well take it then," she screamed. "Cook it yourself," and she tore away from him and ran to the bedroom slamming the door. She must have been crying by the way she ran, holding one hand up to her face the way she did, like a child would do and dropping the bird on her kitchen floor. And Kevin stood there wanting to yell—to hit something if he could.

2

Perhaps he was up twice for water, perhaps more than twice. Each time his head was spinning madly and he had tripped over John lying in the darkness on the floor coughing violently in his sleep as if nothing could quiet what was inside him. But each time he made it back into the bedroom and drifted into sleep again cuddling closer to her as she moved away from him. And his dreams were frightening—full of red colour. The last time he went for water it was light, dismal day, soundless vapour in the Sunday sky. He stood for a moment before the window looking out. The deserted lane, the grey leaf-washed pavement of the town.

He had tried to talk with her as he lay there and after each coming back he tried to improve relations. She was awake. He knew she must be awake listening to him move back and forth from the kitchen, but she was so still most of the time he couldn't tell. And she was silent also, and stiff. He tried again and again and then giving up he fell asleep.

He had frightening dreams. When he woke, it was late in the morning and he was alone in the bed. He tried to remember what his dreams had been but only remembered that they were nightmarish and had scared him. He hoped he hadn't talked in his sleep.

But as he lay there this morning it wasn't his dreams that gave him trouble. It was the night before; it was yesterday; it was all of yesterday. The apartment was quiet, not a sound of them. They must both be gone, and yet he was too comfortable and safe to check, so taking it for granted he lay there thinking, trying to twist away from his thoughts.

Poor Pamela, her little shoulders shaking and John stretched out upon her couch as if he owned it—wetting it, squashing the dead bird's feathers into it and he so sick on the floor. He would never invite one of his friends again, that was the only certainty in it all. And of course the cow; his mother

42

had phoned twice and perhaps again this morning. How could he tell, she probably phoned again this morning and knew all, and the police looking for him. And of course staying away from home all evening would make her worry more. Perhaps she even went so far as to get the police and the police knowing about the incident with the cow informed her. And John making sly remarks all night—not enough to take offence but just enough to count. But, of course, John had needed someone to torment.

He turned the pillow to get its coolness and tried to sleep. His mouth had the stale taste of his sickness and he felt weak. He felt weak enough to know that if he stood he might need something to support himself. But he felt very lucky that he had thrown up, the greatest part of the liquor being out of his system. Yes, out of his system like those red dreams he had —all cleared away.

And he could hear a few cars pass every little while on the lane, and he stared at the clean white walls for a time, the dead palms—a yellowish dead, supported by Christ on the cross hanging on the wall. And the dresser with its woman things scattered on its top, jewelry and powders and things of that sort and a mirror above it with his name taped on it as a reminder to her and the dresser drawers half opened with the room shadows on them. He almost prayed that his mother hadn't phoned, that she knew nothing of anything at all.

It must have been more than an hour later for he had drifted to sleep again with his head sideways on the pillow, and when he woke, he knew it was later, at least an hour later. She was in the other room; he could hear her straightening things around and using a spray of some kind. But even though he knew in his heart it was her in the room because he could not see her he was frightened, frightened to move in case it was someone else. He did not want to call either but lay as he had woken, sober—staring sideways at the wall. There was spittle on the pillow, and yet he did not move his face, and he could feel his heart thumping in his ear. What if it was after all someone else entirely, someone like her mother who had often visited her on Sunday. Many times Kevin had to leave early Saturday afternoon when he had meant to spend the whole evening because her relations were coming down.

He didn't move, for no matter how much he knew it was her, he felt uneasy as if it were a stranger in the other room. It

43

wasn't his bed and if he was to be caught, why then he was the stranger, he would be out of place, he would look ridiculous. If it were her mother come down to surprise her and finding the place in such a mess had taken to cleaning it. But it was her—he knew it was her!

She opened the bedroom door and looked at him. He didn't look but knew she was looking at him, and he closed his eyes pretending to sleep, wanting her to go away now that he knew who it was—that it was her and he really could think of nothing to say. She moved toward him and he kept silent count of her footsteps until she touched him and he jumped.

"Nervous?" she said.

"Where were you?" he asked rubbing his eyes and yawning and lying there as if ready to sink into sleep again.

"I was at church. Andy Turcotte is dead."

"I knew last night—I thought you knew. That's why we were drunk," he said as if he had just remembered it. "Where's John?" he added.

"Took a taxi home—he's as sick as hell."

"Did he throw up last night?" he asked.

"No—but he's got one damned cold, serves him right, you should get one too; that's not how you remember a person, to go out and get drunk—that degrades the person you're remembering."

"Oh shut up," Kevin answered half-heartedly, some disappointment on hearing that John was not sick to his stomach, remembering again how he had been. "It's not right," he continued. "Everyone I know gets drunk when someone dies, so I don't care what in hell you think, and how in hell can you degrade someone that's dead?"

"Degrade their memory," she answered standing in the corner undoing her shirt.

He sat in bed watching her. It was not as if she were angry with him for what he had done but perhaps just disappointed; yes she was disappointed in him—certainly she was and that was a different thing entirely from anger. It made him feel menial and small because he could not combat it with anger of his own. Nevertheless he would try to make amends today, now if need be, for the trouble he had caused. He watched her changing into jeans, combing her hair with a brush.

"So what did you do last night?"

44

"Waited until I got bored with waiting and then went to bed—one free Saturday in a month ruined by your stupidity."

"It wasn't all my fault," he said, thinking how he must not apologize for it but rather make her understand the position he was in. "I had to take care of John or he would have drowned himself—I spent half the night pulling him out of puddles, for God's sake."

"What do you mean, take care of John?"

"Well, his best friend was killed—that's all."

"So?" she questioned coolly.

"So, what do you mean, So? When something like that happens a guy usually goes a little strange."

"For whose benefit?"

"For no-one's benefit—it just happens."

"I presume it was for his benefit," she said again rather coolly. "Yes, to make everyone see how grieved he was, to put on a show for the entire community and dragging you around with him as something of a personal audience. Anyway," she continued smartly, "you did your bit for him and I have to get in at four o'clock." She finished combing her brown hair, straight and shoulder length, and came next to the bed to draw the curtains back.

Kevin looked up angrily at her, not knowing how to say anything more in his defence. She always twisted things around the way they shouldn't be and cut off a conversation when she was on top, not giving him any advantage and then proposed something entirely different so that all would be forgotten. And she stroked the curtain now looking out into the street.

"Did you phone your mother?" she asked.

"No," he said. "Why, did she phone again?"

"Oh I don't know—I was at church."

Yes and he never went to church, never in a long time had he ascended the steps and taken the sacrament. He was born Catholic, had received his First Communion, had been taught by nuns, smelt their beads and heavy black linens, had seen their white faces staring out at him from behind their desks. He had been an altar-boy and at one point had wished to be a priest. But all that, almost forgotten now, had been only one point along the way. He had not gone to church in years save at Christmas eve when she and he would go with his family. He couldn't even remember what priest served the parish

45

now.

"Well, I think I'd better go soon anyway," he said, lifting himself from the bed and putting on his clothes quickly feeling sick even now and waiting for some reply. She made none save that ever-tedious stroking of the curtains. He moved to her and put his arms around her feeling her slight body in his arms and he kissed the back of her neck.

"Did you write to your parents?" he asked.

"I phoned last night."

"And?"

"And what?"

"Well, Christ did you tell them?"

"Yes, I did as a matter of fact."

"What did they say?"

"Postpone it until after Christmas at least but I told them no. They didn't say very much after that. I was kind of hoping we'd celebrate last night," she said turning her face toward him with that look and colour of disappointment, her little wrinkled brow.

"Are they going to come?"

"Yes, they didn't say they wouldn't."

"Two weeks," he said smiling and she smiled and he kissed her. "I'm telling my old lady today."

"Your mother!"

"Ya, my mother—I'd better go."

She looked at him and turned away, the smile erased; looked through the window at the street.

Clinton Dulse had moved his family six years before to one of the few remaining stone cottages on the river. For four of those six years he had fished with a small drifter in the bay, occasionally taking his son with him for company though they rarely talked. He was 56 years old now and fished no longer, owning a small store and operating a school bus for support. He was tall and brown-faced and walked with a crooked sway. He was never loud in any way as if experience had taught him not to be and he rarely spoke either to argue nor to laugh. He never drank now though he used to and he never bothered with his wife now though he used to beat her.

He was a silent man. He had four children, two daughters and two sons, the older boy dead for years and one of his daughters, Sheila, out of the province working and Debby the

46

youngest and brightest at home. Kevin was his only son now and though sometimes they tried to speak to one another they rarely if ever did.

It was Saturday night. He was seated on a stool behind the counter scratching numbers in an account book. The store was already closed, and the naked bulb furnished a poor light so that his eyes squinted terribly and perspiration dribbled on his face. Every once in a while he would sit back, roll a cigarette and relax, blowing the greyish smoke behind him. He would stare at the naked light and think and then after reflection begin to work again.

He was working when his wife came up to him through the doorway adjoining the store to the house. She was a small stout woman a few years younger than her husband. Her hair was greying and her teeth were bad—never taken care of as she would have wished. But for all this her face was soft, white and placid.

"Kevin isn't back yet," she said.

"Ump," he answered with a cigarette in his jaws.

"Well, do you suppose it's that damn old truck?" she asked.

"Truck works fine," he said.

"I hate him out in those woods after dark."

"He knows the woods."

"It's eight."

"He'll be along."

She turned to go and her husband looked up at her, putting his cigarette out in the tray crushing it down not with his fingers but with his thumb.

"We're not going to sell any more dog food or cat food," he said.

"Why?" she asked turning back to him.

"Because nobody needs it," he said.

She went away. A short time later he heard her dialling the telephone and a short time after that talking in an agitated voice. She reappeared.

"He was supposed to be at Pamela's at five, Clinton."

Clinton said nothing. He stood, closed his account book with the pencil still in it and after shutting out the light walked awkwardly into the house. He went into the kitchen and taking milk from the fridge drank from the bottle. Then he replaced it and going into the living-room sat down.

The living-room was small and faded as was the house, and

the house was entirely too small for all the people that lived there. It was a little better with one away but still Clinton thought that someday he might add to it even for his own sake when all his children were gone. He was a good carpenter as he was a good fisherman as he was a good bus driver.

His wife followed him into the room and sat beside him on the couch. A small TV sat on a stand in the corner and they watched it, both watched it, husband and wife, sat there without moving, blinking their vague tired eyes.

But in a while his wife became nervous again and fidgeted for something to do, took her knitting basket down and fumbled through the green materials for the mitts she was doing. Clinton rolled another cigarette and sat quietly watching the picture. And when she could stand it no longer she went to the kitchen to use the phone again. He could hear her dialling again. In a moment she came back.

"He's still not there. I wish you were the least bit interested. He could be lying somewhere shot to death at this very moment, Clinton."

"Well if he is—." He stopped short of saying what he was going to, remembering how many years ago was it he had said the same thing. There was an instantaneous sweat upon him and he looked. Silence once again. The man rose and stretched and looked at his watch.

"It's so awful wet out too," she said. "What if he's stuck somewhere in the woods?"

"He'll be along, don't worry; this isn't the first night he's been late."

He had found that after his operation he always tired early. When he was younger, and not so much younger, even five years younger, a lack of sleep didn't put him out in the least. Sometimes four or five hours of sleep and then up with the dawn just breaking over the white cold water. Or when he was out at night, all night without sleep and then working around the cottage all day long splitting and piling wood. And also when he was coming off drink and knew that he would never drink again he suffered insomnia terribly and was nervous continually, thought at one point he was losing his mind.

Then he became a silent man and quit the boats and then the operation. He tired early and had in his heart an idea that he was fast becoming old—an old man like his brother who

48

lived in the old house all alone.

He brushed his wife almost touching arm with arm but not looking and went into the bedroom to sleep. He wore long underwear even in October and slept in it, slept on his side, always a very quiet sleeper.

He lay there on his side. The light was still burning and the green window-blind was pulled down. He heard the wind, the rain on the outside, the wind strong and then abating and then strong again. He listened to it, enjoying it, hearing also his wife's steady rocking in her chair. He heard someone come in from outside a little later and listened carefully.

"It's him," he thought, "he's home now." But then he heard the youngest's voice and the voice of his wife. He reached up and hauled the string. Blackness; and he lay back in that blackness listening and hearing and thinking. The rain now, like the rain that night with Joseph Paul and the engine dead and he working with the carburetor float and Joseph Paul keeping the drift line away so it wouldn't tangle, cursing at the black swells and Kevin sitting in the corner on a crate of fish stink shivering for he was just very young and not saying a word.

William would have been 38, his wife pregnant with him at age sixteen. He would have been 38 and Sheila now was, almost 30. So he was a father of two families, two different generations of children on whom there was no oneness or family solidarity. The only thing common seemed to be the parents but even they were not common: one, the children of a very young couple and the other, children of middle age, Deborah as unwanted and as unplanned as William had been.

But it was not hatred. He had not beaten his wife in hatred. It was rather an acute understanding at that boyhood age that everything was so hopelessly lost—that he would die never leaving the river to which he had been born. And his wife was pretty and had wanted to finish school but because of William she never had.

So they moved to his family's place and he worked a bucksaw on his father's land and the baby was born. In winter the baby was born and it was a long time after before they had intercourse again. He was very young and wanted others and when he had them he became diseased and had to have treatment and his father never forgave him for his acts.

When Sheila was born, they moved into town and he

49

worked in a garage. He never went to war. He had wanted to so desperately that he sometimes cried because he felt that in it was his one chance. He had two cousins who were lost at sea and at times he wished he were one of them. But the war ended and Kevin was born and one night he found himself an old man with his wife coming in to where he was and sitting beside him agitated, and though she was only 36 and still had her slimness, she was also old.

"William should have been in hours ago," she said.

He looked at her and said nothing. It was nearly Christmas and the floor was strewn with the cheapest tinsel and he was fidgeting with the manger, trying to put it together properly. He said nothing to her; the baby was awake and crying in the other room and she went and returned with it in her arms. She sat again and tried to stop the baby's crying.

"He should have sense enough not to skate on that damned ice."

He said nothing.

"Clinton—he might be dead," she said pale with fright.

"Well if he is," he finally answered harshly, "what in Christ's name can I do about it!"

Now it was ten o'clock. His wife came into the room and snapped on the light. He was not asleep. He was waiting. His eyes were closed and he was waiting. He could hear her undressing. He could hear Deborah in the kitchen preparing herself a lunch. He minded the light only in that she could see him lying there and would speak to him knowing he was awake, knowing he was waiting to be spoken to. But she did not speak, so after a moment he turned around to squint at her.

And she was not looking at him. The door was slightly ajar and she was glancing through it and when she finished undressing and slipping into a night robe she snapped out the light and crawled in beside him. She must have thought he was asleep and the bed sank badly so that they both at some time during the night would inevitably roll toward the middle.

"Where's my tobacco?" he asked slyly after five minutes or so of silence.

"In the other room," she answered.

"Could you get it?"

"Now?"

"Yes—I can't sleep, after a cigarette I'll be able to sleep."

She sighed as she lifted herself from the bed and grumbling a little she snapped on the light.

"Never mind if it's going to give you fits."

She said nothing and returned a moment later carrying the paper and tobacco in her left hand and, handing it to him almost rudely, she crawled under the covers and lay there, her back toward him.

"It's not as if I ask you for my tobacco every night."

She didn't answer and he wasn't the sort of person that would press a conversation. He sat in bed and rolled a finely rounded cigarette. Then in a moment he was up searching through his pants. When he found his matches, he got into bed again and all the while she was sighing. He sat there smoking, thinking of nothing.

"It's not you that has to get up in the morning," she snapped. He reached over her heaviness and pulled the light string and then only the glow of his cigarette and the smell of smoke. Occasionally the wind.

"I wish you wouldn't smoke in bed—it's dangerous."

He did not reply. Then the wind broke out again and the rain also against the trees above the cottage and he pictured the lane in mud and the sogginess of the wood piled in rows at the back of the cottage. He would have to get it in.

"Listen to that night," she said. "He could be stranded out on a night like this, and you sit here and smoke a cigarette."

He crushed the cigarette out with his thumb and covered himself in the warmth of the blankets as if she was not there and not speaking to him. But she spoke on for some time, making him more and more nervous. There would be silence and then she would speak. Then there would be silence again. It was like someone drilling on the nerve of his tooth. Each time she was silent he could not relax, knowing that the silence would not be permanent. He waited. As soon as she opened her mouth again, he would jump a little—even though he expected it, he would feel himself jump.

"—You just don't seem to care one way or the other," she was saying. "You leave it up to me to make all the decisions; leave it up to me to fight with them day and night. I'm too old to fight now. I had my fill with the other two. Poor Willie—if you had taken just the slightest interest."

51

He was going to tell her to shut her mouth but decided against it, since he was never in the conversation from the first, it was pointless to introduce himself at this stage. He remained nervously silent, waiting, and after a few moments more she was silent also, perhaps deciding cautiously that enough had been said and to say any more was to look for trouble. But he had not begun to drift to sleep before the phone rang. Twice it rang—their line.

"Oh Lord," she said with a start and, jumping out of bed, snapped the light on quickly. But before she could go anywhere Debby came to the door.

"Daddy," the girl's voice said. "It's for you."

Clinton got up and went to the phone, his wife plodding right behind him, and Debby ran in front leading. But he moved no faster than usual, that crooked sway that he had as if whatever he was going to find out, he was going to find out one way or the other. He put the receiver to his ear and said hello, and his face gave a sign of recognizing a voice, but that was all it gave and to his wife hovering so close to him at that moment the few words that he spoke were very inadequate. Her face was white with shock, of fear of shock, but it still had that placidness to it, that chubby smoothness. He put the receiver in its cradle after a few minutes.

"Debby, could you make me a cup of tea?" he asked.

"What in hell's name is it, Clinton?" his wife asked.

They looked at each other and he smiled and they looked at each other face to face. She looked up at him intently.

"Nothin' so go back to bed. Nothin'," he said again. "He shot a cow."

Of course the worst thing about the whole affair was that he had not gone directly home after the incident with the cow. If he had, everything at this point would be equilibrium once more. Now it was just beginning. Explain, explain. But if they asked him any questions or if his old man swore at him in anger, he would not answer. He would go to his room or pile wood or something, and after a while everything would work itself out as a crisis always did.

He was travelling the highway along the river toward the stone cottage. The day was very bright and cool and coloured but he did not notice it. He noticed nothing save the glimpses of the highway that he had, the muddy inside panel of the cab.

He hated piling wood into the black cellar, but he knew that soon the wood must go in and that he must help do it. He drove slowly knowing that he must hurry but not wanting to. How he worried his mother. His father worried also but in a different way, and it did not bother him to think that his father worried. His father could occupy his time with something he felt important and never became upset.

For six years now he was downriver and no longer a member of the town, had lost that feeling for the town and enjoyed living where he did. He did not mind the stone cottage either, except it was small and old looking. Yes he had been afraid to bring Pamela there when they had first started going together because he knew just by the way she acted that she came from an expensive place. It was more that she might be embarrassed going to supper with him and his parents and Deborah than him being embarrassed inviting her. But, of course, Pamela was never embarrassed.

He did not know what she did exactly. She was a nurse but he never understood exactly what she did. She told him things, she frightened him; she told him of all the people who were frail and old looking and died there every day. "You never know when you're going to be taken." That was the expression she often used. He questioned her about it, understanding that she loved to be questioned, especially about her work.

She had seen all sorts of things happen, she said, people dropping off like flies all around her, blood transfusions and women with their insides taken out so that they wouldn't bleed to death. She said that that was a very common thing. She said though that most of the people who died were old people who had strokes, and that some of the old men didn't even know where they were half the time. Boys had made passes at her, she said. She emptied the bed-pans of the sick.

Just below his house the river widened from the point, widening into the bay. In spring it was possible to hear the ice breaking like thunder just below and watch the seagulls as they spread their wings above the cold broken floes and the opened water. It was always a very refreshing sight to see. Even the lane caked with mud after the thaw, and the youngsters on the floes, or the younger ones playing hopscotch on the lane. But below the house the river widened into

53

the bay and beyond the bay the gulf. Of course it was impossible to see land looking straight out—only the buoys that warned ore-boats in the night. But the sight itself to the farthest horizon was infinitely appealing to anyone who'd take the time to look.

Kevin looked now. He had parked his truck on the side of the lane and had walked below to where a small rising jutted above the shoreline and was watching the black wintry bay waters and the horizon and the opposite shoreline. All was colour. The day was filled with colour. He stood there looking because he did not wish to go inside without an excuse—some excuse that would account for his activity during the night. He would be questioned and cross-questioned. He wouldn't answer. If he had only phoned them, everything would already be accounted for.

He stood for ten minutes pondering. Of course they must have heard about Andy. That was something of an excuse in itself. Certainly they knew that he had known Andy. But it was awful to think that he would use it as an excuse as he had already done once with Pamela. No, he wouldn't say a thing. He turned and walked up the small grass-wet pathway, and when he reached the rear of the cottage, he noticed his father near the bus. His father was watching him all the time he thought.

"Go-day," he said roughly. His father looked, silently looking.

"Hello," he finally replied, taking the cigarette from his mouth and crushing it under his foot in the mud that the rain had made and then looking back up at his son. Kevin looked at his father also and tried to read his face to see if he could tell in the expression of his father's face. And it was very hard to tell. He couldn't tell and his eyes were the first to shy away.

"We starting on the wood today?"

"We better," his father replied, bending over to roll a tarp out under the bus and then sliding under the bus upon it, almost hidden from Kevin's view so that Kevin didn't know whether it was safe or not to talk any longer. He stood there looking at the bus fearful that he would be ill all day and more that he would have to pile wood when he was ill.

"Okay—well, how long are you going to be?"

"What?"

"How long are you going to be working on the bus?"

54

"Not too long—half an hour perhaps."

Kevin stood there for a moment longer and then went into the house. It was Sunday and there was that Sunday flavour and smell to it which made him think of late breakfast after church. And Sunday was quiet, especially in autumn. The store was closed for one thing and the family sat quietly about all day doing little. Deborah did her lessons and his mother knitted. His father would always work around the yard and then go to bed early in the evening. It seemed that they always had pork or chicken for dinner.

So when he stepped inside it was quiet. He took his boots off and went into the kitchen. Deborah was at the kitchen table doing her lessons and she looked up at him briefly, nodding without talking, and then returned to the scribbler. The radio was playing.

"Where's mom?"

"Lying down."

She was a pretty girl—small but with a tendency to grow fat like her mother. And she was the same age now that her mother was when she was married—sixteen, which made her mother worry constantly over anything, dances in particular, although Deborah danced little and would shy away from a party. "Are you going out?" her mother would say. "Where exactly are you going?"

"Lying down," Kevin muttered to himself and then turned and went into the living-room to sit because he felt that he must. His mother rarely, if ever, lay down and never so early in the afternoon. She must be sick, he thought. She must know, biting at his lower lip in nervousness, which he often did, biting off and chewing the loosened skin of his lower lip. He never looked into a mirror, but he knew how white his face must be for his face was always white like death after drinking.

Rubena listened to it all lying on her bed with the sound of her heart and wide awake staring. She had heard the truck and had heard Kevin talking, first outside with Clinton and then to Deborah in the kitchen, and though she wanted an explanation she didn't know how to face him, nor did she know what she was going to say. Her first impulse was to jump up and run out to him but she didn't do that. He was on her chair now, rocking quietly. She wished to be positive of her

55

voice and of her words when she spoke to him, so she lay there trying to gain composure.

But of course she was upset. All Saturday evening she fretted over the fact that he had not returned and could do nothing but wait in anxiety while her husband remained quietly with his numbers in the store. She went to him twice that evening, but he said nothing and hinted nothing and went to bed much the same as usual.

And then the phone. God how she started. It seemed that he started also, yes, jumped a little under the quilts. And when she followed him into the kitchen, she couldn't catch her breath but saw only his tall swaggering body before her moving at that ever-slow pace. All the while he was calm and tight lipped. Then he turned to her and without the least difficulty looked into her eyes, without the least difficulty said: "Nothin', he shot a cow."

"Where?" she questioned trembling. "Where? Is he all right?"

"Houlden Bellia's cow, upriver," he said, turning away from her and going to the kitchen table to sit.

She went back along the corridor to her room and lay in bed waiting. In an hour or so he came back also and fell sleep as if nothing at all had happened. She didn't sleep that night.

It was not that Kevin was William; he was not in any way except that young wildness that they had. But Kevin was not William; he was more obedient—gentler and kinder she thought. She could understand Kevin. William was doomed from the start to be misunderstood.

They had moved to Clinton's father's. She was sixteen and of a different religion so that everything was new and frightening to her, and she was sick besides. She could not rid herself of the awful shyness she had when talking to anyone in his family and especially his mother. She found herself trying to be friendly and helpful and doing the wrong things and agreeing with everyone even when they talked about religion, which they often did. When she was left alone with anyone, she felt uncomfortable because there was always such a silence between a broken conversation. And Clinton was nice enough to her when they were gathered together, even putting his arm around her at times but when alone he was indifferent. He wasn't happy; she wasn't happy.

The house was large and as cold as a barn when the late fall arrived. She stayed alone in her room much of the time. She had an awful dread of what was happening to her; what would happen when the winter came.

"How do you feel?" the old man would say to her when he met her on the stairway or in the hall. He would look at her kindly and say, "How do you feel" kindly. She would always reply, "Fine—I feel fine," and smile at him a little because she knew he felt terribly responsible in some way for her pregnancy. But she felt like an intruder just the same.

Then there were fears. When she sat alone in the afternoons, she would think to herself how awful the pain would be because she had heard talk and knew from this talk that giving birth was painful. "I might even die," she would murmur aloud. She would shake and try to keep her mind occupied with knitting which she was just learning to do and did poorly. She never bothered Mrs. Dulse with any questions because somehow she thought it improper. When they were alone, Mrs. Dulse would sometimes say,

"You're as sound as a nut."

She would look up at the face of the older woman and through respect think all her fears were groundless. But as soon as she was alone these phantoms would come again. At night Clinton would sleep with his back to her.

It was a few weeks before William was born when the real snow came. Snow had fallen off and on all through December. At times the ground had almost cleared to bare frozen rubble, leaving the fields to the south of their house dead looking. But with the heavy snow everything looked a little more pleasant and the waiting for winter was over.

"Hello dear," he said one night, coming into the room bringing the cold from the outside with him on his woods' jacket and through his hair. He turned on the light and shut the door standing by it unsteadily. There was wine in his hand and on the smell of the cold air and in the glow of his frozen face. He tipped the bottle but kept his eyes on her. She was lying on her back under the quilts so that her swollen part was obvious, and he looked at it and snickered drunkenly, taking steps toward the bed.

"How's the little papoose?" he said.

She looked up at him but said nothing. She wasn't frightened, curious perhaps at where he had been, but not frightened, and she wondered if his father knew that he was drink-

57

ing. He sat down on the bed and stroked at her hair with his cold fingers.

"Where were you?"

"Oh, nowhere—downriver."

"What were you doing down there?"

"At a dance," he said brazenly, almost as if he wanted to test her reaction, but he shifted his eyes so that they stared at the floor. He didn't remove his fingers from her hair.

"It must be nice for you to be able to go to a dance." There was trembling in her words.

"It is," he said menacingly, coldly.

"And you leave me here—I'm married to you, you know." Marriage was a word that she still could not say without stuttering, and so her voice continued to tremble. He turned his gaze back to her.

"So you couldn't come!"

"I'm married to you," she said once more feeling her eyes water, turning her head sideways on the pillow. He drank from his wine again.

"I come in here in a good mood and you start—what in hell am I supposed to do. Look at me," he whispered harshly pulling her hair so that she was forced to look at him. "What in hell am I supposed to do?" He yanked her hair all the more so that she put her hand up to try and pull his hand away, and as she did so she began to cry. But it was from fear and she cried softly so no-one would wake.

Later he finished his wine and crawled into bed with her. They both were soundless for a time and then he began to talk, nonsense mostly, but it was his way of telling her that he was sorry. "We'll probably have a kid with two heads," he said. "Or one that's all wobbly like a rubber band," he said laughingly, making everything a joke. "I'm scared Clinton," she said after he had finished teasing, and she could envision his whole face turning sour, and she felt that she shouldn't have said it.

"Why?" he said after some time, and his voice told her that he was vexed.

"I don't know—I am."

"Why," he said once more, almost lackadaisically. "You're as sound as a nut."

She could hear Kevin in the other room rocking on her chair.

58

Now she lifted herself from the bed and began to dress. She had not gone to church this Sunday, and it was the first Sunday in many months that she had missed. When she finished dressing, she straightened her hair, looked at her calm placid face in the mirror with not a trace of inner anxiety on it, and then left the bedroom slowly.

She entered the living-room just as slowly. Kevin was half asleep and his head rested on his hand. He moved the chair almost unconsciously as if once in momentum it continued to move. He had not taken his jacket off and it was still a little damp, but when she entered he did not move and she made no immediate effort to arouse him. Instead she sat on the couch with her arms folded and watched him without a word. He knew how closely she was watching him, watching his face. About a minute passed.

"How are you?" he finally said, looking over at her, and he could not suppress a nervous grin when he did so. Her face was like marble.

"Where were you?"

"With John."

"All night?"

"Yes—why?"

"Because we got a phone call last night concerning you," she said, looking at him as straight as an arrow the way Pamela sometimes did. He straightened, felt his nervousness grow within him and could not suppress the grin so obvious to her. She was talking about the call and how it made her sick with fright coming so late, and how she worried all evening not knowing where he was or who he was with. But he tried to shrug his shoulders at what she said and could feel his heart throbbing in his ears.

"Who was the phone call from?" he questioned, breaking into the middle of her conversation and stroking at his unclean hair with his hand, thinking of dead Andrew and the night before as if the phone call was something else entirely from what he knew it was.

"You'll have to talk to your father," she said. "You'll have to go with him and see the man this afternoon."

So it was the man then and not the police, he thought. That made him happier, relieved. Yes, it was the man then, and it was as much the man's fault as his. Why hadn't the man yelled, he thought again.

59

"It was an accident you know," he said aloud or rather stammered it weakly.

"I don't care," she said and once again she told him how worried she had been and that he had no right to worry her and had no consideration for her feelings. He looked at her marble-like whiteness as he spoke and was angry with her all at once and looked scornfully at her.

"You don't remember William, do you?" she said trembling, her lower lip trembling a little as she spoke, "you don't remember him but I do. Whenever anyone is out too late, it drives me crazy; it puts me through the same thing all over again and I can't stand it."

He wondered whether or not she was going to cry, and then looking away from her he got up and left the room. He felt stupid and hated her because of it. He went to his room and lay on the bed but he couldn't sleep. In a while he heard his father's bus idling in the dooryard, and a while later his father came in.

"We going to get the wood in?"

"Some of it," the old man said.

He had piled two rows along the cellar wall. Each row he tried to make even with the other, and he was on the third row now. The smell of wet bark in the black cellar. It must have taken some time because through the trap he could see the grey of afternoon and his father was more of a shadow now and the distant sky was darker. He had piled the two rows carefully, and he was on the third row now, piling it carefully on small round spruce supports. He wanted to see no daylight between the individual pieces. It became a game with him —everything in order.

His father was on the outside throwing the pieces to him but stopping to rest every now and then and wiping the sweat from his face, which afforded Kevin just enough time to clear the wood thrown into him before starting it all again. They didn't talk unless a block came too near Kevin's head, and then there would be a slightly embarrassed,

"You all right?"

"It missed."

Then they would be silent again, and the sound of wood hitting against each other on the cellar floor would continue. There was one bulb hanging from the low centre beam and

60

Kevin's eyes were accustomed to it and his hands to what he was doing. He didn't think about what he was doing but that he would have to go and see the man and about what he wished to tell his mother. His father hadn't said anything to him about seeing the man so perhaps they would not go.

He hated what his mother had said about William. It was true he knew nothing of his dead brother save what he had heard in family conversations. "William would always say this about this, or William would always do this;" and it worked on his mind like something short of fascination to think that he had a brother who was dead. Sometimes he even thought that he could remember him, vaguely, of course, but remember some form, some shape of a face, some laugh. But this was all because he had been told things and the things he was told had worked in his memory and he never really remembered anything at all, least of all that his mother had been holding him when she heard the news. Sometimes he thought he could remember. His older sister often called him William before she went away.

So he worked. He liked to think he had energy enough to work forever in that cellar gathering the pieces of wood into long even rows along the cellar wall with the sweat upon him now on his legs and back and on his forehead also. It became so that he didn't want to stop and rest but to keep the forceful flame within him alive by constant movement back and forth from the trap to the cellar wall, even taking the moss and loose bark when they dangled and tearing them away. And his eyes no longer glanced up to his father's form or to the formation of clouds above his father's shoulders, because he worked best with his eyes down, hurrying back and forth.

He would work if need be until he had no room left to work; even though he despised what he was doing, he would work until the black hole was filled with wood from the spruce cuts to the beams, and even and correct, without once thinking all the while he was working until his father finally told him there was enough wood in. It was better to get it done with while he could.

It was no more than fifteen minutes later and the third row not yet completed when his father gave him the signal to stop. He climbed from the trap and stood near the depleted piles and his father stood with him sweating and heaving and panting. Kevin for the first time felt his own exhaustion and breathed heavily also. They entered the house together and seeing that it was after four his father turned to him.

"We have to go upriver." It was the first time he had mentioned anything at all. He seemed neither surprised nor angry. He never questioned at all and this compelled Kevin to talk.

"What did he say?"

"You shot a cow," his father said, still panting and still wiping the sweat from his forehead. "It's Houlden Bellia," his father added.

Clinton stood by the kitchen sink drinking water. He said nothing more and Kevin said nothing, but he felt weak, not only from exhaustion but from not eating, and asked his mother when supper would be ready. He knew he couldn't face the man unless he felt better. Sweat clung to him in a sticky heat.

"At five," his mother said. "And you'll have to clean and change before you go; you also Clinton."

They left directly after supper. They travelled upriver slowly. It was dark and now and then his father would cough and shift himself for comfort behind the wheel. Kevin had taken a bath and changed, but if his mother had had her way, he would be wearing a suit. Clinton also had a new blue shirt on and his hat that he wore only on occasion so that he looked quite comical. To Kevin at least he looked absurd because he was doing it all for him and that seemed unnatural for some reason. His shirt also, which was buttoned to its top-most button, was funny on him.

"Do you know him?" Kevin asked after some time. He couldn't just sit there. It was unnatural the way his father never questioned him. All day long he had never said a thing, not at the bus nor piling wood nor now on the way upriver.

"Yes I do—I do know him," Clinton said. But that was all and Kevin couldn't find the words to say any more because all day he had expected something that hadn't come.

Houlden Bellia had cleared his plate to the sink and was now sitting over a cup of tea at the kitchen table. It would be a cool October evening and there'd be little wind; just the stark coldness and a silence in the woods. He was drinking tea lukewarm from his favourite cup and his pipe with its bowl half full of charred tobacco lay sideways on the oilcloth. A

62

small mutt asleep on a mat near the radiator with its tail curled to its nose. The ticking of the alarum clock that he didn't hear.

Yesterday he had heard the shots and stepped into the clearing when the boy standing above his cow was taking aim again. It was something he had expected for awhile, his land so tight with the woods and hunters in all the time, to the gully and back, sounds of rifles every moment—firing at anything. He put his cows out nonetheless and expected it to happen.

When the boy fired again and again, he didn't yell. He simply watched the boy firing into the cow's head until it was dead and then moved through the undergrowth so that he was hidden from the boy, yet not understanding any of his movements, knowing that the boy might run and almost hoping that he would.

He was glad that he didn't lose his temper and strike the boy. All the while he stood there, he spoke quite softly, and yet in a way felt superior. When he spoke, he couldn't understand his voice because he had often thought of how he'd treat anyone that butchered an animal of his. Yet when he spoke, everything was calm and in that calmness he realized superiority over himself.

Since his wife was dead, he had supper alone, later in the evening than before, and after his plate was cleared, he would often sit until nine o'clock thinking and smoking at the table. Sometimes he would call to the dog and feed it scraps. He cleaned the bowl and filled it again and began to smoke, hearing the clock now and noticing the time. He felt a little tense with excitement thinking that they should soon arrive.

Not that he in any way knew how he was going to approach the subject or what he would ask of them; whether in fact he would condemn the boy outright in a strong manner and ask for money, demand compensation, or whether he would wait until finally they broke out with it and offered a sum. He did not know whether he would refuse their sum and quote his own or whether when they did break, he would accept what they had to offer, make an unwritten contract so to speak and let it go at that. And what if minute by minute he waited and they didn't turn the subject to the cow? He thought that they must at some time turn the subject if he himself didn't bring it about but then again everything was unclear and he knew that all his actions would remain unclear even as they happened. He would have to wait and see.

It was as the previous night. He had supper and waited at the table and it grew late and the storm was bad. He never thought about retrieving the cow. The other cows were in and safe—he had seen to that almost directly after the incident —and he had given the few pigs extra feed, which wasn't at all his habit. But the carcass remained bloated and stiff in the far field, shot wounds in its head. He thought about it but never moved until it grew late. If he had acted quickly he would have had some profit so to speak. But something came over him and he never moved.

Also he knew nothing of what he was doing when he went to the phone, who in fact he was going to phone. He knew only that he must phone somebody. He thought of the police and was sure that that was what he was going to do until he looked into the directory and saw their name and became excited with the idea of phoning them instead. So he did.

It was Sunday night now. He had buried the cow that morning with the aid of a neighbour who had cursed the butcher all the time they were digging much more than he himself had.

He moved from the table and entered the living-room, and the dog awoke and followed him. There was a fireplace with a mantelpiece crowded with all sorts of things—a picture of his wife on their wedding day. His hands had a soreness to them and a redness from digging with a shovel and a pick so long that morning, and when he began to make the fire he felt such an aching in his back. He wanted a fire roaring nicely when they entered and the living-room looking clean so he began to straighten things almost without realizing it much in the same fashion that she once had. And the fire lighted the place at once.

When they came to the door, his father knocked. The man must have heard them pull into the yard, Kevin thought, as all the lights were on and a dog barked behind the door. But they waited and no answer so that his father was forced to knock again, and the dog began barking loudly once more as if to warn its master. Then a slight shuffling sound inside and the door opened.

The door opened and they went inside, into a porch fresh

with the smell of paint and cluttered with storm windows, and then through another door to the kitchen and finally the living-room, the man all the time leading the way and never looking round to see them moving steadily behind him. Kevin watched the swaying of his father as he towered above them both and followed him into the room because it seemed much better to be behind, and when they sat he sat, not with his father on the couch, but on a hard-backed chair in a corner.

There was a fire, and the man went to it and poked at it with a poker. The dog wagged its tail to everyone now and came to Kevin so that he patted its head. The man remained with his back turned for a time poking at the fire savagely. They had exchanged greetings at the door, his father and the man, exchanged greetings but not names, and Kevin did not know whether to introduce his father or not, so he sat patting the dog's head rapidly and waiting for the man to turn around.

Clinton sat quite stiffly on the couch. He had taken off his hat and was fumbling with it in his hand. His jacket was un- zippered and his blue shirt, buttoned to the last button, was plainly visible. He began whistling to the dog softly so that it left Kevin and went to him, and he patted its head in much the same fashion. The man turned to face them now, laying the poker down. He looked a little younger than Clinton, perhaps a few years younger, and he stepped to the couch with his hand extended.

"Houlden Bellia—you remember me?"

"Oh yes," Clinton said, smiling and rising awkwardly to grab at the hand. "You were up here with the fishery once, eh?" The handshake was short and awkward as if neither was used to handshakes and Clinton sat down again. But he kept his smile.

"Oh yes," Houlden answered. "I was sure you'd re- member." And he stood looking down at Clinton with much the same type of smile, but he never turned to Kevin at all, which was something to be expected. Then he sat down him- self on a chair near the couch so that the three formed some- thing of a triangle. All silently listened to the fire which wasn't burning well at all, and Clinton picked up his hat once more and began to fumble it with his hand.

"So you're not with the fisheries no more now?"

"No, no give it up; and you—you still have the drifter?"

65

Houlden asked in return rising to go to the fire once more. He stabbed at it with the poker again, cleared his throat as he did so, and Clinton answered that he had sold his boat and his nets to Joseph Paul and was now operating a school bus.

Clinton stroked at the collar of his blue shirt as he said this, so that Kevin imagined that it was very uncomfortable for him to be there, and harder still since he had to wear that shirt. Kevin never moved at all, not even his hands because he wished no attention to be drawn to himself. He sat still and listened.

"—No I'm out of that business now altogether," his father was saying. It was the second time he had said it in the course of his conversation, and he had repeated other things also, as if it was difficult for him to speak. And he laughed slightly when Houlden muttered that it was best to be out of that business. "Yes, yes," Clinton chuckled looking at Kevin to see if he was chuckling also and then looking away again. "Yes, yes," he said once more as if to reassure himself that he could chuckle when he wished.

The room was much larger than any in their cottage. It was furnished better also, and felt more comfortable to sit in, although Kevin was in no way comfortable as he glanced about it, as he heard his father almost stutter with what he was saying, as he heard the fire snap sparks in a constant struggle to survive.

But there were nicer things in it: far more photographs of people on the walls and a tapestry hanging above the mantel-piece embroidered with wolves running in their pack through the snow as they might have done ages ago and still did far to the north of where he sat. So when he noticed the tapestry, he focussed upon it and nothing else and tried to sense in it the savagery of winter, the starving through the winter months. But the ebbing fire lighted it and made it seem warm, as if the wolves that ran in blackness through the woods howled out the savage warmth within them.

Houlden had given up the fire and was sitting in his chair. Kevin knew he was about to speak his mind because he cleared his throat again and made adjustments to his position. But his father had not spoken in a while and by accident spoke again.

"Who they got up there now?"

Houlden looked at him and collected his thoughts.

66

"Oh, who knows? Davis is still there and I heard about some college guy."

Kevin turned his gaze from the wolves to Clinton. He felt his palms sweating. Clinton looked red and seemed half choked by his shirt.

"Yes," Houlden said. "Some new biologist from somewhere, but I don't see how he can do no better up there."

"Oh he can't, he can't," Clinton said positively. "No sir, you have to know the river; you have to know the river—the fish just ain't comin' up now, not like five years ago—it's not like five years ago!"

"No, it isn't," Houlden said.

"No sir," Clinton said again, sniffing in satisfaction and reaching in his pocket for tobacco. He rolled his cigarette very carefully as if not to lose the slightest bit on the floor. Houlden also took his pipe from his pocket and, placing it in his mouth, fell silent for a time, and then when just enough silence was reached, he turned to Kevin.

"So have you come to any decision yet?" he asked.

The question was forceful enough to make him start. He had been lost in thought, about other things, about the wolves, but he felt he knew how to answer, how he must answer the man who stared at him now with such quiet intensity. He was in the man's house sitting on a chair and had no way of leaving, nor had he any way of lying to the man, or to his father who gazed at the floor with the cigarette clinging to his lip. Clinton shuffled his feet back and forth so that the mutt, lying under the table, looked over at him.

"Ya, well, I'm going to pay you for it," he said.

"Good," said Houlden still looking. "How much?"

"I don't know." Kevin was growing a little nervous under the man's gaze in the presence of his father who still in earnestness stared at the floor.

"How much was it worth?"

"More alive than dead considering I was going to sell it for beef in the spring, and the feed for a year and a half, and what I'm out on the price of sale," he said.

There was silence for a moment and then Clinton looked up quickly.

"Certainly," he said, looking up to stare at Kevin. "Certainly," he said once more, his hands shook slightly as he looked for an ashtray to butt his cigarette. Ashes had fallen on the floor and he tried to hide them with his feet. He rose awkwardly and went to find one. Then he came back and standing in the centre of the room looked first to one and then to the other.

"The trouble is," he said. "They just don't give a heck—they just don't give a—a hell how much trouble they cause, do they?"

Houlden said nothing to this but looked to Kevin.

"No sir," he continued standing in the very centre looking to one and then to the other. "No, no-one can afford to lose a cow. If it were me that lost my cow—if it were me, yes sir, Kevin knows me, he knows. I brung him up better than to shoot no cow, and if anyone shot my cow—." He looked at Kevin now, his face red, and then he looked away again. It seemed that since he had begun to speak, he couldn't stop, and he sat down again nearly on his hat and his face was twisted. Kevin had never seen his father in such a state and was himself perplexed and enraged.

"You see I had me operation or else he'd be out on the boats where I could keep an eye on him. My guts were blocked—you know, intestines and I couldn't crap or do nothing and I used to throw up—you know. So I had me operation and he got away from me."

"I see," Houlden observed. "I see—well we can get this matter straightened out and I think everything will be all right."

"Oh certainly—certainly," Clinton said. "I know Kevin, he'll pay up, you can be sure of that—he'll pay." Clinton looked to Kevin and smiled but he did not smile back. Clinton kept smiling stupidly as if it were his duty to smile.

They were all silent, and Clinton, embarrassed, began to roll another cigarette, sniffed and then broke the silence again. "I'm sure he didn't even think of the trouble he'd cause when he did it, but it's—it's over and done with now so he can just pay up for his mistake, and you did right—I think you did right in calling me."

"Damn! I never meant to shoot the cow," Kevin said finally, looking straight out at the wolves because he was afraid to look at his father, because he was ashamed of his father and because he was afraid to look into the knowing eyes of the man who was silent in his own home. So he looked at the wolves that ran above the dead fire, over the frozen snow, and

68

wished to be hidden in the darkness that surrounded them.

"Who said you meant to shoot it—I don't mean that you meant to shoot it but you did and if you was careful you wouldn't have—."

"The point is," Houlden interrupted, "that as long as I receive compensation everything will be all right, and since you say okay to that, then everything is all right."

"That's right, that's right," Clinton agreed quickly.

"How much?" Kevin said weakly, looking at the man now.

"Three hundred dollars," Houlden said.

"Fair enough—that sounds fair enough," Clinton said, looking at them both. "It sounds fair enough Kevin, don't it?" Kevin nodded but didn't say a thing.

"Oh yes, that sounds fair enough," he said still directing his questions to his son, who did not answer, and then almost directly putting on his hat, and standing, and reaching for Houlden's hand, who rising awkwardly himself seemed too inclined to give it.

Kevin watched both men above him in the centre of the room, each mumbling something about appreciation, and then he also stood and waited to go.

And they both refused tea. It was late by this time anyway, the night cold, so that when they went into the air, he could feel the cold. He walked in front and Clinton turned to Houlden, who was closing the door, and said,

"It'll all get fixed up."

"Oh yes," Houlden said. "It will."

Then they drove home slowly. Neither spoke.

When they entered the house, she called immediately to them and asked them about it, but neither was inclined to speak; Clinton more than Kevin kept dodging her inquiries with the solemn grunts that he made. He did not look to his son and his son did not look to him.

"Well, what did he say—will you tell me what he said, I want to know; is he going to take you to trial? You said that yesterday he said he might take you to trial!"

"When did I say that?" he asked, looking at his mother; his nervous mother with her placid face peering at him while her husband rolled a cigarette and shuffled with his feet.

"At supper—you said it; well, is he?"

"No he isn't; I have to pay him."

"Pay him—how much?"

"Three hundred dollars."

"And how are you going to get that kind of money—I'd like to know how you're going to get that kind of money; you never seem to have a cent. Well it serves you right. We won't be able to help you, so you'll just have to pay it off by yourself."

"So what," he said.

"So what," she said in answer. "You seem to do these things just to torment me, staying out all night—and drinking besides, and don't tell me you weren't, and then this awful mess you've gotten yourself in—what did he say to you Clinton?"

"Who?"

"That man; what did he say to you—I hope you never lost your temper with him."

Clinton looked at her with narrow tired eyes.

"Well, you remember the time at the school with William's teacher."

"Everything will get fixed up," Clinton said.

"Yes, well it isn't the man's fault so I hope you didn't get angry with him—it isn't his fault."

There was such a numbness inside him he went to bed. He lay in the darkness without undressing and could hear Deborah's radio through the thin wall. Listening to the music made him angry so he banged on the wall with his fist until there was no sound of it. Then closing his eyes, he saw only his father stuttering to the man who sat confused and embarrassed in his own home. And he had no forgiveness, only a pathetic longing to rid himself of the voice which kept growing inside—the voice of his father growing—the look of his father in the centre of the room with every drawn muscle in his face. Now it was late—the house quiet; he could feel the stale sweat upon him and it was later still before he went to sleep.

3

There was to be a funeral that he must attend—and he hated the atmosphere of them. He was frightened of the body when he gazed upon it at a wake, and yet there was the wake that he must attend. He had never cried at a funeral and knew he would not cry at this one but that his emotion would be voiced, or made in solemn gestures.

The whistle was sounding for the second time and the sky above the huge stack clouded, the dirt from the stack pouring into it. Between the two small doorways he smelt the stink of burnt sulphur, smelt the thick air, the thick mill air as he walked. He was walking the ramp between two small doorways, and the ramp was covered by the powder of dirt and lime—and as he walked he was thinking of the wake he must attend, and the funeral.

He had been to his grandfather's wake when he was thirteen. The old man died in the autumn, was dying through the summer and died in the autumn. He had suffered greatly during the summer, suffered from pain and heat, lying in white sheets on the bed and would not go to the hospital until the last because he was a frightened man who wished to stay where he had spent his life. Then Clinton went one day and moved him with the aid of his brother, moved him from his room to the hospital where he lived two weeks.

And it was night when his mother told him. He had come in from the river with his sister; they had walked along the shore a mile and the only words Sheila had said were, "Poor Papa" in a voice that sounded distant and old. They had come home by the back path to the stone cottage that was new to them. The inside smelled of apples being cooked, the sweet smell of apples—the comfortable smell of autumn.

His mother met them at the door:

"Papa just died."

Sheila began to cry and it made Kevin uneasy to be there.

71

Then his mother left, taking Kleenex in her brown purse, and Sheila and Kevin sat up until she returned. When she returned, Clinton was with her, and Clinton's brother who sat white faced on the edge of the couch and looked terribly frightened so that Clinton offered him scotch and they began to drink. They were still drinking when Kevin went to bed.

Kevin's uncle Reginald Dulse was older than his brother by two years but was tall and strong looking as his brother was, walked in much the same way—in that swaying gait. As he sat on the couch that evening and drank his scotch in unsteady gulps and looked about him unsteadily—first at Rubena with her wet eyes, and then at Sheila with hers, and finally at Clinton; he seemed to resemble his brother in every way —except that he was the older, and though Kevin did not think of this, it was, in actuality, Clinton who resembled him.

He was not the leader. Everyone knew that. From boyhood he had followed Clinton in everything—had done what his younger brother asked of him. Even in carrying wood Clinton would load and he carry. He had never married and had difficulty with his speech, stuttering when trying to explain the simplest thing so Clinton was often embarrassed when they were younger to have such an older brother with him —going where he went.

"We gotta get a coffin," Reginald said, looking to Clinton.

"We will."

"Are you going to move out to the big house now?" he said.

Clinton looked to his wife.

"No Reggie—we'll stay here."

"There's no-one out there now," Reginald said, looking in that direction.

Kevin went to bed on his mother's orders a short time later, and they were still drinking although the old man had never wanted them to drink, had never wanted Clinton to influence his brother the way he did. But Reginald had always wished to be like Clinton, had always wished to be the same, so when Kevin rose from the couch, his uncle looked at him and laying his right hand on the boy's left shoulder said,

"You know Bena—he looks like William, you know." And then for assurance he looked to Clinton.

"Yes he does Reggie—he does a bit," Clinton responded.

"You bet," Reginald said.

Reginald stayed with them for a week after the funeral and

72

then went home. At the wake he kept close to his brother; whenever anyone gave them sympathy, he would merely nod his head after Clinton had thanked them and going to a chair would sit and wait for others to arrive. He talked seldom. When he spoke, he spoke to members of the family. He talked to Clinton about hunting. Kevin gazed once upon the old man in his coffin as he prayed on the kneeler beside it, and when he did, he saw the white pasty skin and smelled the smell of flowers around him, looked at the small cross in the lifeless hands and thought about himself there with others staring at him. He shuddered because of the thought and was sure people had seen him shudder. He served the funeral Mass.

Often he would sit on the stacks of lime watching the cold yellow water funneling through the pipe below the railing with his wheel cart ready and loaded, ready should the foreman making his rounds come to inspect. He detested the job of pouring lime and today being Monday was the worst for pouring since he was stiff and cold, even with the thought of what he had to do, more so with the thought of it. Once he began to work it would be different. Sometimes he would notch two on the board for dumping one so that by the end of every day he would always have his quota.

He had come in to sit on the lime bags. In the little shed there was only one light but with the door to the railing open the grey morning came through and the sounds of the mill around him, the eternal rumblings of engines and machines—that would never stop, day or night. He heard the curses from the truckers waiting to be scaled, sounding distant in the confusion of machines and the other sounds of the mill.

The water was as white as the morning and still except below the pipe where it turned filthy yellow with the dirt churned into it. It was his responsibility to pour lime into the yellow water, making it clearer when he did. Four hundred bags a day he was to pour though many days he only managed 250 bags. There were three shifts, and he was never found at fault, and also many times he would be called away in the middle of his pouring to do some other task so that always it was at best a very uneven job.

He had made himself somewhat of a little home inside the

shed, in a corner among the pillars secluded from the wind where he could feel comfortable even in the worst of conditions and it was almost a necessity to sit there for a few minutes three or four times a day so that he could gather his thoughts and relax—and though it was nothing more than uneven lime bags piled like a chair, each time he noticed it on his journey to and from the railing where he poured, he would feel an urgent desire to sit there, to lay himself down upon it and sleep so that in time it became the most necessary pleasure of his day.

He had poured two cartloads into the pipe, taking each bag and slitting it open with an axe, letting the powder fall freely and then throwing the empty bags behind him. He had his boots laced around his pants and his gloves tight to his coat sleeves so that no lime would touch his skin as he poured. Already he was sweating in his heavy jacket, and already he was tired, but he poured the third and fourth cartloads without stopping, to warm the engine as it were and make himself run smoothly. He thought of a thousand different things as he poured so that his mind would not be on the business at hand, so that only his body would be where he was. The lime dust was intensified in the shed so that he breathed lime as he worked and could taste it in his mouth. Often that taste would linger far past the alloted hour so that at times he even dreamed of eating the lime.

He tried not to think of his father or the funeral that he must attend. He tried to think of spring and summer, which he did. He thought of summer, not any particular part of summer but just of summer for as long as he could. Swimming naked and clam digging, going with Pamela to the beach and on the sand running with the hot sun drying and browning his skin.

The bags were 80 pounds each; he lifted ten onto the wheeler each time, wheeled them carefully onto the ramp, lifted them off, slit and poured them—went back for others. By noon he had poured a hundred bags, which was far less than he could have poured. Each time he grabbed at one, he could feel the itching lime on his hands, on his knuckles and between his fingers. Also it had seeped into his boots so that his ankles burned like his hands and his nose was plugged with dust.

At the end of the morning he could not stop coughing

because of the dust. Each day was the same, coughing, the small itching burns getting worse and yet he did nothing about it—not even report it to the first aid, which he was required to do. But today at noon he felt that he must do something about it, even if it was to do something else for the rest of the day. He knew it was his right and more his obligation to report it, but he felt that if he did, he would be complaining about his work—and he was frightened to do that.

So he was unsure of what to do when at noon hour he left half a cartload and walked back down the ramp, through the small doorway into the lunchroom and sat, with his eyes watering, on a bench. He did not care to eat, really. He went into the washroom and washed in warm water—washed his burns and the white lime dust still on them. Through the greyish window he could see the chip piles growing, and hear the massive blower throwing chips onto it. He took off his boots and cleaned his ankles and took off his socks and slammed them against the walls. He was not sneezing or coughing now, and actually felt quite comfortable with his boots off because there was nothing to aggravate the burns. Then he put everything on again and went to sit down.

There were eight other men who ate with Kevin Dulse in the small room where he sat. Most of them were older men, but for the most part he felt quite comfortable with them and could talk to them much easier than others that he knew. The eight of them were labourers as he was—having no trade, no background for learning one, and though Kevin had graduated, he also was a labourer. Each day at noon they sat for half an hour and ate sandwiches and told jokes, jokes about women—jokes in filthy language about women and about the work they were doing. Kevin laughed at their jokes and they at his, and there was a happiness in that half hour.

Kevin sat beside the oldest man in their group because the first day he had eaten with them he had situated himself there, and it was something of loyalty that he remain. The old man was always the one to talk first and talk the longest, and Kevin like all the others listened patiently to his jokes as well as his complaints. Some of the things he said were quite amusing so that he was not hard to listen to for awhile.

In fact, they all had their own special place to sit as if it gave something of a family atmosphere. There were four at one bench and five at the other, and if it happened, as it sometimes did, that anyone new entered to eat with them, he would always sit by Kevin on the edge. There wouldn't be as many jokes then.

The old man's name was Clarence Turnbull. He was close to retirement and very slow, moved very slowly, and breathed raspingly—complaining about the labour that he did although he did little to nothing in the course of the day —sometimes going out early with a sore back, especially during the hunting months. He was overweight now and, when his teeth were in his pocket, his face looked sunken and flabby.

His teeth were always in his pocket when he came in at noon—and they were today. There was a growth of stubble on his face that he never seemed to shave, and it made him look grey and old and rough. Kevin was already sitting with the other men with his bucket opened when Clarence arrived to sit beside him. He waved to them and seated himself, saying nothing for a moment and then sneaking his teeth from his pocket into his mouth flashed a smile as if to show them off. They laughed.

"New choppers?"

"Course not," the old man said waving his hand at them. "I'll never get rid of these."

"Why not?"

"Cause these were the first teeth ever made."

They laughed, looking at one another in amusement.

"Sure they were," Clarence continued. "I should know; I made them myself."

"You made them?" Kevin said.

The old man looked at him in great seriousness.

"Of course, but you're too young to know what a person with no teeth is called."

They laughed again and were silent.

"Made them when I was fourteen," he resumed. "I was born with no teeth as most people are," he said, eyeing them all to see if he had their attention and taking sips on his coffee all the time.

"You were born with no teeth."

"I was—I was. I was born with not a tooth in my head and the funny part of it, I never got a tooth. People used to call me names, and I couldn't talk right," he said, laughing at his own joke.

"So you made your own," Kevin said.

"When I was fourteen—and they're still chewable," he said, chewing on a sandwich and opening his mouth to show them all. They laughed again and were silent.

Kevin ate very little, listened to the conversation when it came, to the jokes, listened to the fan blowing above the coatrack in the room, felt the burns still itching at his feet. Half an hour was far too short a time to spend at lunch, was far too short a time to relax. He would go back to the lime and begin again unless he told them—unless he told his foreman or went to the first aid, which he didn't wish to do.

So he sat there pondering for a time over his tea, and now and then the old man would nudge him and he'd smile, or one of the other men would talk to him and he'd answer until he heard the snap of lids and realized it was almost time. The space of time was so short that he had not really rested—in fact, because of the two nights before he was exhausted and nervous and could not bring himself to relax; his mind spinning with all that had happened and all that might happen and the dust on his clothes—the very smell of the dust that he worked in!

"What do you do about these?" he said finally when some of the men were standing ready to go, showing them his hands and spreading his fingers so that the cuts and burns were revealed.

"Where you get those?" Clarence said alarmed. "Working in the pit—you get them working in the pit, my God!"

"Yes," Kevin said lazily, "doesn't everybody?"

"No sir, everybody don't," Clarence said again more alarmed than ever before. "And if you do, then you shouldn't be working there—let me see those—let me see," and he grabbed Kevin's hands in his own and examined them closely, showing them to the rest of the men after he did. "My Jesus boy, you're going to burn your hands off—look at them burns. Basil, look at them hands here." And Basil came closer to look at them. The rest of the men crowded around also.

"Those are bad," Basil said. "I've gotten burns before when salt got into my boots—by Christ!"

"There's burns on my ankles also," Kevin muttered.

"Well, take your boots off," the old man said.

Kevin proceeded to do what they asked him, consciously squinting with the pain that it caused and then lifting his feet

77

for the men to see, and looking at them all.

"I thought everybody got burns in that place," he said.

"Well, everybody don't—only some people and you shouldn't go in there again; when did you get them—look at his ankles; when in hell did you get them?"

"Oh hell, off and on," Kevin muttered. "You can see scars there from other times," pointing to the scars so they would notice. "But if I'm careful, I don't get any."

"Well, careful or not, shit," Basil said. "Get Willis in here and show them to him."

Basil went himself to find the foreman. They were all talking at once now and all pointing to the burns, which made him feel somewhat relieved that he had mentioned it and a little contented that they should be so concerned. But still he was skeptical when Willis entered the room. He had never talked to the foreman, not at least in a friendly sort of way, and he could not get out of his mind that it was underhanded to complain of the work he was being paid for—especially to the man that placed him there. And if the lime burned him, it would burn others just as well, and if it burned others just as well, then there was no justification in complaining. He hated making problems for those who had enough of their own.

Willis was short and very thin and had an almost hawk-like expression to his face—not that it was penetrating; his gaze did not penetrate, nor was it acute or unnerving. If anything it was dulled and eaten by the vapours of the mill in which he spent his life, blended into the air around the chip piles or whatever, so that he looked as if he needed to be painted like the pipes that ran along the cement floors, painted green or red. It was hawk-like in the sense that his nose was the beak that narrowed from his eyes, a long nose and a pointed chin.

It was unhealthy at best, and when he entered the room he looked nervous and unhealthy, gazing at them all hawk-like, very fast and then following Basil to where Kevin was seated. The rest had moved aside so that he might enter the circle, and when he did, he stared down at the boy without really looking at him and then at the burns on his ankles and hands.

"What's the problem?"

"Got some burns."

"How long you been on the lime?"

"Off and on for a while—last winter too."

"You get burns last winter?"

78

"Some."

"Wearing gloves are you?"

"Sure—of course," Kevin said, looking up.

Willis looked around again to all of them and then looked at his watch. The men began moving slowly through the door, glancing back as they did. Only Clarence remained. He was too old to be frightened by watches, and besides he had worked here longer than Willis—had put in more years than the man who ordered him about so that he took all orders in stride. He stared over the foreman's shoulder at the boy.

"Well he sure as hell can't go back to the lime."

"No—no," Willis said. "We can find something else for him to do." And then he added after thinking, "but not today—he'll have to get ointment for those burns."

"I can go to the first aid."

"Not now," Clarence answered, "you may as well go home now; we don't need you here today."

"Yes," the foreman commented, "go home; get those burns looked after and then come in tomorrow and I'll put you somewhere else."

Kevin put his boots back on. They were both looking down at him as he did so, watching the hands as he tied his laces, and when his boots were tied, he stood, smiling a little at the foreman. Clarence began moving to the door slowly, looking back.

"Take care of them burns now," he cautioned as he left. He began to whistle loudly in the hallway.

Willis also looked at his watch and turned to go without saying any more to the boy as if there were nothing more to say. Kevin picked up his lunch bucket and followed him into the hall, walking behind noiselessly, staring at the man's thin unhealthy frame before him. He felt as if he could work the entire afternoon now without feeling the slightest pain, work in the lime or on the trucks or in the shop or half a dozen other places without feeling the pain. When Willis was at the doorway, he turned as if by an after-thought.

"Who's your doctor?"

"I go to Brown sometimes when I have to."

"Well you go to Brown this afternoon and get some ointment," he said. "Bad thing a burn is—you should have told me last winter that you got burned on the lime."

"Yes," Kevin responded, "anyway, I was going to ask you

79

for tomorrow off."

"Why?"

"Have to go to a funeral; friend of mine."

"That Turcotte?"

"Ya."

"Okay then—maybe it wasn't a good idea for you to come in tomorrow anyway. That young guy; was he crazy or what?"

"No, not really."

"Maniac to drive like that."

"No, not really," Kevin said again smiling a little at the expression on his foreman's face.

"Okay then—you be in Wednesday."

Willis turned from him and left, walking slowly. He remained at the entranceway some time listening to the mill—its motors and machines grinding, the smell of its sulphur. When he stepped onto the ramp, the day was still as clouded, the long uneven rows of pulp and the river white and placid under the clouds, the large chip piles under the clouds, the prospect of cold autumn rain.

He came in early Monday afternoon and bathed his sores in warm water. His mother was standing over the dishes in the sink, but he did not speak to her or answer the questions that she asked. He showed her his hands instead, and she started, and then getting a small pan he placed warm water in it and bathed his hands until the water was cool. He filled it again and bathed his feet. She made him hot lunch and he rested for more than an hour.

When he woke, it was after four. He could hear his father in the store talking to a customer and Deborah in the kitchen with his mother. He rose and went out into the hallway. He felt sluggish and tired, but there was very little pain now, and he could close and open his hands without feeling the pain. When he realized the time, he realized also that Pamela would be working and that he hadn't phoned her. He hadn't told his mother anything about the wedding—the plans for the wedding and thought that he must.

So he went into the kitchen. They were preparing supper early as always on weekdays with Clinton coming home ready for supper and Deborah and he eating only sandwiches during the day. He stood by the table and watched them making it, not saying a word to them as they did, watched his younger sister, who would some day look like her mother, setting the knives and forks. Clinton came in from the store and brushed him as he went by. He smoked a cigarette and stood by the sink.

There was more wood to be put down, but Clinton never mentioned it and neither did Kevin. When supper was ready, they sat around—each in their allotted chair and ate for the most part with their heads down without conversation. She had made buns in the afternoon, and they were warm from the oven and tasted good with the meal. Kevin was searching for the right moment to tell her and thinking of the wake; already he was nervous thinking of the wake.

"Your mother tells me you got some burns," the old man said.

"Ya," Kevin answered. He did not look up.

"We got a letter from Sheila today—she might be home at Christmas," Rubena said.

"So you got some burns—where, in the lime?"

Kevin nodded, looking up.

"How long you been working in that stuff?"

"Too long."

They were both silent again.

"Where's the letter?" Deborah asked.

"In the living-room—you can read it later."

Kevin finished with his plate and shoved it from him. Then sitting back in his chair he eyed them all; his father stooped over his place, the rough shave-chapped face of his father. He must help him finish with the wood as soon as possible, work in the cellar until the wood was in, and yet there was the wake, he must attend the wake.

"I have to go to the wake," he said looking to his mother.

"You want your suit?"

"No, no I'll just clean up."

"What happened anyway?" Rubena asked. "I was always frightened of you in that car with him."

"Nothing *happened*," Kevin said, and let it go at that.

"He was drinking," Deborah said eyeing her brother as she spoke. "Everyone at school says he was hammered."

"Everyone at school says that about everybody."

"Well, he was," Deborah said again confidently.

"He was only nineteen," his mother said. "He was younger than you, Kevin."

81

"He was twenty," the boy replied.

"Well, the radio said he was nineteen."

"I don't give a damn—he was twenty."

Clinton left the table a short time later and then his mother and sister. He sat alone waiting, listening to the sounds of the house. He heard his father go outside and in a moment the sound of wood falling in the cellar. Customers came to the store, teenage girls, and he called to Deborah. He did not wish to move. He would have to clean and change for the wake; he would have to meet Andrew's family and gaze upon a corpse. He pictured his father sweating in the yard as he threw wood through the trap, stopping to rest every now and then and looking at the water.

It was after dark now, and the rain that had seemed so predictable during the earlier part of the day had not come. The night air smelled of autumn, the autumn burnings—a tinge of smoke lying on the dark air and over the cut fields on both sides of the roadway, so that everything seemed full with it, and autumn warm.

And the town had that faintness of smoke to it between the rows of small houses and sheds, the burning of leaves in barrels. It was a quiet night, a good night for walking in the streets, through the side streets after dark, or out along the wharf.

He was walking along the lane where their house was, for it was in the house where the wake was being held, and he could feel the good autumn night upon him, and a little nervousness besides, the taste of evening smoke. It was nearing his birthday so that the air and the taste of night seemed more familiar to him than at other times of the year; was more fulfilling to him now that he was walking, and he could remember all the other autumns that he had felt. Only to be in his huntsclothes at the camp, he thought; only to smell the fresh wet air, the rotting of wood or to track along the river with the frost of early morning, stopping to listen and hearing the silent calmness of where he was. His topcoat restricted him as he walked, and he could feel himself sweating as he moved closer to their home.

They lived in a small two-storey badly in need of paint. There were nine in the family—seven children, Andrew was third. People stood in small groups in the front yard whispering lowly to each other, and coming upon them he recognized none that he knew—all older, relatives perhaps, or friends of the parents. He went past them into the house, up the steps and through the doorway. Others sat together in the porch, and some were leaving as he came in.

There was an air of stiffness in it all—a solemnness that seemed to enter the house with him but was present all along, was present with the people standing in the little hallway or sitting despondently in the porch. When he entered the hallway, a man was standing straight, his face expressionless and waiting for people to enter; he shook their hands as they did and nodded his head and let them pass. He was a short thickly set person with a rough, brown-skinned face, and his wife, sitting on a small couch beside him, looked frail and white, watching all who entered with a Kleenex to her face. She did not rise from the couch when Kevin came up to them, but she recognized him immediately and seemed to smile slightly in recognition. Her oldest girl was standing behind the couch; a girl older than Kevin with eyes red from crying that were discernible in the half light—for there seemed to be only a half light in the hallway where they stood.

Andrew's father shook his hand. It was a limp and placid handshake, almost feeble, as if he were tired of holding out his hand to strange mourners that passed through his house, as if he were tired of it all and wished to sleep. There were others behind Kevin now; people coming and going all the time, people who stopped to sit with the family for a moment offering condolences when they did, and Kevin, because of this, wished to pass into the room quickly. There was nothing on his tongue that he might say to them even though he wished there was, and though he heard the whispers of others, he could not whisper himself no matter how he tried. He simply made a gesture with his head.

"This is Kevin Dulse—a friend of Andy's," Mrs. Turcotte explained to her husband. Mr. Turcotte looked to his wife who seemed controlled for the present, and then again to Kevin who did not know whether to smile or nod and so automatically did something of each with his head cocked a little to the side.

"Oh yes, you were here with Andy before, I think."

"Yes," Kevin said, standing there for just a moment longer and then making way for others by passing into the room.

There was a kneeler beside the coffin. The room was small and filled with flowers, and there were candles, large ones burning on either end of the coffin, which was closed. He was trembling as he entered and began to tremble more as he waited to use the kneeler. He did not know why he trembled so, only that he did, and only that he could not force himself to stop. He wished to kneel so he might have something to support himself, but there were others before him and he had to wait.

Then it came to him suddenly that he would never see Andrew again. Never again? He thought about it—never again. It didn't seem at all discomforting, nor startling. He had expected to see the corpse, but perhaps it was better that he couldn't. Perhaps it was better to remember him as he was, as everyone believed that it was. But when had he talked to him last? Already he seemed to forget the face as he stood beside the coffin, as he heard the whisperings of others. They had spent days together in the woods, years at school—never again. He could not realize it; it did not seem wrong or unjust nor important to him at all. Perhaps later it would; perhaps when he thought about it, it would be clearer.

He knelt and blessed himself quickly, looking straight out past the top of the coffin to the wall and then looking downward to the brass handles. They would carry it to the altar front and the priest would walk around it, incense in his hand, four candles burning, altar-boys trailing, holding up his black robes. There they would say the Mass, the coffin at the altar front.

He could not pray.

"Hail Mary full of grace—" he whispered to himself. He was still trembling. Andrew hadn't been to church in years.

He lifted himself and walked slowly to the door. Some were standing in the room. There was a small table to one side of the door with a register upon it, and a lamp. He walked to it and signed his name under the others, scanned the names as he did so, and then lifting his eyes he noticed a small photograph to one side of the book—a small photograph of Andrew taken at their graduation, and when his eyes rested upon the face he became a little frightened, saw the face so seriously staring up at him and remembered him, remembered at once the face and the person. It startled him and he left the house.

The night was even warmer than before with people walking slowly on the sidewalk, the sounds of their talking—some were laughing. He walked along with them until he reached the cement wall near the end of the lane, and he sat upon it listening to the sounds and smelling the good night again. Within a few minutes he noticed Bruce walking toward him.

"When did you get here?"

"I was right behind you—I thought you saw me."

Bruce sat alongside him on the wall.

"He must have been pretty messed up; they didn't even show him."

"I suppose he was," Kevin said, "but it's better that way. Did you see the picture?"

"Ya, remember that night—that was a good night."

"I remember we got drunk and sick," Kevin smiled.

"He started going with Julie then, you know—you know who took her out before then, John took her out before then."

"John?" Kevin said surprised.

They talked a while longer, Kevin telling him about the burns from the lime and having tomorrow off because of it. He wanted to ask Bruce if he had seen or had spoken to John since Saturday but decided not to. It was getting late. He thought of his father and the wood.

"So you're going to the funeral then?"

"Of course," Bruce said looking at him. "Why?"

"Just asked—I didn't see Julie tonight."

"No—they've probably given her something to rest with, at least they always do when something like this happens."

"So you haven't seen her then?"

"No," Bruce said again looking at him perplexed. "I saw John though and he's sick—and he's a pallbearer tomorrow."

"Sick?"

"Well he was in bed when I went over—I wanted to see if he was still as crazy as the other night."

"Is he?"

"He's tuned down a bit, but he's lying in bed, and he never said too much except that he was a pallbearer and didn't know whether he'd make it—and his mother said that he'd better for Mrs. Turcotte's sake. He curses his mother up and down like a madman, you know."

"He does?"

"Told her to get out of the room and stop bothering him and she bringing him up soup to eat. He cursed at her going out the door and she turned around and said, 'Now Johnny,' like some sort of stupid ass. Then when she goes out, he turned to me with that sleazy sort of smile on his face—expecting me to laugh."

"Did you?"

"Yes."

"He jumped into the fountain Saturday night—you know," Kevin said.

"I know, I know," Bruce said.

He leaned back against the side wall near the trap door gazing at the water as he did and listened to his own breathing, the panting of an old man. It was warm for an autumn evening, the smell of smoke on the air and greyness still lingering over the dark water. There were children playing on the shore and the swift coming of darkness, a soreness and a sweat from his body.

The water came in softly to the shoreline. He couldn't hear it now as he could sometimes—he only watched it, watched out into it and heard the sounds of children, the unmistakable echoes from the beach.

He had thrown wood since supper, slowly and methodically through the opening, hearing the dull thud on the cellar floor and then later, each piece hitting on another as it fell. Now he was resting at the rear of his cottage waiting for the darkness of the night. He heard his son leave in the truck, going to some boy's wake that he did not know, that had died too early—died at nineteen, much much too early.

Much like William he supposed. He had not spoken to his son since the previous night except perhaps for the feeble attempt during supper. His son did not look at him at supper and never spoke more than a few words even when he asked about the burns.

But of course he knew what it was his son was thinking, and he knew why. He rolled a cigarette as he thought on it and coughed violently, spitting into the black before him. A dog barked when he coughed and the shouts of children still audible.

Perhaps it was travelling to the man's house as they did. He had been uncomfortable thinking about it all during supper

86

so that he never touched his roast, thinking about what the man would say to him about his son, and then before they left, she asked him to clean and change, as if he weren't clean enough, talking to him in the same fashion as she talked to Kevin—laying out things for him, his shirt and socks.

He made sure he was clean enough, as he always did. His hands and face and neck he washed and she standing over him much as if he was a child, and that too made him nervous, his wife peeking around the corner with an extra bar of soap.

It was as if they were two children going to see a man about a window they had busted; she the conscience of them both because she wished them to look respectable and good. And it was not that Houlden Bellia was important to him, but it was more that she thought that he was. It was that she misunderstood.

And he misunderstood also. It seemed that he could not gather his thoughts at all once he had entered the house, once he entered through the cluttered porchway and into the house, sitting there as the man poked at his fire. And of course Kevin made it difficult, not speaking at all, so that the only conversation came from the two of them. He was never used to conversation, and they had never spoken to each other before in their lives—worked the same river and had never spoken so that he was embarrassed as he talked because they had had ample time for speaking before, if they had ever wanted to.

Or perhaps it was because they were the same type of men, believing in much the same things, and when he stepped into the room he realized that this man had prospered and that he hadn't after all, and that this Houlden Bellia was a man younger than he. If he had been put on trial, he wouldn't have felt more conscious of where he was at that instant nor could he have felt more guilty if he had been convicted of some crime. And yet he knew the man to be no better than he.

But the man knew him also and that was the point. The man, staring at him, knew his history of drinking and whoring, of dropping nets out of season—of where he lived and what he did, of his wife and dead son and that was the point. So that it became not Kevin that butchered the cow but Clinton—it became Clinton that must explain himself to the man.

He butted his cigarette into the black dirt under his feet.

He would throw no more wood this evening. Tired and sore, he could feel his legs aching and a pain at the back of his neck, but he chose to go into the cellar and pile what he had thrown because he wished to work as long as he could not sleep—and it was as yet too early for him to sleep. If he went inside, he would have to speak to her and he did not wish to.

The cellar was dark and small, the faint odour of autumn wetness and rot to it and the one light, the beams low and dangerous for his head. The cellar floor was a little damp, littered with wood chips and bark, and as he worked in it he was constantly bent, piled the wood in rows where his son left off. "And no," he thought as he piled, "I ain't prospered very much for sure." He cursed aloud when he thought.

They did not really look alike, one the wild black-haired and the other so calm, one full of the blood to make him dance half-crazed with a drink and the other more silent, more reserved. Maybe their noses—or something in the eye as Bena said, something in the deep expression sometimes in the eye but nothing else. Surely they were as different as could be, one his dead son, the other his new. And he too was different to each of them as they were to each other. Two generations he had raised—two fathers.

It had rained all that evening, the rain spilling out of the sky so that when William came in he was drenched and shivering feverishly. It was April and the snow was rotting with the rain and the business of travelling through the town in such a slush was not pleasant. William was a boy of sixteen, and he had been drinking—Clinton could tell as soon as the door was opened that his son had been drinking. The door opened into the kitchen of their apartment, a warm kitchen, the walls a cheap pink.

Clinton was drinking also, drinking heavily as was his habit, and he eyed his son in an aggressive frame of mind.

"So where the hell were you this time of night?" He drank as he spoke, eyeing his son from the very corner of his eye. He wished his son to fear him—it was fear that he wanted. His son did not fear him though, did not in fact say anything to him but, lifting the latch on a cupboard, took out the bread and began to eat.

"Where's mom?" he said in a moment, shivering as he was with the wet in his hair and the alcohol he had consumed.

"She went out an hour ago looking for the likes of you and

by Jesus I wouldn't."

"No—you wouldn't, nor would I look for you."

Clinton told him to shut his mouth, and the boy did so, seeming more content to eat. He kept wiping his wet face with the back of his hand and glancing now and then to the table where his father sat. Clinton was drinking wine again, cheap wine—work had not been good. He had a three-day growth of beard over his lean browned face, but the beard was light and did not bother him. He could see his son glancing and was angered by it, and his son could see that he was angered and continued to look. It was an invasion of his private destitution and he despised his son for looking.

"I suppose you don't care how much trouble you cause your mother—her out there looking for you on a night like tonight; she's crazy worrying. I sure as hell wouldn't bother."

"What's there to worry about?"

"The principal phoned me at work—in front of everybody—and says you're expelled for fighting. So what, be expelled; you're not smart enough to go to school anyway."

It was a silly remark, a reflection on himself. The boy said nothing to this; he had been in trouble at school before, and this was just another incident, so he said nothing to his father. He began to smile somewhat mockingly though, as if he realized in himself already the capacity for independence from the wishes of his family. It was a smile that mocked the desperate situation of his father, of Clinton who had lost just such an independence because of this son who stood before him, drenched—his wetness dripping on the floor.

William was tall for sixteen and lean and muscular —looking as Clinton had once. His eyes were set a little close together, dark demanding eyes that Clinton could not stare into or stare down unless he cursed with the process. The eyebrows were thin, coming together at the bridge of the nose. Rubena called it a sign of temper, temper like her husband, so she said and then, of course, the expression of the face. That smart cruelness of it; a sharpness that suggested wild cunning.

And it was in that expression of wild and animal smartness that he viewed his father. Clinton was drunker than he and, hunched at the table, resembled a bear waiting with his paw. He wished to strike his son but could find no absolute reason to do so—knew that his son had been drinking and that he had been out over the town doing what he wished and yet even that was no sufficient reason. That did not anger him. What angered him was the thing's smartness—like a fox, or a cat staring out into the dark and when everything else is blind, seeing something there.

Nor did it bother him that his wife went out in the wet darkness of this night to bring William back, thinking that he was afraid of the consequences of being expelled when any mind could see that he wasn't at all—that he treated it all as a game to plague and torment them both. And she, now walking through the slush to find him, to bring him home, deserved to be fooled the way she was if she was ever really fooled at all.

His son did not move from his position, eating bread dipped in jam and watching his father. They did not speak again until Clinton had finished the wine he was drinking and rose out of his seat to find another. His son watched him all the time—watched him moving.

"Is Sheila in bed?"

"Yes—why?"

"I wanted to know."

"So you know," said Clinton, coming back to him, coming close up to him so that they stared at each other. "You were out drinking—you had no Jesus business out drinking."

"I'll drink when I want; it seems you drink when you want," William said looking straight out, unafraid, completely unafraid.

Clinton flinched in his anger—he had found his reason now; he needed no other reason. The boy stared at him in contempt, contempt on his young hard face looking up at the man about to strike him. Yet there was no fear. Clinton struck him with the back of an opened hand, and the boy, jarred out of his position, went back along the counter. He was sixteen and yet Clinton could not make him fear.

Everything was quiet for a moment. Clinton went back to sit down, feeling guilty about what he had done. Even if the boy had cried, he would have felt more justified—it was his silence that brought the guilt into the room. Clinton drank from his bottle.

"You probably chased the whores," he said after a moment.

"Sure—I'm no different from you," William said, his voice on fire with the rage inside. Then the next moment he turned and left, out into the night again—the wet night, the rotting

April snow.

When she came into the house later, into the kitchen, there was the smell of spring upon her, the look of a tired creature upon the placid skin under the eyes. She moved toward him, sitting at the table with his head upon his arms, stinking of wine—the warm stench of liquor. And she moved toward him slowly as if afraid he was asleep and she might wake him.

"Clinton—I can't find him," she said cautiously, her voice low and controlled as it always was and would always be. "I can't find him anywhere and some of his friends I met say they haven't seen him either. Why don't you look for him?"

"He's here and left—here and left already," Clinton said looking up with a blood flush on his face.

"Where—where did he go—do you know where?"

"Whores," Clinton said mockingly. "To the whores."

Then lifting himself he went to bed without speaking to her again, wishing nothing to do with her—she that reminded him of all his grown life. The small room was dark with that April closeness, and he lay silent, thinking of ice on the water—years on the river, the heated liquor in his veins, the coming of another summer to the town. He was a young man—he was 34 years old, but he no longer felt as a young man should, lying in that darkness listening to the sounds of the station, to a distant train. Later, after William returned, she came in to lie beside him—thinking him asleep.

And the following afternoon he went to the school. It was warm and bright, much of the last snow turning to water on the roofs of houses and in the lanes, so that much of it ran like streams from the station streets to the bottom of the town. There were people out on the sidewalks and about the town walking in the spring weather, and the wind that came out of the nor'west, came over the still-crusted fields and gave a fresh clean air.

The school was grey and large and silent in the mid-afternoon sun. He approached it slowly, wondering to himself what he might say but not knowing. He had shaved for the occasion and had put on clean things, Rubena asking him to put on clean things. He was to meet with William's teacher at three o'clock.

He did not like the look of schools nor the smell of them —the taste in the air. In some sense it was the taste of something bad, the same as hospitals, he supposed. He was out of

91

place in them. It was something very bad. He stood in the long corridor, listening for a time, to the sounds between the walls, those plastered walls with the voices coming through —the brown, closed doors and the lights along the ceiling glowing faintly in the mid-afternoon, catching the dirt and dust in the centre of their bowls.

He stood in the middle of this corridor, glancing from door to door, hearing the inarticulate voices, the faint shufflings within and thought at once that it might be better if he turned and left—went out into the day again, into the warmth of April, the melting snow. The floor was warped in places and now and then the sound of steam within the pipes.

He stood motionless for five minutes pondering. He did not know which door to turn to, which voice to follow, and so he stood, the ancient building refusing all attempts of the day's good light, and the air encircling him with its specks of chalk and dust.

When the bell rang, it startled him, frightened him into moving to a corner as if it were best he be hidden as the sounds grew louder in the rooms. And he stood near a coat-rack in the farthest corner from the stairway so that no-one would notice him until they came to collect their coats.

When they did, they did not notice him. They were laughing young faces that he saw, that pretended not to notice him, all the while knowing he was there—and why. He had no hat and because of the wind his hair was tossed and his wrinkled suit pants and his grey checkered shirt. His worn face and bloodshot eyes as if the small veins within had burst from the alcohol night after night. And all this they saw as they moved past him to take their coats and he was stiff and silent—silent even with the ones he knew. He waited until the building became as still as before and then he moved out into the corridor again and waited once more.

"Mr. Dulse?" a man questioned, suddenly coming from a small compartment off one of the rooms and looking him over as he spoke. He was a short, well-dressed little man with clean fine hair. There was a solemn tone when he spoke that fitted the occasion. Clinton turned sharply eyeing the man, nodding his head.

"I'm Mr. Mayher," the man continued, "William's teacher."

"Oh yes," Clinton returned. "You're the one that phoned me up."

92

"No, that was Mr. Shale—our principal." There was a moment of silence. "I think it was well time that he did under the circumstances."

Clinton kept looking at him, saying nothing, his eyes questioning those of the little man's as if he understood nothing of what the little man said.

"Well, this fighting, and skipping school—perhaps you'd better come inside."

They went into the small room. He told Clinton to take a seat and left for a time. When he reappeared, another man was with him—a tall man with glasses who closed the door and came to sit behind the desk. There was sunlight through the opened window, the bright April day and the sounds of those voices in the lot below—the smell of the soap of the man in the room where they sat. Clinton looked to the man behind his desk, the clean bright eyes of the man of 45 behind the desk, the clean white fingers stroking at his chin.

"You know, Mr. Dulse, we're having quite a problem with your boy."

"Fighting you mean—for fighting?"

"Yes, and other things also. His skipping school, his smoking in the washroom. Mr. Mayher tells me that William is, to put it bluntly, a nuisance in the classroom."

"I don't even know if you knew he smokes," Mayher said softly.

"Oh he smokes—I know he smokes but what can you do—they're going to smoke."

"Well, they're not allowed to smoke here at all," Shale said.

"I know—he shouldn't smoke here for sure," Clinton said.

But he said nothing more, quickly eyeing them as if he had said something wrong. They were looking at him strangely —they were both so different from him that they were looking at him as if he were a spectacle and perhaps he was. He still smelled of that liquor, he thought—still smelled of the cheap warm wine of the night before and they, both of them, smelled of soap.

"But all this has to stop if he wishes to finish high school or he won't finish. I mean he's missed one grade already as you well know—and could very easily miss others."

"Yes," Clinton said. "But maybe he didn't start the fight —you know, maybe he was just defending himself."

They looked at each other and then Shale shook his head.

93

"It was reported that your boy started the ruckus and for no reason—he simply started lashing out for no reason."

"There musta been a reason," Clinton said, raising his voice a little and raising his eyes to observe them both.

"It's happened before," Mayher continued, "he'd be fine one moment and then the next—well the next, he'd start to curse and swing at anybody, almost as if it were a tantrum of some kind and we can't put up with that sort of thing here."

He said nothing. He continued to look at the men, the calm cleanliness of them, smelling of chalk and soap, and he thought of his son and then Rubena—Rubena who wished him to come here to straighten things about.

"You're Catholic?" Shale asked, looking up from a folder that he held in his hand and then looking back down to it. "Does the family worship together; families understand each other much better I find if they worship together."

"We go to church," Clinton said. "Why, didn't you think we went to church?"

"No, of course not—all I'm asking is if William worships with you. It is the responsibility of the parents to instill in their children respect of the Lord," Shale said as if he were preaching to his own congregation, said it slowly and cleanly. "And if William had a proper understanding of religion, then he mightn't be acting in this manner."

"You see, Mr. Dulse, William is off on a bad foot," Mayher continued where Shale left off. "He respects no-one and he has his whole future to think of. Right now he might think it smart but later when he gets out into the world—."

"Didn't you ever fight—everybody fights!" Clinton said sharply.

"The point is Mr. Dulse—he fights constantly. This can't be passed over or condoned," Shale said, looking straight into Clinton's face, into the face clean-shaven and flushed, into the blood-ridden eyes. A sound of busses came into the room, the clean air of April into the room faint with soap.

"Shit, everyone fights," Clinton said not knowing how else to say what he wished to say and looking at them knowing they did not understand or even care to understand what he was trying to say. "Shit—didn't you fight?" he said looking to Shale. "That don't mean you aren't brought up right."

"Mr. Dulse, we don't mean that you haven't brought William—" Mayher attempted to say.

94

"I have never fought," Shale answered calmly. "Fighting is not right and that's why William is expelled—at least for a time."

Clinton was silent. He looked at them both as he stood.

"No shit," he said to Shale. "And what about the other boy—is he expelled?"

"No, we don't think it was his fault—he never wanted to fight with William."

"You know why eh—you know why he never wanted to fight. He was too gutless and you and your piano fingers—you're too goddamn gutless. We go to church just as much as you. No, you can't understand anyone fighting because you were afraid to. So you expel him and you won't expel the other boy."

"Mr. Dulse," Shale said, red-faced and rising, hiding his fingers behind the desk and rising almost up to Clinton's height so that they looked at each other eye to eye. "You're missing the whole point—if you'd just sit down."

"If there was a whole nest of whores outside," Clinton said menacingly, "neither of you'd know how to catch the clap."

When he came up out of the cellar, he was exhausted from piling the wood into the long neat rows that his son had started, exhausted and tired from thinking so that he thought of sleep and wished to go to bed. To lie his head back and sleep, facing no-one for a time. The night was very warm when he came up into the air and closing the trap behind him walked to the front of the cottage, stepping through the black dirt on the fringes of the lane. Once he was to have a flower garden and good green grass and even shrubs around the place and still made a point each fall that each spring he would plant them, plant the seeds and cultivate things to make them grow. But with his bus in the yard and the proposed expansion of his home he had little time to think of doing these things to his lot, and though he might never expand at all, often in bed he planned how he would rip up the back yard to add another room.

He came into the cottage hearing his wife speaking with Deborah as he did. They were in the living-room. He went into the kitchen and busied himself with finding something small to eat though he rarely ate in the evening. He placed the kettle to boil for tea and sat at the table, feeling the heated

95

sweat on his face. The store was closed for the night and his daughter had left a small slip of paper on the table listing various things they were low on so that when the trucks came—which they did every two weeks—they would know exactly how much of everything to order. The store did little business, catering only to neighbours or in the summer to the neighbours and the cottagers down the way, but it was comforting for him to have two occupations, which is how he thought of it, and a little more profit was always more welcome than a little less.

He was eating when his son came in, first hearing the truck in the dooryard and then his son coming into the cottage and going into the room where his wife and Deborah sat. When he finished with his meal he sat for a time listening to the voices talking of the wake, of the young man that had died —and he decided after a time that he too would go in and join the circle for a moment before going to bed. He had an urge to be in the same room with his son even though he knew they would not speak, and so raising himself from the table, his tall swaying form, he moved slowly in the direction of the voices, snapping out the kitchen light.

"I thought you were in bed," she said as he came into the room, placing himself between her and Deborah on the couch. He sighed and shook his head, began fumbling for tobacco, said nothing. Kevin was on the rocker staring intently at the television set. He had paid little attention to his father's entrance, and Clinton did not give more than a glance to him.

They sat for some moments before the conversation resumed.

"Did you see Ellen there, Kevin?" Deborah asked.

"Who's Ellen?"

"She's his sister; you must have seen her before, black hair."

"No, I didn't see her—I didn't go there to see people."

"Were there many visitors tonight?"

"As many as usual."

Clinton had the cigarette in his mouth, letting the smoke out through his nose. He was watching, hearing the short quick answers of his son, hearing his wife say she felt sorry for "that poor woman" as if a reminder to him and her and all of them of some other time that only the two remembered. And his son was speaking in those short answers, tired of the

96

questions—questions that came from things like this.

"It happens all the time," he said finally to his wife, taking his cigarette out and butting it in the tray. "If they're not careful, it's going to happen."

"It could happen to anyone—not only youngsters."

"Yes, yes—and it does."

"The way they tear around school I wouldn't go home with any of them."

"What do you mean 'home with any of them'?" Rubena asked.

"Well, a lot of girls go home with them; it's better than waiting sometimes 45 minutes for that stupid old bus."

"With who—who do you come home with?" her mother asked again.

"I don't," Deborah said. "I don't—I said I don't."

"Well, I don't want you travelling around in those old cars with who knows what."

"I said I don't, okay—hell, Daddy knows I wait for his stupid old bus!""

Rubena said nothing more. Deborah glared at the television a little longer.

"Hell, what do you think I do—travel around all the time in cars or something?"

"No I don't."

"Well you're always saying stuff like that. Why do you say it for then?"

"I don't."

"You do!"

"Shut up!" Clinton said, twisting his position as if he were intently watching the program he wasn't. There was another silence. He began to roll another cigarette. One more cigarette and he would go to bed, to sleep. She was always on the bus; she always sat behind him on the bus—rarely at the back with her friends and rarely with boys, so that he thought Bena's worrying was groundless, that it was groundless and stupid and that it was like a woman to be sick about nothing.

He was half finished smoking when Kevin rose from the rocker and walked by them to the door. He glanced at the boy's left hand and saw the raw fresh blisters, burns from the lime. They would all go to bed now, he thought. Kevin walked to the door and stood there glancing back. He stood for some moments glancing back.

97

"I'm getting married," he said.

The woman was dying. It was inevitable and she in there every day being nice to her—trying to smile. But the woman saying herself out loud at supper time that she knew, that she would not last until Christmas and that she knew. Pamela could only smile and say that it was all nonsense, placing the tray in front of her and elevating the bed so that, in a sit-up position, the woman could eat. And then coming in just before visiting hour to collect the tray and make the woman comfortable.

It was the bladder. She had no hope, of course, and no-one had any hope that she would last until the new year. But she had been home with her family twice since July and then back again twice. Perhaps she was in for good this time, or perhaps just once more they would let her go home. At anyrate she was dying.

It was twelve o'clock, and the streets, with that fine autumn warmth, were deserted, darkened with the leaves that had fallen, and the moon was small and distant in the night. The older houses in the town stood along this street, their high windows and slanting roofs—the old houses of the town where families of four or five generations lived.

She was not tired walking home nor in a hurry. Rather she sauntered, thinking of all the possibilities of the next week or so—of the marriage. She was nervous about it. Her family did not know Kevin Dulse.

They had met two years before—in the winter just before February. She was in training then, living in the brick quarters just behind the hospital. She had thought nothing of it at first, going out once or twice a week with him to a movie or skating and then him taking her to the rear door of the place with the smell of the stack upon the air and both of them cold—the sky raw with cold. He would kiss her goodnight and it was all very casual. She knew that sometimes when he arrived to take her out he'd been drinking beforehand and it made her nervous.

She never invited him when she took her holidays that summer and went to her parents because he would be as embarrassed at going as she would be at having him there. So she never mentioned it at all. Neither did she like his friends; she thought them coarse and vulgar most of the time—

leading him on to be as coarse and vulgar as they.

But he wrote her twice within the week. The letters were very nicely done, as if he had copied them over making sure that all the words were legible, and the words he chose were adequate for what he said so that she felt rather proud when reading them. Often, as he became more at ease in her company, he would curse and go on. She deplored his drinking and told him so. He knew nothing of good wine or liquor but drank the cheapest—the stuff that drunks are made of and once she told him that. He slapped her. It was the only time he had ever slapped anyone, he said. It was hard for him to apologize, but he did.

The past summer she invited him to her home. He refused. She had been to his place countless times—for supper and his birthday and such so that she was angered when he did refuse.

"What in hell's name is wrong?" she said. "They aren't going to bite you."

"I know."

"Well?"

"Well, so what—I just don't feel like going; I've got things to do."

"Like what?"

"I can't take two weeks' holidays from the mill."

"No-one wants you to—just for a couple of days, a weekend."

"No."

So she went alone, explaining to her parents who had expected him that he couldn't get away. It was obvious that they were not disappointed, only their curiosity was, but their relief came in thinking that perhaps it was *over* after all. She could see it in their faces—what future did she have with the likes of him working as a labourer in a mill?

She came in this evening and put her things out for the funeral Mass. Kevin would call for her at 8.30 and she was obliged to go. She had never known Andrew Turcotte very well, but it was only proper, and Kevin had been hurt by what she said about his drunkenness Saturday.

There was still the smell, the lingering scent of John's wetness on the couch, so that she sat on the chair whenever she sat. After placing her things in order and changing into night-clothes, she boiled water for tea and took two pills to

99

help her sleep. She had never taken pills before she began to work in that place. Perhaps it was working with so many of the old and sick. That lady with her bladder and she trying to be friendly. Christ, there was nothing to say.

Cancer smelled. It had its own special type of wretchedness about it. After they had opened up a patient and then closed him again. After he came from his operation in another hospital back to this hospital again. It smelled—she could taste it.

She drank her tea slowly, the warmth from it, the steam in her face. From the window the moon was up over the trees, shadowed now and again by thin dark clouds, up over the river that she could not distinguish. Often she had looked down that river in some futile attempt to see the stone cottage. She did it no longer, just as she no longer scratched his name upon her tablet when attempting to draw. Her brother thought she had a fine hand, had told her to go to a school of arts and crafts, become a designer or something. But she had laughed it off. When she went into nursing school, he said:

"Just like a woman—no ambition."

"Every family has its artist," she replied.

She drank two cups—using the same bag, squeezing it out for the second and then throwing it away. She had taken the partridge out Sunday before church and placed it in the bin, but she was sure the kitchen still smelled of it, just as the other rooms smelled of all the other things. John would not come again, that was certain—he would not be let in if he did.

It was something—a certain power over his friends. Once he asked Kevin to drive him downriver, late at night after skating, after the rink closed and they were parked in the lot talking. He came toward them from the dark. The snow was high in drifts along the edge of the building, and he had come around the building, wading through the drifts toward them. When he reached the truck he kicked the side of it in a playful attempt to make them laugh and shouted at Kevin to roll the window down.

"What in hell does he want?"

"Don't know, nothin' probably."

He stood on the runner looking in at them, smiling with his hand covering the surface of the mirror so that with any excess strain he could shatter the glass. He breathed heat on the window, staring in at them until Kevin rolled it down.

"Go'day—what's up?"

100

John lifted the bottle for them to see, lifted it and smiled, saluting them with it, as it were, and then drinking from it—drinking deep and long and then saluting them again.

"Wanta go downriver, bud—how 'bout it?"

"What?"

"Give me a drive."

"Now—why in hell do you want to go way downriver?"

"Oh—oh I don't know," he smiled and winked at Kevin again. Then stepping from the runner he walked around to Pamela's side. She had it locked as always, so that he tugged at the handle, making faces of disbelief that she should have it locked.

"Afraid of burglars?" he asked when he was inside, adjusting the bottle between his legs and looking over at them.

"No," Kevin said.

"Well, how about a drive downriver?"

"Now—Christ?"

"Why not now—it's early. It's still early and it's only a little way."

"How far?"

"MacDurmots."

"Who's MacDurmots?" Pamela asked, eyeing Kevin. She did not want them to go anywhere—not with him, not drinking, but she knew Kevin did not know what to say and it made her angry. How had he found them—they should have left for the hospital as soon as skating ended.

"That's twenty miles—Christ John, that's twenty miles; why in hell do you want to go way down there?"

"A little party maybe," he said, passing the wine to Pamela.

"No thanks," she said, turning to give Kevin a glance. It made no difference.

"Well, how'll you get back—you'll freeze."

"I'll find a way—you just get me down there; you and her can come too if you want."

"Pamela has to go in."

"Oh yes, Lady Nightingale has to get in," he said as if it were a joke and then saying rapidly, after drinking more of the wine, "I'll pay the gas."

"Shit—I don't want money for gas; I have to get in—you're a crazy bastard going all the way down there this time of night. What if you have to hitch-hike back—you remember those Indians froze down there in January trying to get to the

101

reserve."

"They never made it, did they?" John laughed.

"No sir—and you won't either."

"Well if you don't drive me, I'll hike down," he said after a time.

"I'll drive you," Kevin said, backing the truck out of the lot and turning in the direction of the hospital. "I'll drive you —but you'll have to get back by yourself."

"Suits me," John said.

When they reached the hospital, he took her to the rear door. The sky was cloudless and sharp with cold. Only the cinders from the stack she could smell, wisping out in smoke into the dark clearness, suggested heat.

"Are you really going to take that idiot down?"

"Ya—I may as well; he'd do it for me."

"No, he wouldn't Kevin—he wouldn't."

"Sure—why not?"

"He just wouldn't."

He kissed her. "I'll just drive him there and leave him," he said. She went inside, watching through the window as he left until there was no sight of the truck, their shadows in the truck, going down so far so late with that wine.

After she finished with the tea and rose from the chair she could feel the pills. Her brother once suggested that music was good for sleep, but she never found it so. She set her cup down and went to bed.

"I'll go to the church but not to the graveyard," she thought.

4

It was the land. The whole perimeter stilled by the frost of dawn, and the haze upon the water had not lifted yet. Nor was there any sound, nor the wretched smell that there sometimes was—nor a sound. That was the good of autumn—that is what made it good.

He had woken early and changed into his huntsclothes, following the path, blind with the half-darkness through the alders to the water. Then over the browned sunken pebbles, the frost thick on the mud, ice in places. He walked down the beach, a smile down, to where the brook fingered dully through the rocks and mud. Here he sat upon the cuts hidden by the saplings now grown above them, sat and waited with his rifle cradled on his jacket and gloves.

He waited half an hour. There was nothing—only the brook water slowly moving, like his blood at such an early hour, the smell of the rotting, the rich smell of rotting, with such a fragrance that he wished to sit all day. He glanced occasionally to right and left, the light breaking through into the high wet grass and wooded area to where, at this hungry hour, things were stirring for the day. But no sound—something watching him perhaps, or perhaps he had come too late.

He waited until the last, until it was useless to wait any longer. The sky was clearing, but haze still rested on the water. There was a low tide and the bay was calm. It would be a warm day and perhaps he would hunt again at dusk. As long as he hunted, he had a chance. To smell the clean musk of an animal hide. He walked to the cottage to change.

The bus had gone. He came from the beach by the back path to the cottage and going inside found his mother in the kitchen. She had not dressed yet. When he came in, she turned to him, questioning the clothes with her eyes. Already she was cleaning the kitchen dishes from the table and wiping the stains of breakfast from the cloth, going about her chores at this early hour in her nightdress—hurrying so that she might unlock the store to begin its day at nine. She looked at him a little angrily.

"Aren't you going to that boy's funeral?"

"Yes."

"Well, it's twenty after eight and you aren't even changed yet. Why do you leave everything until the last minute—like telling us you're getting married?"

"I'll get ready."

He hadn't realized it was so late. He went through to his room and without washing at all changed into his better clothes, coming out into the kitchen again as if to present himself to her. She turned once again to look at him, her hands in the sink water—that calm expression on her face —and eyed his hands, the sweat of the gloves and dirt on the burns. But she said nothing, turning back to the sink, looking through the window that in turn showed the lane. He came over hurriedly and using a bit of the water rinsed off his hands, smiling at her as he did for he could not help but smile.

When he reached Pamela's it was quarter to nine. She was waiting for the truck so that when it came she rushed down to him, still vague with lack of sleep.

"I thought you weren't going to show."

"I made it—I was out hunting for a while."

"Hunting, for God's sake, I think you should leave those animals alone."

He did not reply.

"What time is it?" he asked.

"Almost ten to—are we going to join the procession?"

"Not with this."

They drove to the church. It was a long time since he had been here. Everything was quiet, but already people stood along the cement steps in silent expectation. They walked up to them. The day had cleared, and it was more windy here than on the beach, leaves and twigs upon the steps and the cross so high as they walked toward them. The people dull from sleep waiting until the procession came.

"Here it is," she whispered.

It was not a long line, the hearse and a dozen cars or more, but people had come over from the school, many were walking. He was nervous—it was not from cold that he was shaking now nor was it for himself. Julie, he thought, she would be here now and John and Bruce. Men were coughing on the steps, waiting—looking to those who slid the coffin off the runners of the hearse. The bells began to toll. He did not want to see people crying, like Mrs. Turcotte crying or Julie crying. He did not want to see that.

"I'm not going to the graveyard," Pamela whispered.

The church was very large—so many empty pews. When John passed them he glanced a little, holding onto that brass handle Kevin had seen the night before, holding tightly onto it as if afraid of letting go, and then glancing to the steps, watching carefully where he stepped. Everyone followed the

104

coffin in, behind the family.

And again he could not remember. They sat near the rear behind a tall man so they could not see so clearly. He could only see the crowned thorns on Jesus on the cross, peek into the aisle to see the candles and the coffin, an altar boy clicking the chains of the incense bowl. The Mass had started now, the Mass for the dead, and back in the far pew where he sat there was more of the muttering and less concentration. Now and then the brief cold from the outside chamber would make him look around to see through the opened doors where an old fellow stood, as if by habit, peering in, standing at the table by the money-box and magazines—as if he had followed the mourners here and did not know what to do with himself now that he had arrived. Briefly he would open the outside doors every so often to spit up and then upon closing them would resituate himself. Kevin looked at him now and then, then down at the coffin where it lay on its low iron carriage before the altar front.

Pamela kept nudging him to kneel and stand and the frightening thing was that he had forgotten what to do. It had been so long that now, at this mass, he did not know what to do, and each time he turned to view the old man in the chamber, she would nudge him in the ribs. Light through the painted windows on this autumn morning, the steps of the cross each painted separately, and something lying at the altar front that he could not remember, the face from the picture as if they were all together on a dirt road with a glow from the wine.

What if John had let go of that handle ascending the steps? What if he had tripped taking it with him all the way down those steps again. And yet no-one ever let go because there was something inside that was more strange than life lying enclosed in there with the faint smell of decay—how long under the earth would it take to decay? And yet the smell of Pamela at his side mixing with this quiet solemn morning in the church.

He could hear the sounds of the Mass and the short quick cries from some young girls farther down from him and the coughing and shuffling within the pews themselves. The old fellow still standing at the rear coughed occasionally himself. Kevin felt himself sweating, wanting it all to end.

The priest in black, like a nun it seemed. He was neither old

105

nor young, the marble whiteness of his face, a little stout and balding on the crown. When he came down the altar steps to walk around the coffin he cautioned the servers where to stand with something of a subtle firmness in his movement and with his white hands took the sprinkler, shaking incense as he did. Kevin kept his eyes down the aisle or on the old fellow at the back whom he seemed to recognize each time he looked.

"Of your servant Andrew Brian Turcotte into your hands Almighty God," the priest was saying, and he thought of the brook running its fingers through the mud. But when the priest had finished, he turned to the congregation and began to speak to them—to the family, giving sympathy to those who loved Andrew, as he said. Girls cried in little groups it seemed. He spoke plainly and quickly with a conviction that must have come from preaching on that altar year after year, sounding clear and hard, knowing all of what to say.

"When God takes a soul into his hands, it's always hard for us to understand—sometimes too hard, as in Andrew's case, a young man of nineteen having his whole life ahead of him. And so I sympathize with the family today, as we all do, and with those who loved Andrew. But we must remember that Almighty God has a purpose in all that He does—and all that He does is right and just. Who could ever know what the future had in store for this young man? Perhaps there was something in the future that was not so pleasant, and I'm sure that in time the family will realize that God does what is always best after all."

There was shuffling and coughing in the pews and the priest firm and dignified ascended the steps followed by the servers and taking the chalice from the tabernacle prepared to finish Mass. Only the family took communion.

The the Mass was over, as quickly put away and as easily as anything else. They waited for the coffin, followed by the family, before moving into the aisles. The old man had disappeared from the back, perhaps he had just come in to be warm, but at anyrate he was gone when Kevin looked again. Julie walked arm in arm with Andrew's older sister, and Kevin unconsciously tried to edge as close as he could to her, edge toward her. He wondered what she was thinking now, but she didn't seem to be thinking nor was she crying. She moved into the distance and was out the door.

"I'm not going to the graveyard," Pamela whispered. "Are you?"

"No," he said.

"Well, wait until I go down to light a candle."

He stood outside waiting. It was before ten and the day had cleared blue with a wind and a warm fall sun, leaves on the steps blowing this way and that. He watched the hearse depart for the graveyard, for the freshly dug grave, the cold earth and shale removed in heaps along an opened pit. In a moment she returned, coming up behind him.

"Ready?" she asked.

"That stupid old bastard," he said.

"Who?"

"That damned asshole of a priest."

The morning was just another morning in the kitchen of her apartment, the ticking of her alarum clock placed upon the fridge to show the time and the neat row of green plates upon the open shelf. They had finished breakfast and he, lounging in his chair, rested his eyes thoughtfully upon her. She had changed into her house-coat again, opened partially at the neck, exposing the smooth almost reddish skin of the neck. He felt stiff and restricted in the clothes he wore.

"You go in at four again today, I suppose?"

"Yes," she said, looking up at him and frowning. "Yes, damn it—I hope you don't plan to stay on this damn river forever."

"No, why?"

"Because I'm sick of it here already—one year, one year after we're married and that's it, okay?"

"Sure."

"And where do we go from here once we leave?"

"I don't know," he shrugged looking at her. "Somewhere —I suppose."

"That's a great help."

She stood and began to clear the dishes quickly, clattering them as she did. It was eleven now, Andrew inside for an hour, among it for an hour. There was something to be envied about an unexpected death, about something over which there was no control, no medicine. He knew now; in his grave he knew whatever there was to know about it all if there was anything at all to know, and that was the part that seemed so inviting. It was absurd to think of it that way—but Andrew did know while they all prayed and mourned for him whether the praying or the mourning did any good.

"I hate that Jesus priest."

She came back to sit beside him and taking a cigarette lit it, blowing smoke unconsciously into his face, looking at him intently.

"Why are you so upset—it was just a Mass like every other—he had to say something to the family. I think he said what was appropriate. You haven't been to church in so long you're forgetting what a priest is supposed to say."

"Like saying that God was always just and crap like that and that something terrible might have happened to him anyway so it really didn't matter?"

"Yes, why not?"

"He doesn't understand a goddamn thing, that's why not!"

She looked at him with a look of disgust because he had yelled for no reason; a look of disgust and superiority came into her eyes that had come so often before and at so many different moments that perhaps she did not realize it herself. He stood and went to the window, looking into the lane where his truck stood, looking up and down the lane for some moments, the clear fresh October: hunting in the clean coloured woods, the birches, oak and red pine, the smell of spruce intermingling with the smells of autumn rot.

"You know," he said turning, "you didn't know Andrew any more than that priest—so how in hell can you say what kind of a stupid funeral he wanted? It wasn't Andy's funeral."

"So whose was it?"

"It was all put on for the damn family and they felt bad enough without the priest saying he would have turned out bad anyway."

"Oh Kevin shut up—you're talking nonsense."

Perhaps he was, but he could never argue decisively the way she could. But he felt that everyone was wrong about it—girls crying that didn't even know him—Julie not crying at all, the clean priest spreading incense all over. It took courage to drive 90 miles an hour, that was sure, the priest had never done anything like that.

"Well, okay," he said finally, walking back to sit at the table. "Do you think he cared about churches—eh, do you?"

"Who?"

"Andrew."

"Sure he did—in one way or the other everyone does; don't worry, he cared about them even if he didn't go and you care about them too."

"Like so much shit."

"Look, I'm tired of this stupid argument—if you hate funerals, why did you go? Better yet if you hate churches and think they serve no purpose, then why did you go to the funeral?"

They were both silent once more. Pamela went to the sink to take an aspirin. Kevin could envision her thin good body under the house-coat she wore. He was perplexed with what she had said, perplexed by his own feeling of it all. She came back to him again.

"And that priest—you don't think he knows life; he knows life better than you or I will ever know it. Do you know where he's worked? No, you don't. He's worked as a prison chaplain for years; he's been on a reserve and even worked in a mental hospital; he knows the ins and outs. He knew what Andrew was like just by the way he died, that he was good enough and everything but he was young and wild and a bit stupid to boot, going like a maniac around the underpass the way he did." She finished her sentence as if she had said it all, looking at the obvious pain on his face. He thought for a moment, reddened and painful.

"But he didn't know how much he could drink or that he always said he wanted to screw a nun, or that he drove a bike," he blubbered self-consciously.

"What in God's name are you raving about, Kevin?"

"Julie's pregnant," he was about to say but not knowing how to he remained silent, not wishing to let bare that secret, not really wishing her to know, remained with his eyes fixed upon her for a time.

For most of the clear warm afternoon John Delano walked about the town, in and out of shops and stores meeting and talking to no-one. The funeral was completed, the body in its grave and he, at the graveside, watching them lowering his friend and watching also the morbid blankness of Julie on the other side. But it was clear to him standing there with his mind so fixed on her, on her and the consequences of her pregnancy that she did not notice him at all, that he was another of the white half-asleep faces on this white clear day. He knew he must speak to her. He didn't know at what time or place but only that he must at some time go up to her and tell her what he knew.

It was Tuesday afternoon and the town, despite the slow traffic moving, was now a quiet town, the colourful half-naked trees dropping their leaves monotonously here and there, the park silent, the fountain water stilled and stagnant, brown in the cement-sided pool. He was still coughing up and spitting now and then the once-tight cold broken in his lungs so that he could taste and feel his cold more than the day surrounding him.

He walked the lanes and back streets watching those who passed him with solemn curiosity, passing the apartment and noticing Kevin's truck on the lane. It agitated him to see the truck and looking up seeing the closed curtains of the place—her bedroom curtains closed. "I wish the Jesus he'd get rid of her," he thought as he passed and then going a little farther up turned and walked past it again, looking up once more wondering half aloud what would happen if he went to the door. He decided that she, at least, didn't want him there and decided again, after another moment's reflection that he didn't give a damn. Kevin was always so cautious when it came to her.

He walked back into the main street again, crossed it at the general store, an old high, sloping-roofed brick building that had lasted longer than any other building in the town, that had become in fact a monument to the town itself. He walked past it. The first gas pump had been erected here and had stood until just a few years previous and now many of the old men stood along its worn sides as if by some heroic act supporting it. He himself, one summer night, had slept on its steps, not wishing to face his parents nor wishing to give up the good night which his friends had given up hours before.

But they had always stood there, really as long as he could remember, cursing, drinking, laughing, some not so very old, some perhaps as young as he. "If you don't want to end supporting the store, you'd better study," was the phrase Miss Fin would use at school as if one of her students could ever imagine that they would end like that. "But what the hell," he used to think, "what the hell does it matter?"

It was two o'clock now. He crossed the street to sit on a

110

bench, wondering what he was to do with himself for the day—for tomorrow. He had not been called in since Friday, not that it really bothered him, only that he was low on money. But if they called him in tonight he would say he was sick, which, of course, he was. He sat with the sounds of things about him, the clock revolving endlessly just above his head, and was glad that it was over, that the funeral was over without any trouble. Julie opposite him on the pew across the aisle by Andrew's parents not even crying, never making a sound.

It was nothing really but the young explosiveness in him, the hatred in him finally because of what was left unexpressed. He was sixteen and she sixteen, a little older than he and so warm to look at that winter coming from the show house. He followed her from the show house that night making stupid jokes about the snow and how she looked like an Eskimo. She pretended not to notice him but noticed him, had noticed him in the movie when he yelled and threw things and smoked a cigarette in the seat. All the way to the corner he yelled and tormented her, finally pushing her down into the snow, taking her scarf from her and wrapping it around his bare head while dancing all around her all the time. And then he helped her from the snow and brushed her brown coat off and stood with her at the corner until her father came, making more and more jokes all the time and singing wildly—sometimes making up the words.

"I can sing you know."

She simply looked at him. He took her scarf and pretended to blow his nose with it just to make her laugh, and she did —her white fine teeth glittering it seemed, the blonde hair wet, trying to grab the scarf from him.

"Give us!"

"This day our daily bread."

"My scarf."

He put it behind him and she, reaching for it, laughing, her slacks and hair and coat all wet, red mittens reaching behind him for it until finally he assented and handed it to her. She grabbed it and put it around her. "Go home," she said, but he stayed until her father came.

"So you can sing."

"Sure—and play the mouth-organ."

"Mouth-organ?" she laughed.

111

"Why not? My old man taught me—I play it backwards."

"How do you play a mouth-organ backwards?"

"You can—the deep side is at the wrong end of your mouth."

"Oh," she said not understanding. "What does your father do?"

"Works for Smith's construction."

"Oh," she said again.

He had pushed her into the snow to touch her and had brushed down her coat for the same reason—not to touch any part of her but just to touch her. He left and ran home, the coldness of the night making him breathless after a time, his face feeling numb and puffed, singing as he went along.

He found out that her name was Julie and where she lived, what she liked to do and who her father was. It was as if he must find it all out when he questioned his friends, telling them his first exploit with her, how he knew she watched him all during the movie, her eyes forever glancing from the screen to him in the other row, and how he chased her and pushed her down, how he brushed the front of her coat feeling her as he did. But knowing he had told too much and had told it wrong said nothing more.

Then for a long while he said nothing. When he met her in the corridor, his eyes would glance the other way, knowing she was watching him, wanting him to look at her. And he would talk a little louder when he changed classes in the afternoon, passing by her home room never looking in of course, never looking in at her at all. He did not even know why he was doing this, only that he was and that he must do it.

People told him that girls had told them that she talked of him and asked about his marks, and if he was going out with any other girl, and still he didn't speak to her at all even when she was in his presence right directly in the crowd—he would talk to anyone and everyone but her. He turned seventeen in the spring without once asking her out until it became so that he thought, or rather felt, that he had gone so far as never to be able to ask her out.

Finally he decided that he must. Perhaps she had forgotten all about him, for two months on end he did nothing. But he had thought of her all along. And it was not that he thought anything *bad* about her, what he would do with her, not anything *bad*. It was more the fresh good cleanliness that night

112

walking from the theatre, coming from the building to run behind her, tying her scarf around his head and dancing in the snow while she looked up at him from the snow he pushed her into. That is what he thought of—her face, her body in the brown coat as he brushed it down.

She was standing waiting for the bus; her hair was longer now it seemed. She had her back to him, did not notice him approaching her so that he stood for some moments directly behind, kicking at the loose gravel in the lot talking to a classmate that was also waiting for the bus.

"What the hell you doing here Delano—move upriver?"

"Last place on earth I'd move to," he said smartly, looking at the boy and then at her—the back of her. She didn't turn around. And now she knew he was there. Why didn't she turn around, if only an insignificant glance around to show that she knew he was there? He continued talking with his friend about Andrew's new bike, about the spring—the good spring weather.

"I hear that crazy bastard is out driving it now—there's still ice on the road for Christ's sake."

"He'd do that," John replied with a rush of bravery and loudness inside. "He'd dodge the ice, one side of the road to the other and freeze himself to death while doing it."

"What kind?"

"BSA."

"Well, you'd never see me on the back with him."

"Why not?" John said laughingly. "Why the hell not?"

But the bus had come, down from Station Street past the church and into the lot. He could wait no longer now that she hadn't turned around to witness him. He moved closer to her, moving in the line with them until he was next to her, behind her, peering over her shoulder at the books she carried in her arms—history and mathematics. He carried nothing, never did and never would, and as he stood peering over her shoulder he was thinking of what to say. She knew he was there.

"Hello."

"Hello," she said, never turning more than a glance.

"I was thinking of asking you out tomorrow night maybe," he said rapidly.

"Where?"

"Show or something."

She turned round to face him, smiling, a queer little smile

113

on her face, nodding her head. "Okay," she replied, nothing more than a reply, and then moved onto the bus leaving him standing where he was.

He did not know whether or not to take her out. Now that she had assented he did not know how he would be able to talk to her when she went with him. Time had passed, two months without speaking, and it was not the same as on that cold night when he followed her. He would not be able to act the same, and he knew, had it from some feeling just by looking at her, that she also would not laugh in the same manner, react in the same way. He walked home in the brightness of spring feeling stupid, even enraged at himself for giving in and asking her, for standing behind her so long when she knew he was present and yet didn't turn to him.

"Son of a bitch," he said to himself. Where would he take her? A movie perhaps and to the restaurant after and then he would have to hike home with her—he would have to hike up for her also, and then in the hike home again. "Shit," he said aloud.

No, he had done it all wrong from the very start, not talking to her, avoiding her in the corridor, pretending to be uninterested. It had all grown stale and now that he had finally made his move he felt stupid for having made it. It would have been much better, much better if she had asked him or if he had asked her weeks before. He walked home cursing at himself for having stood behind her, edging up to her like some form of weasel without her even bothering to turn around.

Again the next day at school he met her in the corridor at noon. She was walking out of the lavatory directly toward him with another girl, chattering away, perhaps confiding in her. But he had never prepared himself for a meeting with her during the day and became anxious as soon as he noticed her, noticed her and the other girl laughing—perhaps at him, perhaps at him and his stupidity. His eyes shot rapidly to the floor, and he passed them briskly, never thinking to speak until the last, until he was almost by her altogether, and then he only grunted. " 'Lo," he grunted. She gave a faint, almost angry, reply.

That night it was cold, spring cold, and wet and the roads like ice with their water. It was raining when he came to stand upon the corner, leaving at six from his home and running down to the corner so that he might hike to her place in time. Out of breath he stood on the corner where he first stood with her months before, his hand extended to every car that passed. It was a drizzling cold rain out of the sky and the grey rink looked all the greyer because of it, the clouds low and becoming dark. He zippered his jacket after a time and stood there with his jacket zippered to his chin, praying that some car would stop, cursing venomously at the ones that didn't, enraged that they would not stop for him.

When a car finally did stop he was drenched and shivering with the cold. The man only took him to the underpass though, and at 6.30 he still had a half-mile walk to her home. The man let him out, and the car sped off in the other direction, splashing through the mud, the dismal fallen cuts on each side of the road. He decided to walk, actually to run, the remaining distance, somewhat frightened of reaching where he was going. He ran and walked and then ran again, sweat breaking out upon him, upon his wetness. He knew they would never make it to the first movie if they had to stand hiking for any time at all. And the road, the rain falling—he cursed himself again and again. "Son of a whore," he said.

Their house looked much nicer than his own. He peered in at it, gasping for breath, saw figures moving by the broad front window that showed itself to the lane and began moving up the gravel drive toward it, a thousand things stumbling through him—how to act, what to say. He hoped he would not have to wait, that she would be ready at the back porch waiting for him. He came to the back porch and knocked, and the outside light went on and he was let in.

"Is Julie here?"

"Yes, come in, come in—wet night isn't it?" her father said, a man of middle age looking down at him, his belly bulging somewhat. "John, is it?"

"Yes, John Delano."

"Delano—Delano. Yes, I know your father," he said, taking a cigarette to put in his mouth. "Works for Smith."

"Drives a tractor," John said, watching the man looking at him.

"Well, sit down—sit down."

John sat at the kitchen table fumbling with his hands at the table, looking down at his hands saying nothing.

The man went away to call her, saying that her young

friend was waiting, and coming back, sat beside him at the table. Julie came down a moment later followed by her mother and a younger girl that kept peeking around the corner laughing.

"It's awfully wet out, isn't it?" the woman said.

"A bit."

Julie was looking at him smiling stupidly, and he remembered their meeting at noon-hour. He cursed to himself, inwardly cursing while small driblets of water ran onto his neck.

"Well, Percy is going to drive you down," the woman said.

"That's all right," John said, not really knowing at all what to say. "We'll be able to get a drive."

"No—I can drive you," Percy said good-heartedly, "and then come in after, if you like—since it's raining and you have no way."

"Would you like something to eat before you go—something to drink—hot chocolate or something perhaps?" the woman said.

"What?" John asked, looking to her.

"No, mom—we're late enough," Julie said a little sharply.

And so they left, her father driving them, never exceeding the speed limit, talking all the way in so that John was forced to answer.

"Boys oh boys, it's a wet one," he'd say.

"Yes," John would answer, sitting beside her in the front, smelling the perfume that came from her—her eyes straight ahead all the time. "Get some music Julie," Percy said and she fiddled with the radio dial, never looking at either of them as she did.

They went to the movie, but his mind was not on it nor scarcely on her all the time. Vacantly staring at the picture with his arm around the back of her seat, wondering if they should go to the restaurant after—if they would have time. They spoke no more than a few casual remarks, and he kept thinking of her father coming in for them. "Stupid Jesus arse," he kept thinking, "what in hell—I'll rape her or something." He decided that even if they did go to the restaurant her father would be waiting while they ate, looking through the window at them, waiting in the car.

They came out the back way and began walking to the corner. The rain had stopped, but it was still cold, and he keeping his arm around her as they walked. They talked more

116

now, of the movie, laughingly of the movie as if the worst of everything was over, and the old good feeling of a few months previous came into his soul again, and he danced a bit and whooped to make her laugh. He found himself much more comfortable with her now as they were walking, the streets filled with people their age all laughing and whooping. Percy had told them he would be in at ten or so. They did not go to the restaurant, and it was only a little past nine so they walked from the corner to the rink and, hidden in the shadows with his arms around her, talked.

"Don't you have your licence?"

"No," he said, "but next time I'll get a friend to drive me."

"Who?"

"Andy Turcotte."

"Does he have a car?"

"A bike—but he can get his old man's car if we need a lift."

"That's the guy you were talking about yesterday—that crazy guy."

"He's not crazy—I don't know why everyone thinks he's crazy; he can drive. I'm not afraid to drive with him at all, and on the back it's a hell of a lot more frightening than up front; anyway when your time's up, it's up!"

"Don't talk like that."

"It's true," he said bravely, a little thrilled because he had frightened her.

He walked her back to the corner later, just before her father arrived. He did not try to kiss her or touch her, could not bring himself to.

"Well, you get him to drive you next time," she said as her father pulled up.

"Sure," he said.

Percy rolled down the window to look at them.

"Right on time," he said good-naturedly. "Everything go all right?"

"Yes," she said.

But the next week at school it went all wrong again, as if there were two different people in him, or in both of them. Again he refused to notice her—to take notice of her or her friends in their small groups chattering to one another. He stuck close to his own group and talked of anything, reminding himself that he must not make a fool of himself in her eyes by following her around or even glancing her way, or in

117

fact by being persuaded into her house again, sitting there, being asked to drink hot chocolate. And she did not even seem perplexed by the way he acted. When he refused to notice her, she, as if by instinct, very acutely refused to notice him. They walked by each other without batting an eye.

So that it became again all the more difficult to ask her out, all the more difficult to remain indifferent toward her. Two weeks went by before he asked her out again and in much the same manner as before, she accepting in much the same way.

He began to get Andrew to drive him there on the bike after the second or third time, travelling around the underpass with the front pedals scraping the asphalt and then levelling and shifting with the throttle roaring as they crossed the bridge, water in their eyes because of the speed and the clear fresh spring air upon them both.

It was the end of the school year now. Three times they had been to movies, standing on the corner afterward waiting for her old man, and then a few times during the week Andrew driving him up there and she coming out to meet him in the yard while Andrew raced his bike up and down the highway, and they, standing underneath the window in the mud at the side of the house, watching him. And then he'd pull into the drive spreading gravel as he did, the roar of the bike, shutting it down and then kicking it over again in some meaningless exercise that annoyed him but not her. He could see that it did not annoy her. They watched each other, he could tell; they watched each other, he thought.

Until it became clear why they watched each other, but of course it was clear all along, and he never once brought himself to attempt anything, nothing more than a kiss, sliding his hand along her side but nothing more. Until she asked him one evening.

"Who does he go out with anyway?"

"Who?"

"Andy."

"I don't know, some slut or other," he said, vexed.

"Don't use that word," she said.

He hated her, hated himself. She went inside later and snapped out the porch light roughly and Andy, his foot resting on the kick start with the clutch in, and then letting it out again so that the kick start retained its pressure, watching him as he peered in at her on the porch. He came over to the bike and picking his helmet from the gravel snapped it on, looking at his friend who looked at him.

"She's nothing but a bitch," John said.

"Julie?" Andy replied. "Julie doesn't seem so bad to me," and then added, "you'd go a hell of a long way to find something as nice."

Andrew drove him home, stopping to talk for a moment at the door. It was a warm June night, the smell of young birth, of the now-dried mud in his doorway, the smell of oil and gas faintly in the air.

"Well, if you think she's so nice, take her the Jesus off my hands!"

"Are you serious?"

"Yes—you'll be screwed up in less than a week; anyway I'd rather go downriver."

"Who in Jesus is downriver 'cept squaws?"

"Cathy MacDurmot," John said good-humouredly, assessing the look on Andrew's face and hating himself—hating her, wishing he had punched her or punched himself, hating!

There were men on the opposite side of the street leaning against the building, talking to one another and spitting, looking over to him now and then for at this time of the afternoon he was the only person in the park. Groups never gathered here until later in the evening when it was darkened to shadows, or darkened altogether, giving the pleasure of a sanctuary, the feeling of remoteness to those who wandered into it. In the winter the pool was drained, the benches taken away, repainted green to be replaced in the spring.

He sat for some time on the bench staring over at those that stared at him, never flinching while he looked at them, lost deep in his own thoughts, calculating the money he had left and how long it would be before they would phone him for a shift. He still felt miserable with the cold in his lungs and throat, something of an emptiness inside him because of what happened in the morning, and he, with an empty stomach, sitting alone in an empty park. The clock revolved above his head, and he would glance up to it continually to record the time.

After sitting for some time he stood and began to walk around, feeling the blueish-coloured park gravel under his feet as he walked, cutting through the park to the fountain

119

where its discoloured water reminded him of what had happened, of the young saucy ones he had tried to take. He had returned home after the funeral to change and because of the bright warm day had taken only his light checked jacket. Now he feared he might catch more of a cold, have a relapse and be in bed seriously ill. He looked down into the water, making ripples with his hand, trying to sift some of the dirt onto his fingers, aware that people were watching what he did, feeling quite alone.

Perhaps if he went to the apartment he would be able to get in. Not that he thought he really cared; it was more that he knew she didn't want him there. He wasn't going to impose, but he had seen them both at the funeral, had seen Kevin staring at him as he carried the weight of the thing up the cement steps and into the church. He had $2.75, which would buy him eight draft, but, of course, he didn't wish to chance it, not if Randy was working. They had all been ordered not to serve him, he knew; after an incident such as that, what else would happen?

He looked to the clock again and seeing the time walked out of the park and into a little magazine shop across the street, dodging the one-way traffic as he did and muttering curses half aloud, not at the traffic but rather at himself and more for some reason at Pamela and Kevin. "What in shit does he want with her?" he thought to himself, thinking also how everything had changed from the hunting days a few years before. But he would not impose. "He's up to her throat by now," he thought half-laughingly.

And yet there was no-one in the store, only the small books and magazines on their shelves and the old lady working, coming from the small curtained room at the back when he entered and the bell jangled at the top of the door. There was a young dark-haired one who worked occasionally, and at times he had come in on account of it, but she was not here today, only the old one taking her position on the brown stool at the back of the gum counter and peering through her bifocals at him. He did not look at her, did not grunt hello. Instead he walked to the rear of the shop, glancing through magazines, motorcycle magazines and nudes. The smell of the paper—the dust of the place. He never bought magazines or books, not even nudes, not even pornography. It was all a waste of money and time. But he glanced through them now for he had nothing better to do.

He passed as much time as he could here without becoming nervous of the presence of the woman. Then he left, walking into the day again, not going into the park but continuing up the street, crossing once again at the intersection and continuing along. Then, as if in desperation he turned, walked up a side lane in the direction of Pamela's. And all the while he was moving toward the place he was thinking that he must not but all the same was walking up the lane past the pole he had climbed, seeing the truck as he went. Kevin was still there. He walked past the apartment once more, for the second time during the day, seeing the curtains still closed. "Come on boy—hop off, hop off," he thought. He turned round again, came back and stood in the centre of the lane looking at the truck.

Perhaps he could get Kevin to drink some wine with him. At least it was worth a try. Just go back the road with a few quarts of wine, take the guns maybe, shoot a few rounds and take it easy. It was worth a try. If not he'd go to the tavern no matter what, go in and take the first corner table and order a draft as if he had never left the place. Screw them all, he thought.

He waited some moments on the lane. There was nothing really that he was afraid of, but Kevin was always so cautious with her, never opening his mouth, and he knew the mere mention of wine would send her flying into bitchiness, the mere sight of him at the door would be enough. But the hell with her—he was not going there to see the likes of her. Yes, he hadn't gone back the road hunting in such a long time. At one point it had been tradition, each Hallowe'en going into the camp dead drunk with enough rifles and ammunition to shoot anything that moved, and often they did; often in fact, as they stopped by the side of the road to urinate, some bastard would start firing into the woods just for spite. Once he himself had taken Bruce's hunting cap and throwing it into the air blown it to bits with number seven shell and then fallen onto the road laughing as Bruce ran after the shattered bits of material. "You bastard—bastard!" he was yelling.

They had many great times in the woods—of course, all that was past, Boyd and Terry, he hardly ever saw them but still he wished to go, even shooting at bottles—even shooting at bottles was better than not shooting at all. And yet it seemed that no-one wanted it; no-one wanted to retain it but him, and it angered him immensely so that, as he thought of it standing on the lane, he became all the more bitter toward the two of them behind the curtain upstairs.

He moved to the doorway and looked up. The dark afternoon autumn smell of it, looking up to the top of the stairs. He would go up and knock, waiting for a moment; if they opened it, fine, if not, fine again. He entered and waited a moment again, and just before he was to begin climbing, he noticed her mail—two small letters in her box. Picking them out he went up the stairs almost with a sense of duty, as if he were, in the final analysis, delivering some message that was important to them both.

He stood at the top and knocked, but not too loudly, as if following Kevin's example, and waited motionless for a time, then knocked again. It was Pamela who opened it, just what he wasn't hoping for because he had no idea of what to say to her, even with the letters in his hand. She might think he was trying to get around them now—she might think that.

"Is Kevin in? Here's some mail for ya. Is he here?"

Pamela stood before him in her white nurse uniform, shoeless, her white tight stockings. He had never noticed her before, in fact had made it a point never to notice her. Kevin would have loved to hear him say something complimentary about her, and strangely it was just this that made him refrain. He did not notice her now, staring past her, their eyes not meeting as he lifted the letters for her to receive.

"Yes, come in," she said not smiling, not smiling as if it would hurt her face, and taking the letters from him. "Kevin, John is here."

Kevin came from the kitchen saluting almost and smiling bravely. He still had on his uniform of the dead, his funeral clothes ruffled yet still in place, and gesturing toward the couch he asked John in. John took his boots off and walked to the couch while Kevin came over to sit beside him. For moments no-one spoke. The apartment was much whiter and barer looking now. Everything in it seemed so neat and orderly. He hated apartments like that, so neat as not to be able to move, so orderly you feared you were disturbing the very air you breathed. Those stupid comical paintings on the wall, one of boats, one of flowers and one of a stupid old man with a guitar. If Kevin did not leave her soon, he'd be ruined for

122

life.

"Pretty lousy funeral," Kevin said finally. Pamela had gone into the bedroom and was mixing it up with her things in there, the sound of drawers opening and bottles clinking together.

"I never noticed it too much," he said, stretching his legs forward and looking at his friends. "Besides funerals are never very good; I just hope when mine comes around I'm in the woods where they can't find me, rotting under a tree someplace."

"Same here," Kevin said. "They're not going to pickle and preserve me."

"Shit, I don't think Andy really cared anyway."

"No, that's true—but that stupid asshole of a priest should have stayed in the mental asylum."

"What?"

"Oh, that priest—worked in the nut-house for a while so Pamela says."

"Well, let's hope it's the last we'll have to attend."

There was another silence for a moment and then Kevin, lowering his voice, spoke with a small sound of excitement. "See Julie there?"

"Ya, but I didn't say nothin—didn't have the time."

"Well, are you going to?"

"*I don't know,* why—should I say something? I hardly know her."

"You used to go out with her."

John looked at him rapidly and seeing the innocent stupidity on his friend's face squinted his eyes, laughing lowly. But it took him some time to find an answer, and when he did answer he tried to measure his words carefully: "I took her out—I took her out once, I think, before Andy, and that damn well isn't going with her—is it?"

"No," Kevin said abruptly, sitting back to gaze at the ceiling.

Pamela came out of the bedroom staring at her watch with her coat on making ready to leave. She looked to Kevin only as she spoke.

"You're going to drive me, aren't you?"

"Yes, what time is it?"

"Ten to."

Kevin stood and stretched, putting both his arms out to grasp hold of her while John looked on in discomfort. He had

123

only just come, and now he was to leave again. He felt he shouldn't have bothered and rising from his chair went quickly to the door putting on his boots and bending over to lace them up.

"You need a drive anywhere?" Kevin asked as they descended the stairs together.

"I was thinking we might go out hunting," John said inquiringly.

"Oh I don't know; I should get home and change. I have to help my old man with the rest of the wood, and besides it's late, but I'll give you a drive anywhere."

"No," John said. They were standing in the lane now, and John, with a reluctant wave of his hand, turned down it again, thinking he would go to the tavern no matter what it cost. He shouldn't have gone in. But even though it was against his better judgement, he turned once more to them. "Sure you won't come for a draft after?"

Kevin looked at him startled, shaking his head for a moment.

"No, not now, I want to get to bed early anyway—tomorrow night maybe, okay?" he said, and then in a breath and with a somewhat different sound in his voice continued, "but you guys have to give me a party sometime; we're getting married next week."

"What?" John said. He had almost stuttered it, feeling the embarrassed blush of disbelief coming onto his face. "You what?" he said jovially and louder than before to show disbelief, walking back toward his friend who stood with one foot on the runner of the truck.

"Ya, we're getting married—next Friday, a week from Friday, so next week we'll have to get together with the boys and do some drinking."

They looked at each other, and then John glanced quickly to Pamela sitting waiting in the truck.

"Sure, no trouble," he said gleaming and with somewhat of a conscious endeavour patted his friend quickly on the shoulder before turning back down the road. Kevin yelled goodbye to him once more, and he waved his hand without turning around.

Marriage! It came through his mind like a storm, as if the word in itself had something disgusting to it. He walked back

124

through the quiet autumn lanes in the direction of the park. It was growing cooler, much cooler all of a sudden, and the coldness came through his jacket. "Marriage—shit," he thought to himself, "and to her—the asshole!" The men no longer leaned against the building front and so coming up to it he leaned there staring across to the clock, trying to decide what to do. He would go the tavern just before five to see if they would let him in, and if they did, he would go home and hit his old man for money and come back later and drink all night.

The sky had grown white with small cold clouds changing the colour of the trees. It was like Armistice Day now with the smell of the bare white interior of the Armouries, the uniforms of the old legionnaires polished and shining, walking over the barren grounds. The shouts from the officers in the park, the air November-clean with the shouts. And he, too, polished and spit-clean walking with them in his cadet uniform. It was like that, the beginning of winter, the useless saluting and silences for the dead, the smell of rum from the old men placing wreaths, their faces flushed red with small veins, placing wreaths with a dignity that lasted only as long as the saluting and the ordering and the shouts, shaking each other's hand.

He was never going to grow that old—50 only, or 45—that gave him enough time to do whatever he wanted—that was a long way away, a long time yet. Never marriage either. He began to think of it again, of how Kevin was so pleased to tell him, so pleased! Kevin would grow into a useless fat old man placing wreaths. It was so obvious that he began to laugh at it. "Oh no," he kept thinking to himself, "oh no, what an asshole." Where would they live—here? Yes, probably, and what would Kevin be allowed to do—out once every two weeks! Yes.

His face turned sour as he thought, and as he thought he spit, spitting into the same small pools of spit those men had left behind, and all the while glancing at the clock. No man in his right mind would get married so early unless he had to, and if he had to then that was a whole different story, because if he had to then he didn't want to. She was pregnant. "She's knocked up," he said aloud as people passed silently before him on the street, some glancing his way. "She must be." It made him happier to think that; it didn't make him feel so put

125

out or imposed upon by it. Kevin didn't want to, but had to, he thought over and over again.

He looked to the clock, glared at it again and again. Things had changed so much, changed even since the summer. He would have to hunt alone now, and drink alone, especially drink alone, and he hated that. And all except for Bruce he would be alone most of the time, but Bruce never went down-river, never hunted any more. They all had their jobs, he thought again. He was the last of them. For some reason it made him miserable to think that Kevin would get married without her being pregnant, just because he wanted to. "She must be—she must be," he kept saying to himself. Then leaving the building after a time he walked across to the park once more, felt the small gravel of the park lanes on his feet as he walked, kept coughing and spitting as he went along.

He was crossing the park to the tavern now but crossing it slowly because he wished to avoid where he was going, at least for a time. It was nearing five, and if he didn't hurry he mightn't get a chance to go in at all. He crossed the street to the town hall and bent over the drinking fountain, the water no more than trickling out of the spout, and put his mouth down near to it but didn't want to touch it. He heard the town flag flapping above him and looked across to the tavern door, the dark unlit portion of the room. He waited. The wind had risen steadily, making him colder all the time so that he wished for somewhere warm to go and began to cross the street once more in its direction never taking his eyes off the door, but not really thinking of where he was going, what he was going to do.

When he came to the entrance, he halted, standing back in the corner by the telephone looking in. Now that he was this far it was his duty that he go the rest of the way. He could not turn back now and respect himself for it. He stayed half-hidden in the corner so that no-one would see him being indecisive about it, and he stared in trying to tell who the waiters were but couldn't. Finally he walked jerkily into the room, his hands in his pockets, his eyes down.

He took a corner table and flipped a dollar onto it. Then he looked around him seeing only three or four tables occupied in the whole place, one with Emmerson Morrison sitting alone, his draft before him, half asleep. The other men he did not know, mine workers he supposed, out from their shift

126

early, woodsmen perhaps—Frenchmen no doubt, he thought looking at them. He had seen Charlie look toward him as soon as he sat down, and yes, Randy was working the tables, never looking to him at all. They made no motion to bring him a glass, and yet he was too cautious to yell for one. He decided it better to wait.

And he waited for some time leaning his chair back against the wall, staring at them intently, looking at the time. They weren't going to bring him one! He waited. He wasn't going to leave, not for them, not ever. The hell with them, he thought. He began to curse and sigh as he sat there, making no real attempt for his sighs to be heard since he was on a bad footing in the first place. Finally Randy came over to the door to lock it from the inside. "Finish up," he said. Little stone statue of a man. Then turning to John who watched him all along.

"You're out for a week, Delano—it's good you're not out forever but because of everything you're out for a week." He said all this very rapidly and as he was walking, slowly walking back to the counter taking his money pouch off as he went. He had not looked at John for more than a second as he spoke, but when he did, in that second John shifted his glance to the floor.

"It wasn't my fault," he said after him as Randy continued to move away. "It was just as much your fault as mine," he said a little louder, standing up now. Randy simply kept moving away and Charlie looked up from the counter. The others in the tavern looked at him also so that as he moved to the door he thumbed them all. He felt he should say more to express himself but at that moment he couldn't find the words.

"I'll be in next week," he laughed. Then he went into the day again cursing them all and feeling twice the emptiness he had before he entered.

He walked back along the town streets, sometimes going to a closed shop and trying the door handle just for spite, shaking the door and then moving along kicking the dirt and leaves on the street as he went, as the dirt and the leaves blew around him, feeling the chill of early night, the early dark over the town. The park lights had come on, and the streets for the most part were beginning to fill with the traffic going home.

127

The wind was also stronger now, and he could feel it blowing heavily against him, coming down from the nor'east, and when he crossed to move along the main street, he could feel it hitting him full and cold in the face. He kept his hands in his pockets and his face staring at the ground before him, occasionally looking up, but staring more at the rocks, stones and cracked cement sidewalk. He passed the general store once more where the men were beginning to gather already for the evening, passed the canteen. It seemed as if there'd be a storm this evening—the sky dark with clouds and the oaks along the street tossing and cracking with the gale. He turned to his right, walking through a short alley at the rear of the restaurant and came out by the liquor store where he stopped, looking through to the men inside leaning against the counter. "Wine," he thought and became a little satisfied and in better humour for thinking of it.

He went inside and leaned against the counter and asked the waiter to get him some Hermit, one quart, paying for it with a bill and change, counting the money out. He left with it under his jacket and continued walking, this time up the hill past the library and then toward the rink, walking quickly along, the wind even worse—singing softly to himself.

It was the wind that made him sing; he loved watching the trees sway with it, the whole earth grate and move under its force, the northern winter force of it making him wish to be inside, anywhere, inside by a fire looking out to it from a window on the inside. When he reached the corner, he slowed his pace somewhat and then, crossing to the corner, he stopped altogether, the dust and rotted twigs blowing around, and pulled the wine from its bag beneath his jacket and began to drink, throwing the top away in a reckless motion as if desperate for the whole of it at once, to take all the contents of it, guzzle it—feel it in his throat. He kept glancing from side to side as he drank but more often glancing up the road toward her place, her home as if he knew in himself he must see her now. He did not know what to do, was confused at even wishing to go up there. And how would he talk to her once he did? No, it was impossible—they had talked to each other so rarely as it was, even when they were friends, never more than a grunt all the time she was with Andy—even when he went with them downriver to the beach, lying there in the hot sand he would look over and see her wet and browned body, never once attempting to speak. At parties it was impossible to speak. And yet he had thrown the cap away, was guzzling the sweet warm fire into him and becoming more depressed and more exuberant with every second drink. Cars were passing him also, going home from the offices and stores. He waited, looking along the ground to see where the cap had fallen, and once he found it, he jumped upon it with his foot, splintering and crushing it into the hard ground. Then he walked over into the dark shadows, the twilight shadows that the building cast, and sitting up against it finished off the wine, cursing at everything all the while, at Kevin and his slut he thought. He thought of them in the apartment and he bringing up her mail, and he could not help cursing, cursing as the wind around him seemed to curse.

He threw his bottle aside after draining it, attempting to shatter it as he did but it simply rolled down an incline and rested at the bottom of the ditch. He could feel the wine inside him, in his blood, and he rose unstably—dizziness for a moment before moving to the corner once again, and this time he had it in his mind to go to her, almost as if it were a necessary task, some grave duty on his shoulders that he must perform. Every now and then he would raise his arm to a car that passed and then pulling it in again letting others pass freely as he did. He shouted at them all, shuddered with the drink in him and from the cold—felt compeltely unstable all the while.

"No sir," he was saying out loud, "arseholes no sir—you're not going to get me married—not yet, not ever. It's their fault—they want to get knocked up; it's up to them. Kevin, you stupid arsehole!"

And strangely the very best of it was he was talking to himself aloud and raging, but it was to get it all out. And with the wine he felt impulsive, impulsive enough to shatter the windows of the rink—impulsive enough to go to her, and so he kept flinging out his arm occasionally and then drawing it back as if resting on chance, perhaps thinking, "I'll try once every three times—if I get a drive, great; if not, screw it all."

But he was standing only a few more minutes before a small half-ton pulled over. Then he became frightened; now he would have to carry it through. He stood for a moment pondering and then gathering all his breath walked cautiously to the truck.

"Where you going?" he asked the short burly man once inside.

"Up a ways—Renous," the man said.

He settled in and the warmth of the cab hit him and he began coughing almost immediately—feeling himself sweat with the liquor and the cough, terribly weak and frightened now that he was actually going there, but trying to refrain from coughing so that he choked also and could feel the wine coming when he did. The truck moved along slowly, and the wind whistled mournfully about the windows, and the lights were on showing the greyness of the road in the half darkness, and the houses with their lights on along the sides of the road, the smell of the mill, the smell of burnt sulphur rising on the air, the wind carrying it so that its rotted smell was prevalent even in the cab, even to John who was coughing and stuffed with cold.

They rode along in silence until they had gone past the mill, past the underpass where remnants of the accident still remained, and then the man began to speak.

"You have quite a cold there."

"It's a lot better now than it was before—but I had to come out today for my friend's funeral—killed back there Saturday—Andy Turcotte."

"Oh yes—so you knew him did you? It's an awful thing——things like that. So you knew him?"

"Best friend," John said feeling the wine and the weakness from the cold. "I'm going up to see his girlfriend now because," he stopped short—a slight pause, wondering if he should go on, wanting to talk with the wine inside him. The man could smell the wine he thought, and now he was dizzy from the heat in the cab. "—She's pregnant you see, so I'm going up to try to cheer her up, make her feel better."

The man said nothing as if embarrassed and the truck moved slowly across the bridge and up the hill. It was getting darker all the time, the lights brighter with the increasing dark. The man drove along slowly, taking a pipe from his pocket and attempting to light it as they went, the match burning in the darkness of the cab.

"And what's your name now?"

"John Delano—you might know my old man, works for Smith's—he's workin' up this way now as a matter of fact;

130

they're doing some work up Kere before the snow—he drives a tractor."

"No—I don't think I know him."

There was another silence.

"You work in town?" John asked after a moment.

"No, I own a farm up a ways."

"Oh ya—someday I'd like to get a farm. I'm going to get one some day but I get out right by that streetlight up there."

The man pulled over cautiously, meeting the soft gravel shoulder, and John opened the door feeling the wind and the cold again.

"Thanks a lot," he said standing with the door open for an instant and then, waving, he shut it tight. The man took time to light his pipe before the truck moved off.

John felt embarrassed also. Immediately he felt embarrassed for having said all he did and yet it was said and he could do nothing to undo it. So he moved into the drive, walking between the white-painted gateposts of their drive and cursing himself again and again. He was almost upon the house before he realized what he was doing, where he was going and who he was to see.

"If her old man comes to the door and smells the wine," he thought. He looked around to see the desolate highway and felt utterly sick—sick because of the whole day, because he was too tired to go back and hike the road again and because he didn't know why he was where he was, realizing all along that his visit would not be appreciated. Yet what could they say? At least they would think he was trying to be nice. And so he moved to the back porch and knocked on the door, his knees shaking as he did, his whole body nervous and shaking.

The light came on in the porch and the door was opened, and from the door the man, Percy, squinted at him expecting him to speak. He had a cigarette in his mouth and stood in the doorway in his undershirt and sock feet and John looked up to him.

"Ya, is Julie in maybe?"

The man looked at him alarmed and shivered in his undershirt with the gale that had risen steadily, coming at him through the door. He opened the door wider though and looked more intently at the boy before answering.

"No, she's across the way—who is it, oh John is it?"

"Yes."

131

"Well, come in for a moment."

He paused momentarily, reflecting on his drunkenness and the smell of the wine that he could smell himself, before he stepped inside. Then Percy asked him to sit at the table, calling to his wife who came through the doorway from the other room, a room he had never been in with the large window looking out over their lawn. He could hear the sound of the television coming from it, and when she came out her youngest daughter was behind her treading along the way Julie must have when she was that age. They sat at the table around him—their dinner dishes not yet cleared, and he greeted them with a nod of his head. It seemed they looked a little puzzled that he should be here and it made him uncomfortable.

"So what are you doing with yourself now?" Percy asked.

"Nothing—working at the mill off and on, but nothing much. I just came up to see how she was feeling; I mean I saw her at the funeral this morning so I thought I'd come up and see her—see how she was feeling."

They could smell it off him—were gazing at him intently. He looked to the dishes on the table, kept from looking up, muttering to himself that he should not have come. But how was he to leave?

"Oh I don't know," Percy mentioned. "She's quite upset you know but she keeps it all inside, doesn't she Ruth?" Looking to Ruth who nodded, "but she's across the way tonight at Bernice Turnbull's, so old Clarence should cheer her up—you know Clarence do you?"

"Oh yes," John said, "everyone knows Clarence."

"Well, he should cheer her up."

"I don't know," Ruth sighed, "it'll take a while before she gets round to feeling better—it's an awful shock. And poor Andy, it always seemed he was in one sort of trouble after the other, never knowing what to do with himself. I phoned his mother yesterday. 'That damn bike—that damn car,' she kept saying.

"Yes," John said, trying to relax. The young girl had come to sit beside him, and Ruth began to take the dishes away.

"Awful place to let anyone into," she muttered. Percy reached for cards on the little table by the stove.

"Cribbage?" he questioned. John looked up to him, shaking his head quickly. The man seemed to frown, disappointed.

"Oh—no," John said, "I just came up for a moment."

He could see the disappointment rise in the man's eyes, the face turning a little unhappy—the half-white hair on the side of his head thinned and cropped short. Perhaps he was supposed to say Yes but he didn't know that. He knew he wished to go now. The man replaced the cards and stood to pour himself a cup of tea. He knew if he started playing he would feel dizzy from the heat and already he was coughing into his hand, his whole face flushed and distorted with the cough.

"No I don't play it very well," he said half-humourously. The man turned back to him taking his seat once more.

"Andy was a fine cribbage player," Percy said. "You ever play with Andy?"

"Once in awhile—at the camp or something." Actually he could never remember doing so and felt nervous for lying.

"He was a fine cribbage player," Percy repeated.

"Percy's always trying to get someone to play with him—I never will. Sometimes Clarence comes over but you know how Clarence talks."

"Oh yes," John said.

"No—old Andy and I used to have some fine games," Percy said settling his gaze on the boy. John remained seated a minute longer and then stood, hoping he would be able to walk to the door without stumbling, feeling cramped with the people and their talk, wondering what they thought of him as he stood and moved slowly in the direction of the door.

"You don't have to run off," Percy said. The woman dressed too old it seemed, and she stood by the table with dishes in her hand looking at him. Too old looking for a woman her age.

"No," she said, "have a cup of tea or something—Julie'll be along."

"Oh no," John said, "I just came up for a moment; I have to get back down the road now."

He waved and went through the door into the porch, which was cooler and smelled of the night—smelled of the cold autumn frost in the night, the wind, the grating trees.

"Well wait," Percy exclaimed rising from his chair and walking into the porch. He shouldered the boy gently, directing him to one side of the porch, to the clothes-line hatch and opening it pointed across the field. The wind came in, the line was twisted roughly and John was sober again.

"Clarence lives right across there—why don't you go over? I'd like you to; it might be good for her."

John nodded.

"That house?" he asked and Percy nodded, closing the hatch, bolting it and moving with John as he went to the door.

"And thanks for coming up," he said.

John went out, putting his jacket collar up. He went around to the back of the place, passed a small shed that was sunken into the dark, began to cross the field—the well-worn path that separated the houses, that joined them together. "Shit," he kept repeating to himself.

Tall old spruce stood in the distance, and in the distance the whole line and utter darkness of the woods. He stopped in the centre of the path, the cold mud beneath his boots, and looked to the woods, and from where he was he could hear the wind, could hear it moaning with the wind, the trees and starless sky. He was sour now. He had wanted her to cry in his arms perhaps. He had wanted to tell her that he knew and when he was standing on the corner—when he was glancing up toward this way, he was thinking, at least for a moment, of how good it would be. He was thinking of her face and hair, the childlike face and young pregnant body, almost as if he would be her saviour, almost that. And also that she would be ashamed, more than he was ever ashamed, cry in his arms when he told her he knew.

But now he looked at the two houses, from one to the other—then to the woods and the sound of the wind, the warmth of the houses. They did not know, did not know anything that he knew. He could not see her now because he was sober—sober enough to know he had nothing at all to say, that she would never do what he wanted her to do, cry in his arms. It would be like before. There would be no speaking, only the desperate urge on his part to speak, the desperate urge to refrain from being a fool. He had wanted to gloat over her perhaps.

He shuddered. He turned and walked down across the field, making his way through the alders that separated the ditch and field, branches slapping him in the face, almost tripping in them until he made his way down through them and stood on the road. Here the wind was very bad and he crossed the road and began to run. He was running to get the thoughts out of his head, the endless stupid thoughts that

134

came to him, and he ran with the wind at the back of his head so that it wasn't as bad.

Then exhausted he began to walk. The hell with it. He never wanted to see her again, never wanted to be as stupid as to go there again. He tried to hike the cars that passed but with little success, so that he was across the bridge and almost to the underpass before one stopped. It took him into town.

He got out at the corner and walked slowly up the hill toward the station. He walked slowly because his whole body ached, and he wished only to lie down and sleep. If they called him into work he would not go, not until the cold was cleared. Next week he would go. He heard a freight pulling away from the town, the coarse rude beautiful sound of it coming upon him. This is where he lived. He had lived so long by the trains, slept at night with the rough but soothing sound of them that he could not imagine what it would be like without them there. He was happy when he heard it, for an instant, happy and in harmony with the wind on his face and the sound of the train.

He came into his house and did not speak to anyone, looking through the cupboard above the stove for cough syrup and then, taking it, going to his room. His room was small and slanting, his window overlooking the tracks. He did not turn the light on. Closing the door behind him he walked in a circle in the dark, cursing at himself and drinking the warm thick syrup continually. Each time he reminded himself of the evening—of something painful—he would shout out softly to himself. Going over to the window he looked out at the tracks, smelling the air half fresh on the pane of glass. Then he began his journey again in small circles around his room, in the darkness, drinking from the bottle. He thought of Kevin and Pamela again, of what Kevin had said. When he was tired of his walking, he hauled his boots off and lay upon the bed, his jacket still on him, still buttoned halfway.

"The stupid arsehole," he thought. And then he laughed and coughed, almost choking again. "I'll have to get them something nice!"

5

Thursday afternoon when the bus pulled into the yard she went out to him, because it had been prearranged, and waited in the dooryard in her good clothes until he managed to unload himself and come down to her. He was rolling a cigarette and his eyes were upon the paper, the tobacco neatly and tightly fitted, and he walked past her into the cottage so that she had to turn around without a word and follow him inside. Deborah came in behind her, and they all met in the kitchen, the smell of baking just fresh from the stove and spilt flour along the counter not cleared away.

"Well?" she asked coming up to him, "I've been ready for half an hour—I want to get back by the time Kevin and Pamela come."

He looked at her and grunted, placing the cigarette upon the edge of the counter and running the tap to wash his hands. He stared intently out the window as he did this and she calmly accepted what he was doing, waited passively for a reply. He dried his hands on the nearest dish-towel and then looked to the cake as if wishing to sample it. As soon as he looked, she told him it was for the party later. He picked up his cigarette and puffed at it nonchalantly.

"Okay, okay," he said impatiently when he noticed her staring.

She turned and headed for the door again.

"Wait until I bring the car around," he said.

She waited at the door and he went out, crossed the lane to the shed where his car was kept and in a few minutes backed it out.

"Do you want me to ice the cake?" Deborah shouted.

"Yes—good; that pink icing he likes."

She walked carefully across the dooryard, the mud and browned grass of it, afraid of falling and ruining her clothes, half-smiling to him when he glanced at her from behind the

136

wheel. She opened the door and got in, pressing her knees together, afraid that she might rip her stocking on some jagged instrument in the front seat.

"21," she said.

"What?"

"He's 21."

"Oh—ya."

She said nothing more and they drove in silence into the town. It was well after four now, and she wanted to hurry to be home when they came because she didn't want them sitting there waiting. She wanted to have everything ready.

He parked the car behind the post office and on getting out told her to lock her side. Then he stood there waiting for her to come round to him, to his side of the car, and he looked down at her when she did.

"Where do ya have to go?"

"I have to go get him a present and then we have to look for a suit for you."

"Oh no—I don't need no suit."

"For the wedding—they're getting married—you need a suit of some kind."

"I have a suit of some kind, and I'm not going poking around looking for another one today."

"Clinton," she said, trying not to get angry, to control her voice as she spoke, people and cars passing them in all directions, "you need a suit."

He shook his head and as if to show that all further discussion was useless, turned and began walking down the lane, she following him close behind. She followed him down the lane, walking slowly in high heels, keeping behind him as he turned along the main street, meeting people with her head down and never calling out to him at all. When he reached the first cross-walk he stopped abruptly so that she almost bumped into the back of him.

"You need a suit."

He gave her a sour look, and the policeman on duty waved for them to go across. He muttered to her again that he didn't and that the next time she'd have to find her own way in. They were passing the small shops across from the park now, and walking in silence with each other, she angered into such silence because of his stupidity.

"One day," she said finally, "one day out of the whole year I ask you for a favour and you can't even be decent about it."

He said nothing, his tall swaying form now stiffened because of where they were, and he continued to walk almost as if he were trying to keep ahead of her, spitting occasionally to the side of the street. They kept moving in this fashion until they were far down the street, directly across from the rear of the tavern, the green cement blocks of the tavern wall bright with the autumn sun.

"Well where are you going?" he said finally, stopping in the middle of the sidewalk and looking to the right and left, staring through the alleyway to the tavern and the other street. She was out of breath. She had walked steadily and swiftly to keep up with him, and now she was out of breath, panting and looking up at him while he stared past her and people passed them as they stood.

"I need your help," she began. "I could have taken a taxi in but for the fact that I need your help. I never ask you to come shopping with me—but I wanted to get him a good present, and you have to pick it out. I don't know nothing about guns."

"Guns!" he said, looking down at her, his face almost contorted. He reached for his tobacco again and his papers, and fumbled them about.

"Yes, I thought of getting him a gun—a new good one. Oh I don't know what kind he likes, but he's always about in the woods, so you have to help pick it out. You don't have to pay for it—I have the money."

"Shit, money!" he said, "I thought you didn't want him hunting no more."

"I don't mind him hunting," she said puzzled and then remembering, "as long as he don't shoot no animals."

Clinton laughed. It was the first full laugh she had heard from him in a while, and even though it was because of what she said, she didn't mind him laughing.

"You know the type of animals I mean," she continued. "Remember the gun you had and gave it to Reginald, that big rifle—well how much would one like that cost?"

He pondered and then looked at her, said nothing. They began walking once more, and he directed her across the street and through the alleyway where tin barrels rusted in their slots at the rear of the tavern and where the gravel and dirt mixed with the leaves and rot of autumn, and she, in her good clothes, fearful of ruining them, walking through but saying nothing to him because he had at least in part complied with her wishes.

They went into the next street and turned down it. The gunshop was the last building on their right. It was a wooden two-storey place showing signs of decay, the lower floor the shop itself, with its broad front window displaying heads and hides of animals. And the trophies were ancient ones of a bygone era that gave a peculiar closeness to the air as they entered, intermingling with the smells of gun cleaners and guns and steel. There were rows of hunting knives in a long glass case and lanterns hung unscorched by use, clean and ready for use—a taste of oil. In the far corner behind the counter a fat little man in a pink shirt stared through his glasses at them. They entered, Clinton before her, and he went directly to the man while she stayed in the background surveying the place—the hides and trophies: a stuffed squirrel, an owl and a bobcat, a plaque with a salmon taking the fly and the many rifles hanging in gun racks littering the walls.

All the rifles looked the same to her, but of course they always did. The man was talking with her husband, and she waited for a few minutes until she saw him get up from his seat and come around the counter. She moved toward them when he did.

"So you want to buy a .303?"

She looked to Clinton.

"Yes, I guess."

"Well we have a number of them," the man replied going around to the racks and taking one down. Clinton looked at it, opened and closed the bolt, aimed it into the air at nothing.

"Do you have one without the peep-sight?"

"No, I'm afraid not—not in a .303," the man replied, "but you could take it to the gunsmith; there's one across the river that I'd recommend."

Clinton looked at him and looked down at the gun.

"Ya, I'll take it. If my son don't like it, he can take it to the gunsmith."

They walked back to the counter, the old hardwood floor squeaked with their weight, the dark odour of stuffed hides. The man took the gun and wrapped it, tied it with string.

"Boy's birthday?"

"Yes," Clinton answered, looking around as if to inspect the

139

place, as if he'd love to stay longer in it looking. Rubena stood behind him and had already opened her purse to take her wallet out.

"I'll get it," he said quietly.

She looked up to him. "No—," she began.

"I'll get it," he said again, taking his own wallet out quickly and opening it up.

"How much?"

"That's $23.95."

"And a box of shells also. If he's goin' have a rifle, he's got to have shells."

So the man reached under the counter and brought up a box of shells which he added in, making the total come, with tax, to $29.00. Clinton paid him and collecting the rifle and shells turned and walked ahead of Rubena out of the shop.

They went walking back up the street past the tavern, crossing over to the town hall and walking along, the day very bright and colourful and clean, Clinton carrying the rifle with his left hand.

He placed the cigarette that he had rolled earlier in his mouth and stopped under the flags to light it. She stopped with him wanting to speak, for she had been waiting her chance ever since they left the shop.

"Listen, I'll pay half on that gun with you."

"No, it's all right; I paid for it."

"But it was my idea, and I was the one who said he should have something nice."

"So he does and it's taken care of; don't worry about it."

They continued up the road a little.

"Where do you want to go now?"

"I have to get some candles for the cake and I was thinking of that suit for you. Now don't get all mad—you need one."

"I have a suit—I wear it to Mass every Sunday."

"Clinton," she said in protest and he looked at her painfully, "just stop in with me at the men-and-boy's-wear store for a moment and we'll see what they have, and if you don't like anything we'll leave."

He muttered something, and they continued moving until they reached the store where she stopped again in front of the window and looked in, compelling him to stop behind her. There were suits dressed on mannequins for display, and she turned to him.

140

"Let's go in."

But he wasn't even looking or paying attention to her. Rather he was staring out across the park to where youngsters had gathered, chasing each other through it, so that she went up to him and grabbed him by the arm to lead him through the door. His face was sullen as if he had been forced into it by bringing her into town.

The man that came up to them was particularly tiny and spotless. It was hard to tell his age but perhaps as much as 55 without an inch of fat on him. He was too thin in fact and immaculate, but had something of the dust of the store upon him. She could smell the dust on his clothes. He came up to them smiling and asking them questions which she answered because Clinton just stood there looking about.

And this store was an old one, divided into sections catering to the working class with its displays of work-shirts and pants, its steel-toed boots lining the counter in the far room. The man looked Clinton up and down, put his fingers to his mouth pondering and then went away, coming back a moment later with the tape.

"Now what kind of suit did you prefer, sir?"

"I don't really need one," Clinton said looking down at him. The man did not know what to say and looked to Rubena. "I need some new boots maybe; these ones are split right up the back. Maybe I'll take a look at your boots."

"What kind of suits do you have?" Rubena said. She was angry—her face flushed.

The little man looked to them both in a very peculiar way, twisting the long measuring tape around his small clean hands. He answered carefully, almost nervously.

"Oh well, we have some fine suits just in from McGregor, very nice suits for the modern man, pure wool in very fine cuts and we do take-ins without any charge. Just the price of the suit."

"I'd like to take a look at them," Bena said.

"Oh well come over here," the man said, pointing to the suit rack in the corner. Bena followed him, turning to Clinton and waving for him to follow, but he did nothing more than stand straight and stiff where he was. She shook her head violently at him and then turned away. He was just being stupid and she was angry—humiliated.

But when the man showed her the suits, she realized that

141

Clinton would never wear one. They were much too young for him she thought, though she liked them. But Kevin himself had a suit that was much like the ones he showed her —and Clinton would never wear what his son did. She was disappointed.

"No, I don't think Clinton would want one like that."

"No, no—yes I can see where maybe," the little man said, a little man hardly taller than herself. "But I'm wearing one," he said.

"Yes," she observed looking at the broad tie around his throat and the nice yellow shirt he wore, "but I think Clinton would prefer something else."

"Well, we do have others—but perhaps it would be best if your husband came over and looked for himself, do you think?"

"Yes," she said. The man was looking to her and she felt rather embarrassed. He was chewing a peppermint and began to crunch it with his teeth. She turned away from him and went to get Clinton; she came back into the centre of the room where she had left him but he wasn't there. So she ascended the steps to the next section where the work-pants were, and the boots. She looked about the rows of clothes, the wool socks and leather gloves, the smell of the leather. He was gone.

"Christ Clinton," she muttered, looking about. Then she walked quickly down the few steps and past the main counter again where the little man was, looking at her as she passed. She kept her head down as he stared at her, chewing on his peppermint, the clean whiskerless little face that he had. When she was well past him and almost to the door, she turned and lifted her head, and could feel herself blushing and smiling awkwardly.

"He's run off," she said.

"Oh," he answered.

Then she turned and went out the door onto the street.

Into the warm afternoon again, the dusk beginning, the children's voices from the park. She stood on the street looking about from right to left, the oncoming traffic passing. But she saw him nowhere, neither up the street nor down, and in the end decided it best to return to the car.

"Once in a year," she muttered, "once in a goddamn year."

She moved through the park in that direction glancing

142

back occasionally just in case, moving rapidly over the blueish park stone frightened that he would not be there and listening to the voices about her curse. The fountain water was stilled, rising stagnant and filling half the pool, a few scattered leaves floating on the murky brown so that nothing of her own reflection could be seen. And the boys were around her playing and shouting, mud and dirt on the most of them from rolling on the grass. And she could see the mud and dirt and one bleeding at the nose.

"You couldn't even wait for me—not once, not once did I ever ask you—."

She passed by them quickly and was out on the street again looking around at the revolving clock and noticing the time. It was late and she hurried on thinking of the candles now, candles for the cake, so that she passed by the post office altogether and continued up the main street in the direction of the store.

The drugstore smelled new. It smelled of paint and new tiles as if they had just done it over. There was a woman behind the counter, her hair tight grey, pinned at the back and lines from the corners of her mouth directly to her chin and the smell of the newness on her also. She wore a white uniform, almost like a nurse, as if she were a nurse. She smiled and the lines disappeared.

"Yes," she smiled, "I can get them for you."

"And you have cards?"

"Yes, at the far end of that aisle."

Rubena went back the aisle and looked over the assortment trying to do everything in haste, knowing that it was late, knowing any card would do. But she searched until she found one she thought he'd like and taking it and the envelope returned to the counter. Before she reached the end of the aisle she could hear a man come into the store, and then the voice of the woman. When she came to the counter, a man had his back to her arguing with the woman there.

"No," the woman said.

The man said something that she could not quite understand, as if it were hard for him to speak, but she could hear the voice of the woman speaking the same thing and she did not wish to go any closer, fearing that it was none of her business. The woman saw her and motioned for her to stay where she was, and at once she felt stupid for being there at all.

"I'm not going to bother arguing with you—I'm not selling you any." The woman was turning red and the lines were creased into her skin, especially around the mouth as she spoke. She was angry and kept pointing her finger. Rubena felt sorry for her and confused because she didn't know what to do. She thought of turning and going back to the cards but that would not do, not at all. She felt obliged to go to the counter. She stepped a little closer to the man, though he did not see her, and waited.

The man had on a long grey coat, smattered with mud, and his shoes so worn at the sides that he seemed to be stepping out of them. As she drew closer, she could smell him. It was the stench of something sick in the clean lighted store, the perfect aisles, the nuts and candies under glass. It was the smell of alcohol and dirt. He was talking, arguing with the woman but making little sense. She felt sorry for him also and going to the magazine rack stared blankly at the covers.

"You don't have enough money. Look, clean your pockets out; you don't have enough money. That's a nickel not a quarter, a nickel. I can't give it to you—."

The man emptied his pockets onto the counter. "There look," he was saying. "For my knees," he was saying. He threw his money onto the counter, the few coins falling to the floor, rolling crazily this way and that. And he tried to trap them with his feet, staggering backward when he did so and cursing. Then he turned to look for them, a blueish flush to his face and thick spittle on his unshaven chin. He bent over almost to his knees to look for them. Bena glanced to him half smiling but he hardly noticed her. He was looking for his money on the floor.

"I have your candles," the woman said.

She stepped to the counter and paid for her things, the little grey-haired woman taking the money and rapidly handing back the change, while the man looked for his money mumbling curses. She looked down at him seeing the discoloured lumps on his neck, smelling the smell of urine and alcohol. And she could see his change also, scattered about in nickels and pennies.

She could leave now but, though she wanted to, she felt it a duty to stay, at least another moment. And the man was still gazing at the floor. It was indecent not to pick the change up

144

for him but she couldn't bring herself to, as if she'd be collaborating with him if she did. So she waited at the counter and then because his search was futile he too came back to it.

He looked at both women with vague eyes, the sores around his mouth glistening with spit. Bena smiled up at him a little stupidly and he staggered up to her extending his arm so that it touched her shoulder, just touched it, nothing more. Then he looked to the woman.

"I lost my money," he stammered.

"I'm sorry," the woman said, "but I don't want you bothering the customers."

The man looked to Bena with a pathetic twist to his face and taking his arm away from her tried to stand straighter.

"I'm not bothering you?"

"N—no, no," she said looking to the woman, who frowned and kept shaking her head. Bena gripped the card tighter in her hand. "Christ Clinton," she thought. She wanted to leave the store, but she didn't want to leave the woman to deal with him alone, as if she would be doing something nasty if she left.

"No, I'm not bothering—I lost my money," he said looking at her again, the same pathetic twist on his mouth, the sores on his face, his vague eyes staring down at her as if he expected something. The woman shook her head.

"She's not going to give you money—don't go round asking people for money!"

"I didn't; I lost my money—."

"Well, that's too bad but don't go round asking people for money."

The man looked rapidly across to her and cursed. Then he moved to the door slowly, his feet wide apart, mumbling to himself. Bena bent over and picked up the coins. "Bullshit," he was saying. She went over and attempted to hand him the coins, but he didn't notice her and he opened the door and staggered into the street. It was as if he didn't want to notice her, wouldn't take the coins back if he had.

"Emmerson Morrison," the woman whispered, "town drunk."

"Oh," she smiled.

She was out on the street again almost to the post office before she realized the coins were still clutched in her hand. People were passing her right and left, and the grey darkness

145

of autumn night was over the town—all the lights glowing, the shops and stores closing for the night. She looked at the clock and saw the time. They'd be home now, waiting. She turned and moved up the lane quickly, dropping the coins to the dirt.

When she reached the car, Clinton was reclining in the front seat smoking, with his feet up over the steering wheel and his head at the passenger side. She went around and knocked on the window, and he unlocked the door, glancing at his watch.

"What took you?"

"Don't ever pull a trick like that again," she replied, choking with her words. "Don't you ever—I had to explain to that man that you'd run off, and then this drunk mauled at me in a store, but a lot you'd care—a lot you'd care. Sit here and smoke cigarettes."

"What drunk?"

"Just a stupid old drunk, that's all."

He looked at her, said nothing, the smoke rising around his face. He started the car to go.

"Get the candles?" he asked.

They went out just after the darkness to the bay where she wished to walk, and they walked as far down as the spring but the water was high—too high for them to walk with ease and now her loafers were mud-ridden and wet and the bottoms of her jeans wet also so that she told him she wanted to go back.

So they turned and made their way back to the cottage, the calm small waves at times washing up over their feet, the full darkness now surrounding them. And out in the bay the faint buoy lights shining over the water. Everything was quiet in the darkness also, only the sound of them as they moved carefully over the stones, and the lights from the buoys, faint and quiet, and in the distance, in the direction of the town, the huge dark structure of the bridge.

But she cried out when the water came up over them, a cry half of laughter, half of fright, and she jumped upon his back after a time, he carrying her part of the way.

"You'll drown us both—Kevin you'll drown us both," she kept shouting as he carried her veering this way and that over the small slippery rocks, surrounded by the waves on one side and the alders on the other, alders that sloped upward into

146

the dark mass of maple and spruce. She buried her face in his shoulder, and he could feel the soft hair and her short rapid breathing on his neck. She laughed gaily into his jacket now and then.

"Where are we now—are we there yet; you're an awful slow walker; have we made it yet—you aren't going to fall are you? Yes, Kevin watch it!"

He didn't answer her. But of course his arms were tired now and his legs unsteady, and he felt tired. He felt that he should put her down before they did fall, fall into the water or onto the black stones continually grating under his boots. So within a few moments he let her slide off his back to walk beside him on the inside. They were not far from the cottage now, and when they went up the path toward it, he saw the car in the dooryard parked behind his truck.

When they went inside, Clinton was sitting in the room smoking. They went into the room, and he exchanged greetings with Pamela, glancing at the wetness of her jeans and then up to Kevin who nodded quickly before he sat. They sat together in the clean little room, Clinton shuffling his feet and snorting now and then, watching cartoons. Pamela broke the silence once or twice by asking him how the store was going, how the bus was running, and each time he answered he looked to Kevin as if for affirmation of what he said.

"Well that's good," Pamela said when he told her everything was fine. They sat in silence for another few minutes.

"So you're getting married I hear?"

"I guess so,"

"Yes, yes—down here too eh?"

"Yes," she said. "It'll be easier down here—my parents can come down for it. It's only going to be small."

"Sure, smaller the better eh?"

"Yes."

She looked over to Kevin as if she wanted him to say something, but he didn't know what to say. He sat there instead, listening to them talking, to his mother in the kitchen and to the sounds of the cottage, the vague sounds of children outside and Deborah singing in the bedroom down the hall. He wished he had bought some wine or beer but he hadn't. It was his twenty-first birthday and he should have really. But, of course, Clinton never drank anymore. What was the sense of buying it if you were only to drink alone?

147

In fact he had never drunk with his father, not even a sip of wine at Christmas or Easter—not even that. He sat there and was very quiet, his arms folded, pushing the rocker softly with his feet.

"Father Murry—oh, of course," Clinton was saying, "so you're going to get him to do the thing?"

"Yes, we'll have to see him some time next week. I've already talked to him on the phone, but we have to go in and see him."

Deborah came into the room a minute later. She still had her skirt on, an apron over it as if she had been working in the kitchen. She was still singing lowly and she laughed as soon as she entered the room so that Kevin looked up to her.

"How's the birthday boy?" she said. Kevin looked at her and grunted, half smiling.

She sat down beside Pamela and sighed, reaching around behind her to undo her apron. "Supper will be ready in a moment," she said.

"What are we having?" Pamela asked.

"Whatever his little heart desires," she laughed taking her apron and throwing it at him. "The big 21-year-old."

He caught the thing before it hit his face and threw it back at her. He was blushing now—felt it under his skin. He never understood why but it embarrassed him for anyone to make a fuss over him, especially anyone in his family and especially in front of her. Pamela laughed too, and Clinton snorted a little, reaching for his tobacco on the floor.

"Yes, sir," she was saying, "my brother is now a man." Pamela laughed all the harder.

She threw the apron at him once more, and once more he threw it back. Then she stood and came over to him, swinging it around, slapping it about, trying to catch him on the side of the head.

"How's the birthday boy, eh? How's the big 21-year-old, eh? How's the *man*?" she was saying gaily.

The whipping stung his face, but he tried not to show it, and held his hands up protecting himself from the onslaught, cursing at her under his breath. "You wait," he was saying, "you wait."

"Give it to him, Deb," Pamela was laughing, "give it to him."

Until finally he grabbed the thing from her and threw it to the floor.

"There now—go way you little ass!"

She turned to go away breathless from the exertion and then stopped to pick up the apron.

"Chicken," she said. "Chicken—I made little pink frosting for you and little candles."

She was leaving the room now laughing, the apron dangling across her shoulder, and she was mocking him with her laughter, mocking him with the innocence in her voice so that he could not help feeling it—the burning in his face. It make him angry to sit there between his father and Pamela, listening to her, Pamela laughing with her. It made him angry even though he realized she meant no harm, that it was her way—that she was excited and that was her way. "21 little candles," she said as she went through the door. When she was going through the door, Pamela called to her asking if she had an extra pair of slacks.

"I'm not sitting down to eat with these things on."

"Sure," she said and Pamela followed her from the room.

He could feel the presence of his father as they sat in the room alone. That Clinton sat across from him on the couch with his feet curled up under him now and his tobacco out. That they were alone in the room with the silence after so much laughter just before—silence that restricted his breathing, even that, and only the voices from the box in the corner disturbing the air.

He could hear the girls in the bedroom down the hall and his mother in the kitchen. But he stared at the picture in silence and waited, not knowing how to begin to speak or what to begin to say. And his father shifted about on the couch and began to roll another cigarette coughing as he did so, trying not to take his eye off the picture as he rolled and wetting the paper very carefully with his tongue. Every little while Kevin would glance over and then glance back. He was sitting on the rocker but he never moved it back and forth, sat still and waited. Waited for Pamela to come back.

It was late and supper would be very soon. He could feel himself sweating because of the incident with Deborah, the beads of sweat standing on his forehead, along his spine and the heat of anger still on him. He kept listening for the sound of footsteps, but he didn't leave the room, almost because it was his duty to stay—because he felt that if he left it would be wrong.

149

"Did you hear about them wanting to close the season down?" he said finally, looking over to Clinton who now had his arm extended across his eyes, lying there as if he was asleep, the cigarette burning in a small ashtray on the table near his side.

"What?"

"The salmon season—they want to shut it down, for five years I hear."

"Who told you?"

"Guy at work—it'll put a lot of men out of business."

"Ya," Clinton said lifting himself up and staring over at his son, "ya—and no wonder. As long as there's mills on this river, there ain't going to be salmon—no matter how long they close the season. Them mills is ruining everything and you know it as well as I!"

He said it angrily as if he were thinking of his own bad luck on the water. Then sitting upright he placed the cigarette in his mouth and was silent. It had gone out and he searched through his pockets for a match. When it was lighted, he stared blankly at the smoke for some moments.

"What are you doing up there now—not in the lime now?"

"No, in the shop, working with the carpenter—at least for a while."

"Oh ya. Your burns are gone now, cleared up are they?"

"Just about."

He thought of showing his hands but decided against it. It seemed that even this much conversation had been forced —forced from the both of them consciously and nervously, and they returned to silence once again. Nor did he wish to speak about his work, knowing what his father thought about it—how his father loved the water and what he thought about the mill.

"So you plan to live up in town," Clinton said after a moment.

"For a while—the apartment is big enough for awhile and it's close to everything."

Clinton rose and stretched, about to leave the room. He bent over to put his cigarette in the tray and then yawning started for the door. He was going through it when Pamela came back. She came into the room looking as if she had just had a shock, the look on her face that told Kevin she was furious about something—furious at him. She passed Clin-

150

ton, the jeans she had borrowed a little too baggy, and came over to him, looking down at him in the chair—her face white and her eyes narrowed.

"Did you shoot somebody's cow?"

He glanced past her quickly and saw that Clinton had turned and was leaving the room, that now the only person in the room with him was her, and she was staring down at him in such a way that he could not look at her with a straight face.

"Who told you?" he said, feeling a smile of embarrassment coming over him, over his heated face.

"Deborah told me—that you killed a poor cow! She thought I knew but of course I'm the last to find out anything from you—let the whole world know but not me!"

"No-one knows," he said defensively, losing the smile because of what she said.

"Well, you still shot it and I think that's the most childish thing in the world. And you have to pay money also—and how much money do you have? Dammit Kevin you're always screwing up! How much?"

"Oh it isn't very much money so stop worrying about it! And why is it childish, just tell me that. It wasn't my fault! I thought it was a deer. It was right in the woods while I was out hunting and it didn't *moo* or anything." He laughed out loud now because of the way she was looking at him, although he was a little frightened of her just the same.

She turned away from him and went to the window, drawing the curtains back to look out so that she was half hidden by the curtains as she did. He sat for a few minutes with his back to her wondering what she would say. Then Deborah came in to tell them supper was ready and he gave her a mean look almost unconsciously. But she didn't notice it, or at least she didn't let on that she did.

"Supper is being served in the main dining-hall."

Kevin sat there looking uninterested. Pamela turned to her saying that they'd be there in a moment. She shrugged and left the room.

"How much do you owe?"

He turned the rocker around to face her.

"Money? Three hundred."

"Three hundred—three hundred! It took us a year to save what we have, a whole goddamn year and now—," she snapped her fingers harshly, "like that you owe three hundred."

151

Then she went across the room swiftly so that he didn't have time to answer. "You're just as goddamn foolish as John and the rest of them."

He waited for some time lost in thought. Then he moved from his rocker and went to the window, moving the curtain back again and looking through. It was autumn dark, the buoy lights faint red on the distant water, fixed and revolving endlessly—revolving just the same now as when they had walked the shoreline together. He remembered carrying her—the rapid breathing into his neck. But now that she was angry it made all things different, made him angry so that he breathed heavily into the window and cursed aloud. As if it were his fault that he had shot the thing. He turned around just as Rubena came into the room. She had her good clothes on, her good suit for town with an apron tied around her waist.

"Are you coming? Everyone is waiting. There's presents there for you to open from Pamela and your father."

Kevin glanced up when she mentioned his father, looking at her in a peculiar way. Then he shrugged and followed her into the kitchen.

"What's wrong with you two, both going around with faces a mile long?" she asked as they came into the kitchen, looking at him and smiling a little. He did not answer.

Then he moved around the table and sat beside Pamela at the back. She didn't look at him when he sat down, and Rubena noticed it.

"What's wrong, Pamela—you two have a fight?"

"Oh no," Pamela said smartly, eyeing him quickly, "I just found out that bright boy shot a cow!"

Kevin flushed red with anger, could feel himself grow tense with the remark; but he said nothing and did not look at her, as if the pride in him refrained from all comment. Instead he looked to his right quickly, to Clinton who was gazing out across the table as if nothing was going on or being said, or as if what was, was nothing of his concern. Gazing out across the table waiting to be served.

Rubena was bringing the plates over now and gave the first to Pamela, the second to her husband. "Oh," she said as she returned to the counter for the others, "Well, he'll have to pay for it I guess."

"Yes—and with our money," Pamela said pointedly.

Clinton began to eat as soon as his food was placed in front of him, keeping his head to the plate, reaching every now and then for things on the table, for the relish and salt. The stooped round shoulders of an old man.

"Wait, Clinton, for the others," Rubena said, lashing out at him for some reason, "have the decency to wait!"

He lifted his head and put the fork down, looking about and chewing the food slowly in his mouth.

"You're not starving are you?" she smiled.

Then when they all had their plates, they each began to eat quietly, unconcerned with the rest. Unconcerned, without conversation. And Rubena sat tonight at the table beside Deborah—sat at the table with the rest, not standing by the stove or leaning against the counter waiting for orders from the table, nor running back and forth to the store to serve a customer. She sat at the table with them tonight, directly across from Kevin so that each time he looked up he could see her small plump frame, the white plump hands cutting at the food.

"How do my pants fit? All right?"

"Yes," Pamela said, looking across and smiling, "a little big in fact. You'd better not start getting fat."

"I can't help it if you're such a squirt."

"You think I'm a squirt do you?"

Deborah looked over.

"Yes," she said, "I'd say you were a squirt."

Kevin eyed them both. He didn't feel like eating now though he'd been hungry all day. But it wasn't Pamela that had made him upset—or at least it wasn't entirely that.

"You should see what mom got you!" Deborah said after a moment.

"I'll see it," he said looking over.

"What did you get him, Pamela?"

"I shouldn't have gotten him anything," Pamela said.

"I didn't get it—Clinton bought it," Bena said quickly, looking at her husband. "He spent the money," she said looking at Kevin. Again he glanced to his father, but Clinton seemed more intent on eating than anything else.

And again there was silence. He finished with his plate and pushed it away from him, waiting for the rest. He looked above him through the small window over the table and stared blankly at the darkness outside. He wanted to leave the

153

table really, wanted to get in his truck and go to town—alone, wanted to find John and get drunk. He wanted to run about the town singing and shouting because it was his birthday, and that was as good an excuse as any. And he wanted to do what John had done—run through the puddles or swim the fountain, with his hair mud-ridden and the liquor in him. But he knew he never would.

"—Just think," Deborah was saying, "maybe Sheila will phone tonight. She phoned last year on his birthday—maybe she'll phone tonight."

"Maybe she will," Bena said. "She didn't mention it in her letter. She doesn't even know you two are getting married," she continued eyeing Pamela.

"She doesn't?"

"No—not yet, maybe I'll phone her."

"Does she still work in the bank up there?"

"Yes, she's head girl up there in the bank now," Bena said with a tone of pride.

"That's good."

"Yes—I was just thinking of it today. Everyone's grown up now. You two are getting married. She's a head teller up in a bank—Deborah will soon be out of school. Remember when we used to take her and William into the park, Clinton?" she asked, looking over to her husband who grunted while tearing a piece of gristle from his meat but never looked up. "We used to take them into the park every Saturday for the longest time, buy them ice cream and walk about. But you couldn't do that today—not now. Everywhere you look there's wine bottles broken and children no older than Deborah cursing and fighting and drinking. I was afraid when I walked through there today."

"Afraid?" Deborah questioned laughing a little.

"Yes, afraid. The park wasn't meant for that you know. When William was little," she continued eyeing her husband again, "there used to be—well everybody went there then, elderly couples sitting on benches all afternoon."

"So they still do," her daughter replied.

"But it isn't the same. And I remember once when William was three—we lived at Papa's then, and used to have to harness him when we came into town, he was always running about, had so much damn energy. We were afraid we'd lose him in a store unless we did—remember Clinton?"

154

"Harness who?"

"William."

"Oh for a moment I thought you meant Papa," Deborah laughed. Clinton looked up to her.

"Oh for God's sake—William—he had so much damn energy. Kevin had energy too, but William used to tear about and exhaust me. We went into the park one afternoon and I was holding onto the harness but he twisted right out of it and ran ahead of us, I screaming at him at the top of my lungs and he right over to this old fellow on the bench and put his finger up to him: 'Bang,' he shouted, 'you're dead.' I'm sure that poor old fellow had an attack right then. And he always wanted me to take him on the harness—never Clinton —because he could always manage to slip away from me."

Clinton looked over to his wife and was silent. He was chewing the last bit of meat and being a slow eater everyone else was finished. Rubena picked up the plates and began to take them to the sink, Deborah getting up to help her. Kevin had never heard that story before and tried to picture it. He had heard other stories though—stories of William when he was a child escaping the harness and running through the stores, his parents chasing after him—Clinton cursing. But he had never heard this one and tried to visualize the face of the child running in the park. The face of his brother as a child of three.

"Yes he did have energy. Of course he was a lot older than Sheila, but he would never torment her—not like you see some children do," she continued, coming over to the table with the tea-pot in her hand and pouring Clinton a cup.

"Are you going to open your presents now?" his sister asked, standing behind the counter, her hands moving slowly, decorating the cake with candles slowly as if she wished to do it perfectly and glancing up to him as she spoke. He had been looking at what she was doing all along, but looking unconsciously so that when she spoke it startled him a little. "Open them now—there aren't very many—two as a matter of fact," she laughed.

"I don't care."

But she was out already to get them. She went into the hallway and he could hear her rummaging about as if she were carrying something heavy. "I'm saving my money for the wedding," she called.

155

Then she came in again carrying two parcels—one a rifle, he could tell that easily, wrapped in plain brown paper, tied at the barrel and stock; and the other, something—a shirt perhaps. He looked at her moving awkwardly through the door, the rifle looped unsteadily through her arm.

"Be careful with that," Clinton said turning to her, but as he spoke she tried to lift them over his head so that he had to duck a little and raise his arms. "Watch it," he said roughly so that it must have frightened her, seeming to be more alarmed of her dropping the rifle than he was of it hitting his head. "If it drops, it'll ruin the sights," he said. Then he lifted it over and set it against the wall. Deborah passed the other present and sat down.

"Well, are you going to open them?" Pamela said.

"Sure."

He picked the rifle up and tore the paper off, knowing that all their eyes were on him—all except Clinton's who had risen and was walking to the sink, the swaying form moving away from the activity. He stood by the kitchen window looking out.

"Well, do you like it—Clinton picked it out and all, paid for it. And he isn't going to shoot no cows with it Pamela—you'll see to that!"

"Yes—well it's a nice gun," Pamela said.

"Yes—a hell of a nice gun," Kevin said louder—eyeing her, "where did you get it?"

Clinton turned from the sink and walked to the counter. He leaned against it facing his son.

"At the gunshop—though it doesn't have nothing but a peep-sight, so you can take it across river and get it changed. I tried to get one like mine—that's a little heavier than mine, I think, ain't it?"

"No it's great—I like the sight," he said, lifting the rifle to the light and looking through.

"Careful," Pamela said laughing a little.

"Well, your eyes are bound to be better'n mine."

He put the rifle back against the wall and picked up the other present—opening it carefully because it was wrapped carefully. Opened the box and took it out.

"A sweater—oh that's beautiful," Deborah said.

"Yes, that's nice—you sure have good taste," Bena said. "Isn't that a nice sweater Clinton?"

"Yep."

He came back over and sat down, pouring out another cup, staring at the tea as it flowed from the spout, while the rest were looking at the sweater Kevin still held up for them, examining it—feeling the material.

"Yes—you have good taste—that'll look good on him—he won't have to go around looking like a tramp all the time."

"If he'd just take care of his clothes, he'd never have to."

He put the sweater away, setting the box on the floor, then looking back to them. Everyone was quiet again, the sound of Clinton drinking tea, staring into his cup, and the sounds of the cottage—the smell of autumn. But the rifle—the rifle! He could hunt now and every Saturday until the end of the season he would try to hunt. Yes, this Saturday, and the next they would be married—but the Saturday after, and all the weekends until the end of the season. Maybe he and John would go out to the camp.

He thought on it, thought of the excitement of the woods—the excitement he had felt that day when he stood behind the twisted alders looking at the hide, the brown hide standing before him. And that brief split-second of excitement before he fired, and when he fired the faint smell of powder on the air. They were talking now, he could hear them talking again, Pamela and his mother, his mother bringing out the details of his birth and of William's. She did it every birthday and was doing it again, but still he tried to think of hunting, staring at the candles on the cake.

"—But Kevin was born in the hospital and I had no trouble with him at all; I wasn't in labour long at all. Nor with Deborah—eh Clinton? With Deborah Clinton didn't have time to light his cigarette and it was over—just sat down to light his cigarette and it was over. But, of course, with William I was younger then and he was born at Papa's. We didn't go up to the hospital that time because it was winter. There wasn't much snow at first but then just before he came, it snowed all the time."

"Oh," Pamela said, "well, we're not having children for a while—at least not until we get really settled."

"No—you have to get settled," Bena said. Then she looked over to her daughter. "Well, isn't it time for the cake?"

Deborah raised herself and went to the counter.

"Oh yes—for the birthday boy," she said, touching up the

157

candles before she lit them. "Are we going to phone Sheila after?"

"I don't know, maybe," Bena said.

Clinton had finished with his tea and was sitting staring into nothingness. When Deborah began to light the candles, he half rose out of his seat looking down at Kevin as he did so. He moved his chair back carefully.

"Don't you want cake?" Bena asked alarmed.

He looked over to the counter.

"Oh well, I'm not much of a cake eater," he said, looking back to Pamela and smiling a little.

"But you have to have a piece of cake," his wife said. "It's fresh."

"Come on daddy—cake's good for you," Deborah laughed.

So he sat back down and stared into nothingness again. Then when the candles were lit, she asked for the lights to be put out, and when Bena had done that only the small light from the candles showed in the dark, the small flames flitting back and forth as she lifted the cake and brought it to the table. For a moment it seemed as dark as the night outside, as dark as staring over the water.

She was bringing the cake over to him, and he could see her face somewhat distorted from the light the candles gave as it seemed to dance against her skin. He forgot about the rifle now—the hunting, but thought only of where he was and that he should be elsewhere, with his friends perhaps, perhaps drinking with John.

She brought the cake to the table and sat it in front of him. And the flames were burning brightly—only a faint smell of the wax in the room. He could see also the indistinct forms of those around him, of Pamela beside him and his mother on the other side. And then Clinton staring into the darkness, as he was. She sat the thing in front of him so that the heat and light danced on his own skin.

"Big 21-year-old," she laughed, "that's my present." She laughed again.

The candles made the form of a K and it was very nicely done, the remaining candles forming a circle on the outside. She had taken her time to get it right.

"Sing happy-birthday everybody," she said and began to sing loudly for a moment. "Sing happy-birthday Pamela —mom, come on!"

158

And they all started to sing lowly for a moment—all except Clinton who twitched in the darkness waiting. Kevin stood and looked down at it—looked again at them all.

The voices died down again, died into nothing again, and once again Deborah sang:

"Happy birthday to you—you live in a zoo—you look like a monkey—and your father does too."

He looked to his father quickly and saw that his father was waiting silently in the chair. Then he looked to the candles, a fine smell of wax coming from them now.

"My God, I forgot to give you your card," Bena said.

And then he blew them out.

6

But he could not say he was rising with the water, with the waves of the water for whenever he tried to see he was paralyzed and blinded and the taste of salt came into his mouth, heavy and dark and burning—a sense of utter loss except for the feeling of fear that numbed him.

It started with the island as it always did and then with the island it moved away into the sea black and green and he far out in it swimming toward the island, at once seeing the hot sand of the island and then out in the sea. When it left the shore he was never afraid, only the red colour of the sun dancing on him totally red and the boat clean and dry and then the island was far away, morbid and small and dark and the boat itself gone. It was Clinton's drifter. Then he was in the sea—the coldness of the northern strait about him encompassing him with its black depth—hideous liquid encasement!

And the waves were gigantic and swelling. Strong waves that came over him and burdened him, burdened his arms. Each stroke he made against it he could feel himself grow numb and the black liquid rising higher and higher until the swells reached the clouds and closed the island off. Then he

159

was alone in it and he could not feel himself riding out the waves but could feel their pressure and it was as if his head would burst or crack. Everything was dark brown above the water and small and distant, as distant as a row of trees along the horizon and thick with storm. Pregnant with the storm. And far away as he was struggling he could see the iron rusted rungs of a ladder in a green L-shaped enclosure of the wharf. And the fine smell of tar came to him as he struggled and then the ladder grew distant and out of sight.

When the ladder grew distant again it was as if he were in a box long and narrow and it was as if there were something behind him now rising with the swells and he could feel as he turned the black fins and teeth of some gigantic fish swimming behind him, so close to him that he could hear its rasping. He screamed, but as it touched him it didn't touch him. Rather it burst like a mosquito heavy with blood and left a mess on the black waves, more like his father's drifter discharging oil on the waves.

But he could not say he was rising with the water. Then he was near the iron rungs of the ladder in the green L-shaped enclosure infinitely calm and green and deep. And when he went under he did so to see the green deep about him, his feet dangling below with child's sneakers and outstretched in the calmness his left arm floating like a white twisted claw before him, white and hooked and outstretched. Only the pumping sound of his heart, nothing more than the sound of his heart and the infinite water and then below him rusted on the rungs of the iron ladder the tangled mess of construction wire, its barbed points sticking out and trying to reach his flesh.

His bed was moist with the outline of his body. The smell of a cool morning in the room coming with the light through the small box-like window. But when he woke it was quiet and light and he remembered at once the savage pounding of his heart in the black sea—the terrible fish and then the green quiet. It was quiet now and it was still early. The old man was up and about, moving and coughing in the stillness just behind the door. He presumed by the amount of shade, by the faintness of the light that it was still early. In another week they would return to the old hour and the mornings would be brighter and sharper and the evenings would fall sooner and sooner until the very heart of winter. Then he would leave

160

the mill in the dark at night.

He could hear the old man's merciless coughing and the sound of his mother but all this only seemed to increase the sense of quiet within his room, the undisturbed atmosphere of early morning—the weak light that seeped grey and dull over his dresser and the dull mirror upon it. And whenever he closed his eyes again, he saw the half-faded vision of the dream.

It was his mother at the door knocking, and he opened his eyes once more hearing the first of the three morning mill whistles calling over the water as if she had just timed it so —timed it so that precisely at that time she would be knocking. Then he was up, the dream forgotten, Monday again —all things forgotten but the shift he must go into again and again and again, the sawdust and the grinding sound and the taste of the wet cold sour mill again and again.

He came into the lighted kitchen with the warmth from the stove. Clinton had finished eating and was up and ready to leave and his mother had split two eggs and they sizzled, he smelling them with the morning and the oil that generated the heat. His clothes were faded mill clothes that he wore and his boots stiff, hard to get into, shrunken from the materials he walked through—the lime and salt and dirt.

"Tell her to get up—I'll be back in twenty minutes."

He sat at the table without a sound and ate what was placed before him, watching his fork.

"When do you see the priest?"

"Tomorrow—no, not tomorrow—Wednesday. I don't know, tomorrow or Wednesday."

"It's leaving it awful late—you need a practice."

"No—we don't need nothin'."

He finished the eggs, feeling them numb and swollen in his stomach, feeling his stomach churn with the thought again and again—and his mother at the stove flipping more of them for his sister. He stared at his salt-cracked boots, cracked right across the toes, cracked halfway up the laces. He stared at his boots and drank a coffee. The second morning whistle from the mill.

"You should have let me iron you out a shirt."

"Shit," he said under his breath as he rose. He was angry with her for even talking and moved past her, past Deborah who came into the kitchen through the far doorway with her

161

dress unzippered saying nothing to him as he came. He moved out into the light October coolness, the smell of frost on the mud.

The smell of frost on the dead weeds, the mud scattered and streaked along the inside of the cab and the sun barely breaking through the hard clouds over the water, but the water calm, still and even white, the weeds and grass turned down and trampled and dying in all the fields along the river. But the air fresh and the woods silent, perhaps with some expectant hunter propped carefully somewhere in there—in among the trees and alders, in there waiting for the slight, ever-so-slight movement of something that he wants.

The road came no closer to the water except at the causeway where the quiet inlet could be seen, the maples lulled in their autumn colour and the two or three small outboards anchored on slack quiet lines. He passed over it, passed the tall brick chimney scarred black at the base where the huge giant oven sat—black and scarred and unused for years, but giving to the landscape a tall quiet strength that no-one noticed except unconsciously as they moved past it day by day, moved past it and the buried cannons and ghosts of those that made it for some purpose he did not exactly know.

When he reached the mill, the tightness came to him and he knew it was Monday again, and worse, he was just coming into it. The shadows of other men went past him and through the doors, and already the deadening grind and the third morning whistle. Already the trucks backed up waiting, already the dull laughter and curses of the workers as he climbed from his cab to join them.

He went through the door and along the corridor—the familiar timeless smell and into the room where Clarence and the rest sat on the benches around the paint-chipped table. He grinned and waved. No pride in your work, Pamela said. Of course it depended. When he sat down, he felt like sleeping, felt his eyes close and all the muscles relax, the unsteady voices from the other men becoming no more than distant murmurings that made everything inside him wish to sleep.

"Too much screwin' with that young nurse?" Basil laughed.

He looked over and grunted and rested his head back on the cement wall, moving his feet carefully under the bench. There was a slight shuffling when Willis came in, some standing to their feet.

"How's your burns now?"

"Okay."

"Go down with Baps again today—I think he's got some paintin'."

"Okay."

"And for Christ's sake wash out your brushes—every second fucker I send down there has to go to the stock room for new brushes."

He didn't answer. He rose and took his lunch bucket and moved past the foreman into the corridor. He was working with the carpenter again and that was good. He didn't mind doing that. So he went out into the morning again, the sulphur smell, and along the small roadway sloping downward and away from the main building, in the opposite direction from the lime-pit, moving down the gravel roadway kicking the gravel before him.

Already he had the saws going. He was a large old man—as old as Clarence, and every morning at this hour he had his work already begun, working at the same rate day in and day out, ceaseless and quiet and relaxed. He was a careful monotonous talker, a dull story-teller that thrived on telling stories, sometimes with that occasional tinge of humour that made listening worthwhile. And though old his face was strong and independent—his teeth yellowed and chipped but still his own.

The shed was small and filled with the clean smell of sawdust that seemed to cling fresh and yellow in the air. The back doors were open, letting in the morning air and the sight of the boards stacked in rows and held by wire. He came through the front door and yelled above the sound of cutting.

"What's to do?"

Baps turned to face him, already covered with the fine yellow that he worked in, worked in until you could not imagine him looking any different, could not imagine him with anything but the fine yellow covering of dust that gave a different shade to the room and light. He shut off the saw.

"You have to do some paintin'—some sign paintin'—so get out the brushes there and those letter blocks there—and for Christ's sake do it careful! I don't want everything fucked up by you."

"Oh yes sir."

He went to the cabinet and took what he needed and laying

163

it on the floor went over to the plywood cuts that he had to paint.

"Want a taste of snuff?" Baps asked watching him.

"Nope," he said.

"No fuck ya, I wouldn't give you any," Baps said, taking some himself and laying it under his tongue and then smiling with a certain contentment.

He rested the signs on a bench and bent over with the brushes and paint, the block letters scattered about his feet, and the sound of the mill so loud and monotonous that it became inaudible once his work was started. The sound of the cutting of boards. He measured the signs and took a pencil to mark them off and felt good doing what he was doing, wanting to start right in and work at signs all day. But he at once realized he had no idea what he was to paint so he straightened again and went over to the saw.

"What do ya want now?"

"What do I paint?"

"No, you wouldn't know would ya—*No Admittance*—can ya paint that?"

He didn't answer. He walked back to the signs and bent over them again, measuring them again to mark them off.

"And do it even," Baps yelled.

So he did. He mixed the dark red paint and with everything measured and the tin block letters ready he went to work, went to work watching the smooth texture of red going from his brush in fine even strokes onto and into the dry plywood, making a very definite pattern as it did. And it was a fine even red all morning—a smooth fine perfection with his brush. Only the saw and the sawdust, the look of warm fine paint. He thought of nothing else but the evenness and the perfection. Once in a while Baps would saunter over to watch but he would keep working. The sun was warming and drying the timbers that lay outside the back doors and when one sign was finished, before he began another, he would take it and place it by the doors to dry, standing for a moment to let his back relax—to see the clearing day. Then he would be inside again, bent over working. And so he did, worked that way all morning without noticing the time.

Then the saw shut down again, and he could hear the old man gurgling water from his container. He saw that his hands and even his arms were sticky with the paint so he laid the

164

brush upon a piece of board and stood, feeling his aching muscles as he did. He turned and Baps was quietly observing him from the corner with the water jug still to his face and water slopping down over his jaw.

"So ya finally decided to stop—you know you ain't paid for noon hour."

"Ya I know."

"Want a chew of snuff?"

Kevin pondered.

"Sure."

"No fuck ya—you're too young."

Kevin could feel how tired he was now. He felt like sleeping now and his head was spinning. He sat by the back doors with his bucket, itching at the paint that had turned to scabs along his arm. He could hear Baps eating, the tired almost suffocated chewing of an old man.

"Doing any hunting Baps?" he said after a time.

"Ya know, you look like the time our barn was painted," the old man answered, staring at him. "The time me old man asked me to paint the barn and, of course, I never knew any better so I decided to touch up the pigs. No, you might laugh if ya want but I didn't know any better. You look like that now—them pigs. And no I wouldn't do any huntin', not with the likes of God knows what in the woods today."

Then there was a silence and they continued eating. Kevin stared out to where the small island was and upriver from it between the island and the jutting land, the short wild hundred yards of water with its undertow where some in sport had tried to cross, lost and taken under, sometimes their bodies never found. Then across to the jutting land, the graveyard, the first settlers buried there, bottles smashed atop their tombstones—and the stones themselves cracked and decaying. Andy was under now almost a week. Almost a week as forgotten and as entombed and as dead as they were.

"No, how 'bout you?" Baps said.

"What?"

"Do you hunt—or just the women?"

"Oh ya I do a bit—nothing going though."

"I used to hunt the women," Baps said. "Can you imagine that? But the women are getting uglier every day as far as I'm concerned. Yes sir, ugly is all they are. Take your mother now—take Rubena."

"My mother?"

"Yes, your mother. Now you take your mother, she was a fine-lookin' woman in her day. Of course, I was a bit older than she was. But there's nothing around like that now—is there? She got married awful young—your mother. Of course we all did then. But ask her if she remembers me—ask her if she remembers the time I painted the old man's pigs."

Then another silence, then the old man rose and went back to the saw, softly whistling through his teeth and Kevin, though he wanted to sit longer, rose and followed him. The saw started and Kevin went back to his paint. He bent over and began again, the same almost enjoyable tediousness of doing it for he could see while doing it the fine red perfection he was making. But the sun was so warm now, and even the paint itched at times and his head still dizzy from the smell. He wished to be out in a sun that warm, the shadow of the sun on a good dirt road during one of the last good days of autumn.

But he was brought back to his work again by the preciseness involved in his task, by the tin block letters he had to hold firm and disciplined against the plywood while his three-inch brush smoothed and soaked the surface of the wood. And then that vague cracked photograph of a young woman formed an impression while he worked. She was leaning against one side of a small bridge, covered if he remembered correctly. It was a short covered bridge across one of the small tributaries that fed the river. She was leaning back with her hands supporting the soft brown hair of her head almost as if she were posing for something much more precious than a camera. It was a blurred, cracked, scarred picture but he remembered that there was a light duskiness to her face, round and smooth and innocent in youth, and that the pleasant face wasn't smiling and perhaps that is what heightened the quality. The quality of the flesh of the tributary and the scent of the covered bridge.

He finished another sign and brought it to the doors to dry, bringing the signs he had finished and dried that morning in with him. Then he stopped by the jug and took a drink of water, watching through half-closed eyes the bent back of Baps over the saw, cutting off boards and stacking them, the hard rounded back in a faded green shirt. He turned and put the water jug down and was going back to his signs when

Willis came in, stood like a shadow at the doorway, that small hawk expression as his eyes darted around the shop.

"So have we got enough signs?"

"Baps, do we have enough signs?"

The old fellow shut down the saw.

"Oh Christ ya," he muttered looking about.

"Well ya can clean the paint up and go to do some shovelin'," he said looking at Kevin, and then in a moment he was gone, disappearing into the roar and confusion of the mill. Kevin began cleaning up, putting the block letters and the paint away. Then he rinsed his arms down with turpentine and took a rag to dry them, feeling for a moment the coolness as the paint dissolved and cracked on his skin. He was cursing under his breath and moving slowly. Baps stood watching him all the while.

"The day's almost in so I wouldn't worry about shovellin' too hard."

"Ya, don't worry."

Then when he had finished cleaning, when he had washed the brushes and left them to soak, he took one more swallow of water, cursing as it dripped across his throat.

"Hey Dulse," the old man said, "you want some snuff I'll give you some."

"No thanks, Baps," he said.

The saw started up again as soon as he was outside.

For the rest of the day it was the mill again, the grinding smell. He was in the bin and the pulpy mass kept shooting out, he standing knee high and resting on the shovel every so often. Big shovelfuls, he kept thinking. He would cut at the soft mess of it with his spade, watching the shovel blade slide so easily into it and then lifting and throwing, his hands sweating on the handle. His hair in knots itching and sweating. But as soon as he had the pile half depleted again the shriek of the shoot opening, the whine of a mechanical mouth regurgitating something sickly and again the pile would be where it was before.

He shovelled this way for half an hour, seeming to get nowhere with it, cursing at it and at the increasing weight of the shovel. Then he put his left foot into it thinking to himself, If I can bare my boot before the next stock comes. There seemed to be a burning smell in the machine and he worked

167

harder now, the sweat damp on his back. He tried to count the shovelfuls but it didn't work. He didn't want to cheat either —if he dug down in one place, he could bare his foot but that was not what he wished. He wished to have the entire pile at that level. That was what he wanted.

And for a time he tried to do that. For a time he worked harder at it, noticing nothing of the workers around him. His foot was buried three-quarters deep, and sometimes he was unstable as he threw. But no matter how he worked never, never did he win, never did he see the brown and busted fabric of his boot. Each time he thought he might, and each time the grey mouth would open and the pile replenish. Each time it did he felt more tired and more angry than before, another surge of energy because of his anger and the shovelfuls harder on his hands. "Christ," he kept muttering. The he lifted his boot half-way up the pile and then he stopped.

He stopped to rest, leaning back against the slanted side of the bin. The game was over and soon again that grey mouth opened. He watched it piling up now but didn't care, feeling the scarlet flush of heat on his face and the thumping blood inside his head. Elsewhere others also were slowing down, some with wire brooms sweeping down the floor as if they could make it clean and make the cleanness last. He turned and saw the pile again and bending over his foot three-quarters deep went back to work.

Clouds as in the morning weakening the sun and the east breeze slight between the two buildings as he walked across the grounds. Still the sound of the whistle vibrating inside him. He had left the shovel inside the bin and could imagine the pulpy mess burying it, could see the great monstrous mouth opening to cover it. He entered through the small doorway hearing the men, hearing the laughter echo down the cement corridor to him as he walked. He went to the washroom first, washing what he could of the sweat away, of the stink and the dried scrapes of paint still upon his hands, smelling a mixture of smells—the mixture of urine and soap.

Then he went into the room where some of them still sat smoking, their faces cracking slightly to a joke, laughing now and then, laughing loud. Willis was drinking a cup of water, lodged silently against one far corner watching.

"So they had you runnin' today," Clarence muttered.

168

"Yep."

"And you're going to run all night with that little one?" Basil laughed.

"Yep."

He was reminded of it now. But he didn't want to mention it until the men had left. He didn't want them to know. So he set his bucket on the table and sat down beside the old man, watching each one separately as they sauntered out the door.

"How's Baps?"

"Crazy as ever—I don't know, didn't say much today."

"That young Bruce Creamer lad says he'll be outside."

The men were going now but not Basil, not Clarence who still sat clattering his teeth as if he could destroy them when he wished and the fan blowing slightly overhead.

But those were the only sounds now. Then Alton picked up his bucket and moved across to the door and stood there for a moment waiting.

"When was he here?"

"Just a minute ago—says he'll be outside."

Then Basil moved and went with Alton, and the old man too, seeing that no-one was left, picked up his bucket to go. Willis still sat unmoved in the corner, holding the cup of his thermos pinched in his hand.

Kevin rose and stretched, going to the door before turning to say what he wanted. It was as if he had to be at the door, as if the door were an access to not saying it. He stood at the door and turned, viewing the tired pinched face of his foreman in the huge empty room. The taste of autumn lingering in the blowing fan.

"I was wonderin' if I could have Thursday and Friday off—I'm gonna be getting married."

"Married?"

"Friday, ya—so I was wonderin' if I could have a couple of days off."

Willis threw the remaining water on the floor and spit into it. It was comical to see him spit. And then he rose and walked toward Kevin, walked toward the boy nodding as he did, short quick movements of his head.

"Ya, I suppose you'll be needing them."

"Thanks."

"So you're getting married—I hope she's not knocked up."

"Nope."

169

"Bad way to start if she is."

"No she isn't."

He turned away, walking away from the room, Willis walking slightly behind him to the door. But he didn't turn nor did they say anything more once they were outside.

Once outside he walked back to the lot, never turning to Willis who walked behind him. The day was finished and he wasn't tired now. He could think only of the evening and being freed from the plant, freed from the bin and sulphur billowing with the half-grey smoke into the air, churning with the east wind that scattered leaves about the empty lot. So he was not tired now; he was simply happy to be out of it for a time.

The lot was almost empty save for the few cars coming already for the second shift, the few cars remaining from the first. He walked kicking at the gravel, the leaves scattering and dancing with the breeze. Cold autumn breeze that made the river dark, that brought clouds to shadow out the sun. The unending taste of fumes. He reached his truck and Bruce was sitting in the cab, boots against the dash, waiting.

"Where's your car?"

"Didn't bring it—can't afford the gas."

"Cheap bastard you are."

"Christ, I can't afford to run it. I'm putting it away for the winter anyway; take it out on the weekends."

"Like I said, cheap bastard," Kevin smiled, turning the truck about.

Then they turned out toward the town, leaving the tall grey buildings behind, not speaking for a time as they drove. Bruce had his head leaned against the window of the door, looking out toward the strewn pulp logs in the muddy field, the trucks and mountainous chips, the blower idle and silhouetted against the air.

"So we're havin' a party tonight."

"Are we?"

"Well, John says you're getting married to the one, so we'll have to have a party I guess, even if you're nothing but the craziest bastard that ever walked."

"Tavern?" Kevin muttered looking over.

"He don't want to go. He says he's not going back to the place again."

"Well, he must be out for good."

170

"No—only for a week, he's allowed in now. But I think he's broke—the crazy bastard won't work."

"What's so crazy about that?"

"Christ," Bruce muttered but said nothing more.

They turned off the highway, descending the back lane past the dump, smoke from the smouldering garbage, the rusting twisted metal from long-dead cars. They would probably have high winds and then rain, baring the limbs of trees, the birds unprotected during dusk. And every Saturday from now until the end of the season he would hunt. He would hunt alone or perhaps John would come with him. He would go far upriver, maybe to the camp.

"Where then?" he asked, turning from the lane to drive along the town.

"I don't care—I don't give a damn, but we have to get the boys and get pissed. My old man's shed for all I care."

"Great."

It angered him that Bruce would not take his car, that he would leave it home all winter like some miser pinching his nickels and dimes. It angered him that he would work and earn his money just to leave his new and spotless car sitting in the yard, putting it away for the winter like some old man. Like some old man, the inside of it smelling always of disuse.

"Pamela working?"

"Until tomorrow night—well, what do ya want to do? Get the stuff now and go get John or what?"

"That suits me."

The trees were heavy in the wind and the leaves scattering like a storm, cars and people moving in the after hours, in the grey. There were many trees sheltering the street and that was one good thing—rising as they did far above the poles and wires, far above the stores and wires and neon lights. He moved his truck slowly into the lot and parked, edging it toward the rough dirty brick of the building.

Still he could smell the stink of himself from working and once outside the wind blowing the unsheltered dust of the lot into his face. It was like Bruce to be working with the timekeeper at a desk in the main downstairs office. It was like Bruce to be doing that. They went through the doors together and stood in the warmly lighted place, the hardwood counter over which the liquor was sold, the beer counter on the far side, men lined against it in an uneven row.

171

"How much—and what?"

"I'll get the wine and you can get the beer," Kevin said going to the counter and leaning against it. Bruce followed him and stood behind.

"Well?"

"Well, how much?"

"Christ, suit yourself—everyone can bring their own—I'll get some wine for John and I."

"That Jesus gut rot."

"Get some beer—coupla cases."

So Bruce left him and went to the far side, taking two cases and going out. He ordered three quarts of Hermit and followed. He was broke again, and again he was drinking wine. He could already taste the sweet sickliness of it, the warmth and the thickness of it in his throat.

The day had strengthened at dusk, as it always did in the fall, strengthened in the wind and coldness. The grass was brown and dull in the graveyard, and the large white cross with Jesus crucified that looked down over it gave a frozen sterility to it. Behind it the tracks that led away ran, it seemed, into the distant depth and blackness of spruce. But from up this far, up near the station he could see the river turning so evenly from one extremity to the other — from where the two main tributaries cut each other to where, far below the bridge, that dark water hit the bay. And the sky tightening with clouds.

They had come up to meet John. Across from his house the three lines of tracks, the red freight building and the freight cars themselves red and copper-toned at dusk. It gave him a feeling of emptiness as he passed it, a feeling of wanting to go home to sleep. But he pulled into the drive, the browned gravel still carrying within itself the faint look of summer —the faint heat. John came out to meet them, standing at one side of the small blue verandah, waiting. He was in his undershirt, bare feet, hands shoved into his pockets, looking as if he had just come from bed, as if in those hours when everyone was working he had slept.

"Don't they call you any more?"

"I don't feel like working so I don't go in."

"Where's that going to get you?" Bruce asked.

"Damned if I know," he smiled, his mouth breaking out into a yawn as he did.

172

They came up onto the verandah to stand beside him, looking down over the back field of the school, the shouts of
youngsters playing baseball reaching them and the steady
sound of the station and the cars. A smell of fish inside the
house.

Then John stretched and went back to sit on the small cot.
It creaked when he did, a covering of faded orange flowers,
and he laid his head back against the wall seeming to look far
up into the distant sky. They went over to sit beside him, all
silent for a time, John lifting his feet to bring them up beneath him, to give them warmth.

"So what do ya want to do, crack open right now?"

"I think I'll head downriver for supper."

"What?"

"Well, I'll be back in an hour or so—you stay here, get in
touch with Boyd and Terry—tell them to bring some stuff."

John looked over at him smiling slightly and then looked
away quickly.

"Eat at my house," Bruce said.

"No—."

"Well, just make sure you come back."

"I'll be back—in an hour."

He got up and moved off the verandah, neither of them
speaking to him as he did, and moved in short uneven steps to
his truck.

"You want the stuff now?"

"It'll keep."

So he got in and turned out of the drive and headed home.

When he came into the dooryard she was out raking, the wind
blowing the leaves out of their piles and about the grass and
she chasing them around, an old woman with a rake. He
stepped from the truck and walked past her. It was very cold
now and almost dark—very near dark, the cold and the dark
and she in the yard chasing leaves. It was all very funny. Why
did she want to rake them anyway? The lot was small and
dead looking as it was. There was no need to rake.

He walked past her, trying to control his smile but couldn't.
She didn't even look at him though, mumbling to herself and
to the leaves racing this way and that as she stumbled forward
and backward with them, the rake clutched like a weapon in
her hand. He was almost through the doorway before she

spoke.

"No, laugh laziness—a lot you care about those people coming down here and this place looking like a sty."

"You can't rake in the wind," he said going into the warmth and smell of the cottage. There was no sound in here, only the sound of the wind outside grating the trees behind the house and along the lane. But all else was silent. He passed the room and glancing in saw Clinton outstretched on the couch, arm across his eyes and the large circular ashtray on the floor. Then he went into the kitchen to sit at the table. He could hear faintly now the sound of Deborah singing as she piled cans, the sound of cans being arranged upon the shelves.

In a moment he heard the door opening and Rubena coming in. She came into the kitchen panting heavily in her coat, her heavy weight, and her face red from the fresh wind. Still there was that fineness to her placid features, the brown hair soft like the scarred photograph years before against the covered bridge.

"So I suppose you've come in to eat and run," she said going to the stove and lifting the lids of the pots.

He said nothing, observed her as she prepared his food but said nothing. Then she put a plate of stew before him and a cup of tea, going when she had to the sink to begin the dishes.

"Pamela phoned."

"When?"

"Half hour ago—wants to know if you have that time off, says she's leaving Wednesday evening to go up on the train."

"Good."

"Well?"

"Well what?"

"*Do* you have the time off?"

He grunted and went back to his stew. Deborah came through the adjoining door and sat at the table watching him eat. There was the wind again rattling the window and he thought of the outside, of the night, and he wanted to be out there among it—he wanted to be back in town with them drinking.

"You know, I don't know why you can't find the time to clean up the yard this week. I have enough to do in here. Deborah and I can't do it all."

But she said nothing more, piling the clean dishes one piece

174

at a time onto the rack. Nor did he say anything to her—to either of them. He finished with his plate and pushed it away, standing. Then he took one last swallow from his cup and moved quickly toward the door. Clinton still had his arm across his face.

"You be in early—I don't want you out all hours of the night. You hear me, I've enough to worry about," she called.

It was in the lateness of early evening now, the darkness of light, of night spreading in blackness and the lights of the town spreading in warmth and excitement, coming to each of them through the broad split windshield of the truck. The window opened a hair's breadth and the mournful sound with each acceleration, with each pressure of the foot. But the wind had abated in the trees, the trees solid and solemn and bent forward, a forewarning of the storm.

"One more time round—if we can't find him, screw it; we'll go back alone."

"He said he'd be here and with a 40-ouncer of rum, no less."

"Screw it—he knows where the shed is."

"Well, go round once more," Bruce said looking over to Kevin, "go round once more—down to the bridge."

"Screw it," John said.

The streets were dead looking, it being only Monday night, a few girls loitering whom John shouted to as they passed. But for the most part everything remained in that autumn stillness before a storm—the dying moths reluctant to leave the lights. So they drove down to the bridge again, and again up to the back street and across to main, past the post office from which they came, and then all around once more in some tireless, useless demonstration, each of them taking turns with a bottle of wine—each of them waiting and wanting something.

"Screw it," John said.

So he turned the truck this time up past the restaurant, through the parking lot and up the lane toward the highway.

"We're going there now then."

"Yes sir, no more screwing around."

"Good," he said lowly, looking as he passed up to the darkness of her bedroom window, far up to the eaves of the building and then lower to her window.

175

"He'd have to take this way, wouldn't he?"

"Oh he'd have to," Bruce laughed.

"Yes Kevin, you'd better run up and check."

"Screw you."

"Yes for Christ's sake run up and check."

They came out on the highway and headed up, over the tracks, the long hard steel leading away—the priest house, graveyard and church all one, all together indistinguishable each from the other in the black.

And they headed back into the woods, the blotches of woods separated at times by fields and houses. The good unknown woods again. Years ago his grandfather had a camp with another man, and it wasn't too far from the road where they were now, wasn't too far from the new lots that were springing up like sores, dissecting everything. He had never been to it but, of course, only the ruins, if the ruins remained, would exist now. Yes only the ruins and the timeless parasitic plants mushrooming over them. But then it wasn't so long ago, that camp. No, now there would be trees, saplings all round it—or trees even older and sturdier than that, so that only a road, like the old logging roads, could be discerned faintly in the underbrush. But to think they had a camp was the good thing—to think they had a place to hunt and sit their weekends away secluded from the river and the town. The man had taken sick with diabetes—broken bones that never healed, went back to England once to see his brother. Died. So his grandfather built his own camp on the lot downriver. That too was gone.

It was too dark to last without rain much longer, the asphalt causing the truck to rattle as it went alone, the smell of wine and pine freshener inside the cab, the smell of the heat and sweat of their bodies also. She never liked the car-freshener hanging over the mirror the way he had it even though its odour could only be noticed at certain times. But it was not the odour that bothered her—it was the thing itself, hanging and vibrating with each rattle and crank. It was the thing itself she disapproved of so greatly but though it annoyed her it was *his* truck, and because of that he never took it down.

"Wine," John said passing the bottle over.

It was good again, the wine. Last week he had become sick on it—sick on its sweetness that left such a sourness in his mouth, but now the wine was good again—even in its warmth.

He drank the last from the bottle, handing it over to Bruce to throw out. They were approaching his dooryard now, the gateposts white and gleaming, the gravel soft to the tires' weight.

"We'll have to be quiet until we get out of there," Bruce continued.

"Invite your old man out to have a drink," John said.

"Sure."

"Why not—tell him the boy here is getting married."

The shed stood darkly at the end of the lane down in a hollow of the back field where a fence crossed behind it bordering the woods. The house itself was immense, a house of generations it seemed, a house that stood long before the road was anything but dirt. Three cars parked about it and a small waggon at the rear, Bruce's car sitting with the rest, unscratched. To the left the field rose up again and levelled to a small corn field and beyond that in the distance a barn where the lane would finally take you if you wished to go.

The rain had started now, and they were hardly inside the shed before the torrents came, the wind seeming to press again with all the viciousness of the afternoon. It was an autumn rain wet and cold, and the shed though cold and damp from disuse had a protective quality once the light was on —the naked bulb. It was ancient thick wiring. The place was cluttered with old tools—bent hoes and rakes and rusted shovels, hammers across the work-bench made of three pine boards.

"Sit down and make yourself at home," Bruce said coming into it last. The small pane of glass at the far end was being whipped by branches. It felt quite empty to sit there. They all sat close together, but in the corners the solitude crept out to touch them; in the corners where the light didn't penetrate the solitude still lingered. Above the bench the initials B.C. embroidered the rough wood and the date as indistinguishable as the lettering itself scrawled below.

"You do that?" Kevin asked staring at it.

"What—that? Christ no, my old man—1937."

"Oh,"

They began to drink, shivering as always with the drink in them and the cold outside, passing the wine around, each with a beer, swallowing one and then the other—talking little. But that faint sterile look of the place made him uneasy, the

177

look of old paint and hammers—sterile and dead—made him uneasy. The beer was as warm as the wine.

"Why didn't you bastards cool this?"

"Warm's the best way," John laughed. "Anyway, drink it while you can. She'll soon have her claws in you."

"There'll be no claws."

"There always is," Bruce chanted. "Yes bud, we're all going to get screwed some day, but you picked a ripe young age to do it."

He said nothing, looking at their faces that looked back at him in the shadow—faces that smiled with young strong discoloured teeth, faces that were knotted into that peculiar expression, the expression of young men who held conference with the old, that gained before their years a hollow look of cynicism and regret. John's face the cruellest perhaps, perhaps the one that showed most, or least, of what he really felt, but one in which, when it was twisted that way, there was no way of ever being sure.

He turned his eyes away from them and tipped the bottle of wine that Bruce passed over, some of it dripping like water over his cheek. He would reek again tonight from it all, but in his uneasiness brought on partly by the atmosphere in which he sat he felt something else start to swell inside him, something else take root inside. And with every drink he left it growing, slowly at first and then the real pain of it growing.

It seemed that the rain was coming even harder now, even stronger against the small black window, the branches that wrapped and tapped themselves against it. His body was shivering and stiff. When he passed the bottle round again, he lifted himself steadily and walked tightly to the window. The room was lower here, the roof of the shed slanting downward near the back so that it wasn't very many inches from his head. Nails stuck out from it dangerously and cobwebs supported themselves on the nails and in the corners. He stood for a moment with his face to the window watching and hearing the water slide across it, sipping at his beer in small mouthfuls as he did, feeling already that growing pain and energy as he drank.

Then they called to him, and he went over and sat finishing the one pint and taking another, feeling the warmth of it through the bottle. The wine was going round again.

"You know," Bruce began, taking a swallow of wine; then

178

he stopped for a moment to think, twisting his top lip below his bottom and pondering. The click of the bottles and the rain, the half darkness of the shed. "You know—well Christ, how long do you plan to spend at the mill?"

Kevin looked up from the floor and shook his head.

"Why?"

"It just seems a bad thing to get into too long—look at half of them up there—Alton and Simard and anyone you want to name. Everyone working up there until something better —until it's the only thing they can do. I don't want it for me."

"It doesn't have to be," Kevin said, looking up once more. The heavy bent back of Baps over the saw, the unending lime and the persistant mechanical mouth. "You can make it what you want—and leave when you want."

"Like Alton, always going to leave—tomorrow, next month—tomorrow."

"Well shit, I don't plan to stay there long after I'm married."

John looked over grinning, passing the wine as he did—last of the second bottle. It was not good to mix cheap wine with beer. It was never any good.

"Tell us what you're going to do—she's knocked up, isn't she?"

Kevin took the wine and held it to his mouth, tilting his head back and his eyes away from them again.

"I could tell the day of Andy's funeral she musta been knocked up."

"How?"

"Oh I just could."

"Well, you're wrong—she isn't."

They looked at each other a moment, and then their eyes shifted. Then they were drinking the beer all three of them, guzzling rapidly. He wanted her to be—he hated her so he wanted her to be. Baps over the saw and old Clarence with his teeth chattering. He could feel the pain of drinking taking root, wishing to say it all—unable to say it but wanting to say it all.

"Well then, where are you going?"

"We want to save some money and go—next year some time. We'll be earning pretty good money and then in a year we'll go."

"Shit."

179

Bruce was busy opening the last quart of wine, fumbling with his fingers on the cap.

"Good luck anyway—if she's pregnant or not," he said, passing it over, and then when his hand was in mid-air as if remembering something that he wished to say all the while, he turned his head slowly to John. Kevin took the wine quickly, frightened that it might drop, and held it to his mouth. Bruce was straining for what he wanted to say and for that moment the empty silence. Not even the rain beating against the back window—not even that. It was as if for a brief second he had wanted to say it, forgetting who was in the room, and now that he realized who was there was not so sure. It was as if he were pondering whether to say it or not, knowing finally that he would.

"You know that Julie is preg—."

"Yes I know, I know," John said quickly, looking at him, an almost sad look. "I know—what in hell do you think was screwing Andy up—or *anybody*?"

Then they all settled back again. Then they began to speak of other things—things that were better, that they could laugh about—things that they remembered from school and other places, from hunting, from dances, to emptying people's traps and boiling the lobsters on shore. The drinking continued—the room seemed warmer.

"Well I hope she'll let you out anyway. Screw it, we have to go hunting again."

"We will—Jesus we can go back to the camp next weekend for all I care—the week after I'm married, for all I care. I got a new .303."

"There's deer back there," Bruce said. "My old man said there was two doe, a buck and a fawn back there all summer—used to cross just below the camp where that little island is."

"Well, I don't want your marriage fuckin' everything all up."

"It won't."

Again there was a silence. The harsh shadows in the corners, the ancient wiring and the glow from the light. All this swam before him as he drank. He would give up drinking wine once he was married—he would do that because cheap wine was never very good.

"So do you know what Julie's going to do?" Bruce asked,

looking over to John.

"Oh shit I don't know—anything I suppose."

"Maybe someone should go up and talk to her."

"I already did," John said.

They both looked at him.

"What did she say?"

"Nothin'."

"Does her old man know?"

"How in shit should I know—listen they want to get pregnant; it's their own goddamn fault not ours."

He drank rapidly from the wine. You could smell the sweetness of it lingering in the shed, the fruit of it as they passed it around. He could feel the fire of drinking inside him now—the fire of the wine and beer and the pondered slurred speech. But he felt he could not say what he wanted even when he spoke.

"How is it their fault—it's just as much our fault as it is theirs—without Andy Julie wouldn't have gotten pregnant," he said.

"Well it's up to them, isn't it?" John said. "It's up to Pamela if you get her pregnant. It's all up to them."

John stood and stretched and took another beer to open. Then he went out the shed door and stood to the side, urinating, singing as he did in a rough and unclear voice—the words themselves unclear.

"You almost drown out there," he said coming back, water dripping across his straight black hair, his jacket and pantlegs drenched.

"You had a brother that drowned, didn't you?" Bruce asked looking at him.

"Long time ago," Kevin said. The outstretched limb and the child sneakers and the water green and silent.

"Shit, years ago," he continued. "I never knew him."

"How old was he?"

"Eighteen or nineteen or something like that."

"Ya well, a guy could drown tonight."

Water had come in when the door was opened, some wetness on the floor—wetness tracked in.

The wine was finished now, and they set the two empty bottles on the bench, continued slowly drinking the warm beer. There was a point he sometimes reached when drinking—a point when he knew he would be able to go all

181

night dancing and singing and drinking. He wished to dance and sing tonight. He wished to do that now, setting his head back to guzzle the beer, the bitter-sweet taste ot it.

Baps bent over the saw and Clarence with his teeth, and Willis moving slowly through the corridors melted into the very greyness of them, and the blower and the shoot and the lime.

"You know those old guys would die in a week if they weren't there—if they couldn't go there every goddamn day—old Clarence won't last a year when he retires. They have nothin' else to do."

"Ya but I don't want to get into the same fix."

"Either do I and I'm not going to—but still it grows on you after a while."

"It's grown on you two already," John said shaking his head almost as if he were disgusted—almost that. "You two will stay here for the rest of your lives going in every morning and coming out every night—so that in 50 years you'll look back and that's all you'll have to remember."

"And what will you have to remember?" Bruce said defensively—nervously.

"Well I'm not going to marry any slut at 21, nor am I going to shovel shit all my life."

The word. There seemed to be a pause directly after it was spoken, but it lay in the air—its harsh flat sound lay on the damp. The shed with the musk of dying autumn, the word so true to the narrow shadowed room—true to the wet and the smell of the wet and the timeless ancient wiring, the defaced wood. The harsh flat full sound of it and now a pause after it was spoken as if they all were waiting for the meaning of it to sink through the warped boards out into the night to be forgotten.

John half raised himself in reaching for another beer, his eyes darting over to the case immediately after he had spoken. Kevin took another drink of his. It had seemed to go flat from too much waiting.

"I suppose you mean Pamela is a slut then, and I'm marrying one."

They looked at each other, Bruce looking at them both, but John's face now was blank and white, a small sneer that thinned his lips to nothing. It took him a moment to speak.

"No I don't mean that—but *you'd* take it personal. It's just

182

an expression. I don't know her well enough to call her anything and I don't really care if I do. It's just an expression that
I use."

There was a silence after this. The clinking of bottles together.

"It's just an expression—I call all women *sluts.*"

"Forget it," Bruce said, imposing himself between them,
into the conversation that was tight and restrained, and pop-
ping the cap off another beer as if to remind tham all why
they were there.

"Well they aren't."

"What?"

"All women aren't sluts—so I don't know why you call them
that."

"Sure they are," Bruce said laughing. Laughing neither low
nor loud but laughing into the damn emptiness of it all. "For
Christ's sake, Dulse, you'd think to Christ he'd meant everything he said personal."

Kevin stood and grappled for a beer and went outside to
urinate. Out here the wind, the lane so black and wet with
mud and the house—the distant upstairs lights of the house
with all the curtains drawn. The seclusion and warmth of the
house with its lights on. He stood against the edge of the shed
drinking all the while, watching as he did the trees just behind
the shed grate and tear in the wind, pinned as they were by
the rotting fence. And the wind in his own ears and hair. The
rain blowing into him.

He urinated long and stood guzzling as he did. His face was
lifted to the black wet now and his mouth twisted from the
bottle as beer went up his nose. He sneezed and coughed and
spit, cursing, spitting into the loose unhealthy-smelling mud
that ran up against the shed's side. From inside he could hear
them laughing above the night. Faint sick light through the
warped sideboards but the good beer into him now.

"Holy ol' Jesus it's wet."

"It sure is," John laughed. All laughter now, all goodness so
that immediately he could forget the immediate past until
some other time. "Have another beer," John said, taking one
out for him to open and handing it to him once he did. "Don't
worry, bud," he said as he handed it across as if something
more than sympathy had risen from deep within him, as if
some feeling had risen he could never express when sober

183

and contained. "I know you know what you're doing—and I know she's probably a fuckin' good kid—so don't take anything I say personal, for Christ's sake don't do that—cause holy shit Kevin, I'm tellin' ya, holy shit I don't mean nothin' personal."

Then there was laughter again and the jokes came.

"Me ol' man might hear us."

"No, not now, they're all upstairs—I seen the lights so they're probably all in bed."

They continued drinking, throwing the empties this way and that into the case. The second case was opened, a faint coolness to it from sitting as it did in the cool damp shed. The wetness of his pants had warmed into his skin, but he was shivering now. John in his stilted language broken and slurred by what he had consumed. It was hard to follow all that was said. It was good to drink.

"I love that bitch—that fuckin' little bitch, and you know it and Bruce knows it and Andy knew it too. But what in shit can you do? Ya can do fuck all."

Then he did not know what John was saying. He took another beer and stood to walk about. It was raining less now, less on the window, the black pane. The wind had died calmly also, but he could still hear it—could still hear the rain. He walked about now. He did not know what John was saying. Then the three of them went outside again. He felt cold on his wetness, and Bruce at the side of the shed slipped backward landing hard on his back and spilling his beer.

Then they all laughed and stood facing the tar-smelling side of the shed.

"Who's this, John?" They were close together at the side of the shed.

"Who's what?"

"The little one you were talking about."

John looked over at him.

"Julie—the bitch," he said. He said it in a voice quite unlike his own, and he was shivering—his face and lips all shivering. Kevin said nothing at all. Not because he was surprised. It was more an excitement, an excitement about it all, and he shivered also. Then they went inside again.

"You knew it anyway," John said, wanting to talk now.

"No, bud, I didn't."

"Well, Bruce knew it and so did Andy and so does she."

184

Andy in it for a week now, among it, almost that, and the juices inside her churning together, mixing within themselves to create something. But he didn't know *that*. It was the church, the stained-glass windows, the passions of the cross. He saw her there and edged over to try and get closer, but Pamela not knowing why he wanted to move up the aisle so quickly held him back, firm pressure with the glove. And the thorns on the head of Christ, the incense and the smell of the soft October morning, the thick lump decaying inside being wheeled about on rollers.

"—But ya can do fuck all," John was saying, looking across to Bruce and now and then lifting his bottle as if to proclaim the absolute toast. "No, you bastards have got it all—good jobs, at least ya must like them a bit. You ya bastard are gettin' married."

Then he pondered as if trying to express the inexpressible and sat stooped for a moment, clutching the beer between his folded hands. A silence—the rain still falling, the wind.

"And yet I wouldn't give a two-penny damn if she was knocked up higher than I don't know what—so if Pamela's pregnant you shouldn't worry about that. Screw it anyway," he said finally, finishing the bottle down and thrusting it against the shed door.

"Quiet John."

"Well let's go to town anyway—I'm not sitting here all damn night."

He was angry now at all he had said, all of it, hating it all, for he stood and kicked at the empty case as if to get it out. Then he took another beer.

"Come on, let's go ta fuck to town."

But they stayed in the shed a little longer holding onto the night. Then he brought out his mouth-organ and began playing it, harsh and deliberate, his eyes sad and narrowed. He played one tune after another, unconscious of what he was playing, stamping his feet with it. They all stamped their feet and sang along, and things got rougher again—better. He played well. The harsh rough sound of it grating and untrained, into the ears and heads and minds of Kevin and Bruce. It was good but they were too noisy. So they left and got into the truck again. It was colder outside now than it had been with the full flight of the the rain. Only a drizzle left. They laughed and talked.

185

"So John, listen John I want ya to be the best man now—so ya will, won't ya?"

John lifted his arm and hugged him.

"Sure, bud, sure—if ya didn't ask me I would have kicked your head in."

"Well, ya will now, ya crazy bastard. You don't have to do much, just stand there beside me."

The road was wet and desolate. He drove slowly, John between him and Bruce. They were all drinking the last of the beer, and John still had the harmonica going, stamping his feet against the floor. The pine freshener shaking with the rattles and the music loud. They were all shouting. It was good to shout. Outside the highway before them and behind stretched into the bald and empty dark—darkness like when only the lights could be seen across the bay blinking at an ever-steady pace. The dark fish-smelling water. There were no other lights except those of the truck showing a few hundred feet of highway.

So they went into town again, driving around the square and in and about the lanes, wet and leaf-spattered and still. He drove past her place but there were no lights yet. Then down along the main street to the restaurant. Its lights still on and a few still loitering on the inside though he couldn't tell how many—the stained window wet and foggy from the rain. They parked in the lot beside it.

John was quieter now, no music left inside him. He put his harmonica in his shirt pocket and buttoned it with slow careless hands, sitting in the middle as he was with his legs straddling the stick shift and his head turning from right to left. There was one pint left, and they passed it about until it was empty. Then John threw it past Bruce and it landed in the lot and smashed.

"Yes sir—well that's that."

"Yes sir, it is—you hungry?"

"I'm hungry ya, hey Bruce you hungry—wake up ya crazy bastard—ya hungry?"

He grunted that he wasn't, keeping his eyes closed and his head half down, leaning against the door, his arms wrapped about him and his hands hidden beneath his jacket. John looked at him for a moment and then lifted his head up by the hair, laughing silently.

"You hungry?"

186

He shook his head and threw John's hand off and cursed, laying his head where it was before. So they sat for a time in silence, listening to the rough idling of the truck and watching the streets for a sign of someone, though the streets were empty and dead, the buildings large and silent on the empty streets with only a few cars passing almost soundless on them.

"Well come on, let's go get something to eat," John said.

Light and warm, the restaurant gave the heated smell of food, the smell of fryers in the back. On entry the heat hit him in the face but unlike other times he didn't mind it. It was good to be out of the drizzle and away from the shed. Other voices coming from other booths. There were faint black scratches on the tile and the music soft, almost reluctant, coming to him from the tuned-down speaker on the side of the yellow wall. He could feel himself going drowsy with the heat. The smell of other dinners.

They ordered and waited, both staring past each other for a time listening to the music, the soft melancholy music from the speaker on the yellow wall. And the wall, in fact the entire restaurant, was in colours that made his eyes squint for a time. His hair wet from the rain dripping upon his collar and a tinge of the afternoon's stink till upon him. The red leather booths, grease-streaked and torn. The thick scent of food throughout.

"So you really want me to be best man?"

"Of course—wouldn't have it any other way."

"Good."

Then the music changed to a faster and better sound though it was still as low and as regulated as ever. He stared at the white, wet, almost shrunken skin of his friend.

"Did you really mean that about Julie?"

He wanted to know—it was as if he had to know now that the secret was partially divulged. John glanced over in a tired drunken fashion, rubbing the side of his cheek with his large right hand, reddening it as he did, making it as red as the cracked knuckles on his cold right hand.

"Oh shit I don't know—she's a bitch."

"I never even thought you knew her until Bruce said you used to take her out."

"It was me who introduced her to Andy," he said slowly. "I don't know—I took her out once or twice but that's not it." Then he laughed, "shit *love*, I don't think there's any damn

187

thing anyway—but sometimes I wish I was still going out with her." He stopped laughing, his face almost peaked in its whiteness, wet skin drawn tight over his bones and again the right fist rubbing at the side of his cheek and down to his lower lip. Eyes half-closed with drink. "Like last summer I knew he was putting it to her every night and I wanted to go up to her and slap her ass. None of my goddamn business, is it? Then we'd be laying on the beach and I'd look over and her top half down—Christ I can't speak to the bitch. Now she's knocked up anyway—."

"That don't matter."

"I know but I can't *speak* to her—not now anyway, shit," his head down again and his right hand went up against his wet black hair. He was silent for a moment.

"But I'm gonna say this—Andy's dead now and everything, but Christ I'm only sayin' what is true, sometimes he really pissed me off—sometimes I just had to get out of his sight or I knew I'd slap the bastard—ya know what I mean."

"Ya, that's like everything."

"And it had nothin to do with Julie—I mean there were lots of other things too. I mean the poor bastard's dead now and I really liked him—really fuckin' liked him but some things about him just pissed me off."

When the food came, they ate—gorging it in drunken mouthfuls, not speaking. Until they had finished, they neither spoke nor looked at each other, both of them fixed only upon their plates. Other voices in other booths and the sound of the music—soft again and restrained.

Then he stretched his legs out and shoved his plate away and picked up his coffee, gone sickly white with the milk in it. He stirred it again and lifted it to drink, the sharp heat of it burning at his tongue and the too-sweet taste of too much sugar. He looked across to John still gorging—slopping onto his fork the mouthfuls of beef that seemed to drip in its own blood. The jaws of his friend moving. And then the other jaws, *his* jaws—part of it now. He couldn't help thinking of it again.

"Well, he knows what it's like to be dead. You know there is something to be envied in that."

John looked up startled a little.

"What do you mean?"

"I mean at least he knows whether there's anything else."

188

"There isn't."

"Well ya never know until you're dead."

"There isn't," John said again, pushing his plate aside.

"Did Julie say much when you were up there?"

"Nothin' no—I can't talk to her. I want to but I can't so I didn't stay long up there. I'd just like to know what she's going to do."

Perhaps they were too tired to walk any longer. He was tired and had to work in the morning. Her lights would be on now or perhaps she'd be sleeping. But it was late now and she'd be in. Maybe he'd go to see her later, maybe that. He took his time to finish with his coffee, so long that it became cold at the last mouthful.

"You ever going to go in again?"

"Maybe in a while—next week if they call. Shit I don't want to work," he smiled.

Work. The sound of the mill coming down across the water. It would wake him again. Again. But yes, they couldn't remain here long—not long. A year or so. But they couldn't remain fixed as he saw and knew so many would. Felt that so many would. The waitress came with their separate checks, the faint rustle of the fabric of her uniform, white and stained on the white and the fingernails broken, a little unclean. He had his face down now, trying to ward away the grogginess—the dizziness. The bloated feeling of the beer. He tapped with his spoon against the side of the empty cup, remaining fixed in his thought. The bloated smoke out of those dark chimneys gone almost purple in the air.

John shook his arm and he looked up, moving his feet back against the seat. The white tight skin on the face of his friend, over the cruel lifting bones of the face.

"Look," John said, raising his arm to signal as he did.

"What—oh Boyd."

He came over to where they were sitting, walking unsteadily, his pants hanging too loose upon his legs, and stood gazing down at them, the red hair curled short and tight upon his head. He was wet and smelled of it. Smelled of strong liquor and drunkenness. His eyes were glazed and in his tall young massiveness he almost stooped to look down at them, smiling as he did. A girl had followed him in but remained near the ice-cream counter at the side.

"Where in hell were you?"

189

"Back the road—where the hell were you?"

"I was around town all night waiting for you—ya bastard."

"Well Kevin and I looked."

"Shit."

He slumped into the booth beside John, bringing as he did a bottle from under his jacket and shaking it so that the liquid inside was disturbed, so that it rose and fell with the swaying motion of his arm.

"This is what's left of it," he said.

"Any mix?"

"There was," he smiled, searching himself on the pretext of finding it. "But there ain't no more—order a Coke. Kevin, order a Coke."

He felt groggy already and now they wanted to drink more. But perhaps he could go all night tonight, perhaps like sometimes he would reach that level, and then after that level he could go all night—drinking more and finding more energy as he did. Yes maybe that. He ordered a Coke and then decided to order another.

"We're closing in fifteen minutes—you know that," she said.

They began to drink again, taking it in mouthfuls and using the Coke as a chaser—the mouthfuls burning so that he couldn't breathe, only wanted to cough it up, cough up his guts and then the chaser cold and stabilizing.

"We better check on Bruce soon."

"Screw Bruce, he wanted to sleep, let him—watch now, keep the bottle down for fuck sake—she's lookin, Boyd, she's lookin' right at ya."

Boyd put the bottle down and passed it over, giggling as he did so that he spit up—it coming out his nose. "Shit." And then the girl he was with moved from the side, moved toward the table. No-one really noticed her until she was standing there beside them looking down.

"Well what are ya going to do, stay here all night? I wanta go find Ann. O my God, you don't know him do ya?" she mocked, pointing her finger at John.

"Yes I do, why? Sit the fuck down and shut your mouth."

"I wouldn't sit by him—he'd rape me."

John didn't look at her, didn't bother, as if not bothering was the remedy for the situation. She remained standing —her hair long and filled with the filth of the season, nylons twisted on her too-thin legs and her wool skirt short and frayed. Her jacket unzipped showing a thin pink blouse. And in every motion she was like the week before. Her face dirt-ridden and saucy, but dirt-ridden only by makeup carelessly employed. As if she had taken grease and rubbed it across her eyes so that it made stains to destroy the girlish purity of her flesh. Young and saucy, he thought. The nose snubbed by rubbing it with her hand. Drinking herself.

"I'm going ta find Ann."

"Sit down, shit."

John tipped the bottle, drinking long, not caring now for the waitress who kept glancing their way, not caring it seemed—taking the second Coke immediately after and almost draining it. His face was flushed again, looking sick.

"Do ya still swim the fountain?"

She sat down beside Kevin now to wait. Still John didn't look at her or answer. At home she would be lying, thinking, waiting in her bed. Not asleep yet. No it took her a long while to go to sleep. Perhaps he would go up later, the good perfect sweetness of her bed.

The waitress went over and shut out the light, locked the door and came back to them.

"You'll have to leave—we're closing."

An older woman came out with a bucket and mop. So they stood and paid and left, the outside air cool and good when it came upon his skin, the freshness and smell of the town. The drizzle had settled into nothing now and they went over to lean against the box of the truck talking loudly and cursing. Cursing into the black fresh night air of the town. There was still some left in the bottle. They were all very drunk now. The girl remained a few paces away—watching.

"Who wants it?"

"Finish it—it's yours."

"John?"

He took from it again but not it all, handing it back for Boyd to finish. Then he cursed because there was no Coke left, and he had to swallow it straight. Kevin looked blankly at the both of them with his hands in his pockets, hunched and shivering, and then, now and then, to the small frame of the girl standing in the middle of the lot.

"I'm going to find Ann," she said.

"Come here for Christ's sake—Ann's with Terry."

"Ya well, I got to find them."

Boyd lit a cigarette and leaning up against the box stared at her, the twisted nylons on her too-thin legs. Then he made a lunge for her and she screamed, at the same time laughing as he hauled her in toward him roaring as he did, roaring in playfulness with all his massive drunken weight.

"I said come 'ere, didn't I?"

"You're as bad as he is," she laughed, " 'cept you don't swim in fountains. Watch it or you'll burn me with that smoke." She twisted away from him somewhat as she spoke. "Gimme one."

So he took the pack out and handed it to her. She lit one and inhaled deeply as if it were an exercise she must do before them, must prove to them that she could. And the smoke filtered out through her nose into the quiet air. She smiled now, the vague emptiness in her face.

"You shoulda seen him last week," she said. "But I like you," she smiled pointing to Kevin.

"He's getting married," Boyd said.

The girl stood stunned. Her mouth opened with the cigarette still dangling inside. Then she stepped back two or three paces to observe the lot of them. Then she took another deep inhale from the thing and blew the smoke rapidly into emptiness.

"Well holy livin' Jesus shit! Married! Fuck you're just a baby. And you two tried to pick us up last week—well holy livin' shit."

"Like so much shit we did."

"Ya, ya did—a course you never jumped into the fountain or tried to rape us, but you were both lookin' for it."

"Like so much shit," Kevin said again.

He wished to laugh at it but he couldn't—the young small ignorance of the thing, blowing her smoke into the air as if no-one had done anything quite like it before. He wished to laugh at the thing, standing as she stood with her frayed skirt up to the bones of her thigh, with her nose and face snubbed and her nylons twisted from doing it in the dead unhealthy burdocks, with her eyes pinned on him as if she had discovered some great crime—something unhealthy in him that made her positive of her strength. The stench of the river on her bones. He couldn't laugh at all.

"Shit," he said under his breath, turning from her to Boyd. "Well what are we going to do?"

192

John stumbled to the side of the truck to urinate and called back over his shoulder that he wanted to go downriver.

"It's too late now John," Kevin said.

"No it isn't," he shouted back, "not too late at all, the night's still fresh. This is the last night with the boys, bud."

"Going to show it to us," she laughed, watching him. He turned around to her zippering himself up, spitting as he did so but not at her, only on the ground, only so that she'd know where he wished to spit.

"Well I'm going to find Ann—the little bitch said she'd be here, leaving me alone, Jesus fuck," she said, throwing the butt away.

There was calm for a moment. No-one spoke or moved. Then Boyd lit another cigarette, puffed on it strongly so that it fired hot and red. Then he took a bill from his folder—ten dollars and handed it to John.

"What's this for?"

"It's a game—put it over the back of your hand as tight as you can and then take this cigarette here and try to burn a hole in it. If you do, you win the money—if not tough luck, the only thing you've got is a cigarette burn."

John looked at him and then took the money, placing it tight across the back of his large right hand and taking the butt in his left held it a few inches from the bill. Kevin had never heard of it before. But there was some trick to it, he was certain of that, and he was certain also that John would try it. John would try anything—he was certain of that.

John lowered the fire carefully onto it. He winced sharply and drew it back. There was no hole in the bill.

"I put a hole in 'er she's mine?"

"Right."

He blew on the fire until the sparks flew from it disappearing into the night. Then he lowered the cigarette again. He held it longer this time—even when he winced he held it not wanting to draw it back. He almost cried with the pain before he brought it away.

"You'll burn your hand off John," Kevin cautioned.

He said nothing. He resituated the bill and dragged on the cigarette to make the fire come. Again he put it on his hand, holding it there until Kevin could almost feel the scorching himself. When he drew it away the bill was still intact. The girl was laughing now. Each time he put the butt to his hand she would laugh and dance around, her thin wild unshaped body dancing like a shadow over the lot, coming back to yell and taunt him in his pain. Kevin said no more. The fourth time he tried was still useless.

"It won't work," Boyd said, "it doesn't work, John."

John looked at them both and then glanced to the girl. He breathed deeply as a drunken man will breathe, as a man in pain. He cursed strongly, shifting the bill quickly on his hand and then, as if to take revenge on her, on himself, on them, swung the cigarette butt down firmly, the pressure of his thumb and index finger driving it downward onto the bill so that Kevin not only thought but felt he could smell the flesh underneath. And he held it there, holding it, holding it until his eyes watered and his shrunken skin turned sick. Then he flung it away and dropped the bill—his right arm and hand gone rigid. He closed and opened his fingers slowly but what he felt made his face contort so wildly that Kevin was sick himself.

"Jesus John—let me see."

"It's all right—it's okay," he managed to say. "Let me see the bill; did I make a hole?"

"No," Boyd said picking it up. "You can't—it can't be done."

There were five large raw burns. They had broken the flesh in five distinct places, almost like sores that have postulated from some disease. He showed Kevin his hand and it was trembling—all the nerves in it trembling, his eyes still watering. He cursed again and again.

"Do you want to go home?"

"Shit no—it's all right. The night's still fresh."

It was scorched flesh and dried liquid under the skin and red unhealthy-looking moisture around each burn. Kevin thought he should go home—but no, he didn't want to. He wanted only to enjoy the night.

"Maybe you can put something on it."

"Put some butter on it," the girl said quietly.

"It's all right," he said.

The girl turned to Boyd again.

"I'm going to find Ann now—no more screwin' around."

"Can you drive us Kevin?" Boyd said. "I know where they are—down over the bank."

Kevin nodded.

194

"You'll have to get in the back."

"Well we certainly don't mind that," Boyd laughed, grabbing onto her and lifting her high—lifting her high so that her skirt hid nothing of the small tightness of what was underneath, so that she squealed and laughed again as he carried her and lifted her and laid her down in the box. Then John laughed and hugged Kevin again.

"The night's still young," he said; "let's go find Ann."

They got into the cab, John going around to the passenger side and pushing Bruce over, doing it almost angrily.

"Get over, ya gutless son of a whore."

Bruce was very drunk and very much asleep. He rolled into the middle and slumped there and Kevin, shivering now so that he couldn't control himself, started the engine again, letting it idle for a moment, hearing the squeals of her in the back, her that he didn't know in the back of the truck, her skirt lifted high lying in the back.

"Christ, my hand," John said.

He drove out of the lot and headed the long way round, going down to the lights and turning toward the bridge. But he couldn't see all that much what he was doing, and John now with his harmonica out playing it madly again. The dizzying stilled darkness of the cab, the turning streets empty of all but washed-away leaves that stained them with faded colours, and the streets turning into dizziness and greyness spinning in his head. His thoughts spinning as if he must leave, go somewhere, be quiet for a while.

When they came back round and up past the square, John was singing loudly above the rasping of his harmonica, above that. He grabbed the stick shift with his burnt right hand, the harmonica dropping to the floor. "Plant 'er," he screamed. Kevin shoved in the clutch to let him shift. "Plant 'er," John laughed. Dizziness and Bruce slumped against him rocking with the motion of the truck.

"Let's throw him off her—the slut."

They were going down on the paved stretch by the water now, the Legion darkly silent, and out over the water the buoys that he didn't really see. But they were travelling faster now, and every time he glanced he could see the sickness of John's right hand burned and blistered on the shift and then up to the dizzying wetness of the road. "Yes sir again, plant 'er." John laughed and they shifted again and then down onto the dirt road below the bank, the crooked black rock and weed jutting above them—high above them and then below the ancient sinking timbers of the wharf. But he didn't see this. It came into his mind—she lying in bed silently clean; *slut* he would call her, *slut,* like the one stinking in her wet filth in the back, the dirt of her thin young legs. *Slut,* he would think of her always, after the marriage—years from now. Something dirty because he didn't wish to understand, because Julie didn't understand with him. He could feel the liquor turn and rage inside him. "Let's throw him off the one, Kevin—plant 'er, plant 'er." So he turned the wheel sharply toward the wharf, and the truck lurched and felt heavy, lurched and slid over the soft shale of the ditch between the roadway and the gravelled lot, the exhausted roar of the engine under him. But when he turned the wheel again it didn't work; it wasn't working. It wasn't working. He waited for the impact of something—the truck sliding—he waiting, thinking so rapidly he ceased to think—and the brake and the clutch and the wheel with John still on the shift, but it wasn't working. And then he felt empty and sick before he even realized he felt it, and the truck was up along the ditch now. And then there were branches so that he ducked and closed his eyes, branches and dirt and something like an explosion before it stopped.

It was all silent. Too silent, and then the nervous laughter breaking from John. It was a nervous frightened laughter that couldn't be controlled.

"Did we wake ya?" he said to Bruce, "did we—sorry we had ta wake ya."

"What the fuck—."

"Accident," Kevin said.

John and he got from the truck. It had struck more than one tree, but he didn't know how much damage.

"You all right"?

Boyd was already standing alongside the box, dazed. Gash across his eye, Kevin thought—yes, gash across his eye.

"Your eye's cut."

"It's all right."

Then he heard her crying, saw her crying uncontrollably, hunched as she was in one corner of the box, crying like a child—no more than a child crying, and he didn't know what to say. Saw that she was more than half naked and hunched,

196

crying.

"She all right?"

"Ya I think so—what the fuck happened?"

Kevin shrugged. She was crying—a child.

He went back along the cab looking for damage. There was too much damage and it was too dark. The one streetlight was too far away to be useful and the moths flitting up against it after the storm.

"Your whole front end looks pretty bad," John said coming around.

"Shit."

Bruce was out of the cab now, vomiting on the side of the road, and once more the weakness and the emptiness came to the very pit of his stomach.

"Hey Boyd, stop her from crying."

"What the shit can I do?"

"Do something—stop her the fuck from crying."

"What'll I do?"

"Dress her or something—take her home; nothing we can do here anyway."

But the girl wouldn't let him, told him to go away and began to dress herself. Then she came down from the box shaking and crying, but she wasn't hurt. Kevin could tell at a glance that she wasn't hurt.

"You're all crazy," she said but her voice was not saucy anymore, more pitiful in its sobs than saucy, and she left them and headed up the road alone.

"You better go see she gets home."

"Shit."

Then they started walking back together, leaving the truck where it was, Bruce still heaving in his sickness, spitting now and then, John still playful, trying to be playful—making jokes.

"She can't be hurt," Boyd said.

"No I don't think she's hurt."

"She can't be. I got the whole thrust of it and she was using me as a cushion."

"You better phone a tow," Bruce said, "and report it to the police."

"I can do that tomorrow—I'm in no shape to do it tonight."

They came up into the light. It was the town again and the sweet after-smell of the rain on the air, over the autumn water

197

and the fresh air calm and waiting. Waiting for the frost and snow. He knew if he lay down he might be sick. She half naked in the truck. Pamela sleeping soft and clean. Christ he thought, Christ.

"Your arm's bleeding Kevin."

"I know."

7

For two days it had been coming and going, letting up and coming so that the tree limbs stood bare and black. He had to go out along the lane because he wished to hear no more, and when he was by the stove smelling of the oil he could hear, though he didn't want to, the sound of them from the other room. No matter how restrained they had tried to make it. But it was like that coming and going and now that it had started again—the rain spilling, the trees waving and the fields flat and wet, he felt the raw of it on his head and the muddy looseness underneath his feet.

The lane took him right to the water and he stood for a moment staring out over it, the rain clouds shadowed all across it, shadowed above him also, the pellets stabbing at his leathered face. The sand and rock and dead logs of the beach. Then he turned and went back to the cottage. She had left the boxes. The weather would rot them useless so why hadn't she done it right?

He opened the doors of the shed and leaned against the car, looking at the cottage, waiting, rolling a cigarette as he did, the wetness of his hands wetting the paper. Across the lane the black soaked bark behind the cottage settling for winter. And the sound of the rain on the tin roof.

But he didn't want to hear them—didn't want to hear her careless voice, or him shouting back at her in that suffocated whisper. So he stood for a long while staring into nothing, now and then rubbing his broad flat hand across his chin.

It was very late and they were both in bed when he came in.

And if he had been thinking he would have known something was wrong. But he was lying with his eyes straight to the ceiling, and the boy came in and along the hallway stumbling.

Because he was listening only to her breathing. But he felt perhaps he did know something had gone wrong. When the boy came in he came right to their bed without speaking. He was trembling and gone white. When he told them, his lips were trembling as if he might cry or laugh or both. He was white and wet and shaking. Then as the boy was telling them, he remembered the empty soundlessness, that there was this time no sound of the truck. He didn't speak. He simply stared at the boy white and trembling and saw in the half-dark room the left arm hanging limp and streaked blood along the knuckles.

"My God, my God there's always something—there always is," she said jumping up, the smell of sleep gone sour on her flesh. She turned back to him and her eyes were flashing. For a second. Then she turned to the boy. "Where did it happen, where the hell did it happen?"

"In town," he said, turning as if to go out again.

He did not get up. Instead he lay there stiffly, absurdly waiting for the sound of the truck. It was as if he had gone rigid when he looked at the arm and now he only wanted to wait. The boy went back to the door and turned with his hand on the switch.

"No-one was hurt," he said.

"Who were you with—who were you with? Was Pamela with you?"

"Where's Pamela?"

"No John—John and Bruce."

Then he turned and went out. She followed him out and he could hear them talking, hear her talking in the kitchen. He did not get up. Then the sound of Deborah in the other room yelling, getting out of bed with a thump and thumping along the hallway to the kitchen.

"You're bleeding—your arm is bleeding," Rubena said, almost shouting.

And then it was no longer the sound of the clock beside him on the night table, nor the sound of the season above the house. It was something else. It was as if he were still waiting for the sound of the truck to rumble into the dooryard. The face of William—the man at the door gone white and Rubena holding *him* in her arms gone white. The stupid tinsel still in his hands, the small white manger with its angels overturned. The same feeling passing over him as he lay there almost waiting for the sound of the truck.

But the sound of his wife and daughter in the kitchen. He lifted himself from the bed slowly and searched for his tobacco. He put on his pants and rolled a cigarette before going out to them. He lit his cigarette before going through the door.

"You should have gone to the hospital," she was saying.

He went into the kitchen and glanced down at the boy. Then he went to the counter and leaned against it, listening to her voice. Deborah standing in her loose pyjamas and Kevin sitting at the table on a chair. The heavy stench of liquor that he noticed only slightly as he looked over, glanced at the wet dishevelled hair. But he could not feel anger, he could feel only some numb kind of fear, seeing as he looked the softly oozing blood.

Rubena was at the cabinet taking things out. She was the only one talking and talking loudly though no-one was listening. Then she came over to the counter and put the things down, went to the sink to run water.

"You should have gone up to the hospital—why didn't you?" she kept saying, her voice falling and rising. "Why didn't you go up to the hospital! You might need stitches. Well, take your jacket off—Deborah, help him with his jacket—out all hours of the night, you're lucky you all weren't killed."

Kevin stood uneasily and took the thing off, looking to no-one, moving his arms slowly out of the thing one at a time and then letting it drop onto the chair. He rolled his shirt sleeve up and looked at the cut across his arm, the blood smeared and dried across the gash but the gash still bleeding slowly. It wasn't bad, Clinton thought. It wasn't bad; it needed only to be cleaned and wrapped.

Yes only that. He went over to the cupboard and took down the pot for tea and then went to the sink to wash it out, getting in her way as she scurried back and forth.

"What are you doing?"

"Having tea."

"Oh yes, have tea," she said.

But he didn't mind her. He plugged in the kettle and

200

waited beside it. When the steam came, he felt the moist burning on his skin; watched her as she prepared the bandage.

"Drinking again," she kept saying as she worked, her daughter standing over her shoulder, looking down saying nothing; Kevin saying nothing. When the water was ready, he put it in the pot and let it steep. And if he could only rid himself of the voice coming into him, hearing it as if he were witnessing it all again. Still kept thinking of the truck.

He waited until the tea was steeped and poured out a cup. But it was still too light, the steam coming up into his face as he watched it hit. He stood by the counter and rolled another cigarette and drank the tea, watching, looking at the side of his son's head, the wet knotted hair.

"Why don't you make coffee?" she said looking over to him.

"I don't need no coffee," Kevin said.

"You'd better take tomorrow off."

"No—I have Thurs—Thursday and Friday off."

She finished with his arm and stood to her feet slowly, one hand clasping onto her knee as she came up and the knee gone red. The flabby muscle of her arm. She took the pan and ointment back to the counter, and the girl turned and went back to her room. Then there was silence, the sound of late night in the small warm cottage, the smell of the kitchen and the stove.

Then she went over to him again, her white face as if it were about to break into tears and Clinton only watching from the distance, pouring out another cup of tea.

"Who were you with?"

"I told you."

"No you didn't."

"I told you—John and Bruce."

"And you were drinking! I can't even stand close to you, the smell is so bad. You could have all been killed—all of you. And that boy just dead—no more than just dead and you're out trying the same trick. You're supposed to have some sense—," she said breaking off, her eyes flashing again, flashing angrily over to Clinton as if he were supposed to speak.

"It was an accident, that's all," Kevin said.

But it did no good to talk now and even if he felt he must say something, he couldn't. The boy was tired and drunk, frightened perhaps. It did no good and he hadn't any idea of

201

what to say. Only the blood and the sight of the blood and the thought of the rusted skates, the cold slow churning under-belly of the ice. But it wasn't the truck; it wasn't that. He wasn't angry about the truck, but he kept staring at the twisted knots of hair, staring into them at the side of the boy's head. Thinking. And it wasn't the *old man* stepping down from the truck, coming around the side of it and calling him over. It wasn't that. But now the boy angry and drunk sitting on the chair and Rubena standing above him speaking.

"Well," she was saying, her voice a little lower now, "I don't know what you're going to do after you're married. This is twice in a week you've been in trouble. *Don't you think?* I don't think you care what trouble you cause. Is the truck in bad shape—why can't you drive it? Is it that bad?"

"No it isn't. I'll get it out tomorrow," he said.

"Does Pamela know?"

"How in hell do I know?"

"And you blame her for getting mad at you. How can you blame her?" she said, stepping back to lean against the stove with her arms folded and staring at him as if she expected an answer. He rose awkwardly and groped for his jacket, moving sideways through the door, not looking to them as he went. Trying not to stagger.

"Get me up for work," he muttered, going back along the hallway to his room.

He went along the hallway to his room, and Rubena followed him in, speaking lowly but intently all the time. Clinton also went back to bed and, lying with the light on, waiting for her, listened to the creaking of the house.

When she came in, she didn't speak, turned off the light and turned her back to him. He had expected her to speak. He lay for a long time and then rolled another cigarette in the dark, letting the smoke out loosely into the dark above his head. Hearing her constant sighs and turnings as he did.

But he didn't mind her. He was trying to rid himself of the feeling and couldn't, of the man and the ice and the rusted skates. Of the face in the dark red before his eyes. And even when she began speaking, it didn't matter. It didn't matter to him at all what she might be saying even though she was talking so loudly that he couldn't remember for a moment, didn't know for a moment which one it was that day with Joseph Paul.

202

"For Christ's sake," she was saying.

He butted his cigarette and lay back to sleep. The rain was very soft on the cottage and sometimes the wind. But it had come again and he couldn't rid himself of it, tossed and turned on the bed as if to rid himself. "He was wearing skates we don't know he was there with them but he didn't come up and there's no lights and Emmerson run to get the police but we don't know!" And Rubena:

"Oh Lord Christ."

And the man:

"So sir maybe you should come down—maybe he's come up and is all right, ya never know 'cause my brother went under once on a sled and he come up and everything so maybe—."

And Rubena:

"Oh my God Clinton, oh my God."

And the man:

"So sir, maybe—."

And Rubena like a child clutching with her arms and holding onto the baby and then putting it down and clutching him:

"Oh Clinton, maybe you'd better go."

Wanting to rid himself of the man and her, of the helplessness and in the dark going down with the man because she wanted him to. Going down to stare into the dark and vast unending windswept expanse of ice. But it did no good. Nothing! Nothing did any good; so he sat up to have another smoke and heard his son in the other room emptying out his guts.

But it was like that now, coming and going for a day or two, spreading the wetness and dirt about his sunken lot and behind it down about the saplings and alders that ran almost to the water. Everything dark and flat. He stood against his car for some time throwing his exhausted butts into the puddles on the lane and every little while staring at the boxes soaked and full of leaves that Rubena had collected and left in the centre of the lawn. Then he became tired of waiting and went over, moving them to the side of the house. Why hadn't she done right?

He came round to the front again, his arms and pants wet with the water, and he saw the taxi and her getting out. He waited for her to reach him, watching the parcels swaying in her arms.

"Is Pamela down?"

"Yes."

"Good—I want to show her this."

He took the boxes from her and they went into the cottage quietly. There was no longer any talk coming from the room. He set the parcels down and waited for her coming in behind him to go in first.

They were both sitting opposite each other but there was no sound now, none of the smart and saucy answers there had been before. The boy sitting on the rocker and she on the couch with her small legs tucked under her, her short skirt not covering the thigh so that he glanced away as soon as he nodded, glanced at the boy who stared at nothing.

"Well I have something to show you," she said.

"You do—you got your dress, oh good let me see."

Clinton sat at the other end of the couch and Rubena ran into the hallway to get the box. "—Now I don't know," she was saying, "you'll have to tell me the truth—I was in a hurry so you'll have to tell me the truth."

She brought the box and opened it, taking a blue dress out and holding it up. Like an excited child he thought. Glanced quickly to the girl for her approval.

"Oh Bena that's beautiful."

"Do you like it? I don't know; I was going to try to get shoes to match but I just didn't have the energy—so I'll wear the shoes I have, I guess."

"Oh yes that's—show it to Debby."

"Do you want me to try it on?"

"Sure—Debby come here and see your mother's dress!"

So she went into the room to try it on. He rolled a cigarette and waited, staring blankly. Kevin in the rocker, his shirt sleeve rolled up and the bandage showing. She was smoking a cigarette now, her small white hands, her good clean body under the skirt that he couldn't look to her because of. Vicious she had called him, vicious, as if she could think of no other word, he supposed. And the boy cursing out and stamping up and down so that even in the kitchen he could hear. But they were quiet now, the voices gone out of them, dissolved as if it all had never taken place. But still the memory wrenching in his skull.

"Were you down to see the truck?"

"No. They towed it out so I'll go down tomorrow. There isn't much damage—front end is banged up a bit."

They were silent again. Then she came in with the dress on, seeming as she walked almost too heavy for such a thing. He stared at it apathetically and she looking down at him. He didn't know exactly what to say. It was as if some pressure had tapped him on the skull.

"It's a good dress."

Then Deborah came in and said it was *adorable*. "Doesn't that look good on her, doesn't it Pam?"

"Yes it does," she said.

"I got shoes for you," she said, still looking to him; "you'll wear shoes won't you?" she laughed.

He grunted and stood. He wanted to change out of the wetness. He wanted to lie down now. Perhaps the boy was getting married too soon, perhaps he was. He didn't know. He only knew that he could not look at her the way she sat, that he always felt uneasy with her as it was, the small cold hands, the proud small face and the goodness of her smell. And it was as if Rubena had no-one else to talk to, talking to her the way she did—talking to her about William and the past.

He went into the bedroom and she followed, unzipping the dress and taking it off.

"We're going to have the reception at Anderson's," she said. "Pamela's mother said she'd take care of it and I ran around ordering everything tonight and I'm tired out," then lower, "you're going to give them the car for the weekend, aren't you?"

"Yes," he said, lying back and putting his left arm over his eyes. Maybe to just rid himself of the thought. Maybe just once the good softness. "Yes," he said, "they want it tonight also," he said. And again wishing to rid himself of it—wishing to sleep so that when she went out through the door he didn't hear a thing.

"But I didn't mean it," she kept repeating.

He was silent and did not look at her, pretended not to hear, pretended to be watching the road so carefully as to have nothing to do with anything she said. And the more she said it the more coldness passed through him, the more his face set into a hateful complex rigidity. But the more he was obstinate the more she spoke, the more her voice filtered through the thick unused air of the car, the stale smell of his father's stale tobacco and the inside dark.

Then she too was silent, turning her face to the window and away from him. Only the sound of the wipers in the rain and the thin steam of the hood seen in the lights ahead. Then the coldness left him, and the heat of agitation rose again inside. But he was silent for a long time, his eyes following the road only.

"Does he look like Clinton?" she asked.

"You'll see."

"He's older than Clinton, isn't he—how many years?"

"You'll see."

So she put her face to the window once again.

"I hope you're not going to be like this all night?"

He was silent for a moment.

"I hope you're not," he said.

"Well I said I was sorry but if you can't admit that you were a damn fool then I'm not sorry at all. If you don't think getting drunk and driving trucks into the side of a tree is retarded, then I'm not sorry at all!"

"It was a party."

"No it wasn't—it was a drunk."

"It's the same thing," he said.

"Oh Jesus Kevin—it is not the same thing."

"What is it then?" he said, angrier now because she knew how to make him angry—she had made him angry all evening. "You keep saying that but you won't tell me the difference—you roar and scream at me and my old man has to leave the house it's so bad—'cause he doesn't want to have to listen to your bitchiness all night, but you don't make no sense—you just keep roaring and screaming."

"I just thought you were different," she said her voice not raised at all, which infuriated him even more, having in it the tone of sympathy. "I just thought you were different enough to know the difference."

"Different from what—different from what?"

"Different from all your so-called friends that go out to get hammered and tear around town in cars thinking they're having a great time—a party!"

"Well if I can't go out—if I can't get together once in a blue moon with friends and have a few drinks then screw you

206

lady!"

"You see, a few drinks! If you had a *few* I wouldn't have minded, but no! Every time you go out with them you end up getting pissed."

He laughed in his frustration and didn't reply except for muttering curses under his breath and stepping on the accelerator so that the speed climbed and they could feel the vibration and the looseness underneath the wheels.

"Slow down Kevin or I'll get out."

"I'm only going 50—shit, you've driven with me before."

"That's what I'm afraid of—so slow down."

So he took his foot off the pedal and let the car coast over the thick mud and the loose fill of the road, coast until they were barely crawling and then he turned to her.

"This all right?"

"Just fine," she smiled.

"Shit—yes for you it would be. Anyway it was my party and everyone gets drunk at them—so what in hell am I supposed to do, be in bed every night at ten o'clock?"

"It isn't your getting drunk at your party that I minded. You don't see Kevin—you just don't see. It isn't that I minded—it's, Christ, it's everything else. Your mother tells me all the time how she worries. She lost one son—you don't even think of that—no not at all. And being drunk is one thing but to get into a car and go 90 miles an hour or something is just asking for God to reach out and tap you on the shoulder."

"So what?"

"So what, shit—you sound just like John."

"John, John always John, what the fuck you got against him anyway?"

She glared at him and would not speak. For a long time they were silent again. *Slut,* he would call her. *Slut.*

"So it's probably the last time I'll be around with them after I'm married, after you get your claws into me!"

"Claws!" she said, looking over to him again, her voice rising. "Claws, what in hell do you want to do—be seventeen all your life? Those guys are acting now just the same as they acted then—and in ten years if they're still alive they'll be acting the same damn way. They'll never change no matter what happens, fires or floods, they'll still be hanging around the streets searching for money to buy wine. You have to

207

grow up— those days are over. Some time you have to!" she said.

"Why?" he said looking at her. And every weekend from now until the end of the season—every weekend if he could. "Why do they have to change—what's the big reason!"

"Because."

"Because why?"

"Because there's no reason to do what they do—that's why."

They turned off the dirt road onto a smaller lane that led up a small hill and levelled off, and as it levelled the house could be seen dark and rising in the immediate distance. They drove into the gateway and stopped and sat for a moment in the car. Two lights shone from the upstairs and the light from the kitchen. On the other side of the lawn the hen-house and back from it in the field a barn with the roof sagging in the middle.

Then the forest behind that, the forest enclosing all round.

"How much land does he own?"

"Not very much—my old man owns it with him and it isn't very much—my grandfather sold most of it before he kicked."

They went to the door and had to wait some time before they heard footsteps coming down the stairway and along the corridor to them, footsteps much like Clinton's, shuffling and slow. Then the door opened, and when the old man saw who it was, his face cracked into a small grin and he told them to come inside. They followed him into the kitchen and he stood by the stove and they sat.

"Reginald, this is Pamela—I don't think you've met her yet."

"N—no, I haven't," he said slowly, smiling a bit and stepping a little closer to the stove. His hair was shaved shorter than Clinton's and it seemed to be darker. His face was dark and leathered and strong looking, hard wrinkles across his brow whenever he looked at them, as if he wasn't quite sure why they had come. Perhaps he looked younger than his father, even though he was two years older; perhaps he did look younger. He stood there awkwardly for a time not knowing what to say.

"How's Bena?"

"Good," Kevin said looking up to him. "How's everything with you?"

208

"Oh go—good, I keep myself busy."

"That's good—we've come to invite you to our wedding."

"Oh," he smiled awkwardly looking at the girl. "You're gettin' married then?"

"Friday at two."

"Oh—I see," he said looking at the girl, smiling even more. "I'll have to come, yes I'll have to come."

"Good," Kevin said.

Then he came over from the stove and pulled up a chair. When he did this, he kept his head down, looking at the table, his eyes on the brown board table.

"This is a big house," Pamela said looking about.

"Oh it's big enough I guess," he said and then turning to Kevin: "you tell your parents to ge—get down here and visit me sometimes," he said with a certainty and a seriousness Kevin didn't expect and not knowing how to answer simply nodded.

Then he turned back to the girl. He was talking very carefully as if not to stutter but even then he sometimes did.

"Yes—a big house. They might tear down the house 'cause they might be putting a new bridge across the lower river here and it would cut across here then."

"They've been talking about that for years."

"Well they've already been to see it you know," he said turning back to the boy; "it's that government there—they're all stealin' our money anyway." Pamela nodded and looked over to Kevin who was staring past her at the opposite wall.

Then Reginald got up and went into the pantry and closed the door behind him, and Pamela looked to Kevin again until he looked to her.

"We have to go."

"Not yet—not yet."

"We have the priest to see and I have a train to catch," she whispered.

Kevin didn't answer.

A minute later he came from the pantry, closing the door behind him as he came out and carrying with him a quart of wine. He set it on the table and went to the sink to get glasses, bringing them over and sitting down.

"Would you like a little?" he asked looking to her.

"Ye—yes a little."

He opened the quart and poured out three glasses and

handed them around, taking his to drink quickly. Pamela took a sip and kept looking at Kevin. He didn't want to notice her—didn't want to look. He drank his glassful and shoved the glass away.

"So you'll come up for it?"

"Oh yes—I—I'll be up. How's your father now—how's Clinton?"

"Good."

There was a silence. Pamela took another sip, seeming to take more of it this time. Then she too put her glass to the side.

"Well Kevin, we'd better go—I have to catch a train," she said, turning to Reginald to explain.

"Oh—a train. I've never been on a train," he blurted. "Where are you going?"

"I have to go home—I'm coming down with my parents tomorrow night."

"Oh."

He stood and went back to the stove and watched them as they stood to go.

"Did he tell the truth," she asked once they were outside by the car, "that he's never been on a train?"

"How in hell should I know? He's a bit retarded anyway and he stutters. Maybe we should have stayed longer."

"I know," she said, "but we'll come down again."

Then they got into the car and drove back upriver, and she sat next to him as he drove.

The small church where the service was to be held stood a mile below the cottage on the right side of the highway. The house stood on the left, farther down and closer to the water than any of the other houses about it. There was no barn and no shed, just the house, small white and immaculate with the grass so close and clean and a flower-bed below the picture window.

He had never been inside, and now that they parked the car beside it he could feel the swollen knot inside him begin to grow, could feel the nerves tighten across his flesh. She got out and walked ahead of him to the door—her small fine legs moving ahead of him to the door. Turning back to him to smile, her smile beckoning him on.

Father Murry came as soon as she knocked, opening the door and smiling to invite them in.

210

And they went inside, into a small dark corridor and then across it to a small study. He closed the door behind him and turned again smiling as he did.

He was not a large man and his hands were very white and clean. His black shirt without the collar showed the chapped redness of where the collar sat upon his neck, and his clean-shaven face was flushed red, the fine red veins underneath the smooth fine skin. He asked them to sit and when they did he went to sit behind his desk.

"Well I never get many visitors," he laughed. There was a smell of dinner off him—the smell of beef or stew or late dinner pervading every gesture that he made, and even the study had in itself the faint heat of dinner on the stove.

"So you've decided to get married—Friday is it, at two?"

"Yes Father," Pamela said.

"Good—well there'll be no problem there. Big wedding?"

"Just the family," she said.

"Oh," he said, looking to her and then over to Kevin who shifted his eyes when he did and felt stupid doing it. Doing it because of the way the man looked, because of what he was—cooking his own dinners and living alone. Because of what he was, the picture of Jesus above his head. "Oh well that'll be easy," he smiled, "and you have your marriage certificate—without the banns you need one."

"Oh yes," Pamela said.

"Good—now I'll have to ask you some questions in private, so ladies first. By the way I don't think I remember your name," he said looking to the girl.

"Oh—this is Pamela Kingston," Kevin said, feeling a bit stupid as he said it.

"Yes, yes—well Kevin if you'd just go out into the corridor for a moment."

"Sure," he said rising.

He went back to the corridor and sat on a chair by the opposite wall. There was no sound from the study—no sound at all. The corridor was small and led to the kitchen. Another picture on the wall and a statue of Mary that glowed faintly in the dark, sitting on a small table beside him, her white and blue in the dark glowing out to him. Mary and the plastic beads and the curtains pinched back and the unwholesome smell of Mammie as if her very veins were roasting in the fire. But everything here had so much the smell of cleanliness to it,

211

even in the smell of the meat, even in his gestures and the pinched redness about his neck. He waited, wondering what they were saying inside. Wondering what he would have to say.

He waited five minutes before she came out, his head down staring at the floor when she did. She came over and tapped him on the shoulder and he stood.

"Your turn," she smiled.

He walked in slowly, feeling that if he walked too fast he would stumble, feeling as he walked the uncertainty in his gut rising to take control of the movements that he made. He sat on the leather-back chair closest to the desk.

"These are just some standard questions that have to be asked," the priest said.

"Yes," he said looking above him. Jesus and the thorns and the Bibles and cathechism and the smell.

"You're Roman Catholic?"

"Yes."

"You know of no reason why you can't marry this girl?"

"No."

"You know of no physical or mental handicap that might in some way prevent you from having children?"

"No."

"That the children conceived from this holy state will be brought into the Roman Catholic Church and taught this religion?"

"Yes."

Julie walking up the aisle, he tried to move close to her to see but couldn't, tried to move close to her but was held back by the firm pressure of the glove because she didn't know why he wanted to move there, to see perhaps if she was showing, to see the thing inside growing, and Andy no more than a lump inside being wheeled about on the carriage.

"No, I know of no reason."

"There is no secret you are holding from this woman that might impair the relationship?"

"No, I know of no secret."

Andy never in a church in years, he tried to say, Hail Mary full of Grace, the Lord be with thee—he tried to say it but didn't.

"Then that's all—nothing to it," the priest said.

Then the priest got up with him and walked out into the

corridor where she was waiting. Her small fine legs. They stood in the corridor talking for a moment about the parish, the old church.

"Well then, I'll see you two Friday—are you nervous?"

"No," they answered.

"No, no there's nothing that you should be nervous about. I've been marrying couples for longer than I care to remember and there's nothing to be nervous about."

Then he showed them out.

They drove up the road slowly past the cottage and into town. They were silent for a long while.

"Did you tell him that you had some big dark secret?" she said, nuzzling up to him.

"Sure, why not—and I told him all my kids were going to be holy-rollers 'cause there's nothing better than holy-rollers, and I told him if God was alive the last place he'd be found would be in a church."

"Did you now?"

"Sure I did."

When they reached her apartment, it was a quarter to ten. She had fifteen minutes to meet the train, and he stood in the living-room while she changed into her slacks and brushed her hair at the mirror. Stood there looking at the small prints of pictures on the wall. The good clean room and pictures on the wall. She came out carrying an overnight bag over her shoulder.

"Well come on, we have to go or I'll miss it."

So he drove her to the station. Already the train had finished watering when they came up—the short spouts of steam rising from its underside, the churning of its diesel in the confusion of the dark.

"You have your ticket?"

"Yes I have my ticket."

He got out and walked before her across the platform to the car. It was as if inside him he wanted to tell her about it now, but he didn't bring himself to; having not told her yet he couldn't. And the sound and the smell of oil on the tracks, the long black shed stretching away from the station to right and left.

"You know maybe we should take the train out Friday," he said.

"Why?"

"I don't know—just maybe we should; it'd be better."

She said that she didn't care. Then she kissed him and told him she'd be in tomorrow night, that they would drive down and be in by eight. And again the knotting in his stomach and again the nerves tightening on his flesh.

"You know," he said, "poor old Reginald—we should have stayed longer, you know."

"We will," she said, "we'll go down next week some time."

Not that he really wanted to—not that he really wanted ever to go down but that maybe he should. Maybe he had to do it.

He waited until the train moved away and then drove home. He backed the car into the shed slowly because his old man always, when he had time, backed it in. Then he went into the house.

He could smell the stench of wax on the floors and saw the chairs from the kitchen cluttered in the hallway. And she was bent over in the room scrubbing it down also. Working this late to get it right, working like a pathetic old woman on her knees to get it right.

"It's not as if they're going to live here," he said.

"Well what do you want," she snapped, "the place looking like a sty?"

He didn't bother answering. He went to his room and lay in the dark. This time in two days they would be somewhere. It would be all over, all of it, and he would be somewhere with her alone.

He heard his old man cough in the bedroom down the hall and the sound of the radio in Deborah's room coming to him faintly through the walls. It was not like it was going to be a big wedding. He didn't have to be nervous about a lot of that. He lay with his right arm over his eyes. They said when he went to school he was very slow and quiet and shy, that he couldn't make friends and always wanted to go home. And they said then when he began to write he wrote with his left hand and the teacher lashed him with a yardstick every time he did. That is what they said. They said she beat him across the left hand with a yardstick every time he did, and he would come home and never say a word about it. But he never passed grade four and still could not write more than a scrawl for his name. They said it was the teacher who made him stutter the way he did; that is what they said, that the teacher didn't have the sense to realize he was slow. That she didn't have the sense to know there was nothing wrong with writing with the left hand. And now tonight he talked about the government, as if he knew anything about the government, as if he knew anything *at all*. And then going to the pantry that way and coming back with wine, and closing the pantry door. Christ, Christ, he thought, coming back with wine as if they were to celebrate there and then.

8

It was so hot that day that the whole road had a haze over it, so hot that the dust of the lane and the sky were one in the thick denseness of it. And the dust—the dust went onto the maple leaves and clung there because of the trucks hauling fill out to the highway, throwing the dust up under the mudguards and the mudguards flapping. The dust filtering into the air behind and clinging finally to the bush and maple leaves along the side of the road. Growing about his fence along the opposite ditch.

There were tandems and even Kenworths on that road all morning. Those old boys with the big throbbing sound of the muscles inside their hood churning out along the lane and packed sky-high with fill. He watched from a chair nearest the window, the window open so that the stifling dead air clung to the mesh of the screen, and coming in clung in a half-damp odour on his skin and about the unevenly shaded room.

"Look at them," he called to her.

Once she came to the window to look but nothing passed as she did, loose strands of hair coming down from her face that way and she wisping them back with a short upward breath from her mouth. Outside the tulips he planted in the bed and the clinging vines growing good on the brick chimney. Then she turned and moved away and then they came again.

"Do you want the fan?"

"Not now."

215

"I'll go upstairs and get it and you can sit on the porch."

"Okay," she said, again blowing the wisps of straw-like hair away from her face and going into the kitchen and through to the porch.

He climbed up the stairs and went along the corridor to the far bedroom where they slept. The smell of face-powder and heat rising together. The sound of a fly batting itself against the window, between the window and the screen, first one way and then the other. The fly that buzzed inside the light fixture the night before when they lay naked atop the sheet was still inside it crawling in a slow unconscious circle as if its wings were dragging. The taste of her powder and the heat. He unplugged the fan and brought it out with him. The sheet ruffled the way it was when they pulled it over them when it got cooler.

She was sitting in the old chair in the porch, staring vacantly through the dusty window at the drive, the dog lying quiet just beside her feet.

"Here?"

"Good."

He plugged in the fan and set it on the small green picnic table beside the chair. She told him to move it farther away, so he moved it back.

"Here?"

"Good."

She leaned her head back and slanted it so that the breeze blew into her face, the thin dry lips of her face and the wisps of greying hair. That hair all grey now and the thin grey legs lying motionless on the sheet.

Then he went back and watched those trucks coming out of the pit, pictured the payloaders digging in and rooting out the fill. All morning they came and no letup to the heat. Then at noon he made sandwiches and tea and brought it into her. They ate together quietly with the whirl of the fan churning the air onto them, the odour of his sweat drying with the fan.

"I'm going out with the canoe," he said. "I have to get out so I'm going out for a while."

"Okay."

"Do you want to come out—just down the river a ways, no further than Donaldsons' camp—only for a while."

She shook her head. He frowned when she shook her head, so she smiled, the small half-decaying teeth. She kept shaking her head as she drank the tea.

"Are you sure?"

"I don't feel like it now—some other day."

"But a canoe ride is just what you need."

"I don't feel like it now." Still smiling as if she were nervous about saying no.

As if she were nervous so he didn't ask her again. He went inside again and she came inside with him. He sat for a long time in the chair and then went out and cleared the dishes and began to wash them. Dishes left from the night before.

"Aren't you going?"

"No."

"Go on."

"No."

"Oh Houlden, go on—go on, go on," she said.

He threw the dishrag down and went out into the heat and down along the river, crossing the lane and along the footpath to the water. The smell of pine and spruce and maple in the heat, cone seeds busting out because of it and not a motion or a slant. Nothing but the suffocated stillness and the trucks in the background calling out to the quiet deadness with their throbs. Now and then a bird flitting to another branch because he was moving down.

He took his canoe and went down along the river, the sun glinting on the half-browned water. But, of course, the heat on his back now and the inch of water itching at his bare feet tucked under him in the bottom of the canoe. And all along the river it was soft and still July. There would be a fire yet, a bad fire he thought. He went as far as Donaldsons' and brought it in there. Waited for a long time, watching the lingering brown current, the heat and closeness of the air seeming to dip and touch the current as it rolled, seeming to be some substance that he could reach out and carry in his hands. He could feel the sun burning at his shoulders through the thin material of his shirt. Maybe if he said, "Let's take a picnic and find a nice cool spot, because it was no fun for her, no fun in the canoe at all, she always sitting there stiff and staring just ahead at the water. I'm the pilot and you're the navigator, he'd say. He stood and walked up into the clearing and sat on the open porch of the camp, the silence of it with them gone, the water looking black and cool from this point and the sun no better, so that the blue boards of the

217

porch burned in the heat, burned his sleeveless arm as he leaned back upon it.

It was like sickness to lie there and yet it was like sickness to move—to want to move. His head was spinning, and yet he didn't bring himself to move for a long time. Until it was after four and a slight breeze came. He got off the porch and walked back down, and the sickness came to his stomach and his head. He pushed the canoe back out and went back up, all along watching the side, the baked clay sides of the river and the shadows of the dried spruce over the water.

It was cooler on the path going up, but he was too sick with the heat to notice. And the trucks still crossing on the lane, the dust spoiling up behind them and settling on the leaves. Choking slightly with the dust as he crossed behind the trucks and went back down the drive and onto the porch.

There was the sound of the radio in the kitchen and the fan still whirling on the porch, the clinking of its blades as it moved back and forth, taking the heat in with it as it moved. The air softly scattered this way and that, the dog against the chair-leg slapping its tail on the floor. The uneven silence with the uneven stench of heat.

He went into the kitchen and leaned against the door, taking the pipe from the table and clapping it between his teeth, looking into the room where the slight breeze blew against the curtains of the open window and again the throttling of trucks moving with their fill. She had done the dishes and left them in the rack to dry, the dishes from the night before and the cups from noon.

"Martha," he said softly.

The dog came into the kitchen and stood behind him panting. He went back onto the porch and turned the fan off, coming out again and walking through to the room.

"Martha," he asked softly, standing at the bottom of the stairs with his hand on the banister knob, with his grey eyes looking up to the top where the banister railing ran along the upstairs hallway. "Martha," he called. It was not as if he didn't *know*; it wasn't even that, because it was along the hallway or inside the room, or inside the porch when the fan was going. He kept calling, not moving from the stairway.

It wasn't the fear of the quietness within the place, with his voice calling out into the soundlessness of the upstairs, with the waves of his voice stirring in the heat. It wasn't fear so

218

much as the pain of knowing and the feel of the grain of wood. He took his hands from the banister and returned to the chair, staring out to the lane, to the maples leaning against the fence on the far side. The clinging of the green vines. He sat in that chair for a long time and increasingly could feel a trembling throughout his frame that he had no control over, and yet he tried to hide it from himself.

The unexpected emptiness perhaps. He waited long, a clot of thirst growing in his throat and the shaking, dampness clinging to his underarms. He lit his pipe and waited until he couldn't bear any longer the emptiness and the shaking. He rose and went to the banister again, placing his hand there again. "Martha," he shouted. The dog came into the room and stood watching.

"Martha," he shouted. "Martha," he shouted.

He climbed the stairs, stopping halfway up to call again and as he called again looking back down, the woodbox by the fireplace, the wood in order and the poker leaning against the box's side. He climbed to the top where the air clung to the rail and the walls and the oval picture of her father on the wall, clung inside the spare bedroom, the grey naked mattress and the dust beneath the iron bed-frame. An iron bed-frame with twisted legs.

Then he looked to the far bedroom, the door half-ajar, the still fine light of a summer's heat. A contrast to the darkness of the hall. He stood for some time with his hand against the railing, with the warmth of the pulse inside him racing violently inside his quiet arm, with his grey eyes fixed against the door and the clotted growing inside his throat. He did not call out again. And he knew—knew because of the fan and the dog and the music filtering faintly through the silence, climbing to him from the kitchen radio making it all so soundless and dead. But he did not want to know, did not want to go in there at all. Wanted to run out and ask one of the truckers to come with him, wanted one of the truckers to go inside there and to come out and tell him with his hand still on the rail and the heat of his pulse still racing inside. Wanted to be told by anyone else at all because the doctor had said, "Martha is very sick; if she gets upset, you shouldn't get upset—if she gets upset, you should realize she is very sick." Wanted it to happen that way instead of the way it was.

He wanted to stand there until darkness, motionless as he

219

was. He felt that if he didn't move, if he waited until darkness, he could go into the room. But then he felt his hand along the rail sliding forward and knew that he was moving toward the room, knew it all with a sense of pathetic weightlessness. Everything heavy left him; all that was in the hallway and along the streaked wall left until he reached the doorway, until his hand came again from the railing. Then the weight of fear as never before. Because of the fear he could not move for many moments. Because his eyes weren't controlled by his thoughts, he looked at the hinges and then through the crack, wanting to see without going in.

But then he did, so quickly it startled him—went inside, rushed over to the window and slammed it down so that the half-dead fly trapped inside came up again in frantic buzzing, batting itself against the window and the screen, the smell of her face-powder and the heat, the taste of the heat, the taste. And then with not more than a glance he made his way to the door, along the hallway and down the stairs. But all the time he was phoning and all the time he was shouting into the phone he saw her staring from the corner, slumped against the bed.

It was said that their will was so great. He knew it. The way they followed up the water coming in from the ocean to come up along the river. And fighting everything as they did, splashing madly up out of the water to make the jump. It was said they would lie at bottom gathering into themselves all the strength they had—and wait and wait. Then they would begin at a point and make the run, gathering, gathering something frantic inside to come up out of the water with the surge they had gathered. Once up they would topple over or topple back, continue onward or slant on their side at the bottom again. Those that failed would try once more, exhausted they would flick their tails up and out, never reaching, never quite reaching. Battered and bleeding in the attempt.

Those that continued would spawn, would loosen their eggs or sperm into the soft mudbank of the stream, loosen in their progeny the life within their flesh. As if some great release to existence they were fated to give came with something destructive within them all. As if, he thought, something comical within it all.

He waited in the porch because he could not sleep. The sky

cleared and the sun came up red without him ever noticing it. Only once it was light did he realize it. He looked at the time and settled back with a blanket over him. The smell of paint still lingered from the storm windows that he had put up the day before and outside the clumps of browned grass flattened by the frost. Frost on the windows seeming to kindle in the fresh sun. A clear fresh day.

Perhaps he shouldn't have asked for money from the boy. It was foolish to think that, he knew, but he felt a guilt inside himself for asking for money. Money from a boy who had no money. If instead he had simply talked, simply talked to the boy about it. He would feel better now if he had, for the anger had passed altogether leaving only a sympathy for the son. And his father the way he was that night.

"I would have shot him," Ken said as they dug that day, the carcass bloated and stiff. "I would have so help me, I would have shot the bastard."

He listened then but now he had no anger left. And the boy was coming up today. When he dug, the pick burned his hands and he thought of her all that time, all that time as he glanced at the walls of gravel and shale and he standing deeper and deeper inside it. Her eyes, he thought, her eyes dug out with the shale between them. Oh Christ, he thought because he could not cry—never could cry.

And still could not even as the thought and the horror of it clung to him at times so that he could not sleep. He used the spare bedroom now, and still at moments like this he could not sleep.

He slept all morning. At mid-day Rubena came in and shook him so that he woke. But he lay there for a long time drifting occasionally back into sleep until she came into him again.

"Get up now, I want to clean your room. And you have things to do—you have that man to see."

He rose and went out into the kitchen. The place was spotless and reeked of wax. He stood for a time by the sink with his eyes half closed. The sky beyond stood out raw and tasteless, the lane and field rutted by the frost that had penetrated and had not lifted. Everything looking cold and clear.

"Do you want breakfast?"

"I don't care."

"Well what are you going to eat?"

"I don't care."

"I can mix some pancakes to put on if you want."

"Good."

He turned and stood watching her as she moved about, his eyes still half closed and a thumping in his head, along his forehead just above the eye. He glanced to see the time. One more day.

"Do you have any Anacin?"

"Why—is your arm bothering you?"

"No."

"Well?"

"Well, I have a headache," he said not looking at her. She went over to the cabinet and took the bottle down, handing it to him and then going back to the pancakes. He took two tablets with a glass of water. Then he waited in silence until they were ready and went to the table to eat.

And all during breakfast she kept asking about his suit. "Does it fit?" she kept asking. He would nod his head, too busy to speak.

"How do you know it fits—have you tried it on?"

"No," he said.

"Well how do you know it fits—my God you might need a new one for all I know. You should have a new one anyway."

"I've hardly ever worn it," he said. He finished with his plate and stood and walked down the hallway and into the room.

"You and Clinton both," she kept saying from the kitchen, "you and Clinton both should have new suits. But I'm too busy," she added after a pause. Then she came into the room and sat beside him. He leaned back with his hand rubbing at his forehead, paying no attention to her.

"I took his down to the cleaners," she said. "I hope to God yours is clean."

He sat there for a moment and then stood and walked quickly into the hallway again, going to the closet and taking down his heavy grey coat.

"Does he know I'm taking the car?"

"Yes—and you be back early. And for God's sake stay away from the tavern today—with those people coming down and all."

He put the coat on and went back to the door to glance in at her. Everything was spotless in here too; and the way she

222

looked at him, as if she were pleading for something when she did. And all the time she spoke, the words came out of her soft and yet in their softness something pleading and forceful.

"You're stupid to worry so damn much," he said. He went back to the door and went outside.

"Well someone has to, don't they now," she yelled as he went back.

It was biting cold, after midday, and silent. So damn silent with the sting of the cold, the cumbersome heavy winter coat that he wore uncomfortable, everything inside him uncomfortable and sick. Worry, worry, that's all she did, he thought —all the damn thing did.

He took his father's car and went into town, driving it slowly, watching the water. With days like this the ice would come soon, the snow before the ice, the tracks clearer in the snow. The water was quite calm and white, waiting for the ice. Everything waiting now, silent and burdened with frost and calm—everything for a few more weeks. Perhaps really the coldest time of all.

When he came into town, he drove round for a time, passing by the lot where they had his truck. But he did not go in. He knew he had to see the insurance adjustor but he didn't want to—not today; today he wanted to do nothing more than be alone, and yet he had the man to see—had to pay out for the cow. Money that wasn't his. Money that belonged to the both of them. He did not want to go there either, wanted instead to be alone. But today he had to go.

The way they gathered after every accident. He had seen it, been there himself most of the time, watching them drag the car into the lot and then climbing over the mesh fence to get a closer look. Always wanting a closer look. The blood, they would say. Look at the blood. The handle would be covered with blood, the hood and the seats, and the stench of alcohol and the glass mixed with the clots of blood, and the twisted metal so you could envision the flesh tearing in that one moment, the eyes seeing the flesh tearing in that one moment. There would always be blood and in the summer the heat rising up out of it and the stench of the inside. And in the fall the faint warmth rising out and the quiet decay. But they always came round, always came round to gape and talk and be excited by it all. There were very few deaths in winter, he

223

thought, more deaths in the summer and fall.

He did not want to see his truck because of that and there was no more damage than the front end really—the front end and the sides. But what if he went inside to look and saw on the seat or the door handle or along the windowframe his own blood streaked and cold and drying in the deadened frost? What if he went to look and saw that? He drove past it once more and then turned in a parking lot and headed toward the centre of town.

He parked the car and went for a walk. The coat felt better on him now, closer to his skin with the warmth that it gave, but still the itching cold at his legs, through his jeans and into his legs. He crossed to the park and sat on a bench watching the people pass in all directions on the quiet streets, huddling into himself for warmth.

Then in a few moments he stood and walked stiffly out of the park, crossed the street again and went toward the bank. He would draw the entire amount that he owed and take it back in his pocket, hand it to him and leave. That was the best way to go about it. The sooner it was over with the better. He would simply hand it over and say he was sorry and leave. Never hunt that area again, at least not this year. Instead, for the rest of the season he would hunt in toward the camp, or back toward the Mines or somewhere else entirely. He should have run. When the man slipped behind the spruce he could see him moving, occasionally he could detect the figure moving toward him from behind the trees. And the carcass behind him with its punctured, blooded face and eyes. He should have run down across the field. He should have then, and now as he walked, he cursed at having stood silent as the man came out and toward him, walking slow.

He went into the bank and took it out, all that he owed, and shoved the whole amount into his jeans pocket and went back onto the street. The faint steady sun and the biting day, the trees hanging with their branches naked and grey. He walked back up the street thinking to himself, hearing the whistle of an ore-boat coming in. As soon as it was over—as soon as the whole mess was over. And he would find out. He would find out what she was going to do. Perhaps he would go see her and ask her what she was going to do.

He passed the general store thinking this, so that he saw nothing of the man coming out behind it and walking toward him stumbling. He saw nothing of the man until the slow deadened movement of the arm reached out to him and placed the hand upon the shoulder of his coat. The same man in the urinal with the wine—the same man stooping over him now, breathing heavily into his face.

"Yes," he said unconsciously. Then stepping back so that the stink of the breath wouldn't reach him, the cold heavy sores about the side of his head, the eyes reddened and busted out. "Yes, bud—what can I do for you?" he said.

The man stepped closer and put his arm across again, extending it to him so that he felt he shouldn't move. The man kept moving closer, moving his lips as he did in some pathetic demonstration, in some ugly and pathetic demonstration, as if he wanted, while he moved his lips that way, to speak out loudly and clearly but as if when he twisted his lips no words would come.

Kevin felt his nerves tighten. He reached through his pants to find change and brought out the bills crumpled together. The old man gaped. He kept searching until he found some change, the old man still gaping, and clutched it in his hand while shoving the bills away.

"I wan—I wan—I wan," the man was saying.

"What?" he kept saying.

"I wan' a poppy."

"It isn't the eleventh yet," Kevin said looking up. "It isn't the eleventh yet."

"I want a fuckin'—you don't know shoot me, you don't know shoot me, you fucker—I don't know," he kept saying with his right arm steady upon the shoulder of the boy and people passing them a little to the side.

"It isn't the eleventh yet," he kept saying.

The man kept muttering.

"It isn't the eleventh yet."

The man kept looking.

"You don' know, ya fucker—you don' know, I don't know—shoot me, ya fucker—you don't know." Then he spit and hammered his left fist into his side.

Kevin handed him the change. The man looked. His eyes narrowed, flickered, and he kept muttering his nonsense. Kevin put the money in his hand but he kept muttering his nonsense.

Then he moved away looking back. Kevin shook his head

225

and went to the car. Old bastard, he kept thinking.

He drove out of town and up along the highway. The nerves and the tightness and his head still aching. Only once, one time in the middle of the summer, had he seen John lying beside her with Andy out swimming. Perhaps she never thought at all of what he was thinking. Not at all in the way he thought of her lying there with her body strained with the heat and sand. Only once and now it was hard to remember whether or not they were talking, whether or not that day they ever said anything. And still the face of the boy—the photograph on the table when he signed his name.

It was a day that reminded him of the cold sterile shale along the mountain slope that he had hunted that year, the weekend before his birthday. The shale without a smell to it, only the frost covering it and the silence disturbed by his boot crunching into it as he climbed. And off to either side the huge rocks smoothed out in the cold. Nothing came of the trip but now this day was like that day because it reminded him of the almost lonely purity in the freezing of the ground, the lonely biting cleanliness before the snow with the sun's pinched heat like reddened patches on the ground, giving no warmth but only the soft glint of colour.

When he reached the house it was three o'clock. He took the car off the lane and parked behind the truck in the dooryard. He did not get out for a minute, pulling the money out of his pocket and counting it, once, twice, making sure. He knew the man wouldn't count it—wouldn't touch it for more than a moment. Wouldn't look at it until he had left.

He shoved it all back and went to the door to knock, knocking and turning around to view the lane and the fields and the barns rising all steadily together in the cold. In a minute he turned and knocked again. The dog barked and came to the door, putting its paws up against it, scratching. Then he turned and saw the man coming round toward him from the corner of the barn.

"Good-day," the man said.

"Hello."

"Bit cold."

"Yes."

The man reached him and with his eyes turned a little to the side, went ahead of him into the house. Through the kitchen again and into the room. He took a corner chair and

226

the man pulled one up and sat beside him. He stared again at the wolves running above the mantelpiece in the cold. They looked deader now without the fire, even the half-bright glow from the dying coals could give them the heat they needed to run. He looked past the man who was looking at the dog —talking to it. Then he pulled it from his pocket.

"Here 'tis," he said, conscious of the bills crumpled like so much waste-paper in his hand. He handed it over and the man glanced at it and him with the same small movement of his eyes. Tired eyes, old and grey in the silent house.

"Oh good," he said, taking them and placing them in a bunch quickly in his pocket as if he were nervous about it. Kevin kept looking behind him to the wolves.

"I thought you'd be writing out a cheque."

"Oh no," Kevin said startled a little, feeling stupid.

"That's good," the man said again, rising up as he spoke. "You want something, tea or a beer or something?" he said.

"Oh no."

"A beer maybe—I was just going to have some tea. Don't rush off," he said going back into the kitchen; "no don't rush off."

Kevin sat in the chair. He heard the kettle going and waited. It was after three now. The man came back and handed him a beer. Then he went back into the kitchen. The kettle stopped and in a moment he came in again.

"You aren't working today," the man said sitting down. Kevin sipped at the beer wanting to take it in quickly, knowing that he couldn't.

"No I have the day off today—I'm—er—getting married tomorrow."

The man looked at him; he was drinking the tea and the steam was rising and he glanced with his grey eyes beyond the steam to the boy, swallowing and taking the cup from his mouth all before he spoke.

"Oh all the more reason to have a beer. A girl from around here then?"

"No, no—she works as a nurse at the hospital though."

"Oh a nurse," the man said.

They continued drinking, the silence between them growing.

"Getting married," the man said again, swallowing again. "My wife just died here a few months ago," he said.

227

"Oh."

"Yes—we'd been married, let's see, 24 years next March."

"Oh," Kevin said again, drinking the beer down harder to get it in.

"No children though," the man said.

"No," Kevin said looking about him at the dog tucked in the corner on its mat, its ears half raised to the sound of the man's slow voice.

The calmness about the place at mid-afternoon with the quiet light slanting easily through the window to the side of the fireplace, and without the fire or the warmth of the lights the place looking cold and out of sorts.

"You know we all do crazy things like that, shoot cows and such at some time or another—and pay the price too. As long as we pay the price," he said slowly.

"Yes," Kevin said, finishing the beer now and setting it down on the floor.

"I rode an old mare into the ground when I was seventeen—sweat and hair coming off in patches, off its back. That was a crazy damn thing to do. But you can't really feel bad about things like that because everyone does them."

"Yes, well I'm sorry I killed your cow."

"Well it's done with now. So you're getting married. You going to live around here?"

"Yes."

"Work at the mill?"

Kevin nodded.

"That's a good place to work as any," the man said standing.

Kevin stood also and followed him to the door. The ticking of the small clock in the kitchen and dishes in the sink. The man placed the bottle on the counter and went through to the porch.

"Well good luck," he said, "and I wouldn't feel too bad about doing what you did because we all do crazy things sometimes. As long as we're honest and learn by it," he said.

"Yes," Kevin said. He went out and along the lane back to his car. He could feel the man staring at him from the porch and over the fields and dirt lane, the quiet cold spreading slowly into late afternoon, the maples lulled in their nakedness at the fence's other side, the naked alders like fingers spreading out.

He spit into the dirt and followed to his car, the eyes still following him he thought. Married 24 years, he thought. But they had nothing to talk about because it was over —everything was over and waiting for winter. The frost pushing its fingers into the ground. He got into the car, the smell of stale tobacco rising from the ashes in the tray. He felt the eyes were following him as he backed it out.

9

Staring into the mirror he could see his face blotched and roughed with those so many scars and contours of the flesh that he had known over the years, that he had seen form and develop like minute ticks upon the skin, so slowly that he had never noticed their development at all. And now he watched himself as his right hand slid upward to tighten the notch of his tie, watched the blackened hair over the browned knuckles of the hand curve in that smooth line to the fingers or away as the thin knot became thinner on his throat. It don't look good, he thought.

He stepped back from the mirror and stood sideways undoing the jacket button and examining how he stood with the tie falling that way, tight and narrow over the whiteness of the shirt. The jacket sleeves up too high as if his elbows were catching them. The pants seemed merely to hang on his too-long legs yet straight and clean and set in their crease so that they made his legs look stiff. He buttoned the jacket again and kept looking. When he buttoned it it pulled his sides too tight. As if now for the first time he noticed it—as if before, wearing it to Mass, because she had said nothing about it, he had never noticed the pulling or the shortness of the sleeves.

And yet it was his face. He went back to it, turned toward the mirror again and looked at the so finely implanted leather streaks upon the skin, as if the skin had made them there the moment he was born. And he loosened it again, unknotted it and stood back once more. A long stringy man he was with a stooped powerful walk. He tore the tie off and redid it, more carefully this time, trying to get it right, tucking the shirt collar just under the jacket after he had and staring closely again.

It don't look good, he thought.

He pulled the tie tighter again and stood there for a long time. Then he went to the bed and, bending over carefully once he had sat upon it, picked up the shoes she had bought. He put them on, smelling the cleanliness of them as he laced them up. Seeming to confine his feet even though they fitted. But it was because they were new. He sat on the bed staring down at them for five minutes, looking at the right shoe and then the left, left to right again. They were good, new, the smell of fine leather and the glint of black polish. Then with a sigh he stood and went back at it, trying to get it right before he went out to her, trying to get it right or she'd say,

"It doesn't look right and I knew, I knew just as well that day in town when I begged you to get one, when I begged you to try one on."

But even with his shoes on it still didn't look too good. Hell it's only for one day, he thought, cursing at her under his breath as he did, cursing at himself. The things made him feel awkward. He straightened himself up and looked at it all as calmly as he could. He wasn't satisfied. Even when he shaved the face would be rough and the shirt frayed and the sleeves, as if the elbows were hauling them about.

So he turned away from the mirror and looked at the shoes again. He moved one foot ahead and then the other. The old pantlegs seemed to catch. Then he stood on one heel and then the other as if to supple them out. He walked the length of the room three times, each time staring into the mirror as he passed it, and turning his face abruptly as he did. It didn't look good. He came back to the mirror and straightened everything once more, tried to get his tie right again and the jacket, open or buttoned? "Shit," he kept muttering. Because it wasn't the suit that didn't fit him, it was he that didn't fit the suit.

He went back to the bed and sat for a moment and then stood, turning out the light to go out to her. He walked slowly down the corridor to the room.

When he came into the room, she was already walking about the boy, inspecting—a piece of dust here, a loose thread

230

there. And she had pins in her mouth as if she were going to do the curtains—like at times when she did the curtains. It was seven now and they'd be here; they'd be down soon enough. He wanted to be out of it all when they came, as if when she came in with them, he'd be embarrassed to be seen like that. As if because it was *her* coming in with the good young scent of her, he'd seem foolish. Kevin had his chin in his throat, looking at the floor all the while she was scurrying about, mumbling more to herself than anyone else.

"It don't look good," he said quickly coming in. She looked up and grunted. He went over to the window and stood there with his back to it watching them, feeling the cool of frost and night gathering and touching and coming through the pane. He could feel it along his shoulders and the back of his neck. The thick brown leather of his neck. There would be snow soon for sure, a clinging to the ground, the melting off and the clinging once again, hardening and thickening in the fields. He waited and watched her.

"Well it seems all right," she was saying. "What's Pamela wearing, do you know?" she asked.

"Something I suppose," the boy said.

Deborah came into the room and sat on the couch looking up.

"When are they going to be here?" she asked. No-one answered so she asked it again.

"Oh I don't know—eight," Bena said.

"Why is everyone so grumpy?" she said.

"No-one's grumpy," Bena said.

"Are you going to wear your suit tonight?"

"No."

"You should," she said.

The boy looked down at her and than at Bena. Then he stepped away from her and straightened his head, moved his neck back and forth as if looking about.

"It's all right," he said looking at her. She nodded.

"I think so—there's nothing I can do about it if it isn't."

"Good," he said. He moved away from her to the door and went through it along the hall.

"What do you mean it doesn't look good?" she said turning quickly to him.

He was startled and didn't answer for a moment, kept listening to the sound of his son along the hallway walking.

231

"Oh I don't know—it's okay."

She came close to him, close enough so that he could smell the same smell of perfume that he had smelled while sitting beside her in the pews or driving to town in the car. The same faint lingering on her half-reddened flesh, against the pale skin rising out a little red. But not the redness of underneath—the redness of something she put on. Put on because *they* were coming down, just as she had waxed and cleaned and made small-cakes and bread because they were coming down. Asked him this afternoon to buy something *good* to drink for them because they were *her* people coming down.

She stood close to him looking up, inspecting the tie knot and the shirt, the jacket buttoned and tightened to his sides.

"No, well I warned you," she said stepping back. "But there's not a thing to be done about it now. It doesn't look that bad," she said. "A little old." Like him, like his chapped face protruding out of it, like something with moss growing over, as if all the years had gathered up and busted something out above the collar, which was his tired eyes and face and half-bitten jaw. He looked at her and stepped away from the window and walked to the couch.

"It's all right," the girl said looking at him as he sat.

He sat on the couch, the circular ashtray below him on the floor. He looked about for his tobacco and papers and rolled himself a smoke, she staring at him all the while. It was good to smoke.

"You know it's half these shoes," he said.

"What's wrong with those shoes—now I paid good money for those shoes and they fit you so what's wrong with them?"

"I don't know. I don't think they go good with my pants."

"What do you mean?" she said.

"I don't know."

"Well there's nothing wrong at all with those shoes —everybody wears shoes like that. Do you think something is wrong with them, Deborah?"

"I can't tell—I don't think so."

"Well I don't know—I paid good money for those shoes," she said drawing back and staring.

"Oh I won't die in them," he said looking down, dragging off his cigarette as he did and letting the smoke through his nose. "No I won't die in them."

"If you didn't have such long legs," Bena said.

"It ain't my legs—there ain't nothin' wrong with my legs."

He butted his cigarette and stood looking down at the crease of his pants. She was still looking, her right hand to her face, her fingers tucked against her lip. He walked to the door and turned.

"Well it's only for one day and I ain't going to worry about it."

"Oh it's all right," she said looking up to him. He felt stupid because of the way she was looking.

He went into the bedroom again and took the thing off, hanging it on the hanger carefully and changing into the clothes she wanted him to wear that night. A dark red sweater that he had worn only twice before. He changed and looked at himself again and then lay down, reaching for the string to snap the light. It would be winter again soon—winter. He hated it on the road in winter, always frightened, always fearful of the children laughing and going on behind him in the seats. Because he was the driver and he was a good one at that, but if anything happened—if he happened to skid with those behind him playing in the seats.

He lay there in the darkness, motionless in the clothes she had put out for him to wear, motionless with the thoughts of her coming in with them tonight. "How long will they stay?" he had asked at supper, looking up from the cup, the tea half-cold and the milk like skim on the top of it so that he had to stir it up again after he had asked.

"I don't know—they'll have something to eat I suppose. I don't want to sit there and rush them out," she said. "What did you get to drink?" she asked.

"Stuff," he said.

As if she were afraid that he didn't know what to get to drink. He had spent $16.00 to get it for them and he wouldn't taste a drop. He lay there looking at the ceiling. The voice of the girl with her in the kitchen, running about, doing things right. He had put the champagne in the fridge and the rye in the cupboard and had taken the beer to the cellar. If they wanted the beer Kevin could go and get it. He didn't know about the champagne; he didn't know about that. One quart of that stuff was worth three quarts of wine and it tasted no different. He had heard that but he had never tasted it before and never cared to. She was frightened he had bought wine or something. She was like that—frightened.

233

He didn't sleep and soon he began to sweat, lying there that way, with the sweater and the shirt buttoned right up. He undid the top button. His legs were crossed and for the time he lay he never moved them at all.

Then she came in and began to change before him. She sat on the bed to put more of that colouring onto her face and took lipstick from her purse to put on. She smelled of it all. As if, if he tasted her he would get the taste of powder instead of flesh. Like those days at the church picnic in the summer when the heat of the grounds brought it all out even more. She put the lipstick into her purse again and brought out cigarettes.

"Smoke these tonight, will you?"

"Why?"

"Just because."

"You'd think it was the King and Queen."

"You can smoke these tonight and at the wedding too."

"I don't like them—you know I never like them."

She sighed and stood and going to the closet reached for her shoes.

"I'll have to wear these darn things to the wedding tomorrow. I should get another pair—I only have one pair."

"Nothin' wrong with those," he said.

"Well you smoke those," she said, "and get up now; they should be here any minute."

He lay on the bed and undid the packet and took one out. He never liked them; he would rather go without one than smoke them. He tore the filter off before putting it into his mouth. Then he stood again and went into the room, buttoning the tops as he did. The browned and leathered skin of his throat.

They all sat for some minutes without a sound. Only Deborah breathing hard every little while and standing to go to the window, and he breathing the smoke out of his mouth and into the waxed air. Then she stood herself and went into the kitchen. Kevin sat stiff and white in the chair, his hands clean, his hair clean, his young cheeks smoothed and reddened by shaving. He sat there in the rocker looking down. Clinton rolled a cigarette and smoked it. Then she came in again.

"Did you take those boxes away?"

"What boxes?"

"The ones with the leaves that Deborah and I had to run around for."

"I put them out back."

"Where out back?"

"By the barrel," he said.

"They aren't going to take a tour you know," the boy said looking at her. "Did you get beer?" he said looking to him.

"Why?" she said.

" 'Cause I might have one."

"It's in the cellar," Clinton said.

"You're not having one now anyway," Bena snapped, "not until they come—fine thing now they come and everyone sitting around guzzling beer."

The boy sighed and cursed under his breath. She was nervous; she was trying to make everyone as nervous as she was. It was past eight now certainly so perhaps they wouldn't show until the morning. Deborah came back from the window and sat again on the couch. Young and with a tendency to grow fat like her mother.

"I don't see why he can't have a beer," she said.

Bena said nothing more but stood a little from the doorway observing them all. Deborah's good clean face smiling as she said it.

"I don't have a present for you yet," she added. "I'll get something soon—before Christmas anyway," she laughed.

The boy said nothing. The boy said nothing because he was waiting, as if it took everything inside him to wait now.

He didn't hear the car or the engine shut off before he heard the voices coming. They must have driven the car in right behind the bus, and when they were getting out of it their voices came through to him. Deborah stood and ran out to the door. He heard the voices coming along the yard and then the real sound of them inside. He stood, because she had told him to stand, and waited, the back of his legs firm against the couch, ready to sit down again, the edge of his left foot hitting against the ashtray on the floor. The boy stood also and moved a bit closer. Then they were coming into the room— she first and then a woman and a man and then a girl. Deborah came in behind them all.

He stood there with his hand extended, not more than glancing quickly. The woman was thin and nice he thought, and the man stood beside him as if he wanted to talk about it

235

all. She was laughing now as she brought the boy forward so that he almost bumped against them. She was laughing. She kissed him quickly.

"Mom, dad—this is Kevin." Then she added laughing, "Kevin this is my mother, my father." The boy shook hands, his face colourless except for the slight redness from shaving.

They stood there talking, all of them talking, and then the voices waned so that all the air seemed to settle undisturbed. He reached for his cigarettes and began to smoke—the ones she had given him. Then they started talking again, the voices lower and friendly, but no-one sat down and he wanted to sit down now.

"Well Kevin, we had hoped to meet you earlier," the woman said.

"Ya—I know."

"Yes, it's too bad you didn't get up," the man said.

It was because there wasn't enough room. If every spot were taken, there'd still be two or three standing.

He was sweating again and the man was standing beside him, the smell of lotion and the fine bright eyes. The woman was slim.

"Yes," she was saying, "you should really have come up—don't you think, Mrs. Dulse?"

"Oh yes—but you never know about Kevin," Bena said. "Deborah, get a few chairs from the kitchen," she said. She was looking to him as she spoke, the voice coming out of her soft, but he did not know why she was looking at him. The man was speaking about the road.

The girl went out and Pamela went with her and they came back with three chairs and set them below the window. Then they sat and were all quiet for a moment.

"Who's this—your sister?" Bena asked.

Pamela looked over. She was sitting on the couch alongside her mother, Bena on the other end.

"Oh no—that's Barbara Members—my bridesmaid."

"Oh I see."

The girl smiled. She was sitting at the other end where the chairs went by the window. The girl smiled. Tall and brown with a narrow jaw.

"I see," Bena said again, "are you a nurse too?"

"No, Teachers' College."

"Oh a teacher," Bena said.

236

They were silent again. He was sweating—because of the sweater and the shirt he was sweating.

"You'll meet our son tomorrow," the woman said; "he's supposed to drive up from the university."

"Oh I see—what does he do there?"

"It's a long story," the man said.

"Oh I see," she said.

"Not really," the woman said, "he's going to try to get into law if he makes the marks."

"He goes from one idea to the other," the man said rubbing his right palm against his knee and looking to her. Then he looked back quickly.

"That's a damn bad road into here."

"Yes, in the spring it's real bad," he answered, taking the smoke into him and not letting it out for many moments, sitting stiffly. It wasn't the same. It was never the same with the filter on it. He could never get the taste, the loose tobacco that he liked to chew. "But I don't know why they don't fix it," he said.

"I probably threw my car out of line," the man said, rubbing his right palm back and forth on his pantleg.

"It wasn't that bad," Pamela said, "Barb and I never found it bad."

"You two slept," he said; "it's bad."

"You must all be tired then," Bena said.

"Not really," the woman said, "we stopped at the motel anyway. Well, is everything ready for tomorrow—it must have been hectic on you."

"Oh no, I got by—we're having the reception at Andersons'. She's an old woman and everything and doesn't mind at all helping out. She's got a great big place there to have it in—it's only about a mile up from here."

"Yes, well it isn't going to be a big weddin' anyway," Clinton said; "it's better to have a small weddin' anyway." She had a necklace around her throat and her dress long and green hung on her that way, making the room seem unsuitable, the couch on which she sat unsuitable. She was younger than Bena, yes, younger than them both. And the man with just a little fat at the belly, and his hair thin and smooth.

"Yes," the man said, "and how are you Kevin—are you ready?"

"Ready as you'll ever be, eh Kevin?" Deborah said.

237

"Yes," the boy said looking at the man, not at his sister, looking at the man and then at the woman who was listening to Pamela on the couch.

"I think Deborah's more excited than anyone," Bena said.

"That's not true," the girl said. "I'm not."

The woman looked up. She had been talking to Pamela. "I've heard a lot about you," she said.

"Oh."

"About school."

"Oh yes, Deborah does good at school," Bena said. "She always did good."

"What subjects do you like?" Barbara asked looking over.

"None really too much," the girl said slowly.

"No she does real well at them all," Clinton said. "She does better'n anyone around here at school."

"Kevin did good," Bena said.

"Oh yes," he said, "Kevin did good—if he had a applied himself he would a done good," he added quickly. He glanced to the boy and then the woman. The boy said nothing.

"That's the trouble with them all—they don't apply themselves, like our Richard doesn't apply himself."

Clinton smiled and stood and went to the ashtray. He brought it back with him to the chair and sat again, stiff-legged, and lit another smoke.

"You got to apply yourself," he said.

"Trouble with Richard is he gets settled into one thing and wants to change."

"Oh Harold, that's not true," the woman said, laughing as she said it.

"Kevin did good at school," Bena said. "Anyway his schooling is over now."

"Yes it's over now anyway," Clinton said, biting into the filter as he did, because he didn't like the filter when he smoked.

They were silent again, the woman staring up vaguely to the ceiling, her mouth pinched that way as if she was not thinking of what she was looking at. Her mouth pinched and her thin cream-coloured skin.

"Well, do you like it where you work?" the man asked. "Pam tells us you work at the mill—what do you do up there?"

The boy looked over. He had not spoken all evening, and it was as if he didn't want to speak, didn't want to be there in the

238

room. Because it was *he* they were there for and he knew it; it was he they were wanting to see and hear and talk to. He looked to the man and his words came out slowly, talking as if he wanted to say it right, choosing his words to say it right and yet speaking lowly with his face reddening as he did.

"Anything and everything," he began, "but it's all right I suppose—I mean I don't mind it and the pay's okay. The pay's good enough and everything and the hours are good too—it isn't like working at the mines or anything. The pay's good."

"You think you'll stay there then?" the woman said. She had turned her head toward him, a small brown birthmark showing on her neck just below where the necklace went round.

"For a while—I mean it's up to Pamela too. We were thinking of moving away some day—going somewhere else. I might like to go to Technical School," he said, "but we have to decide."

Pamela was looking at him now. He stopped talking and looked to her and then quickly to Clinton and the man sitting there together.

"Oh well, you're still young yet," the man said.

"Yes, that's true," Clinton said. The boy turned his head away.

"Of course it depends," he said. "I don't know just yet—I think I can stand it up there a while longer."

"Oh it's a good enough place to work," Clinton said quickly.

"Yes," the man said, "they're both young yet."

"Well, there's nothing wrong with that," the woman said.

Bena stood and went to the doorway. That faint scent off her as she passed him. "Well I better get you people something to eat," she said.

"Oh don't put yourself to any trouble."

"It's no trouble," she said.

He stood also and went into the kitchen with her. The stove had been going on low all evening and the room was warm with it, the outside looking black. He stood there for a moment watching her as she hurried about setting the things out on the counter with the wax paper over them. She didn't look at him at all. He stood watching.

"You think they want something to drink?"

"Well ask them."

"You ask them."

She looked up at him, her face white.

"What do you mean *me* ask them?"

"Hell," he said under his breath. He went back through to the room and stood by the doorway looking in, their voices coming to him, Pamela and Barbara talking.

"You people like anything to drink?" he said. "I got some rye here if you want some rye."

"Okay," the man said. "Susan do you want a rye?"

"Yes," she said.

He went back out and moved around her, taking the bottle from the cupboard. Then he went into the store and back to the cooler for mix. He came out and Kevin was standing beside her in the kitchen. He opened both bottles and began to mix the drinks.

"Where's the beer?"

"In the cellar."

The boy went to the latch and opened it, going down. He came up just after the drinks were mixed and put the beer on the table.

"It's not too cold," he said.

It looked as if he were white and sick. When he came over for the opener, it looked as if he were sick. He didn't speak. He took the opener and went back to the beer, opening three pints and carrying them inside. Bena picked up the plates and started to take them in.

"I bought champagne," he said, "but I don't know about that."

"We don't have no champagne glasses," she said.

He went inside and they were eating. She had pulled up the small table and had set the plates on it. He handed them the drinks and sat down, taking a cigarette again and lighting it because he wasn't hungry and didn't want to eat.

"Aren't you having one?" the man said.

"I don't drink no more," he said holding the cigarette just out from his face. "I had an operation and it's better that I don't drink."

"Oh," the man said looking.

"Well, have something to eat now," Bena said.

He wanted to tell her that he didn't want anything to eat. He butted the cigarette and went to the plate, taking a sandwich back with him. No voices now, only the sound of eating.

240

He held the sandwich in his hand a very long time watching them. Pamela had gotten up and stood beside Kevin. They were drinking beer slowly but neither was talking. He shoved the food into his mouth and chewed on it again and again before swallowing. Then he lit another cigarette and waited.

"Well," the man said, "by this time tomorrow it'll all be over." He turned his head to look at his daughter as he spoke. She had her left arm around his neck staring down at him but neither was speaking.

"Yes," Barbara said, "by this time tomorrow you'll be an old married woman."

It was that he looked sick, Clinton thought. It was that he looked pale and sick.

"Yes it will be," she said. "I'm glad you only have to go through it once."

"Oh there's nothing wrong with going through it," the man said turning back.

He turned back and smiled, and then put the drink to his mouth, swallowing it off in one gulp as if he wished to be through with it and then setting the glass beside him on the floor. They had finished eating now and everyone was silent. He turned back to his wife. Bena got up and went to the kitchen again. For five minutes they were silent.

"Well, do you think we've bothered these people long enough?" she asked finally.

"Do you want to go?" he asked.

"I think we'd better."

"Don't rush off," Clinton said.

"Well, it's a long day tomorrow," she said rising. The man stood up also. Bena came back from the kitchen.

"Are you going?"

"Yes, I'd better get her home to bed before midnight."

"Oh yes," Bena said smiling slightly.

They went out to the door and he followed them to it, following behind her, the good youngness of her body slightly ahead of him as they walked.

"Well thanks for everything," the woman said, "and we'll see you people tomorrow. Goodnight Kevin," she said. The boy was standing behind them in the hallway. Pamela turned and came up to him.

"I'll see you."

"Ya."

241

"At the altar," the man said.

Then they went out, their voices quiet in the dark.

He went back into the room and rolled a cigarette. The place smelled of wax and the voices still seemed to be there. He heard the car as it moved away. Then he went down the hallway and into the bedroom carrying his tobacco with him.

He undressed and lay there smoking with the light on, hearing her with Deborah in the room clearing the things away, glasses and plates. But, of course, it was only for one day, and he could wear it for that long. But it was *her* also even if only for that day. He heard his son between the walls and then Deborah walk along the hall.

She came in. Yes it was like in the summer on the picnic grounds with the heat making it more noticeable. Her scent was like that now.

"I was going to make coffee," she said.

"They didn't want none," he said. He butted his cigarette and rolled on his side. Then he began to cough, coughing for a long time. She snapped out the light and rolled in beside him, with her back up against his back, unmoving. If he had thought of special glasses, he would have got her some, but he never thought of it when he bought the stuff. But perhaps he should have bought some glasses. He didn't know that. He only knew that it was a hell of a lot more expensive, and no-one was going to drink it, that it would be the last time he ever bought it. He lay on his side until the coughing stopped and then turned on his back staring out into the blackness above his head. He could hear his son in the other room tossing on his bed. He didn't know why he mentioned about school. He didn't know that. It was because they all were talking and he was talking. He knew he shouldn't have mentioned it.

"Well they're not bad people," she said, as if it cut the silence above his head.

"What did you expect?" he asked.

10

"When did he decide it?" Kevin asked.

She brought the sausages over and set them before him, burnt black on the skins and the smell of them.

"Soon as he got up."

"And she went with him?"

She nodded, sat down at the table and stared at his plate.

"You won't like them 'cause I never cook them right."

He began to eat, tasting the burnt skin. They were still whiteish on the inside.

"They aren't done," he said, shoving the plate away.

"Well I don't know—if I had a left them any longer they would have wizzled all up."

"You cooked them too fast," he said.

He got to his feet and went to the kettle and began to prepare himself tea, staring out the window when the kettle was plugged in and watching the lane that looked cold and autumn hard. "Went into town," he murmured, "Christ."

"I can make you some more of them," Deborah said. He came back with his tea and sat down again.

"No."

"You'll have to get used to that anyway," she laughed. He drank quietly listening for the sound of the car.

"What time is it?"

"Almost twelve," she said.

"Christ."

He drank only part of it and then took the cup to the sink and threw the rest out, staring up the highway for a moment. There wasn't a car.

"What time is it?"

"Twelve."

"Shit."

He went through to the room and lay across the couch. It still lingered with the night before. The curtains still drawn as if she hadn't even bothered to come in here since. The conversation still lingering in his head and the broken smile of his father. He lay face down on the couch, seeing the blackness and breathing quietly into it.

Then he heard her. She came into the room and drew back the curtains and sat upon the rocker watching him. He hadn't turned his head the slightest, and yet he knew she was watching.

"Nice day for the wedding."

He did not answer.

"Where are you people going on your honeymoon?"

"Nowhere."

"Nowhere?"

"We don't *know* where," he said louder. He didn't stir. "Somewhere, I suppose," he added.

"Yes well, mom's going to be mad if she finds out you didn't eat; I can cook more you know. You can cook them yourself if you want."

He sat up and looked across at her. She had her nightgown on and slippers that seemed too large on her feet.

"Did she say when they'd be back?"

"No—you know dad, she just ran out after him and got into the car, so I don't know if they will be back."

He rose and stretched and went to the door. "I'm going to lie down until they come."

He went to his room and threw himself down. Then he rose again and took his suit out and laid it across the chair. He leaned against the small dresser. It was grey inside and out and there wasn't a sound. There wasn't a sound, so that if he listened carefully he could hear the stove in the kitchen, the oil fire churning out the heat. He stood there staring blankly until he heard the car.

Then he went out again and along the hallway to the room, went into it just as they were coming to the door. Deborah went out to meet them, brushing past him as she did.

"Did you get one?"

"No, he didn't," Rubena said. "Fine time to try to get one —the morning of the wedding when everyone has things to do. I wouldn't a minded—I wouldn't a minded if I hadn't begged him last time he was in town. Well he can wear the one he has is all I say."

The old man walked past the door and through to the

kitchen without a word, Kevin watching him as he went. He walked bent at the back and stiff, his long arms hanging and bent outward at the elbows, his shoulders rounded. He wouldn't look good in a suit. She and the girl came into the room and sat on the couch, and she looked over at him smiling slightly.

"Well you're up—you'd better get ready now."

"Lots of time yet," he said.

"You'd better take a quick bath and get your suit on now," she said. "You don't want to be late."

"I ain't going to be late," he said, looking across at her small lips almost hidden in her face smiling that way. She turned away from him and looked to the girl.

"I got myself some shoes," she said, taking the package held in her arms and tearing the brown paper off.

"Oh great; where did you find them?"

"At that place I got my dress—so I went in and looked again. They're good enough anyway I think." She bent over and placed them on her feet carefully, slightly lifting the right foot and then the left as she did and looking down at them as if she were contemplating something.

"Oh I like them," Deborah said. "They'll go good."

"You think so?"

"Sure they will."

"Well I'm just sorry I couldn't find him a suit. If he had just had sense enough to know the last time we were in town."

She took them off. Then she told Deborah to start getting ready so there wouldn't be a last-minute rush like there was always when they went to Mass.

"What time is it?" he asked.

"It's going on one," the girl said standing. "Do you want to take a bath now?"

"You take it—I took one last night so it'll hold me over," he said. She went out and into the bathroom singing, her singing finally drowned by the sound of running water. It was one o'clock now, one more hour now.

Then Clinton came inside and sat, taking his tobacco out and rolling a cigarette, rolling it evenly and roundly and staring at the loose tobacco ends when he did. The deep tired wrinkles extended on his face. He lit the thing and sat back, and when she told him he'd better get ready, he merely nodded and inhaled, glancing to the boy.

245

"You want the car do you?"

"I guess so."

"Well you two go on and get ready," Bena said.

She got up herself and left the room.

"Kevin, you should be down there early," she said calling back.

It still smelled of the night before and the chairs still beneath the window in a row. He didn't want to move now because he felt suddenly that if he were to walk his guts would take control, that he would be weak from it and dizzy. She would be at the altar—he would meet her there, she would walk up to him and extend her hand then the priest, and the sacraments and the smell of the wood. Then it would be over and they would move down the aisle again. Then they would go and be alone. So it was just one hour and then they'd be alone.

"How's he gettin' up?"

"Reginald—don't know."

"You should have asked him when you were there—you should have asked him that."

"I didn't think of it."

"Well I may as well go down and get him now."

"I think he'll get up okay."

"He's probably down there waitin' so I may as well go down and bring him up," Clinton said. He butted his smoke with his thumb into the circular ashtray on the floor, with his head down staring at the exhausted smoke rising from it slowly. He said nothing more and stood, and then he walked through the door and out into the yard. Kevin heard his sound in the yard, spitting up and getting into the car. He didn't move. He didn't want to run out and say, "You'll be late goddammit—you'll be late goddammit," so he didn't move. Until she came into the room again with her blue dress on her unzipped and the scent from her through the room.

"It's quarter after—now where did he go; where did he go?"

"Get Reginald."

"Get Reginald! Get Reginald! There's always something, there always is—now he's gonna be late for it; he's gonna be late. He doesn't think of no-one, he never does," she said going over to the window and looking down the highway, her neck twisted that way to get a better look of the highway as if, at this time, she could merely by looking signal him back. "Get Reginald, Christ, that man!" she said. "He isn't even changed yet," she said. "He hasn't even changed."

Kevin stood and left the room, leaving her to herself. He went into his room and took the suit and then made his way to the bathroom, knocking on the door when he did. The tub was draining and she was singing again. Her voice singing that way. As if everything was good. She came out with a towel wrapped around her and ran past him down the hall.

So he went into the bathroom and washed, felt the water on him, on his neck and face. And each time the water hit him it felt better, each time more cleansing than before. He stood there splashing himself with it again and again. Then he straightened and took the towel. It was filled with steam, the bathroom, the faint enclosed warmth still rising from the sinking water in the tub, the window fogged and the pink half-closed curtains just above him hanging limp. The taste of a woman perhaps.

He put on his suit, standing before the mirror a long time after he did, straightening and restraightening his tie. Then he got into his shoes and walked out. She came out to him as soon as he did.

"Well, let's see how you look—yes all right, good—you'd better comb up your hair a bit."

"It's combed," he said.

"Well, I phoned John and he and Bruce are coming now to get you—so you won't be late."

"Phoned John?"

"Yes I did. God knows when he'll be back tearing off that way."

"Phoned John," he said again. "Shit."

"Well it's that or have you walk down. You have to be there early you know."

He went into the room again and sat. He could feel his stomach starting up. He could feel that awful pressure building up along his temples again. As if when he had dashed his face with the cold of it everything for a second had stopped, and now that he was sitting there trying to be quiet it all came up again, started again. They came into the room and sat with him, waiting for the sound of the car. And with every car that went by he felt his nerves.

"What time is it?"

247

"Just after 1.30."

The lean gaunt shape of his father driving down. The lean bent shape of his father and his father's brother coming up late. And his mother and his sister quietly waiting with their dresses on staring into the vague unquiet silence of the room. "Christ," he muttered to himself, "Christ, Christ." Because perhaps his father hadn't even thought of anything when he left.

"Now don't forget to thank Pamela's mother," Bena said quickly so that it startled him, cutting into the air the way it did.

"Why?"

"Because you're supposed to," she said.

He left the room and went outside, standing on the lawn, his shoes flat on the hard ground. It was a grey biting cold through his suit and the small wind blowing and flapping his unbuttoned jacket back. He went round to the side and stood watching the overhead sky, the clouds moving at a steady pace across it, going nowhere. He put his arms together for warmth and leaned carefully up against the cottage with his eyes closed. Then he turned and headed back seeing the car pulling in as he did.

They came right up behind the bus blowing the horn. John was the first out and he ran over to him, his face glowing that way, his black hair fine and straight and combed. They came up to him and John grabbed him by the shoulder.

"Ya ready?" he said, almost shouting it, his face flushed that way.

"As I'll ever be, I guess," Kevin answered. "What time is it?"

"Shit I don't know—we better get you down there though—come on."

That same suit, Kevin thought. That one when they were carrying *him* about.

"Just a minute," he said. He went into the cottage again and to the door of the room. "They're here—I'm going now," he turned to go out. "If he doesn't come back, you people walk down. I don't want everybody being late," he said.

"Don't you worry," she answered, him going through the door.

They got into the car and headed down, he on the outside watching the fields along the way, saying little. Bruce drove slowly, hunched at the wheel almost like his father would

248

hunch, *was* hunching now.

"Here's the ring—don't lose it," Kevin said handing it to him.

"Don't lose it—Christ," he mocked. Then he took a bottle from his jacket and opened it.

"Want some?"

"Are you bringing that in?"

"Why not?"

Kevin shrugged and took a drink. It was straight and he choked on it. They were both half-drunk, he thought—both of them were. He handed it around and they pulled off the highway and up to the church.

"You bastards drinking."

"What did you want us to do?" Bruce laughed. "Come to your wedding sober?"

They sat in the church lot waiting. He would have to go in soon, into the vestry to wait because it was later now, because it was almost two. John took the bottle again and gave it to him. He took just a little and handed it away again.

"What's wrong—nervous?"

"No."

"Like hell—we got a quart of vodka here, going to help us with it after?"

"Sure."

He wasn't listening. He was staring up at it, cold and white and silent carved out of it all and standing that way so solid on the ground. The tip of it reaching its cross high out into the sky that way so high above himself as if who had ever built it had danced in the air while doing it.

"Like hell you will," John was saying. "Like hell you will."

He turned back to them, their faces blushed with it and their eyes glazed sitting with their suits on waiting.

"Well we'd better go inside."

"Anything you say," John said.

"I'll sit here until they start coming," Bruce said, taking the bottle again and putting it to his mouth.

They got out and went to the rear door, John just behind him walking slowly. When they came around the rear, the wind was up blowing at the grass, the gravestones sitting in the cold, and behind them the woods standing empty and naked. They went inside and up three short steps to the vestry. The priest and the altar boys were already there.

249

They stood for a moment in silence watching it all. The taste of the dark wood and the incense, small figures of Jesus and Mary and almost ancient yellowed pictures on the wall.

And it was quiet besides. Very quiet so that he could hear people coming in from the frost and going into the pews.

"What time is it?"

"Five to," the priest said coming over. He introduced himself to John, looking down that way, his eyes a little narrowed. Knowing perhaps. And even with his collar on that pinched redness along the upper neck as if he always shaved too close. A certain quality of cleanliness about it all, about the robes he wore and the dry white hands.

"Well you know what you have to do."

"Yes," John said.

"Just step forward and place the ring on the plate."

"Yes," John said.

"No, there isn't going to be anything to this," he said looking at Kevin. The music was playing now, coming out from the organ upstairs, drifting down to him through the quiet. For another moment they both waited stiffly, quiet, each of them quiet and lost in thought. His father going out that way, never thinking.

"You better go in now," the priest said straightening the robe with his hands and looking to them. "Just go up to the altar and stand because they should be up front by now ready to come in."

They went through the door and walked to the front of the altar, slightly apart from each other, and when they reached it, John stood with his hands folded just slightly to the side. He saw faces when he entered but he didn't see. He hadn't taken the time to see if *they* were already in the pews. He stood facing the front looking at the cross. And every sound and shuffle behind him he heard, the coughing and the shifting of weight in the seats. He felt cold now, as cold as if he were outside with the wind. Then the music started again.

It wasn't that he didn't wish to turn around; it was more that he couldn't bring himself to, with the music playing that way and the sound of people standing. If they aren't here, he thought, Christ. And yet he didn't look around even when the priest came out to the altar and kneeled, and he knew then that she was standing just beside him with Barbara on the other side. Realized then that he had taken her hand and had

250

stepped up to the kneelers at the front. Feeling the small white coldness of her hand. He supposed she was nervous about it all. But perhaps when she looked at him, her eyes told him they weren't there—that they hadn't come. She had a dress with a hood on it and her fine hair seemed to flip about her neck. He looked at her standing beside him and then looked to the cross.

He heard nothing of the priest, watched him going back and forth the way he was. But he heard nothing of what he was saying. Only the people behind him now and then coughing and he trying to discern whose cough it was. Because if they hadn't come. Or if they had come late. Then he stood before them and John stepped forward and put the ring on the plate.

The priest stood before them instructing them on what to say. And he put the ring on her saying this, squeezing it over the knuckle, hearing that voice guiding him before he heard his own and his own sounding distant and out of place. And then she was speaking, saying the same words, her small face pinched in some nervous expression as if she were frightened of every sound she made, of her own fine voice that climbed above them, to the woodwork and the crosses and the slanted windows above the altar. Raised and gone through those windows and out into the day.

Then they both kneeled and signed.

"See there's nothing to it," he whispered calmly to them, smiling slightly.

The Host tasted flat and sour in his mouth.

And taking the Host they stood again waiting. He went back to the altar to flinish the Mass. It was over. And yet he could see the fine dust filtering before him in the dull light of the church, the white robes hanging on him that way, and the Host sticking to the dry roof of his mouth. He hadn't heard what she had said or what he had said to her. It was the priest speaking—not them, not ever them. It was the church and the taste of the Host and him speaking in it. But not them. Not her speaking to him.

Then they turned and she put her arm through his. Still he was uncertain when he began to walk, uncertain of his gut and legs. And when they turned, he saw them sitting, all of them sitting in the front row looking up. Bena and Deborah in their dresses and Clinton in his suit. Reginald smiling, looking up.

"Thank God that's over," she whispered coming out.

They went outside and stood there. People came out and they stood on the cement steps shaking hands. Very few people she knew, he thought. Friends of his mother who had come to watch.

"Let me take a picture of you two," Deborah said. "I have to take a picture."

They stood there and people brushed them coming out, shaking hands. It was cold now and the wind was raw, seeming to tear at him. Clinton came out to them and stood off to one side watching while Rubena kissed them both, her perfume in the wind, brushing her lips against his cheek. And then her family came out.

"Well Kevin—you're one of the family now," the man said.

"Yes."

"You'll have to come visit us now," the man said.

"Oh yes—I guess we will."

Everyone moved off the step and headed into the lot. They waited for a moment longer and went down also, the small loose gravel flattened by his shoes.

"Who are we going up with?"

"Mom and dad I suppose," he said.

He took her to the car and she got in, Reginald and Deborah already waiting, and then he walked back to John and Bruce.

They were sitting in the car passing it around and when he came over they handed it up. He took a small drink and gave it back, eyeing them.

"You two are coming up to Andersons'?"

"Don't know," John said.

"Well you'd better come up."

"We'll be along."

"Well as long as you come," he said.

He went back to the car. The wind was very bad and he was cold and uncomfortable in what he wore. He got in beside her, and Clinton came around from the rear of the church, walking slowly looking at the ground.

"He said sorry he can't make it."

"Why?" Bena asked.

"I ain't sure—just said he couldn't."

"Oh well," she said turning back to them. "Well it's over

252

—are you glad?" she said.

"I didn't even know what was going on," Pamela said.

Clinton turned the car around and headed up, driving slowly, her parents driving behind them. There didn't seem to be another car now, another movement on the road. It was dead autumn, everything dull and quiet.

"I didn't know if I was going to make it," Reginald said looking at her.

"Oh."

"No—I didn't know if no-one was gonna come down and get me or not this morning," he said quickly, laughing.

"Oh," she said.

"No but Clinton come down and got me, and we had to race up," he said.

"Well that's good," she said. "I'm glad you came."

"Yes," Deborah said, "well I got one picture and I want some more."

They drove a mile past the cottage and turned to the right. A large two-storey with a large verandah standing as solid to the ground as the church stood. They got out and went inside, through the verandah and along a hallway to the living-room. Her parents came in behind them and they stood talking. Clinton and the man in one corner talking.

"Who's this?" Bena asked. "Is this your brother, Pamela?"

"That's Richard," Pamela said.

"Oh you look alike," Bena said.

The boy had come in last and was standing close to Barbara by the door. He looked over and nodded, and then came up to Kevin with his hand out.

"Congratulations," he said. He was taller and thinner and his hand seemed bony. It seemed to go a little limp in Kevin's hand.

"Yes," Kevin said. "You made it did ya?"

"I guess so," the boy said. Then he turned to Pamela. "So where will you two be staying?"

"In town."

"I'll have to get up and visit some time."

"We'll have to go see you," Pamela said. "How are you making out?"

"Same old shit," he said. Then after a moment he went back and stood by Barbara again.

They stood in small groups talking. Just the families. John
and Bruce hadn't shown and that was all right because both of
them were drinking—would be almost drunk by this time. So
they stood about talking, every now and then Deborah snapping a picture of them or Bena, or Reginald who was standing
beside the two men silently watching and Clinton smoking
from the package she had given him.

But Clinton hadn't come over to them at all, and each time
he looked their way, he would seem to look past them, behind
them to the picture-window that showed the rear lawn and
the woods on its border. Then his head would go down again,
and he would continue talking every little while glancing to
the man. Reginald standing silent beside them with his hat
cupped in his hand, his tie twisted on his throat.

"It's after three now," Bena said. "Do you think we should
eat now? It's a cold plate you know."

"It's up to Pamela—do you want to eat now?"

"I think we may as well," Bena said again.

"It's fine with me," the girl said looking at them. "I mean
I'm not that hungry anyway."

"I don't think you have to eat very much—the plates are in
the dining-room. Do you want to go round and tell them
now?" she said. "Maybe you should go round and tell them
now."

"Yes," Pamela said.

So they went to each of them, Kevin behind her. Then they
moved into the dining-room through the two broad doors
that separated the living-room from it. The curtains were
open, showing the drive and the light coming into the room
over the white table-cloth and the plates upon it. They sat and
began to eat, Reginald sitting by his brother at the far end and
her parents sitting beside Richard and Barbara on the other
side.

He kept staring at his plate. He wasn't hungry. Each time
he raised his fork to put it in his mouth he could sense how
sick his stomach was, how full it was, and that if he took
another mouthful he would be sick. But he kept eating slowly
because it was there and he knew he must finish it. The cake
resting upon a small cabinet at the side.

No-one toasted or did any of those things. Perhaps they
had forgotten. It was John's responsibility anyway and he
wasn't present. He wouldn't have done it anyway Kevin

thought because he wouldn't know how to do it. So they ate at the large round table, each talking to the other as they did.

"Where are you two going tonight?" Mrs. Kingston asked, "or am I asking the wrong question?"

"We don't know yet as it is," Pamela said.

"No we don't know right yet," he added looking up.

"It's probably a secret," Deborah said.

They were silent again.

"They can stay down home if they got nowhere else to go," Reginald said quickly as if to get it out as quickly as he could, looking up for the first time from his plate and realizing perhaps as soon as he had said it that he had said the wrong thing—uttered the wrong words. Not even perhaps knowing why. Not even that. He looked at them all quickly and then at his brother who hadn't looked up. Then he put his head down also and continued with his plate. The stupid hat he wore resting on the back of his chair.

"Oh we'll go somewhere," Pamela said.

When they finished with the plates, Mrs. Anderson came out and took them up, going into the kitchen again. Then Bena got up and went out with her for a moment, coming back to ask them if they wanted tea or coffee. They carried both pots in and poured. Then she brought the cake over sitting it in front of them.

There was the sound of yelling outside. It had started just when she was setting the cake in front of them. No-one paid any mind to it. It was something that came with weddings he supposed. But he knew by the loud talk and the sound of the yelling who it was. He had his back to the window so he couldn't see. But it was all of them out there, he knew that. No-one paid it any mind.

They stood to cut the cake.

"I want a picture of this," Mr. Kingston said.

He told Deborah to close the drapes and she did, the yelling rising up when she did. They were standing. He felt weak again and stood as stiffly as he could to try and ward away the weakness—the yelling. Then they took the knife and began to cut, smiling out at him while he snapped a picture—smiling out stupidly that way.

"Now kiss the bride," he said. "One more picture—kiss the bride."

She was smiling. Bena was smiling. The yelling still outside.

255

He turned down to her and kissed her quickly and the man snapped another picture, the light of it blinding his eyes for a moment. The despair because of the shouting of his friends. Then they sat down and handed the cake round.

"I'm gonna keep mine I think," Reginald said.

They were eating the cake and the old woman came in and handed them an envelope.

"It's from them outside," she said. She laid it by his plate and went out again.

"God knows what it is," Pamela whispered.

He stared down at it, not wanting to touch it. Not wanting to open it at all in case it was something. In case it was what he thought it was. "Christ," he muttered. There was no sound now. They might have gone. He was hoping that they had just come up to give him this and leave. But he didn't know. He only knew he didn't wish to open it.

He picked the thing up and felt it, but still he didn't know. It felt like money but it could have been something else. Then he took it and with his hands under the table flipped it open, looking down at it.

"Well what is it?" Richard asked.

He took the money out and counted it.

"$30," he said.

"Well, that was nice of them," Mrs. Kingston said.

"Yes," he said.

He held the envelope up and put the money into it again, shoving it away in his jacket pocket. He ate the cake slowly.

They drank tea and coffee for a time after everything was finished, talking to each other about the wedding, that it was a good day to have it. Reginald sat silently at the far end listening, his hat on the back of the chair, the cake folded in a white napkin beside his cup.

"Well I'm glad you liked it," Bena said. "I really didn't know about the cold plate but I figured at this time of day it was better than rushing around for something hot."

"Oh everything was great," the woman said.

"It was," Clinton said. "It was good for short notice and everything like it was."

"Well I'm going back down to your place to change," Pamela said standing. He got up and went out with her down the long hallway and onto the verandah, the rockers and couch smelling faintly old in the light that came through.

256

When they went outside, he didn't notice it immediately. It was she who shouted first—her voice that way small and shrill when she was angry. But he didn't say anything about it. He went over to it first, the wind tearing at him, blowing his jacket back that way and his hair twisted with it now. He went down the steps and crossed the walk and then along the drive to it.

"Look what they did—look what they did," she was saying. "Goddammit," she was saying.

He felt that they were all behind him on the steps watching. He told her to be quiet but she wouldn't. "I knew it," she whispered. "I goddamn well knew it—and your father's car."

He looked down at it. They were watching from the steps, the wind up, coming at them all, the clouds moving silently in the silent sky, the house strong against it all as the church was strong. They had taken the tires off and had set them sideways under the axles. They had taken shoe polish and spread it across, written signs and question marks all across. "Christ," he muttered. He turned back to her, she shivering in the dress she wore, Barbara and her parents and his parents on the steps. And they had left—they had left because no-one was in sight—only the day and the fields and down below the road the water spreading whitely, calm and cold in the wind.

Clinton and her father came up and stared down at it. Then Richard came and stood beside him. She had turned and gone back inside. They weren't in sight. If they had stayed to help put it right again, if they had stayed but no they weren't in sight, none of them. Just the sight of the day and the odour of gas seeming to drip from it, out into the wind.

"Christ," he said. Because they hadn't stayed.

Clinton bit off a filter and put a cigarette into his mouth. It took him a while to light it in the wind, the smoke drifting out quickly once he had it lit.

"A bit of a mess," the man said.

"They always act foolish at weddin's here," Clinton said. "We can get 'er fixed," he said.

"Do you want us to help?" the man asked.

"No my brother and I can get 'er fixed—you go on down to the cottage," he said.

The old man went around to the passenger side and opened the door and bent over on the seat. Then there was something strange from the inside, a voice seeming to come from the back of it and the old man rose up and stepped out of it quickly. The smoke still clinging in the air.

"They got a pig in here," he said.

Kevin said nothing. Clinton opened the back door and bent down again. Then the voice of it squealing as if its throat were about to be cut, as if the old man were about to bring it to the block.

"Just a little one," he said.

Kevin opened the other door. The smell of it on the seat, the dirt from its hooves and the piss, the smell of the piss and it looking both ways—first to his old man and then to him and then turning and squealing and jumping across the seat when Clinton made a dash for it. The dirt and the smell of excrement and piss. Then it was out by Kevin and into the yard running in jagged circles, wanting somewhere to go.

"Christ," he said.

"We'll get 'er cleaned up," Clinton said.

Then Reginald was outside running after it, his tie flapping up over the back of his neck and his short greying hair flung out by the wind.

"You people go now—don't worry 'bout it," Clinton said, throwing the butt away now.

So they got into the other car and drove to the cottage, all of them cramped against one another in the car. In the cottage it was warm, the sound of the stove gently churning out the heat.

"Do you know who it was?" Mrs. Kingston asked.

"Some guys I know," he said, a tight smile breaking on his face.

They had given a pig because he would call her slut. He would call her that and it was him. It was him!

He went along the corridor to his room and changed into his work clothes, mill clothes that felt good on him again. Then he went out into the room, Pamela sitting with her mother and Bena.

"Well it was a good wedding for that," Bena said. "Where are you going?" she smiled.

"I'm going up to help them." Outside the air—the light of the sun slanting inward upon them all.

"Oh leave it to them," she said.

"They'll get their clothes ruined," he said. The good feel and smell of the clothes upon him now. He went to the closet and took out his large grey coat and threw it on. The wind blowing the alders along the side of the path. He came back inside and looked at them.

"It'll probably be a good hour," he said.

"That's all right," Pamela said.

"Do you want a drive?" the woman asked. "Harold can drive you."

"No—I can walk it in five minutes."

His old man hunched over at the car working at it now. He picked up the tobacco lying there and shoved it into his pocket. Then he went out the door. The wind tossing into him and the sun glancing just above the trees. He went out to the road and began to walk it, walking slowly with his head to the side, spitting away from the wind the dried taste inside him. He wouldn't have minded except for that—the voice of the thing squealing. Below him the water white and dull. The voice of the thing squealing that way, the smell of its excrement on the air. But it would be frozen soon, the water and the earth. The empty thudding of his boots along the ground now, the roadway stretching almost black, and he turning and spitting now and then, the dried taste inside.

The first five chapters of *The Coming of Winter* were awarded the Norma Epstein prize in creative writing in 1973.

Library of Congress Catalogue Card No. 74-76154

ISBN 0 88750 128 1

Cover by Michel Leclair courtesy Department of External Affairs travelling print collection. Book design by Michael Macklem.

Printed in Canada by the Hunter Rose Company

PUBLISHED IN CANADA BY OBERON PRESS